# *Texas Victory*

by

Denzel Holmes
and
Tom Schliesing

*Texas Victory*

Copyright 2003
by
Denzel Holmes
and
Tom Schliesing

Cover art and illustrations by Loraine Blount

ISBN 1-932196-09-9

*WordWright*
*.biz*

P.O. Box 1785
Georgetown, TX 78627

Printed in the United States of America

*I claim German blood only by adoption, that is, the process I experienced while writing this book.*

*First, to my adopted German brother, Tom Schliesing, who conceived the idea and the story, contributing the bulk of the castle technicalities and the historical research to the project.*

*Second, I fell in love with the great German leader, John Meusebach, who succeeded in negotiating with the Comanches to create an enduring treaty, and whose wisdom boosted the morale of his people through all travail. This book is to you, Herr John. Forgive me if we had a little fun at your expense.*

*In previous writings, I owed so many debts of thanks that I found no room to acknowledge the pillars of my life: Margie, my wife, and my Maria, always the stabilizing force during my runaways. And to a host of other family and friends whose encouragement is prized beyond measure, and whose anticipation, I hope, was worth the wait.*

**Denzel Holmes**

*I see a little of Jim in*
*Prince Carl, and a little*
*of Margey in Maria!*

*To great friends always,*

*Denzel*            7-22-07

*Dedicated to my ancestors,*
*Carl and Elizabeth Ackermann Schaefer*
*and nine children, who landed with other immigrants of*
*Prince Carl von Solms-Braunfels' German Immigration Society at*
*Indianola, Republic of Texas, November 1844.*

*My great grandmother, Johanette, was born to Carl and*
*Elizabeth's oldest child, Fredericke Schaefer, at Camp Agua*
*Dulce, January 6, 1845, making her a citizen of the Republic.*

*Carl was responsible for transporting two bells to New Braunfels,*
*later used at the First Protestant Church.*
*I honor my ancestors and their acquaintances with the use*
*of many of their names in this story about*
*German pioneers in Texas.*

**Thomas (Tom) G. Schliesing**

# *Chapter 1*

Kronprince Carl Franz von Altmann dismounted below the cobblestone walk that led to the arched double doors of the medieval castle. His two comrades in arms marched silently at each side, and stood rigidly as Carl pulled his coattails downward and dusted his tunic. He lifted the heavy brass knocker and pounded twice on the scarred oak surface.

Shortly, one of the heavy doors creaked open. A candle emerged followed by a white-haired head. "Yes, sire." The voice held a vibrato but its note was music to Carl.

"Gustav, do you not know me? Has my father waited supper for his firstborn?"

The old man narrowed his rheumy eyes and lifted the candle. "Herr Carl! Oh, thank God. We had reports of your death."

Carl stepped into Gustav's open arms. The two hugged warmly, Gustav's head at Carl's chest, though once they would have met eye to eye. The old man had taught Carl the art of riding and enticed him with tales of battle.

Pushing free of the embrace, Carl fought a melancholy tear. "And my father? Is he well?"

Gustav clung with his free hand to Carl's sleeve and gazed upward. "Ah, Carl, I had hoped the duty would never fall to me to tell you. Prince Christian went to his Lord a year ago. It was more than his poor heart could stand when word came that you were killed in battle. I'm so sorry."

Guilt, sorrow, and anxiety surged in Carl's chest. He deeply loved his gentle father. The man had already delegated many duties of prince to his firstborn. Now, on return from war north of Austria, Carl would have to assume the throne as well as the mantle of grief.

He stood shaken, both unable and unwilling to speak for several minutes. He felt sympathetic hands on his shoulders as Wilhelm and Ernst, his close lieutenants, spoke soft condolences. He struggled to straighten his tall frame, and keep his countenance firm. "The principality. Who has reigned?"

"Your brother, Julius, the next heir beyond you. He has..."

"Acted in my stead. Of course," Carl said tremulously. He exhaled, unable to subdue a sigh.

The old man hesitated. "Yes, well, of course it is acting because now you have returned. It is good. But I must tell you that Julius arranged for the council to convey the title of reigning prince to him, and the priest has likewise ordained him as such. The festivities lasted a week."

Carl's face flushed. "Law requires a lapse of five years before the title *Reigning Prince* can be transferred from the rightful heir. Of course, he would take charge of the council in my absence but there is good reason for the law. And in this case, the deceased has risen from the dead! Where is Julius?"

A faint smile lit Gustav's eyes. How often Gustav had admired Carl's bravery and privately mocked Julius as a hopeless coward. "I will fetch him from the bedroom and his new bride. Please forgive that I have not invited your company inside. Are you comfortable?" Carl nodded as his mentor proceeded toward the stairs.

Carl turned to Baron Wilhelm von Bieberstein, his chief assistant throughout the campaign against the Slavs. Wilhelm wore the Van Dyke beard and wax-pointed mustache, like Carl. Unlike Carl's dark eyes and black hair, Wilhelm bore determined gray eyes and brown locks, showing a new fringe of white at the temples. Carl wondered if his own appearance confirmed fatigue, like Wilhelm's, after the two year absence. They were near the same age, and their eyes met level, more than six feet above the stone floor.

"Willi, you and Ernst take a seat." He motioned toward the stuffed chairs encircling his father's antique oak desk. "This may take some time."

"Herr Carl, I know protocol as well as you. We came here before greeting our own wives and children, as required by the respect one shows a prince. Likewise, Ernst and I will not sit as long as our Kronprince stands."

Carl smiled weakly, knowing the two men wouldn't take chairs. He would sprawl for a few seconds on the overstuffed chair which bore the family crest. He would rise before Julius entered the room.

Ernst said, "Herr Carl, will there be trouble over this issue; the title of prince? You know your command will support you with all energy, starting the moment Julius descends the stairs." He pointed toward the winding casement.

Carl smelled the ancient stones and the hint of moss as he glanced up. Ernst, with the piercing blue eyes and blonde hair, was younger and stockier. Carl felt closer to Wilhelm, but knew that Ernst's valor in war was akin to his own. That assurance gave him comfort. He'd felt it before.

Ernst, had screamed approval at Carl's orders, and rallied his company in countercharge to the Slavs while other commanders pulled back. As a junior officer Carl had narrowly survived a retreat on the Rhine and witnessed the slaughter of most of the routed soldiers of Field Marshal von Heflin's command. He vowed that if he ever commanded, he would not retreat from pitched battle. Shooting defenseless soldiers in the back was too easy. He wouldn't give the enemy that option. He never entered battles recklessly, but fought without hesitation those he believed he could win, else he held back for another day, a better advantage.

"There will be no cause for military action," Carl said, less sure than his voice suggested. "We knew reports had been sent home that we had been killed in battle. We should have anticipated some kind of civil action in response." His eyes flashed. "I'm not thrilled that they held a week-long fest in the face of my father's death and my own reported death."

No wonder his command had reported him killed. He had pursued the superior Slavic army, which made the mistake of retreating, for a hundred kilometers. He had given no quarter and expected none in return. He had the advantage and refused to give

3

it up. He engaged the adversary daily, starved, dehydrated and humiliated them when their ammunition ran out. By the time his jaded soldiers and horses relocated their own camp, ten days had passed. Now a year had transpired since that day, two years since he last saw the Principality of Altmann, his wife and two children.

His body grew comfortable in the deep cushion as he pondered Helga. Now, at age 46, he had a son of thirteen and a younger daughter. Helga was the first woman he had courted who loved him, it seemed, without regard to his title. And, God, her beauty had stunned him from the first.

They had wed fifteen years ago. How he had wasted his early youth in wars that held no importance for Altmann except for the widespread terror he'd seen in his subjects' faces as battles to the east came closer. And patriotism or adventure, he knew not which, had once again swept him into the fray.

"A childish venture," Helga called it, acceding to the iron will of her husband in his decision. Even then, he found her desirable. His children accepted his departure more readily. At least, they understood the important position held by their grandfather, Prince Christian Johann Victor, Reigning Prince of the Principality of Altmann, Grafestein Schwartzenberg, Grand Cross of the Royal Order of Munich, Ducal Order of Maximilian, Knight of the Order of St. George.

Abruptly, Carl hoisted himself lest he be found sitting when Julius appeared. He stalked about the castle's lesser hall. Most of the furnishings, including the wall hangings, had not been present when he last spoke good-byes to his long-widowed father, Prince Christian. Now the décor was changing as had the chargé d'affairs. It had been a long time since Carl thought of his mother. But had she lived, she would have had something to say about Julius as Reigning Prince. Prince, indeed!

"Carl?"

The youthful voice jolted Carl. He turned to see his brother descending the ornate staircase. Family loyalty and genuine love took precedence over his mixed suspicions. He adjusted the scabbard at his side and lunged to greet Julius in a bear hug. The two remained speechless for moments after they broke the embrace.

Julius stood an inch taller than Carl. His yellow blond hair and short beard matched his colorless, expressionless eyes. His shoulders loomed broad above a thin waist and narrow hips. Village frauleins, often those in the company of Carl, cast longing eyes to the striking brother more times than Carl could remember. He hardly cared anymore, though he never had quit augmenting public appearances by wearing military uniforms, pressed and polished to perfection and by maintaining a posture and demeanor consistent with future princedom.

As Carl drew back he recalled the birth of his younger brother. At six, from his room Carl heard the squalls of the new arrival down the long upper hallway of the castle. He joined in the excited festivities and the delight of townspeople as the lively infant was presented publicly and privately time and again. Even at Carl's young age, he knew the meaning of *firstborn*, a future position that his brother could never hold. As the years passed, Carl resolved to position his brother prominently in government so that all could see his love, his respect. At the proper age, Carl left home to be schooled in military affairs and expected that Julius would follow in six years. He did not.

Julius spoke dispassionately. "We thought you were dead. It has been a year since word came."

"Ahh, the first lesson of war. Stay alive! It's the fact that counts. Not the thought. Right?" He laughed nervously, dreading to speak of their father's death.

"Gustav told you that Father has died? We needed you most desperately in those days."

"The main thing is that I'm back now, young brother. We must talk at length soon. You must brief me on all events of the principality." Wanting to avoid any semblance of confrontation, Carl lightened the subject. "Right now, I must see Helga and the children. Gustav said 'new bride.' Please explain."

"Yes, I married Lucille from the mountain village. It was only the second festival since Father died. You knew that Mathilde died?" Julius referred to his first wife, who had become an invalid shortly after the wedding. Carl hadn't been told but assumed as

5

much despite Julius's readiness to speak of all other concerns first. Carl remembered the young Lucille, a haughty, raven-haired beauty who showed no interest in commoners. She had smiled often at Carl though he was married and twenty-five years her senior. At that time, she showed no interest in Julius.

"I'm saddened by the loss of your precious Mathilde, but my true congratulations on a fine choice in Lucille. Do you see Helga often? Is she well? How are the children?"

"I fear I may have neglected them. Though I've extended invitations to all gatherings, she does not attend. I trust she is well, my brother. And you? Are you well?"

"Well but tired." It seemed a good moment to probe his brother's intentions. "I hope you have the affairs of the principality in good order so that my burden will be light."

Julius patted his brother's shoulder. "All is well, Carl. All is well."

After courtesies were exchanged with Carl's lieutenants, Carl abruptly muttered his good night, which, he reflected, may not have camouflaged his growing ire, and they tramped to their horses.

The shadow of the always-snow-covered peak now completely darkened Crystal Lake which stood near Carl's block stone house. The Village of Altmann, in the Province of Southern Bavaria was a beautiful spot. He parted company with Wilhelm and Ernst and rode past Julius's modest former residence and felt rage disrupt the anticipated pleasure of seeing his family.

ଔ  ଔ  ଔ

Helga opened the door. Her night attire cast a frailty about her light frame. Yet her durable beauty struck him. Her dark, thick, radiant hair and high cheekbones accented a perfect nose. She yelped with delight and clung to him in a crushing embrace. She called to their daughter Elisabeth to come downstairs to greet "a stranger."

Carl smiled. "Will you not call Hans? I must see my son."

"He has been ill for months, husband." He knew her use of the

6

word as a term of fondness. "We'll go to him when Elisabeth is greeted."

At that moment, a wide-eyed Elisabeth appeared on the stairs. She flew into his arms. How she had grown! She was becoming a young woman. She had the dark features of her father, and often he reveled in the praise given her beauty by townsfolk.

When the tears of joy ceased, Carl asked Helga, "And how has your health been, my frau? Has life treated you well?"

"I'm fine, but better now that you're home."

Elisabeth was more frank. "Mother has not been fine. She faints and she won't allow me to fetch Doctor Schmitt. She insists on performing too many chores, though Hans and I try to help. Well, Hans did help before..." Her trailing voice concerned Carl.

Upstairs, they entered Hans' room. His mother approached, woke him gently, and when he could comprehend, told him his father was alive, well, and home. When the lad rose from his feather bed to stare at the strange soldier standing in the door, Carl shuddered at the sight as he remembered the athletic boy and his muscular frame.

He now seemed a different person altogether, a ghost of his former self. His blue eyes were sunken so deeply, Carl thought for a moment they didn't exist. Hans reached with toothpick arms toward his father but didn't offer to step from the bed.

Carl repeated over and over his pleasure at being home with his family. He assured the boy that he would snap out of this lingering effect from fever, that it was common to lose body weight after such a bout. He was convincing. Hans rallied and continued the conversation at length, expressed his desire to re-enter the games, walk the streets, climb the mountains, get on with military school.

When Helga and Carl retired to their bedroom, Carl had gained a certain reassurance. He had convinced himself and Hans. In the warm comfort of their bed, he held his wife of fifteen years closely and spoke softly of her beauty, his loneliness for her voice, her body, during the long campaign. Her frailty faded as strong arms encircled Carl's neck and pulled his face into hers. Her body showed surprising power as she pulled, full length, against him.

Carl's own weary frame found new energy. He recalled the first time with Helga, how his frame trembled in anticipation and desire. A pleasurable shiver raced through his chest and arms even now. His hands roamed. His heart surged. Their mouths joined spontaneously. Nothing was lost from the two-year absence, not even from the young love of their wedding night.

When the passion ended, neither moved from their positions but fell into the embracing, welcome, sleep of true lovers.


Carl served breakfast to Hans upstairs and offered to help the boy sit in the parlor for a long talk of the future. Hans declined but said he was feeling stronger, perhaps this afternoon.

After breakfast, Helga continued the family small talk forever as Carl had seen her do to avoid subjects dealing with his departure. He hugged her shoulders and assured her he wouldn't leave, asking her to explain her views on the happenings since the death of his father, the village, the principality, and his brother's schemes.

She said, "I've not seen Julius since the priest anointed him with the stolen title. I attended because I wanted him and his phony new wife, as well as Father Gaspar, to see my displeasure."

Carl urged his wife to sit and patted her hand in approval of her effort. "You know Father Gaspar had no authority to do that. It has no effect in law. And even if I *were* dead, Julius could preside over the council but he couldn't assume the title for five years."

"But, my husband, you know the villagers well, and if the priest does something, anything, they are loath to go against him. They fear for their mortal souls."

He leaned back. "Helga, why do you suppose he performed the ceremony?"

"I believe he thought it unimportant to wait. He truly believed you were dead. We all did." Tears welled. "Then perhaps someone profited from a bribe. God forgive me but I suspect your new sister-in-law was behind the plan. He was frightened by the fear of what would happen to the village with Slavic threats and no leadership. But I admit, I'm but guessing."

8

"Julius would be a great one to lead the defense against Slavic threats, a coward to the core. I'd never say that if my father were still alive."

"Carl, my darling, please find a way to resolve the dispute without violence." She touched his knee. "Perhaps when you face Julius in public he will quickly relinquish."

"I hope you are right, Helga. I'll not take back my title by force. I'll have the support of my people, the sure way to depose an impostor peacefully."

Carl planned to take Wilhelm and Ernst and return to Julius in the middle of the business day (so that witnesses would be present) and assert firmly that he, Carl, was back. He expected Julius to hand over the controls of government to him immediately as the rightful heir to the title *Prince of the Principality of Altmann.* But word of his arrival had spread like wildfire through the night. Visitors of all ranks began arriving at his door. He decided to seize the opportunity to sound out his subjects.

As minister of grievances for his father, the townspeople were accustomed to Carl's quick, but usually just decisions. This day they fell into the old pattern as though he hadn't been gone for two years. They welcomed him back and openly supported him, unconcerned that any conflict should arise in the transfer, but few wanted to dwell on that possibility.

The people excitedly discussed the circulars and rumors of great numbers of Germans throughout the provinces who planned to emigrate to Texas in the New World. Many had already left, selling all possessions in the old lands to raise the fare. Even Carl's cousin, Prince Carl von Solms-Braunfels, called Solms, had teamed with a protection society and led a new wave of immigrants. The promise of land and freedom abroad offered a promise too great to resist.

Carl listened with subdued impatience, finally deciding to approach the power issue through the most diplomatic route first. He would go to the church, make confession to Father Gaspar, take communion publicly, then call the priest aside to persuade him to reverse his earlier error. With Helga's assistance in repairing,

9

washing and pressing his and his lieutenants' uniforms, they made great ceremony of their mounted march down the cobblestone street to the church entrance. Carl sent Wilhelm inside to announce his arrival.

Townspeople gathered with awe-stricken eyes, heads leaned to view the trio, mouths partly open. Carl held a straightforward countenance and spoke to no one during the ten-minute respite. His subjects stood in mute silence, respectful. When the chapel door swung outward, Carl lifted his hand and gently removed his black, spiked helmet, decorated with polished brass, and crowned with a billowing ostrich feather, it's pink softness waving in the breeze. He gently tucked the headgear under his arm. Old Father Gaspar came forward, slightly bent at the waist, appearing tense, apprehensive.

He greeted the prince. "Herr Carl, I heard that you returned. Thanks be to God. It is good to have you home." The priest extended his hand.

From his horse, Carl looked down at the old priest. "I cannot take the hand of a man of God until I have confessed my sins and received absolution. Will you so bless me, Father?"

"I will, my son. I will."

"Good, it is only then that I can rightfully return to my duties in Altmann."

Father Gaspar's expression never wavered. Instead, he extended a hand to usher his visitor inside. Wilhelm and Ernst followed close behind.

In the confessional, Carl spoke forcefully, his words memorized, taking advantage of his powerful tenor voice, a talent which, doubtless, aided his military leadership. "During the two year campaign, I often thought of sins of the flesh, Father. Forgive me. There were those in my camp who challenged my orders, and I bore malice for them to the point of committing murder in my heart. Please forgive me, Father. In battle, I could have held back from slaughtering the enemy in retreat, but I allowed passion and anger to overcome the fruits of the spirit, and I killed more men than necessary to win the battle. May I be forgiven, Father? I have not been a husband and father to my family in the ways that are spoken by the Lord. Duty called me away. I promise to make recompense. Forgive me for I have sinned."

The prayer went on and the people heard every word as they gathered in the sanctuary. When Carl and Gaspar emerged, the priest waddled straight to the altar and uncovered the communion dishes. Carl knelt and performed the sign of the cross as his lieutenants did likewise beside and slightly behind him. After the priest administered communion to the trio, Carl again performed the sign, both kneeling and standing in a bowed posture. Then he rose to military attention and stepped to a pew and sat while the entire congregation received communion.

The ceremonies ended, and the people filed by Carl and shook his hand, many making gestures of welcome, some worriedly, some happily. He nodded politely with each spoken word but kept his face rigid.

When everyone had left the church, Carl turned to Father Gaspar. "Father, I will need an audience with you concerning my stately duties, if you please."

"Come into my office, my son," the priest offered, and then turned in mild surprise to see the two junior officers following close behind. The priest settled into his seat and steepled his fingers. The three officers took chairs in front of his desk.

"Father, I understand that in my absence, and in certainty of my death, you performed a ceremony which gave church sanction to my brother's claim as rightful heir to the title 'Prince of the Principality of Altmann.' Am I correct?"

"That is essentially correct, Carl." Gaspar's eyes drifted as if to camouflage his thoughts.

"Good. Now that we see your error, I respectfully request that you make public the knowledge that you rescind the ceremony. Of course, I'm sure you agree that your action as clergy is not binding for legal purposes. But I have too much respect for you, the church, and Almighty God, to act out of concert with what you have done. My request is for the good of the principality."

The priest shuffled. "Herr Carl, you must understand that what the world views as binding and what God so views are sometimes, oft times different. The Church enters no covenant without careful advance scrutiny, much prayer, and the blessing of the Holy Father in Rome."

Carl rose from his chair as his face flushed. "I do not understand. Are you telling me that this act was blessed by the Holy Father in Rome? What has he to do…?"

"Please control yourself in the Lord's house," Gaspar lectured. "You ramble close to blasphemy of the Holy Father. I will explain. Now, first, your brother asked me to perform the ceremony. At first I was reluctant. But two reports came from the front. The first reported you missing in battle and presumed dead. Soon another report came saying simply that you were dead."

"My brother requested the ceremony before the second report!?" His face darkened in fury.

"My son, we cannot continue if you cannot control your basic instincts with certainty. If I may go on." Gaspar leaned back uneasily. "The church has been in a most difficult financial position since before you left. Perhaps if you had stayed home, as most men, the economy of the Altmann would not have become so desperate. Promises were made to rebuild the crumbling roof. You witnessed its poor condition when you were here two years ago. Now it is new. Our people no longer worship in danger."

"You deposed me as prince to pay for the damned roof? You ought to…"

Father Gaspar stood to face the prince. "This meeting is over, Carl! You are not repentant. Your confession was a mockery of God."

"I'm sorry, Father. Please understand my position. I truly want to hear all you have to say. I am sure that my beloved brother is ruling with great finesse." Carl's voice rose with every word, as did his anger. "Though he married again long before his days of mourning were gone…a much younger and more attrac… "

"Do not damn your eternal soul, my son! I will permit you stay only because you need to hear what I am going to say next."

Carl sat.

"Once the ceremony was performed with all church blessing, a complete record of the transactions along with a generous donation to the Vatican was packaged and sent to Rome. In due time, a note of thanks came back which stated that we had acted wisely and correctly. That note can only be construed as the irreversible will of the Holy Father. I am truly sorry, Herr Carl, but the action of the Church cannot be reversed. You must accept God's will."

Carl, beyond anger, was dumbfounded. He knew he dare not open his mouth again because he would fail to suspend or retract his words. His lieutenants looked to his lead. He rose and stalked to the door. He turned and said calmly, "My confession was sincere."

They rode to the grand beer hall. Carl ordered Schnapps and rushed each drink, hoping to get too drunk to act on his impulses to go to his brother's house. No! His father's house. No! Carl's rightful house, and do violence to his once beloved brother. Violence that would end with murder.

*Kronprince Carl Franz von Altmann*

# Chapter 2

Near noon Carl regained stamina enough to think of leaving the house. Uncharacteristically, he had no firm plans for approaching his brother, no memorized script. But again villagers poured through his door as Helga grected each one and showed them to her husband's suite. Carl addressed each guest formally but didn't rise from his chair as he would if his head didn't pound.

Some sought redress for grievances as though Carl were still minister and prince. Many wanted to engage his wisdom on the sordid state of the economy. He rushed them through. And an even larger number droned endlessly of the exodus from German lands of cousins in other principalities, asking if Altmann may sponsor such a migration in the future.

He indulged them. "Tell me the wonders of the West, Luge. You seem so schooled." *I will jot names and chastise these who betray my need with the desire to flee.*

But their blunt honesty, their lack of fear of his reprisal, their enthusiasm, confused him, and the numbers of professional men and master craftsmen who showed interest impressed and dismayed him.

His questioning led to three shallow conclusions: His people believed the government of the state as well as the principality should help in such a venture. Second, since Carl had been deposed locally, perhaps he would have a personal interest in leading such a migration. Third, they viewed Texas, in North America, a Utopia where one could grow rich by taking advantage of all opportunity. At the mention of liberty, Carl bristled, since he viewed his own discretion and wisdom as sufficient for the people.

When Doctor Heinrich Schmitt, his trusted family physician, entered his suite to discuss emigration, Carl held him for a thorough questioning. "I can appreciate your interest, Herr Schmitt. You must have many patients who cannot pay your fees. Better for us all if such folk crossed the ocean."

"Not at all, Herr Carl. True, some may prosper by staying behind, but those who go will enjoy the greatest gain. There are many drawbacks, of course. Money is the first need, for the journey and to survive until crops and other goods can bring revenue."

Carl pounded his clay pipe on a polished oak block. "Herr Schmitt, you sound so excited I could almost believe you are one of the peasants who would board the first boat." He leaned back in a pleasant laugh.

Schmitt smiled and shook a finger in Carl's face. "Ah, not a peasant, but my heart is tempted. I could pay my own way and care for my family. But I will never do such a thing for one reason."

"The reason?" Carl packed aromatic tobacco into the pipe bowl.

"While finances are a major need, so is proper leadership. Our principality is among the best led in all of Southern Bavaria. I should say, 'was the best led.' A society of immigrants would require similar rule, even more so."

Carl said, "What of my magnificent brother, Julius, the *ordained* Prince of Altmann?" He waved a hand about his head. "Take him with you. I will gladly contribute him to your cause."

Schmitt's lips tightened. "Herr Carl, please do not jest of such matters. It troubles me greatly that just such an incompetent will find his way to the head. The professionals and the trade masters will abandon the idea and leave nothing but the unskilled, illiterate, poor, the beggars for a voyage to disaster. There is only one way the venture could succeed."

"And what is that way, my friend?" Carl said, his first puff curling lazily.

"If *you* should lead the movement."

Carl drew his thick eyebrows close. "Schmitt, Schmitt! You know well that I have troubles at home. It is out of the question."

Schmitt leaned across the desk and lowered his face while holding his eyes steadfast on his prince. "Your troubles at home would vanish the moment the ship leaves the shore."

Carl felt flattered by the compliment, but leaving Southern Bavaria? Leaving Altmann? "You know me well enough that I never quit a fight. I have unfinished business here, and much of my remaining prime years could be consumed in resolving it."

"I know, Herr Carl. I know," Schmitt said with dejection. "But I had to say these things to you. The seed must be planted. You will keep an open mind?"

Carl rose and circled from behind his desk, placed his large hand on his friend's shoulder. He gazed intensely then said, "I will promise to keep an open mind but you must make me a promise, too."

"What is that, my prince?"

"You will keep a closed mouth concerning this conversation."

ឌ ឌ ឌ

With the day gone, Carl cast aside the conflicts of the preceding hours and tried to enliven his family with his undivided attention. He helped Hans down the staircase and pillowed him on a stuffed chair as Helga brought in a roasted ham from the detached kitchen. He dug out his accordion and played rusty polkas while Elisabeth danced in circles spinning her full skirt, singing in harmony with her mother. Carl could tell that Helga didn't have the energy for the merriment but knew she wanted to cheer Hans. As Carl watched his daughter and wife, he glanced often to Hans who continued a forced smile. *How utterly ridiculous to think of emigrating to America when my family is ill. Schmitt's proposition is out of the question.*

He rose the next morning disgusted that he had shown poor leadership by letting two days pass. *It was a mistake to go to Gaspar first. Once Julius is set aside, Gaspar makes no difference anyway.* He summoned his lieutenants.

They entered the town hall as they had entered the church, dignified, stiff. Learning that the Altmann Village Council was in session, Carl turned in military march down the hallway to the council room. He swung the door wide, entered, and allowed

17

Wilhelm and Ernest to step forward on either side. Julius sat at the head of a heavy oaken table speaking to twelve councilmen. His words froze in his mouth when he saw the trio enter.

Townspeople sat near walls waiting to petition the council. Terror seized their faces. They leaped to their feet, turning toward the door.

Julius addressed them nervously. "There is no need to leave. Council is in session." They paid no heed. Instead they stampeded past Carl and his deputies and scurried through the still open door.

Carl stepped to within saber striking distance of his younger brother, touched the handle of his engraved Damascus weapon, then moved his hand away. He distinctly saw Julius's head dart downward, then to the side before the younger regained dignity. Carl gave brief thought to the fact that among the happy visitors to his house since his return, he counted none of the appointed councilmen among them.

Julius maintained his silence. Carl began the dialog. "Brother Julius, men of the council, in my absence your faces have changed. Indeed many seated in these chairs are different from when I left two years ago to defend your homes and families. I now report to you that my campaign was successful. I lived for another day. And in the sorrowful death of my beloved father, Julius has seen fit to lead you as acting burgermeister.

"My first official act will be to recommend a medal for his services. Now, as Kronprince of Altmann, I will assume my proper place at the head of this table...if you, my dear, younger brother will kindly lift yourself from the chair."

Julius not only lifted but ran like a rabbit to the back exit before stopping. When Carl didn't pursue with his sword he rested his hand on the door handle and turned. He tried to speak but wheezed a subdued squeak instead. "The ch..." He cleared his throat. "...chair is a matter for council to decide. In fact, they have already determined that I should serve..."

Carl stepped forward. Julius's words stopped and he ripped the door open. Carl expected to see an armed guard enter to defend the cowardly leader. Instead, a woman entered, a finely dressed woman of stunning beauty – Lucille. The sight of her flustered him beyond words. He realized suddenly that he had pulled his sword halfway from its sheath though he had sworn to his wife he wouldn't resort to violence.

Lucille's stern black eyes exuded hate. "Is there an issue here, Julius?" his wife asked, in full control of her demeanor, staring at Carl.

Julius stammered. "He wants to regain the title of ..." Carl moved forward again. "Uhhhhh! Uhhhh!" He crouched his tall frame and cuddled himself to his wife's bosom like an oversized child.

Carl slammed the sword back in place, sure that his embarrassment didn't show. "Thank you, my younger brother. You have properly abdicated the position of acting burgermeister. I'll now assume my duties."

He turned his back to the pair and seated himself as head of the council. Wilhelm and Ernst positioned themselves rigidly behind him. The screams from the doorway would have awakened their father as well as Julius's recently deceased Mathilde. Lucille charged the chair as Carl had seen crazed Slavs charge his troops. He rose in defense as her hand swung madly at his face.

"You are no prince! My husband is prince. You can't come in here after you're dead and take..." Carl's quick left hand fended off Lucille's right. Her left hand arched viciously. When Carl caught it easily, fingernails extended and gashed the back of his hand drawing blood. Her screaming insults never ceased. Carl controlled both her wrists, while his deputies sought a way to help from behind her. She kicked at her brother-in-law brutally as Wilhelm and Ernst dragged her away.

"Unhand my frau!" Julius stammered, not moving from his doorway position. "You, you have no right to handle a woman in such a manner."

Lucille screeched, "I am the princess! Tell them, Julius! I am the princess! Tell them!"

Carl let go while maintaining his stiff stance. His battle voice rose above Lucille's tirade. "Frau Lucille, you will speak with dignity in the presence of the council. Julius, you will move to the far corner of the room until you are spoken to."

19

Lucille panted and struggled. Julius hastened to the vacant corner as though he had committed a misdeed before his tutor. Carl commanded the council. "Give me the decree which has caused this confusion."

A councilman on his left opened a satchel and shuffled through papers, then passed a small, bound parcel to Carl. He took the binder and noticed blood droplets from his hand had stained the pages. He read the first lines, noting that the action resulted from Carl's death, but it went on to say that the declaration was unanimous and irreversible. He raised his eyes and surveyed the councilmen. "Is this how you would vote today?"

When they remained silent he elevated his voice. "I asked you a question as your Kronprince. Is this the way you would vote today? And do you want to be ruled by a decree stained in blood?" He threw the document toward them. A few drops of blood splattered the closest councilmen. One winced whiie the other wiped his cheek.

"No, Herr Carl, no," came the subdued reply from a few while others shook their heads with downcast eyes.

Carl gaveled the meeting to order. "The first order of business is the reversal of this ridiculous irreversible decree." He sat.

Lucille found her voice and screamed. "Only the unanimous consent of council can act in contradiction to the law! Only the unanimous council!"

Carl fell for the trap. "Very well, we will draft the wording later. All who will vote to reverse the decree which was based on the false premise of my death please raise your right hand." He held his own high.

Ten of the twelve councilmen meekly raised their hands. Carl glared at the other two seated side by side. He said, "All opposed now raise your right hands."

The two procrastinators remained motionless. Carl proclaimed, "It is done. The unanimous vote of all participating councilmen declares the prior order void. I will assume my duties."

"No! It's not unanimous. All twelve must vote as one. The lawyers must give their opinion." Lucille's struggle against Wilhelm and Ernst seemed almost successful. "The Southern

Bavarian legislature must rule. Julius, come take your seat! You are still prince. I am princess."

Carl realized there may be a legal technicality and was positive that the ruling would go in his favor. As he looked down on the burning claw scrape on his right hand, it continued to bleed. Lucille had nicked a vein. *The only act of violence has been committed by the wench.* Carl knew if he would retain rule of the council today, he could only do it by force. He also knew that would work against him with the lawyers and the legislature.

He addressed the council. "Gentlemen of the council, I was born to be Ruler of the Altmann Principality. I have prepared myself for the duties and the title all of my life. The dignities bequeathed me by my father and grandfather are such that I will not conduct the business of council while blood pours from my body and detracts from the solemnity of the occasion. Nor should *anyone* conduct such grave business who would, in the presence of all, inflict such a grotesque wound on a rightful heir.

"I will set about to put in order all legal matters related to my claim. I will now take my leave. For those ten councilmen who voted affirmatively in rescinding the decree, I declare to you that this meeting is adjourned."

Carl moved unceremoniously toward the door as several of the councilmen rose to leave behind him. Wilhelm and Ernst saw their chance and released Lucille. She shrieked, "The council is not to leave! The council is not to leave. Julius, take your seat quickly! Stay! Stay! Eiiiieeee!"

Carl glanced back from the outer steps to see ten councilmen separating to go home. The two who withheld their votes remained in the meeting room with the dubious pair who had, doubtlessly, paid them handsomely for the position they had taken.

# Chapter 3

Carl's early childhood, his training and experience in adulthood, had prepared him to rule. He hated the role thrust upon him, that of going to lawyers and politicians, hat in hand humbly seeking redress. Rulers should give, not receive redress. He had sought a favorable legal ruling from Helmut Schalter in Munsburg, the Justizhorde for Southern Bavaria. The best Schalter would do was to issue a legal brief which neutralized Altmann's government pending a ruling by the Southern Bavarian legislature.

Immediately, Carl heard rumors from his supporters that Julius and Lucille had declared that Carl had betrayed his principality by causing its people to be without guidance in a period of terrible political unrest.

"I have betrayed?" he shouted at Schmitt. "I have betrayed? If those idiots would abdicate as they should, the principality would be with government, the best it has had in over two years!"

Helga, who had taken to sitting in on his meetings with Schmitt, urged him to control his temper

"I'll avoid violence, my frau, but you must understand also, that I'm a man first, and a prince second. I'll defend my honor. I'll not cower from attack. And I won't be bullied by any coward on the streets, in the highways, or in the houses where my requests must be taken. Speaking of cowards, I need to visit my beloved brother right now. Not that I would take pleasure at seeing him leap into the arms of his honey laden wife when I shout 'boo!' at him."

"Yes, you would take pleasure!" she answered as Schmitt chuckled. "Carl, you must not go there. You're too angry. In fact, your only pleasure these days is in frightening Julius. Please, Carl, go to Leitendorf and asked Prince Streib to present your case before the legislature without delay."

ෆ   ෆ   ෆ

Prince Streib of the Principality of Lietendorf was a distant cousin of Carl and legislator to the Southern Bavarian assembly. Carl had never liked Streib because of the man's evident stupidity, however, Carl was sure Streib would side with him against any liberal factions that sought to bring down all princes. In fact, Carl was keenly aware that the reason the illegal decree hadn't been promptly reversed on his return was because of political unrest throughout Germanic lands. Stronger and stronger protests, including isolated violence, had erupted supporting various forms of democracy, presenting an ominous danger to all principalities. Those who supported the decree may well have hoped for such a fall here, not that they held any fondness for Julius. Simply, they perceived Julius as easier to topple when the time came.

Carl, Wilhelm and Ernst found Streib, not in Leitendorf, but in Munsburg, where he spent all his time, whether or not the legislature was in session, ignoring his own principality, leaving a juvenile daughter in charge.

The short, rotund prince received Carl's company with his usual phony aplomb, fussing over their comforts, introducing them to everyone, even strangers, then settling into his leather cushioned chair and ordering schnapps for all. A comely chambermaid entered with a silver tray laden with an outrageous assortment of bottles. She laid it in front of Streib as she bent low to reveal an ample bosom. She gave a familiar smile to her employer then shuffled out to bring crystal glasses. Streib's pig-like eyes followed the lively form until she disappeared.

"Ah, yes, my cousin Carl. I trust that in your travels, an adventurer such as yourself has learned how to live." He smiled and looked to the just-exited doorway. "There is more to life than the next war. There are finer things than fighting."

Carl felt nauseous disgust with his sixty-year-old cousin's self indulgence and wanted to get on with his agenda. He noted that the old toad hadn't even asked the intent of the visit. When the young

23

fraulein, Berta, returned with the glasses the lass curtsied properly as Streib introduced her to everyone, but she reserved her devastating smile for Streib. He dismissed her with instructions to come back occasionally to see to their needs.

*Likely the imbecile fears she'll have time to cavort with her young liaisons if he leaves her too long.* Carl fumed.

"Cousin Carl, I've learned how to rule a principality, serve in the legislature, remove worry from my heart, and put in its place pleasure. I have even learned that women can lead effectively if properly coached by men from the wings. My daughter Franzen leads the Council in Lietendorf, such a pleasure and a relief that I don't have to bother with the petty day to day issues of the peasants. Many in the legislature worry of the liberal uprisings in the land. I tell them to live life. They fret too much. Do you not agree?" Streib grinned broadly revealing the gap of a missing tooth which Carl remembered from earliest acquaintance.

"Yes, I suppose you are right, Herr Streib, provided we princes don't simply shift the worry to someone else's shoulder. When that day comes, there are no more German princes. That would be a sad day. Would you agree, my cousin?"

"I trust that you haven't come to spoil my mood, Herr Carl." He grunted as he leaned to pour the drink. "Surely you have nothing amiss in the quaint little kingdom where you rule. Tell me, do you have a fraulein on the side?"

Carl held his response until the vibration of rage settled. "Not my style, cousin. I'm still in love with my wife. Helga is quite beautiful, you know. Please drink your schnapps so that my purpose won't seem so ominous." Carl perceived that the simple man couldn't face responsibility when cold sober.

Streib downed his drink and looked for the fraulein to refill it. He poured another. "You have heavy burdens? I had hoped your visit was one of pure friendship."

"I will bear my burdens, but you can be of help to your loyal cousin in the most trivial of matters. Have you not heard that my brother Julius has claimed my title in my absence and now doesn't wish to abdicate?" *He, too, has a wonderful female assisting him.*

"I…I suppose I've heard. Surely you've worked out that small affair. You are the soldier, are you not?" He leaned back in hyena laughter.

"I swore to my wife that I wouldn't use violence to return to the rule, though I've been tempted. The Justizhörde tells me that an item must be passed by the legislature in order to rescind the decree of Julius. I trust only you, Prince Streib, to introduce such a measure. Never would I stoop to one of the liberal representatives who would betray the rights of princes."

Streib frowned. "Can you advise me of exactly what you want? I'll call a scribe tomorrow and you can make your wishes known to him. Tonight, we celebrate!"

Prepared for the occasion, Carl produced papers from his coat. "I've taken the liberty to write it out for you. This proposal cites the exact decree, then explains how to rescind each section according to Southern Bavarian law. It leaves no room for error. You would need but to submit the paper for legislative consideration. Of course, a few well chosen words on your part will speed it to final passage."

Streib took the papers and fondled them like a child making paper dolls. "Perhaps you could take a quill, cousin, and jot down a thought or two on what I should say."

"I've already taken care of that. You have the final page."

"Ahhh! You are thorough. I could use you on my staff. If all else fails in Altmann, you can come here and work for your beloved cousin." Another staccato laugh, then he tossed the package onto the table and lifted his drink.

Carl met one of Streib's clerks before departure and, at the risk of offending his princely cousin, moved to scoop the papers from the table where they still lay from the night before. He gave them to the man, explaining at some length their intent and importance. He left with a slightly improved feeling that the process would go through.

Expecting progress on his request within weeks, two months passed in which Altmann had no government because of the Justizhörde's moratorium and Streib's inaction. The working class and the poor grew desperate. Carl placed an article in the local newspaper explaining the situation and emphasizing that Prince

Streib of the Principality of Lietendorf agreed to present legislation.

Other presses, including Munsburg, copied the item. Streib evidently felt the pressure of the press release and presented the measure, forgetting the prepared introductory script left by Carl. His confused colleagues hesitated to call for a vote pending further study.

Carl couldn't believe months had passed and he still floundered in the confusion caused by a ridiculous misunderstanding. In the drinking hall where he spent more and more time he said to his friend, Beckler Roth, "Wars have been fought over less than this issue. I would gladly go to war rather than deal passively with waiting. I've visited my farms, my sheep meadows, mills, my vineyard. I'm completely caught up on business affairs. Now, I drink…and wait."

"Herr Carl, why don't you give up your claim? You look drawn and tired. Sooner or later, you'll commit murder against your own kin. Then you'll be put away where you can never be ruler of Altmann," said Roth, a wiry part owner of the tavern, a favorite of Carl, and heir to a small forestry fortune which enabled him to shun work.

"I may be put away, but some would go down with me in the scrape." The thirty-year-old's short, curled beard and arched eyebrows suggested a near smile at all times. "Look at you, Roth. You have me speaking as though I'd really do such a thing. You ought to be ashamed. Sometimes I wish I could go back to my youth, start all over, start a new Altmann, rebuild the castle my father and I dreamed of."

"Back to your youth? You're not old. Not a man in Altmann would face you in a duel. None in all Europe! You're in your prime. You can do anything you set your heart to."

At home, Carl related the conversation to his friend, Dr. Schmitt, and laughed.

Schmitt didn't laugh. "Roth is right. You are strong. It's not too late to start a new Altmann or to build the castle of your dreams. You are the one who is wrong, wrong to hang on to the past. Old princedoms die from within, Carl. You will die with them if you stay here. They are starving from too many people and not enough work. Princes throughout the states are much like your cousin Streib. They will hang on with their fingernails until they hang by their necks. The winds of change are upon us."

Carl's face flushed. "Shut up, Schmitt. You anger me. You don't consider my circumstances. I have a son who'll become prince. I cannot abandon his hopes."

"Ah, Carl." Schmitt's light frame shuddered. "Forgive me for offending you. What I must tell you now is what I should have said at the beginning. You won't long have a son. Hans is dying. He will not live until the autumn."

# *Chapter 4*

Carl's heart sank. He had ignored his seriously ill son, too caught up in his own agenda to pay attention. Helga, too, had appeared increasingly tired and relied on Elisabeth and the maid. She seldom addressed their mutual concern for Hans, saying simply at day's end, "Speak to your son before you sleep."

Hans failed to awake from his near constant sleep a few days after Schmitt had spoken of it. After the funeral, Carl directed that all visitors be turned away. Expecting Carl's mourning to last a few days, Helga and Elisabeth languished for two weeks. When he asked Elisabeth to fetch Dr. Schmitt, she became terrified that he was seriously ill.

Carl emerged from the long meeting with Schmitt looking pale but well. He told Helga they would talk. At dinner, they glanced to one another in pleasure that he ate like a deprived wolf. They adjourned to the parlor and sat with knees touching.

"My loves, you know I have great respect for Herr Schmitt. He profoundly affects me with his views. But what I must tell you is my own thinking. Please never blame him for my folly or success, whichever it should be."

Elisabeth's face drew tense. "Father, please. Your health is the issue. What has he told you?"

"Health?" Confusion creased his brow. "My health is fine. No, I am thinking seriously of emigration to North America. There is great promise in that land and, it seems, none at all in the German states in these times."

The two women smothered him with hugs, kisses, and joyous tears. He returned their affection warmly. "Settle yourselves, my loves. Allow me to continue. I think not only of myself but of the thousands of my subjects who would likely follow us to the new land. We'd have much to prepare, perhaps too much. Perhaps it cannot be done. We will see. But first, I must know if you will support such a venture. If you will not – cannot – I will not go further."

In reality, Elisabeth had no say in the matter. Carl could even choose to disregard Helga's word but Carl and Elisabeth both waited for Helga to speak.

Helga sighed in relief that Carl's health was not the issue. She wiped her eyes. "I first ask myself if I'm strong enough for the voyage, but perhaps the change in climate would be good for me. Often I have pondered if the dampness of the land has caused my illnesses. I wonder if Hans would have lived had he been born in a different place. What do you think, husband?"

He pulled her close. "The area I would choose is the southern land – the Republic of Texas. Schmitt has convinced… No, I said I will not blame Schmitt. But I believe him. The climate is warm, even hot for most of the year. The winters seldom see ice or snow. Not as much rain falls there. Because our colony would be so dependent on agriculture, these features make Texas superior to Wisconsin, or Missouri, or Pennsylvania where many Germans have already gone.

Helga said, "Is Texas not a part of the United States as are the other places?"

"No, it is an independent republic. There is even the possibility that if enough Germans could emigrate there, that we would control the national politics, form a German republic on American soil."

"So that's the real reason you want to go. Carl, you'll be making a mistake if you let your desire for power overrule your good judgment."

"No, no! That's not the real reason." Her response disappointed him. "Besides the weather being good for you and much better economic conditions, the freedoms to strive to attain are unimaginable. We have lived in comfort because we belong to the ruling family, but I would gladly give up my claim to Altmann to see a few thousand of my subjects better themselves. But Schmitt does say that the colony would need good leadership above all else. He says I am the man to give it."

"And if you are not, it is Schmitt's fault, correct?" Helga laughed while speaking.

"No, no, no! I just hate to say in my own words that I am the man to lead." Carl was laughing with his wife when he finished the statement. They hugged nervously, knowing they hadn't enjoyed such pleasure in months. This felt so right.

Helga asked, "And how would you leave the issue of your stolen principality? Would you allow Julius to continue?"

"I've been in my room for many days and have hatched some eggs. We may be able to play the strife with Julius to our advantage."

Helga's energy soared as their chat went on into the night.

Elisabeth, at first appalled began to smile. "I feel myself warming to the idea. Surely, if I cannot persuade my friends to join us, you could talk to their fathers." She leaped and hugged his neck.

They covered the topics of finances, ship charter, passports, travel and arrival provisions, dangers, setbacks. Carl delivered a confident answer to each question.

ೞ    ೞ    ೞ

When Carl began revealing to his confidants the sincerity of his thoughts for emigration, their response overwhelmed him. Schmitt grew delirious with enthusiasm and offered to take charge of any and every effort.

"Schmitt, above all, you are my first lieutenant. Spread your workload. Enlist everyone in the cause for raising funds, the overriding concern at the outset. Organize an immigration society to raise funds from every source which could conceivably benefit, those who go as well as those who stay behind. Merchants and manufacturers who could gain trade. You understand."

Schmitt nodded in full agreement. "And the governing bodies that stand to rid their borders of much poverty, the volunteers themselves who own assets or could borrow from relatives."

ೞ    ೞ    ೞ

Money sat within one of the *eggs* Carl had hatched – the castle's treasure – gold – hidden in the basement floor. His father had told him of its existence only because he was heir. Positive that Julius didn't know of it, even Carl had no idea of its value.

Carl, Wilhelm and Ernst donned their uniforms and rode about the highlands locating soldiers from their command. A cavalry of twenty trotted straight to the Altmann castle in broad daylight. Gustav answered the innocent knock before Julius could know his brother called. Two castle guards inside caught unaware because of the absence of threats or confrontations for months, quickly laid down their weapons.

Julius stood, startled, in view of the door as Carl bolted inside. He screamed. "You have no right! Lucille!"

Carl charged the quivering man and struck him in the chest with both fists, knocking him to the floor. Carl's voice rattled paintings on the wall. "Shut your mouth, swine! I will tolerate not one word from you. My men will bring your thieving frau to join you shortly."

Julius, curled in a fetal position, began a whimper, then a sob, then a gurgling, terrified cry.

Carl pulled the saber and raised it full length. "I said, shut your mouth! Childish crying will get your throat cut!" His military training and battlefield experience taught him to never hover with a sword. As soon as it's raised, it comes down with all force. He trembled with temptation.

Wilhelm and Ernst, enlightened from the first time they restrained the energetic Lucille, sent four troopers upstairs. She refused to place her feet on the stair treads, so the soldiers carried her by the arms locked tightly at her sides, taking repeated kicks from her thick healed shoes. Carl winced in sympathetic pain and subdued a chuckle as he watched the screaming descent.

When his troops had wrestled her to a position directly above her cowering husband, Carl ordered her on the floor.

She screamed. "You will not put me on the floor. I don't fear your threats, you decorated pig."

"Arnold, bind and gag her," Carl commanded his young blonde corporal.

31

"What are you going to do to me? The government will have your head. You are no longer Prince of Altmann." Broad bands of silk secured her arms to her sides. "You would not be allowed this authority if you were. I am prince...princess. The council voted...rrrrr." The gag plopped easily into her ever open mouth as they tied the scarf securely. They deposited her form so that she looked adoringly into the eyes of her terrified husband.

Julius asked meekly, "Carl, what are your intentions?" He began to hyperventilate.

"Relax and enjoy your temporary principality, brother. My house in which you live still holds many of my possessions. After a thorough search, I'll leave. We'll talk calmly and peacefully another day of our differences."

The soldiers dislodged bricks from the basement floor where Carl directed, shortly unearthing a metal clad strongbox two feet square and eighteen inches high with hinged handles on each end. They issued an audible groan when they lifted it from its grave. Carl draped the prize with a blanket to exit the house.

ଔ    ଔ    ଔ

Schmitt reported that a daily stream of indignant peasants and workmen filed into Julius' residence after that day, demanding work, demanding food, voicing their discontent with the lack of council action. They protested the tax burden, asked for Carl's return.

A similar crowd besieged the legislature in Munsburg, petitioning for Carl's reinstatement, and money. Schmitt reported Streib near madness from the flow of fierce dirty faces into his chambers.

Carl gauged reactions to the public pressure through the feedback from Schmitt and others. When he deemed the time right, he drove again to his cousin, Prince Streib. "Cousin, tell me it's not true that you are stressed. You assured me in our last visit that you've learned to live, relax, enjoy life."

Through glazed eyes, Streib cried, "I have no time for myself. Wherever I go they find me. It is madness. Carl, you have a way with people. Many of these are your subjects...were your subjects...could still be your subjects. I will help you get your principality back. I will do anything. Tell me what to do to get them off my back."

"Ah, my prince, I too have learned to live, relax, enjoy life. I took your advice. I'm not sure I want my position back." He sprawled in the cushioned chair.

"Carl, please, there must be something you can do to help me. I fear an uprising. Please help me. Please."

"I was trying to help you when I brought the legislation." Carl rolled his hand easily. "It's good for the princes to be in a strong position. Do you agree? Why, my cousin, did you take so long? Why, indeed, is the article not already passed?"

Streib wheezed. "Carl, you must understand, we must follow strict protocol. An investigation was held," he lied. "The legislature sent for Julius. He brought a beautif...his frau with him. She spoke to the legislature at some length and impressed the legislature with the programs for reform which she offered. She appealed to them as honorable men to leave the original decree in place. I tried to persuade them. Most were convinced, by me, but still it didn't come to a vote."

"I am sure Frau Lucille can be charming in her fine clothes bought with my father's money. Did she charm you as well, Streib?"

"I must admit that at first I found her disarming. But I was strong, Carl. You must believe me! You must help me settle with these commoners. I want rid of them." He wiped schnapps from his chin.

Carl leaned back. "Many of these commoners, my former subjects, wish to emigrate to North America. Unfortunately, they have no money. So, dear Streib, you are stuck with their daily demands for the rest of your days. Their smelly bodies, both dead and alive, will grace your mansion, your offices, your courtyards as you stroll with the lovely, what was her name...oh, yes, Berta."

"Ahhhggg! Berta has left me. She was stupefied by the constant throng, pushed, disrespected, fondled. There was no time for me. I must get her back. Carl, please help me."

"Are the other legislators similarly harassed?"

"Yes, they are ready to do anything."

"Would they cherish the day if the vermin were shipped out to America never to return?"

"Y-yes, they would," Steib responded. "Why do you ask the question?"

"Would they find it a relief if I gave up my claim as Prince of Altmann and disappeared forever?"

"My cousin, I do not wish for you to disappear. You are the one man who can control this mob. But, yes, I suppose the legislators would find it a relief."

Carl fixed an intense stare on the rotund prince. "If I stay in Altmann, I'll fight for my right to rule forever. Economic conditions are getting worse for the working class, even the masters and the professionals. They'll not improve until revolution sets Altmann and Leitendorf on their ears. But if the legislature would support their travel, and mine, with funds from the public treasury, arrangements could be made for our departure to North America."

"Our departure? You would go with them?" Streib appeared stunned.

"Only with a generous monetary backing from the benefiting government."

"How much? Not that I can cause it to happen."

"Prince Streib, I have no doubt that you can cause it to happen. You have boundless powers of persuasion. In addition to other modest sources, we'll need approximately 200,000 guilders to make the voyage." Carl's knew his figure was ridiculously high, a starting point for negotiation. "And we must have it in time for the ships to reach America by mid autumn."

Carl called on other representatives in Munsburg to assure that his message didn't die with Streib. Within days, newspapers throughout Southern Bavaria carried headline stories suggesting the government might fund emigration grants and credits.

ɔʒ  ɔʒ  ɔʒ

Schmitt returned home with great excitement. "A dozen manufacturers and even more merchants have committed support." He wouldn't allow Carl to interrupt or congratulate him. "And, Carl, the ships used by the Society for the Protection of German Immigrants In Texas, Prince Solms-Braunfels' colony, are available in Bremen right now."

Hardly realizing the contagion had trapped him, Carl traveled by rail to Bremen on the north coast and signed contracts, placing a huge deposit of his own money to guarantee that a thousand immigrants would be ready to sail by September 15, 1845, three months away.

Headed home he told Wilhelm and Ernst, "You've been with me in battle. You know me well. But that was the bravest thing I ever did, or the most stupid."

To himself, he said, "That damned Schmitt."

# Chapter 5

Heinrich Schmitt had known Carl since childhood. His father had been Prince Christian's physician. Now, Schmitt continued in the tradition and ministered to all who occupied the castle, even Julius. He was the same age as Carl, shorter, slighter in build, fair skinned, light brown hair, as were many of his countrymen.

When Carl returned from the seaport, Schmitt greeted and praised him for acting on the commitment for ships. Schmitt said, "Solms-Braunfels almost succeeded in extracting travel funds from his government. Your efforts with Streib may be rewarded."

Carl said, "If that pompous ass, Solms, can get funds, I should be able to do the same."

Schmitt thought, *How could Solms be any more pompous than you, my princely friend?* "Good, then you understand that you must employ the utmost diplomacy."

"My strong suit, Schmitt. I will go straight to Julius, as I did Streib. The timing is right. He should be ready to cough up a goodly sum to assure my departure. I can hardly wait to see the expression on his face when I hint that I would leave the principality."

"Herr Carl, you have met with Julius twice. On both occasions, violence erupted. Not your fault, of course," Schmitt lied, "but I suggest in the matter of extracting funds, it may be better if I go."

Carl acted hurt. "My friend, you would deny me the pleasure of a visit to my dear brother? Are you opposed to closeness in families?"

Carl could hold a stern face, but he couldn't fool Schmitt. "In this instance, closeness will be preserved if I make the visit."

CR CR CR

When Schmitt entered the castle, Julius leaped with glee. "Doctor Schmitt, I am so pleased to see you. Come in. I will summon Frau Lucille. She is in need of your services. She is having difficulty breathing and a great rash has erupted around her waist."

Lucille appeared momentarily, ashen faced and breathing in shallow gulps. Schmitt ushered the pair to the private room where he had often examined family members. "Frau Lucille, we must loosen your corset and lower your dress from the shoulders. Turn your back to me."

Stripped to the waist, Lucille waited for the diagnosis. Schmitt, the most professional of physicians, fought inner turmoil to think objectively as he applied stethoscope to the smooth skin and observed her v-shaped back. Though he needed to listen to her lungs from the front and examine the rash, he didn't allow himself.

"Julius, please help me. We will fasten Lucille's clothing." Both men struggled to bring the back buttons and loops into alignment.

As they finished, Lucille's short breaths returned.

Schmitt spoke. "Frau Lucille, your clothing has shrunk. I am positive there is no affliction upon you which would not find relief should you see your tailor." *She has gained weight from opulent living. Wait until I tell Carl.* He produced a jar of skin ointment.

"Julius, I must discuss a matter of business with you. I feel you will be most pleased."

"Certainly, Herr Schmitt. You and Lucille will come into my office."

Lucille excused herself to change clothes, admonishing her husband to hold the discussion. She returned in a silk gown, enveloped by the fragrance of the medicinal balm.

"Julius, I have a possible solution to the political difficulties of the principality, in fact, the difficulties of all German peoples. But each domain must be willing to help locally, even sacrifice. In the case of Altmann, we could solve two problems with one simple solution.

"All public bodies are assisting the people in emigrating to the Americas. Altmann must do the same. We could relieve ourselves of the poor and at the same time create western colonies for trade. Altmann folks favor the Republic of Texas in North America for emigration."

"Yes, yes, Herr Schmitt. Perhaps we can help, if the legislature would give us our title and authority. But what if they should act against us? Carl would not be smart enough to help the emigrants. I would be tempted to take the boat myself if he is reinstated."

Schmitt shuddered at the thought. "You have not heard the best part."

Lucille leaped on the statement. "What is it, Herr Schmitt? What?"

"We could resolve the issue of your title in the same way. I have personally heard Carl say he would give up his claim to the title, if sufficient funds were made available for the emigrants."

Julius frowned. "My brother is not that magnanimous. Why should he do such a thing to help the poor?"

"Because, my undisputed prince, he would go with the emigrants. He has visions of grandeur in America. A new Altmann, a new principality. But lack of money will never let it happen."

Julius and Lucille looked to one another, their worried faces turning to smiles. "There is money. How much do you think?"

Schmitt wouldn't allow the amount of his extortion to be set until he had explained the magnitude of the venture, including the almost certainty of Southern Bavaria's support, the merchants and manufacturers who stood by, the modest means of the people. The pair gained enthusiasm after every exchange of questions and answers. Schmitt described with eloquent detail the return of pristine hillsides, a robust economy, and the healthy tax base once enemies, poverty and disease were shipped across the Atlantic. When their excitement reached a fever pitch, he under-calculated the other resources and exaggerated the departing numbers, drawing on paper a remainder of funds Julius and Lucille must make up.

Their hopes turned to despair when they saw the amount, but Schmitt encouraged them that the final figure could be far less if they urged businessmen to help. Also, speed was important. Ships must sail in time to reach Texas before winter.

Schmitt promised to return and see to Lucille's health and to further discuss emigration as he packed his case and left.

ය   ය   ය

Carl allowed his friend to run out of voice as he told every detail of the visit. He wriggled in his chair and thrust his face forward hanging on every word. Schmitt said, "There, I have told you all."

Carl clasped his hands. "Tell me again about Lucille's rash. How many kilograms has she gained?"

As the month of July closed, Schmitt had organized The Society of Altmann Immigrants. He often asked Carl to travel with him to visit key people, those who would want to join in the voyage and those who would invest in the venture for their future profits back home. Carl established a registration office for all volunteers. He required that for every third farmer, an artisan, master craftsman or professional must also enlist. And for every three farmers and one craftsman, he could allow one family with no means or skills at all.

"And if we're still not fully booked to fill our ships, travelers should be accepted on a first-in-line basis." He hadn't meant this directive as public knowledge, but the walks outside society headquarters soon saw lines of poverty-stricken peasants.

Of the Society's twenty-man committee, half planned to go to the new land while the other half hoped to gain by staying behind. All were professionals or businessmen. Mueller, Schultz, Krug nodded in agreement along with Schmitt. Doctor Albert Hagerdorn likewise approved.

Carl wrote to the President of the Republic of Texas asking immigration permission, even requesting free land. Meetings usually dealt with money and provisions, estimating per-family needs. Carl argued that Schmitt's figures were too low, both individually and in total.

Schmitt began to regret his insistence on Carl's leadership. He knew the prince always thought in terms of making the voyage and the settlement easy on himself. *Of course, he wants to think like a pompous prince. If he orders it, it should be done! Period.*

"Herr Carl, we need to set minimums, not maximums, on the number of emigrants, the number of professionals and craftsmen we must have, and the finances. Bear in mind that you have already committed a great sum of your own wealth. And wisely so. We must not fail now."

Schmitt sensed that everyone agreed but some were reluctant to voice it in Carl's presence.

"Wisely so? You cajoled me into doing it," Carl said quietly to Schmitt. To the committee, he said, "Yes, but lowering our sights from the ideal is not wise until we hear from the legislature…and from my dear brother."

Mueller spoke. "You are both right. Let us make priority of those items. Time is crashing down upon us. Dr. Hagerdorn and I will go to Prince Streib. Dr. Schmitt, will you approach Julius again?"

"Yes."

"Wait, Schmitt," Carl broke in. "As your chosen leader, I must make these contacts. I have prepared for the role since earliest childhood."

Schmitt flushed. "You have prepared for it an entire three months, Carl. No, you must not approach your brother. And if you go to Streib, take Herr Mueller and Dr. Hagerdorn with you. Please."

"And where is *your* great diplomacy when you speak to me, Schmitt? I was making a small joke at your expense."

ରେ ରେ ରେ

Carl traveled to Munsburg with Mueller and Hagerdorn. They remained with Streib three days and nights until their measure was introduced and passed by the legislature. The legislature appropriated 100,000 guilders, half in cash subject to a promissory note and half in the form of credit at New Orleans a year after the colony arrived in Texas. Terms heavily favored the government but everyone understood that if the commerce of the colony succeeded, the obligation would be forgiven soon enough.

Schmitt approached Julius and Lucille. They wrote a draft on their bank in Altmann and made Schmitt sign papers conditioned only upon Carl leaving Southern Bavaria. The entire note would be forgiven when he relinquished his Altmann citizenship in favor of Texas.

When all collateral was toted, including the estimated value of real property to be sold by the travelers, the society saw on paper a figure three-fourths the amount they had hoped. Carl pushed from the table and stalked about the room without a word. Schmitt motioned, when Carl's back was turned, for the others to remain silent. At last Carl stepped outside.

Schmitt spoke. "Let him cool, gentlemen. I believe he'll come around. The sum is near to the minimum I had earlier recommended, though we never acted on it. How could we, with such a strong willed leader? If you agree, I will urge him with all force to accept our condition, and sail, subject to one thing."

"And that one thing, Herr Schmitt?"

"Permission from Texas. It still has not arrived."

The members nodded and grunted affirmatively as they heard the door creak.

Carl entered. "I suppose transactions have taken place behind my back. Would you kindly tell your director what it is you have voted in his absence."

"We have not voted a thing, nor will we do so without your presence, Herr Carl. But I speak for all when I say, we want to go through with the venture." Schmitt rose from his chair. He stared coldly into Carl's eyes. He paced. He looked back. Carl glanced over the waiting faces, his impatience showing. Schmitt finally spoke as he turned directly to Carl and pointed. He raised his voice. "Will you lead us?"

Carl pulled himself to full military attention and faced the table. "I will lead! Will you follow?"

With no committee effort, the village seemed to know. Peasants emerged from every shadow, hand carts and great packs on their shoulders. They wouldn't leave. Carl and Schmitt, as well as the other committeemen, were at wit's end as to what to tell them. They knew start time would be critical if word came from Texas. The people must be ready.

A month passed. The letter came. The people cheered wildly. The committee tallied 801 souls for departure by ox and horse-drawn wagons and afoot for the rail head at Munich. Rumors floated that another 500 were enroute to Altmann from neighboring provinces–all dirt poor, unemployed laborers. While passage was booked for a thousand, Carl knew that immigrants would continue to pour into Texas after the initial landing if they sent any hope of success back home. He and Schmitt agreed to try to hold the present party to size and move on.

A mile out of Altmann, a running horseman hailed the procession from behind. Carl ordered no slowing. He and Wilhelm spurred to intercept the rider.

"Roth!" Carl greeted him cheerfully. "You have brought us your fortune? Thank you, my friend. I will write to you from the new country."

"I brought you Roth! Did you really think you could leave me behind? I will establish a proper biergarten in the new land. Who could be more qualified? I know I am not listed on your manifest, but you must make an exception."

"I make the exception. I will introduce your soft hands to hard work on the voyage and in Texas."

Now, Carl could claim most of his close friends in the procession – his uniformed officers and former soldiers recruited from the rural areas; the smiling families of Elisabeth's friends; Helga's charming sister and her husband, Katheryne and Christian Linnartz, a successful farmer. Schmitt straddled a strong gelding beside Carl near the head of the caravan, his Eva and five daughters drawn in their oxen wagon behind Helga and Elisabeth.

"We will camp on the open plain for the first time," Carl said to Schmitt. "Good practice for the task ahead in America. I have assigned guard duties, not that we expect Indian attacks this time."

"The cook teams, I have appointed. A little music will follow dinner," Schmitt replied. He dropped behind Carl's prancing stallion as though to remind his charges.

As evening settled, Carl heard the musical clangs and thuds of horns and drums before the wagons stopped. He turned in the saddle to see Schmitt chastising the musicians for rushing their act, anxious to set up even before cooking. "Germans! Hmph."

# *Chapter 6*

Outside the depot, Carl fumed to Schmitt on learning that train fare for man, beast and freight totaled slightly higher than budgeted. "I had reasons for insisting on adequate finances. Do you not now understand?"

"I always understood. Perhaps something along the way will be less costly," Schmitt replied cheerfully.

"Yes, our labor and produce, most likely," Carl scoffed and stalked away.

"Carl, wait." He stopped as Schmitt caught up. "We cannot continue this way. We will not reach Bremen as friends, much less Texas."

"What do you mean, Herr Schmitt?" Carl's boots clomped. "I speak the simple truth and you are offended. One would think you are the director of this expedition as often as you've coerced me to change my mind."

"You are the director! No one questions that fact. If I have helped with your decisions, I must say they have been good decisions, but you are the one who has made them. If anyone errs in a small way it should not be cause for Germans to fall into decent. Are we not Germans? Do we have no need for solidarity?"

"Yes, above all we are German." A gloved finger stabbed the sky. "We must never forget that. We must act as one when we get to the new land and on the voyage as well. I'll emphasize this to the people. And, Schmitt, I apologize for being short with you. Tell me one thing, Schmitt."

"I accept your apology. And what is the one thing you ask?"

"Do Germanic people never argue?" A score of fellow travelers watched amused as the prince and the doctor engaged in tumultuous laughter as all waited to board the trains.

Carl fussed over the draft cattle and the horses in separate cars, especially the treatment of his own horse. Each time, attendants assured better attention to detail – twice daily feedings, daily brushings, prevention of fighting between horses in adjoining stalls. Each time he heard grumbling as he left.

He complained to the train commandant. "Tressler, the train moves too slowly. Only fifteen kilometers per hour?"

Tressler said, "The rails are in poor repair on curves, speed is dangerous."

At the scheduled stop, Carl led his horse out of the car, saddled him and rode a kilometer up the track and returned. "Commandant Tressler, the tracks are in fine condition. Try for twenty kilometers."

The trip suffered no mishap to man or beast and no serious illnesses broke out. They continued on schedule and could reach Bremen with a week to spare. Then the speeding lead train gently derailed on a curve near Fuida. Tressler sent men scurrying up and down the road to set fires to stop the approaching trains.

"Schmitt, the oncoming locomotive must retreat anyway. Take it all the way to Bremen and tell them to hold the ships." Carl unwrapped his arms from Schmitt's shoulders as the small doctor hastened to comply. *And I'll avoid your accusing mouth during this four-day delay.*

ᘓ   ᘓ   ᘓ

Bremen, inland on the River Weser, bustled with ship activity. The tall sail vessels – the Weser, the Ferdinand, the Herrschel, the Apollo, and four others – bobbed lazily in the water awaiting their mission. Carl's committeemen paid protocol to the Texas Consul's office though no consul was on duty, and the officials there voiced agreement with the departure. As they exited, what seemed a welcoming band of forty families, native to the local state of Hanover, greeted them cordially. Carl waved, smiling, and disappeared into his quarters.

The welcoming natives approached Schmitt. All spoke at once, anxiously inquiring about available space so that they could join the voyage. Schmitt sorted through the noise, asked a few questions, then sent his daughter, Margarethe, to get Carl.

The committee gathered at the door of Schmitt's room where he told them that the Hanover natives seemed to have their papers and supplies in order, though they lacked leadership.

As Carl and Margarethe approached, Schmitt heard the prince declaring, "There are the matters of funds and loyalty." He quit speaking when he saw Schmitt watching his approach.

Schmitt stepped back for Carl to take charge, but Carl turned his palm upward and folded his arms, meaning that Schmitt should continue.

Schmitt rephrased what his daughter had told Carl, and added, "Gentlemen, we didn't fill our quota in Altmann and the surrounding principalities. We have space for another two hundred travelers on the ships, all fellow Germans dedicated to our same principles. They will eventually find their way to Texas. Much goodwill could be achieved by inviting them to join us." He waited for *Old Pomp und Prunk* to bellow his objections.

Carl said, "My thoughts exactly, Schmitt! I will require but one item, easily handled by me. I will speak to them as a group and extract their loyalty to me…to our society. They will understand that in Texas, they form a colony with us, not Solms."

*Oh, hell, could the loyalty not be built during the voyage?* Schmitt thought. *He cannot hold them to such a pledge anyway once we are on Texas soil.*

Carl stood on a platform above the pier. The strong wind and noise of the docks couldn't drown out his voice. "Folks of Hanover, I am Prince Carl Franz von Altmann, director of emigration. You seek what we seek – a new life in a new land. Therefore we have much in common. You must direct all questions and petitions to me. You must meet the following conditions for consideration for passage on our ships. First you must have all emigration papers in order, good conduct citations, birth certificates, marriage license.

"You must have, individually or collectively, adequate funds to equal, on average, an amount of 300 florins per family for your fares.

"You must have documentation of your professions or skills from your native state. You must be of good character with no criminal record.

"You must understand that your allegiance is to me, that is, to the Society of Altmann Immigrants. You are no longer subjects of Prince Solms-Braunfels and the Society for the Protection of German Immigrants in Texas. You will be required to take an oath. In Texas you will continue with us to our new location. You will not defect to become independent or to rejoin the Solms colony."

Schmitt thought his leader would never step down, laying more and more requirements on the pilgrim travelers. When Carl finished, he called for a makeshift band to play and sing a number of marches and folk ballads. Schmitt mouthed the songs impatiently. To his surprise, every family met every requirement smiling. They had already gathered their monies in common, at least enough for the anticipated fare. They signed the oaths of allegiance to Altmann without blinking an eye.

The committee inspected the ships for safety, the food supplies for quantity and quality. Solms, they learned, had complained about foodstuffs so severely before, the merchant suppliers didn't dare short this voyage, not knowing that a different, even naïve, prince was in charge this time. The committee could delay departure but not indefinitely. Carl expressed pleasure with the cabin provided for Helga, Elisabeth, and himself, handsomely furnished, roomy, a porthole, positioned near the bow of the flagship, Weser. However, the horse stalls did not please him at all and he ordered carpenters into service to build his bay stallion a suitable suite.

ভ   ভ   ভ

Carl held Helga's arm gently as she crossed the gangplank onto the Weser. Elisabeth clung to his other arm, continuing a chatter with her friends, Christine and Magdalene. Helga seemed unafraid of what lay ahead. They exuded confidence. As their subjects cheered, the ships moved slowly down the river. Well into the North Sea, the Weser began a painstaking turn to the west.

47

Helga broke into tears. "Is Altmann no more, Carl?"

"Altmann is forever, ahead of us in the new world. You will see."

The ships harbored in Plymouth, England, giving Carl a final chance to communicate with the others. A baby had died on the Ferdinand, no other deaths reported, no serious illnesses. They sailed south and turned west again as they circled Eddystone Lighthouse and departed the shores of Europe for the last time.

The alternate smells of the sea and aging food remained constant companions on the high seas. Captain Holbein reported to Carl two weeks later that they had crossed the halfway point toward New York Harbor. Carl guarded his words to Helga, seeing a distant unease in her eyes, not wanting to set off real fear. Other than sea sickness by many on board, including Carl and his family, the claws of death stayed sheathed.

The widely spaced ships landed over a five day period, at New York Harbor. Passengers disembarked but remained at the port both by Carl's orders and by American law. Helga declined to leave her berth, saying she wished to see no land except her adopted home in Texas. Carl and Elisabeth, with an entourage of Elisabeth's friends and their parents, toured the docks and bought costume jewelry and trinkets of American craft, the first they had ever seen. They enjoyed savory fruits and meat from vendors, taking an ample assortment back to Helga, who accepted only a simple apple.

As the ships passed through the Florida keys, a tropical wave caught them in open water and threatened to cast the vessels toward the shores. Seamen joined in the ocean sickness of their passengers which made control of the crafts difficult. The storm passed, but Helga remained bedfast through the docking in New Orleans. There, Carl asked Schmitt to join him on the Weser. From her hot face and occasional delirium, Schmitt feared Helga suffered from more than seasickness.

The committee, headed by Krug, reported to Carl. "Twenty passengers, ten of them young children, have died. Herr Ackerhof and his frau both perished leaving five children. We appointed a guardian family with a promise of compensation from the society.

"Collectively, the captains reported ten marriage ceremonies performed on board although the betrothed had represented themselves as married before we left Altmann, or Bremen. No single women were permitted – legally – you know."

Carl forced a faint smile as Krug continued. "With favorable weather, the ships can reach Indian Point, which our predecessors named Carlshafen, in a week."

&#x0186;&#x0298; &#x0186;&#x0298; &#x0186;&#x0298;

Schmitt ministered to Helga daily with no results. Her fever soared. Two days out of port in Texas, Schmitt told Carl to expect the worst and saw the man rage against his instincts to break into tears.

"Can you not do something? Is there no cure? Perhaps a medicine would keep her alive until she sees her new home. Schmitt, you have never let me down. You must not do so now."

Schmitt gripped Carl's hands. "Carl, my friend, you must prepare yourself to be strong. The entire venture pivots on your courage. The people must see you rise above grief. They will be as devastated as you when we…if we lose Helga. They see their own strength in her unconditional support of you. Now you must be both your own strong self and Helga as well."

Schmitt saw Carl's knees sway with the deck's motion and felt the man's pain, hardly able to control his own sorrow. But he walked away without further words.

Before land came into sight, Schmitt heard a primal groan such as he had never known come from the cabin of his prince as he approached. He knew what had happened and thought of leaving Carl alone for a period to vent his grief. Close as they were as friends, he knew the ceremonious leader wouldn't want to be seen in this state. He entered anyway.

Carl had dragged Helga from the bed and onto the floor, had her cradled in his arms, his legs sprawled forward, his face inches from hers as he spoke like a child pleading for her to respond. Schmitt glanced about for Elisabeth, relieved at her absence. He sat down on the floor behind Carl, not announcing his entrance.

Carl alternately talked to his dead wife then looked blankly at the wall or through the porthole. He rocked her in his arms like a mother would rock a child. Schmitt waited.

It seemed Carl would go on this way forever. Schmitt reasoned that the cadence must be broken to keep Carl from slipping into a state from which he could never recover. Most of an hour had passed. Schmitt whispered, "Carl." Then again, "Carl."

A long moment, then Carl said, "How long have you been there?"

Rather than feel embarrassment at his indiscretion, Schmitt felt relief. He knew Carl was strong enough to wish Schmitt hadn't witnessed the scene. That was good. Schmitt replied, "All the time, Carl. Could I help you place her on the bed?"

"Yes."

The act completed, Schmitt said, "Take all the time you wish. I will find Elisabeth. Then I will bring her back here. I will make all arrangements for the sea burial."

"No, she will not be buried at sea. We will wrap her body tightly in canvas and her final resting place will be on Texas soil. She wanted to go as much..." Carl lost control. Schmitt left.

# Chapter 7

Carl couldn't shake the guilt that resulted from the great silence between him and Helga which seemed to pervade every sanctuary. She hadn't questioned, though her eyes betrayed fear. He hadn't spoken, dreading that he would make matters worse. He sensed that Elisabeth blamed him for her mother's death, though she spoke few words to render that conclusion. He expressed his love to her often. But he knew her frends, including the Schmitt girls, delivered the greater therapy.

As he had done for much of the voyage, Carl conversed with Captain Holbein at the helm. A veteran of death at sea, Holbein's dark eyes and beard-shrouded face seemed to put death in perspective, dedicated to the task at hand.

"How long now, Captain?" Carl asked, slapping his hands on the rail, staring ahead.

Holbein drew on his pipe, laid it aside and rolled the wheel port side. "Good seas ahead. Maybe two days. Of course, only one ship a day can land. Never risk the vessels sailing too close to one another. You will notice that for much of the voyage, we have not even seen the other ships. That is for safety. One at a time! Once we dock, the others will follow. May take a week. More if there's wind."

The Weser landed on Holbein's schedule with no sign of panic among the sailors. Carl wrapped an arm around Elisabeth as he stepped to the plank to disembark first.

He held a set expression and made daily appearances among the immigrants as official in-processing went on. Elisabeth clung to his arm always, seeming to sense that Carl represented both her parents now. Unexpressed sympathy showed in his subjects' faces.

On the third day, the third ship, Ferdinand, docked. Carl told

Schmitt, "We should bury Helga this evening. The ships land too slowly to wait for a grand funeral celebration. Besides, we have no priest or minister."

"Good thinking, Carl. I shall never forget your rage when I suggested we invite Father Gaspar to join us."

Carl glanced toward Schmitt and grinned despite his grief. "Gather the committee, their families. Herr Christian will read over the grave site. Have Krug and Shultz build a sturdy wooden cross. Inland, I will commission a suitable stone. The immigrants' cemetery sits on the western hill."

Cg   Cg   Cg

The last shovel of soil mounded the grave, and the party waited Carl's lead, then turned down the hill. Light rain spewed ice crystals and whipped in the wind, adding to the gloom of the late shadows. Forcing his mind back to business, Carl asked Schmitt to assess the society's need for wagons.

After two days, Schmitt reported. "It seems early immigrants bought up all available wagons and animals. We can search farther out."

"Solms must be the greediest man in Texas," Carl complained. "He has raped the land of all provisions and made our plight difficult. He has in all likelihood gobbled up the best sites for settlement. Stop me if I challenge him to a duel when we meet – if we meet."

Schmitt voiced the committee's concern. "We may be forced to seek Solm's charity in the form of temporary shelter at New Braunfels. If we choose to settle west of him, we will have to make purchases of land from his people and the Texans there."

Carl scowled at the word *charity*. "Wilhelm, take ten men on a scout for land. Go to San Antonio and New Braunfels. I'll give you a letter of good faith assuring the society's backing. Lease or purchase land up to a league in size if you deem it suitable.

"Schmitt, set our carpenters, blacksmiths, wheelwrights scouring in all directions for materials to build wagons to add to those we brought.

"Gentlemen," Carl glanced toward the darkening sky. "We must have our colony inland before year's end. The weather turns on us even as we speak. And we must have more wagons. The Hanovers fear they are to be left behind."

And they would be. Carl felt a growing anxiety that he had a tough decision to make. He wouldn't risk taking travelers overland without wagons for nighttime cover and protection against Indian attack. Indeed, the Hanovers would carry lowest priority.

From his packing crate podium he shouted above the rain, "Travelers from Hanover, do not let the rumors alarm you. Surely we will find or build enough wagons before we move inland." He sensed from the size of the crowd that some had already bolted from the colony. "I must stress that wagons will determine the safety of all. If we are short of oxen-drawn vehicles, you must remain at Indian Point temporarily. The colony will return for you as soon as we establish our winter location, but I do not anticipate this happening."

The scowling faces of the second-class society members blazed a memory into Carl's mind. But one comely fraulein continued to smile from directly below him. He had seen her someplace. "I hold your membership in the society in high esteem, and I want the best for you. I will not misrepresent any facts to you. For that reason, I stand before you now."

He hoped his honest approach would count to secure their loyalty. He stepped down as the fraulein continued smiling, seeming to seek his acknowledgement. Berta! Streib's concubine at Munsberg. She turned to leave.

"One moment, fraulein. Tell me how you managed passage with our ships. You are not married."

She smiled showing rose in her cheeks, dark eyelashes and blue eyes. "Herr Prince." She curtsied. "But I am married, so say the papers which brought me."

"And where is your husband?"

"Alas, he was not true. He left soon after we landed and went in search of his cousins on Chocolate Creek. He said he would divorce me and marry one of them. He considered it a favor that he had made me his frau long enough to come to America and start

53

afresh. I hated to lose him. I was becoming attached."

*You attach quite easily. God forbid that your next attachment does not wreck a happy home.* He said, "And who cares for you now?"

"I am quite comfortable, thank you, my prince. All the men…people have been most gracious in seeing to my needs. If you should require the services of a maid in your quarters, please consider my application."

Others heard the conversation. He shuddered at the thought of bringing Berta into the log quarters, built by earlier immigrants, where he and Schmitt lodged. He said, "My cousin in Munsberg told me you left because you were harassed by the populous that came to his doors. How is it that you joined those people to sail across the ocean?"

"Your cousin must have misunderstood. I fell in love with a young man who came to the courts."

"I see. And he became your husband for the voyage."

"No, that was another."

"I see! Behave yourself, Fraulein Berta. And you will do well in Texas." Carl terminated the conversation and marched away. Was there no world where the oldest profession didn't find a place? New Altmann, indeed.

ᘓ ᘓ ᘓ

Carl felt pride and dread as he watched the carpenters pour into the work of building wagons from scratch, materials they had rounded up around Indian Point. Not nearly enough. Even if the column heads northwestward, they could hardly expect to break ground for spring crops. Solms's colony had succeeded through immense advance planning. Carl's, it seemed, had been a lurch into darkness, an impulse, a mistake.

He surveyed the encampments of earlier immigrants, who, for reasons of sickness, lack of transportation, and poverty, couldn't move inland. Sorrow showed on emaciated faces who had learned that the Altmann ships were independent of Solms. Carl didn't linger in their camps.

"Stay away from the earlier arrivals," he urged his people. "They carry diseases, and their piteous pleas will weaken our resolve. I also saw children serving able-bodied men who sat on kegs. I suspect they were left behind because they refused to work."

Schmitt added, "Many are not German. There are several Czech and Slav bands along the creek. "

"Czeck? Slav? That explains it!" Carl screamed. "It is no longer a request. All will avoid them subject to severe penalty." He now had more reasons than ever to move out, none to stay.

When Wilhelm and his company returned from their inland survey, Carl assembled the committee, not waiting to hear the report privately. He knew with certainty that one way or the other, the colonist must leave, unless they wanted a new director.

"We will not waste time, gentlemen. Wilhelm will give his report. Please take a seat. Herr Willi, please proceed." He scooted chairs hurriedly and was the first to sit.

Wilhelm appeared tired, sad and nervous. "My report will be brief, gentlemen. I have little to tell. We could not purchase or lease land in such a short period. Perhaps it could be done out in the Comancheria, but time would not permit such distant travel nor would I subject our people to such dangers. That land lies beyond the protective line of Texas frontier defenses. You will agree, Herr Carl?"

"So, what do you have to report? You have given us what did not happen." Carl's exasperation showed.

"The German Society at the village of New Braunfels offered charity if we can prove our solvency and industry. The acting director said…"

"Charity! You told the ass, Solms, we would not accept charity, of course?"

"Prince Solms was not there. He established the colony and left within months. They have a new leader, Count Otto von Meusebach. He, too, was gone. Some thought he was traveling about seeking credit for the society, and trying to settle old debts. It seems costs greatly exceeded available funds."

"But you told them we wouldn't accept charity. Correct?" Carl seethed with impatience just below anger.

"Actually, I accepted. Please, allow me to explain."

Carl leaped to his feet. "Yes! You will explain, Herr Wilhelm. And be quick about it!"

"The land President Jones spoke of west of New Braunfels is adequate for a temporary encampment from where we can make proper studies for permanency. The colonists will lend shelter and food to assure our survival until we move out. We would even have time, if we settle there for the winter, to break ground and start crops for the summer. We cannot accomplish even this much if we wander through the winter. And we may die of starvation."

"We will not die!" Carl screamed. "I will not tolerate such words from you or anyone. I will not allow our people to die. I will die first. But if the committee seeks my resignation, you have it." Rain, already sputtering, started pouring again.

When Wilhelm didn't resume, the moldy chamber fell into ominous silence. Carl didn't want to speak again but no one else would. He said, "Willi, is there more?"

"I have made a record of the details with the council at New Braunfels if you care to hear them."

"That will wait. I want to think. I will give the committee my recommendations within a day. Herr Wilhelm, Herr Schmitt, please remain with me for a while." Carl sank back into his chair as he dismissed the gathering.

With the three alone, Wilhelm said, "My prince, my captain, I deeply regret that I could not bring better news."

Carl extended his hand, "My dear friend, the fault lies within me. I always think I could have done better than you, or you, Herr Schmitt. I must admit, in this case, no one could have done better." He leaped from his chair and paced. "God, that rain! Is Texas always like this? It is not the lack of land to settle that will defeat us. It is the weather." Seated again, he eased his head onto his hands on the table.

Schmitt spoke tenderly, "Texas is not always like this. There will be better days. Carl, the New Braunfels offer is not charity at all. It is a lifeline. We have the means to reimburse them, at least in the beginning. Will you consider it?"

Carl raised his troubled face. "I will do more than consider it. I will accept it. Tomorrow I will tell the people. Tonight, let's go home."

Schmitt and Wilhelm each placed a hand gently on their leader's shoulder as they moved for the door.

Carl responded to their touch. "My friends, if I am wrong in this decision," his voice trembled, "I was wrong to have ever been born."

# Chapter 8

Carl read the water-smeared papers Wilhelm had left, then re-read them. The details, as Wilhelm called them, were vague. No remuneration was mentioned, shelter was offered "such as may be available," land outside and west of the colony "can be purchased from rightful owners" with no mention of who these persons were. Neither Wilhelm nor the papers mentioned amenities on the lands – water, tillable soil, structures. "What a fool I will be," Carl pondered, "to find the land totally worthless. Then we will truly become charity recipients, unable to move on."

Maybe he could move north and deposit his followers in the non-colony settlements in Austin and Fayette Counties en route, with hope of a better report in the spring. No, they would adhere to the land and their countrymen there and forget about the colony. He could not, would not risk it.

In dread, he plunged onto the muddy street that morning. Altmann immigrants startled him in their rush, euphorically praising his decision to move out. They rang his hands, turning him left and right. Obviously, he concluded, when Schmitt and Wilhelm left the meeting they immediately told others that Carl had no choice. He would accept the New Braunfels offer, the camp would soon move.

Anger emerged above the moment's glory. He should tell the well-wishers just the opposite long enough to call a council meeting and give the members a good dressing. But time was too precious. With a slight break in the rain the air dropped to near freezing levels, but the colonist didn't slow.

Carl personally counted the vehicles. One hundred thirty-six wagons, half loaded with hardware, tools, food, and half with women and children, stood hitched to two hundred seventy-two oxen and an equal number of horses and mules. Another sixty oxen and ninety horses were ringed in remudas as reserve – not enough. A hundred ten men rolled their two-wheeled hand carts forward. Most had families at their sides, some did not. Other families had fashioned backpacks for both males and females over the age of ten. The hum of activity assured enthusiasm. Maybe Carl would overlook his earlier declarations. The stragglers from previous voyages approached with rolled blankets and forced smiles.

All families of the original Altmann Society had animal powered vehicles for man and freight. The Hanovers, as Schmitt named them, were among the hand cart contingent. None of the stragglers were prepared. In addition, the freight wagons were greatly under-teamed with animals. Heavy wagons should have six oxen, lighter ones, four. Two could pull peoples. Everyone understood that able-bodied men and boys over ten, would walk and lead the animals, not adding to the weight inside. Many women and girls voluntarily did likewise. Without consulting the committee, Carl ordered Ernst and the guard to separate the Hanovers and stragglers from the Altmann contingent.

When those threatened with abandonment saw what was happening they set up rebellion in every possible way. They begged, fell on the ground, cried, refused to move. Others held their muskets in menacing postures. Ernst organized mounted charges against them. Stubborn, some were knocked from their feet. They recovered and stood their ground crying out for Prince Carl to negotiate with them. Carl sat on his horse at a distance, not moving. When Ernst charged them a third time, muskets broke into disjointed fire from the Hanovers, striking too guardsmen and killing a horse.

Ernst rallied his force in tactical retreat, posted them, and rode to Carl. "I need a direct order from you, Captain," he said. "I will act as you command."

Carl had drawn his sword, not for a charge, but as a commander to direct battle tactics in the field. When Ernst spoke, it was the first time he noticed the weapon in hand. He instantly knew why Schmitt was calling, "Calm yourself, Carl. Calm!"

Carl asked, "Do the Hanovers have a leader?"

"I'll ride back to them and ask."

"No, I will go. Thank you for your valor, Ernst. Stand by."

Schmitt went wild with protest. "Carl, for God's sake, don't expose yourself to danger. If ever we needed you, it's now!"

As in other battles, Carl subdued his fears. He rode toward the Hanovers. Armed with his sword and a single shot horse pistol in his belt, he knew he had no chance if they threw down on him. Still he trotted nearer and nearer. The cool air didn't prevent a sweat from breaking on his forehead as a vision of Elisabeth, then Helga, came and went. Twenty feet away from the closest of the Hanovers, he pulled up his horse. "Do you have a leader?"

Minutes passed with no answer though the throng began whispering among themselves. A man stepped forward and said, "Gossett will speak for us," and beat a hasty retreat into the crowd.

"Please step forward, Herr Gossett," Carl called, trying to neutralize any emotion in his voice. When the moments again lingered, Carl added, "I mean you no harm, Herr Gossett."

Felix Gossett, a large man both in height and weight, emerged with his palms raised upright. "Prince Carl, the people are most desperate. The shots were not ordered, but were spontaneous in the face of perceived danger. We apologize sincerely. We know you to be a reasonable man."

Carl interrupted. "If you will aid me in a grave matter, I will reconsider my earlier position.

"Anything at all, Herr Prince. Anything. We will do it."

"There are a hundred or more stragglers who want the same thing you want…to join our caravan. That is impossible. If you and your people will discourage them by any means you have, assure that they do not follow, you may join the procession with your hand carts and packs. You understand there is no more space in the wagons."

"I understand. We will discourage the stragglers. Consider it done."

"Your work starts at this moment. Have your women and children push your carts alongside the wagons. Your men are to hold back the unwanted."

"Done!" Gossett didn't wait for formal parting remarks but set to work spreading the men. Carl lingered, impressed with the precision and speed of Gossett's actions and his people's response.

As he rode toward the caravan's head, he realized he had erred. He had given no parameters and there were obviously in Gossett's crowd a few hot heads. Schmitt and Ernst sat mounted waiting for his arrival. He pushed his horse into a trot and closed the distance. He opened his mouth to speak. Shots rang from behind as Schmitt looked beyond him in alarm. He wheeled his stallion.

The Hanovers were charging the stragglers head on and had opened fire. The stragglers were in route. Twenty or more men knelt to reload their muskets while another twenty charged past them continuing to fire.

Schmitt screamed, "My God, Carl, I cannot believe you ordered those poor people to destroy fellow Germans! You idiot! Dare you offer your resignation again it will be accepted, or asked for. You are a dammed fool. Fool!"

Ernst, the soldier, studied the conflict. "Stop, Schmitt! Stop! It's not as you say."

Schmitt retorted, "Don't give me that military manure. You're a copy of this fool!"

"Schmitt! Stop! Look at the action. Not a straggler has fallen though the Hanovers have fired fifty shots by now. Look, and shut your mouth."

Carl was positive Schmitt was right from the moment he unleashed. He hardly heard the scurrilous insults that followed. He would have agreed anyway. Never had his depression dipped so low to be ripped upward so fast by Ernst's declaration.

"Is it true, Ernst? No one is killed?" Tears prevented clear vision.

"Not one, Herr Carl. Who is their leader? We must decorate him."

Carl sighed audibly. "You see, Schmitt, not all my decisions are so bad. Gossett acted exactly as I commanded him. Yes, Ernst, we will decorate him. Move the wagons!"

Schmitt showed greater relief than Carl, grinned sheepishly and turned his horse to follow his prince. He and Hagerdorn ministered the wounds of the guards. One had a broken arm, the other a bullet-ripped side.

Immediately, wagons cut deep ruts in the mud and slowed to a crawl. Carl and all the committee rode up and down the line encouraging the men who leaned against muddy wheels straining every muscle. Women and children dropped from wagon seats to help. Schmitt's Eva wanted to join as did Elizabeth. Carl and the doctor wouldn't allow them although Schmitt's daughters, Margarethe and Therese, jumped down to help anyway.

Carl ordered the guard to dismount and help with the wheels. Committeemen began to do the same. Carl knew the men were acting to please him. He felt proud. He would join them on the ground except for his fine uniform. *Besides, they expect the prince to maintain a decorum.* He would use his voice to continue encouragement.

Toward evening the train had moved two miles from camp, and the travelers could still see the fires of the stragglers. Carl rode ahead and found a high plateau that would serve as a camp He rode back and galloped along the entire procession shouting, "Camp is a mile away. Lean to, men. You are doing well. Your prince holds you in high esteem. Keep up the good work. You will be proud."

Yet the wagons seemed to move even slower, then stopped. A boy, about nine, rose from the mud below the oxen he was leading and shouted in Carl's face, "If you would get that uniform muddy and help us we might do better."

Carl laughed and told himself, *I suppose I am too proud of myself. I'll do it.* He stepped from his prancing steed, underestimated the depth of the muddy water under his boot, and fell face down with a mighty splash. Ongoing, buoyant laughter seemed suddenly to die as his ears pulled, dripping, from the pool. He rose without ceremony and sloshed to the wheel of the wagon led by the smart-mouthed kid.

"I, too, can work, young man. I will give you an example. Lead the team true while I help your father." Carl leaned into the only wheel not already covered by a family member, lost his footing again, but, this time, didn't go out of sight underwater. The wagon wheels sucked as they rolled free, the team moved forward.

"Keep them going, youngster. There are others I must help."

A cheer went up from the front and rear wagons, people close enough to see the happenings. Carl worked his way down the line, helping each one. A renewed energy surged through each family, and wagon after wagon eased free from the mud's grip. The whole train moved forward again not stopping until it reached Carl's high ground.

Family after family filed past him in camp and praised his effort. Many said politely that he should not have taken on such labors, but he knew they lied. He hadn't seen such response to leadership since the beginning. Elisabeth alternately rubbed his shoulders and hugged his neck. Tears streamed as she giggled at her father's wardrobe, her first laughter in Texas.

Though the day ended successfully, Carl knew he had endangered the immigrants by not posting scouts and guards well ahead, and a plan for a quick call to arms if danger lurked. He also realized he should space the wagons farther apart. Today, when one wagon bogged down, all behind came to a stop, then sunk in the mud. Scouts must watch for the best routes. He needed to make duty assignment for encampment as well.

Felix Gossett approached the prince. "Herr Carl, the Hanovers were much impressed by your performance today."

"And I was much impressed by their performance earlier. My lieutenant recommended you for decoration. Tell me, Herr Gossett, will the stragglers follow us?"

"We posted a rear guard to stop them. We will rotate each day. I am determined not to lose the confidence you placed in us."

Overcome, he hugged his new friend warmly. "You seem to have a military sense. Have you training?"

"From earlier days."

"And your men all have muskets. We may find them useful if hostile Indians show themselves. Can they hit their enemy as well as miss when they chose?"

"Alas, Herr Carl, I must confess, the reason I disturb you on this night is to seek your help. My men have no more bullets. We spent our last lead on your soldiers. Please forgive me. Could you see fit to lend us a few rounds, or some lead stock so that we can mold our own?"

"My God, man!" Carl gripped his arms. "You mean you would have killed the stragglers had you not been firing blanks?"

"I do not know," Gossett said, gesturing helplessness. "I requested the men to fire high simply because we had no bullets. Had our muskets been armed, I cannot say how I would have directed."

"Oh, thank God. You acted correctly, Gossett. I should have ordered you to hold the stragglers at bay without bloodshed. I overlooked giving you this small detail. And Gossett, you should use the term *ordered*, not *requested*."

"But Herr Prince, I was only their leader after you rode up."

Carl broke into pleasant laughter. "Then, I appoint you vice director in charge of Hanovers from this time forward."

Carl ordered that all Hanovers be fed in the greater circle of wagons. Instruments came forth and a muddy dance followed dinner.

Though Carl could remember few times when he was more tired, he called a committee meeting and appointed scouts and guards. He instructed his men to space the wagons with one to five hand carts between each two wagons. He had heard that some Indian tribes understood the Spanish language and inquired if any of the committee knew Spanish. Dr. Hagerdorn did.

Carl's fluffed helmet plume was matted to the crown. His red, gold and green uniform was gray-brown with mud. He dropped all pretense of wearing it starting the next morning, emerging from his tent in the work dress of a farmer – the sword and pistol still buckled on. He told the committee, guards, and scouts that although they had rendered valuable service in pushing wagons, matters of safety precluded such efforts on a daily basis. The caravan delayed start until scouts could reconnoiter the best direction.

The train progressed four miles the second day toward Victoria where they would intercept the Guadalupe River and parallel it, for the rest of the journey. Carl joined the rutted road and wagons on foot once more. The spread of wagons helped. When one got stuck, one got help. The others kept moving.

"Civilization of a sort. A welcome sight," Carl told Schmitt as they entered Victoria. "Pass the word that prices for all goods will be high. Washing clothes and bathing are our main needs."

City Marshal, Jay Johnson, introduced himself at the mercantile. Carl immediately inquired of Indians. "I should tell you," he said, "that someone spotted Fleetaumountec, a Comanche chief, near Gonzales. Has some fifty warriors with him, they said. He wears a buffalo skull headdress and a red American shirt in cold weather."

"Can you advise me on how to defend ourselves?" Carl asked, feeling his spirits sag.

"I think your caravan is too large for an all-out attack. I'd say you are in little danger if you stay closely bunched, and post guards at night."

They rolled out of town on their sixth day since Indian Point. The marshal's advice to bunch the wagons blunted Carl's earlier success in spreading them. He decided danger lay farther from civilization, and he kept the wagons separated for another six miles, approaching the bank of a swollen creek at sundown. Clouds overshadowed the camp and a windless rain began in earnest. The next morning drizzle continued and the creek ran wider than ever. Reports of sickness deluged Carl, dashing the last of his enthusiasm.

Progress stopped dead. The immigrants dug graves on the nearest high ground and buried another dozen travelers, including two able-bodied Hanover men who had pushed carts.

Carl told Gossett, "Assess the contents of the carts, eliminating all but the most vital of necessities. Germans are forever saving what-nots, family heirlooms, and musical instruments to the exclusion of cast iron skillets or tin utensils."

He should know. One of his own wagons bore Helga's hand carved oak and mahogany piano and his heavy coat of arms brought from the old country. "Use your best judgment, then stuff the remaining goods in the wagons."

Elisabeth slept each night with her Aunt Katheryn's family, but was quick to rise and move to the lead wagon, one of six hauling Carl's personal property. Wage earning teamsters drove them all. Elisabeth often handled the reins as the men stepped to the ground to move wheels, their own or others. Ernst spotted a log raft floating down the creek with the aid of four men with poles and a makeshift rudder. He hailed them to the bank. They threw him a rope with which he towed the craft to land. He had correctly guessed the boatmen were German. He asked them to transport him and his horse to the opposite bank so he could ride ahead to survey conditions. From the point of departure on the near bank, the craft drifted downstream a half mile before making land on the opposite shore.

He returned to Carl. "Captain, all land as far as I could ride and return was nothing but a sheet of muddy water as though a million cow tracks had widened until they joined each other in an endless lake."

Carl grew short with everyone – Schmitt, Wilhelm, Ernst, the committeemen, Elisabeth, and Gossett. He captured any who would listen. "I cannot even find this silly creek on the map. How could it be so ominous now? Unload a wagon and drive it into the water. We must test the depth."

A few feet from shore, the wagon upended as it and the oxen were swept away toward the roaring Guadalupe River. The drivers swam ashore exhausted and chilled. Wives, laughing while crying, draped them in blankets and walked them to the wagons for dry clothes.

෬ ෬ ෬

Carl told Schmitt, "My decision was wrong. We are destined to perish here on the bank of Cruel Creek. Some will survive, but the colony will never exist."

Schmitt, angered by Carl's negative attitude said, "You're right, Carl. It was a poor decision. There will not be a New Altmann, a new life. Forget your star struck dreams of a castle in Texas."

Carl glared at Schmitt. He smoothed his waxed mustache and clawed at his pointed chin whiskers. "I will tell you one thing, Schmitt, the wagons will cross that stream three days from now."

*Shall I call you Prince God from here on?* "Of course, Herr Carl. As you say."

"Quit agreeing with me, Schmitt. You have no right to make light of my dilemma. I tell you the water will recede and we will cross."

Schmitt sensed delusions in the statement. But he held to his earlier approach. "And I'm sure the ten thousand acre lake will dry before our eyes as we approach. Right?"

"Damn you, Schmitt. No! We will die on the other side. But I will die laughing at this silly creek which could not defeat me."

Schmitt elected not to press his luck. But he hastily warned the other committeemen of Carl's intention in case they had to physically restrain the man from acting foolishly.

On the third day, Cruel Creek's waters reentered its banks, and the caravan spent the entire day in a painful crossing. Carl and Schmitt held another, similar, conversation regarding the shallow rain-lake that spread before them. Carl said they would strike out in three days. Schmitt agreed.

ങ     ങ     ങ

The wagons crawled and all able-bodied persons on the ground, slogged through the mud, with water to their knees. Carl's personal assistance helped but the people's earlier enthusiasm for seeing their prince get muddy faded. As evening waned, Carl ordered sufficient oxen hitched so that five wagons could be dragged out of the mud lake, and a cook camp made on dry ground. The rest would spend the night in the mud.

After dinner when no musical instruments emerged from the wagons, Carl harshly ordered the musicians to strike up. They did, but no one danced, and after a few folk tunes, they disappeared back to their families. Carl turned to his tent in distress. The tension of the creek crossing, then the great mud flat, which they occupied, and the threat of Indian raids were more than the immigrants could bear and still feign cheer. It was more than Carl's words would bolster. Never were they more vulnerable. He collapsed on his cot. He shot upright. Had he surrendered? Was

Schmitt right? How dare that man imply that his leadership was weak! He rushed from the tent and spotted Mueller and Schulz talking calmly outside their tents.

"Mueller, Schulz, we need a committee meeting. We must post the guard and establish shifts. The unharnessed animals and the lifeless wagons must be closely protected. Help me call the men together quickly." Schulz turned toward Carl so slowly that Carl thought for a moment the man was imaginary, a bad dream. This was not really happening.

Schulz spoke. "Herr Carl, the guard is on duty. The cattle are in close containment. The wagons are watched. It is all by your precise orders. Are you all right, Herr Carl?"

Carl felt his head swim for a split second before he heard the voices of Mueller and Schulz above him. They urged him to speak, straightened his tangled legs, raised his head, and called for Doctors Schmitt and Hagerdorn.

"Pneumonia, do you agree, Doctor Hagerdorn? We should arrange for his constant care by the women."

They ignored his feeble protests, recognizing the symptoms of delusion in lung patients, and made a comfortable bed in his own lead wagon. They also agreed that it was not rare for a pneumonia victim to remain active until he collapsed, not acknowledging any warnings.

Carl lost track of time in his wagon bed, conscious only of sunrise when his body functions demanded relief. Needing the aid of women on this most simple of duties embarrassed and angered him.

When Schmitt came to visit his patient, Carl demanded, "My schedule demands Gonzales in a week. You are field commander, Schmitt, but you come back to me each morning and evening for orders. Understood?"

Schmitt smiled and agreed with him, neglecting to tell him the wagons remained in the same spot where they were when Carl fell. "We're making distance as good as weather will permit, Herr Carl. You are to recover. Don't worry."

He rasped, "Don't tell your director not to worry. I decide whether to worry. It has nothing to do with healing. You did not answer me. I forgot my question…"

"I answered. You asked if we were making good distance. Indeed we are."

"Good, good. Has Willi or Ernst seen Indians?"

"No Indians. Our caravan is too large for them to attack," Schmitt assured.

ʒ ʒ ʒ

On a knoll above the cypress and pin oaks which surrounded the small circle of wagons, a company of ten warriors watched.

Chief Fleetaumountec sat tall upon his black and white pony. The horned skull of a buffalo cow added another foot. His red shirt was hidden under a beaver robe from which his bare right arm extended. White and red paint adorned the arm as well as most of his broad face. Fleetaumountec's name, a corruption of French, Spanish, English and general misunderstanding, meant, to the Americans, *Fast on the Mountain.*

He said, "The travelers are helpless. They stay in the mud like ducks. Their guard moves with the swiftness of a three-legged turtle taking half a sun to move from one end to the other.

"Horse Eyes will attack the rear wagons at dawn. When the guard is drawn to that place, I will take Queno and his warriors and set fire to the chief wagons in the circle. These ocean people do not know the Comanche way. When their chiefs are dead, they will try to make a peace. We will pretend to accept their offer. I will give the signal, and we will kill them all saving a few squaws for ourselves."

Queno spoke. "They are not the people of Captain Jack?"

Fleetaumountec pointed directly at his son. "No. Captain Jack cares nothing for the ocean people. They do not speak his language. Do you ask because you are a coward?"

Only an Indian fool would fail to fear Captain Jack Hays of the Texas Rangers. Though Fleetaumountec hadn't clashed with the notorious white warrior chief personally, he knew well the ranger's record for destruction of Indians against all odds. Bands that recognized this enemy retreated with all speed rather than take him on, but many a warrior seeking to build a reputation relished the chance to harvest Captain Jack's black hair as a lodge trophy.

Queno scowled, "I fear no white! I ask because Captain Jack is in the field. We saw his horses, and crossed his tracks two suns ago."

"His puny band rode west. They are in San Antonio now where they eat with squaws and drink whiskey. Are you ready to strike at dawn?"

Queno said, "I ride where Fleetaumountec rides."

# Chapter 9

Carl heard the shouts and shots from his bed and rose abruptly. The pain under his ribs slammed him back down. He gasped, "Elisabeth, look out and see."

Elisabeth peeked from the cover flap and turned. "Too dark, Father. I see nothing, but it must be at the rear, over a mile away. Don't waste your strength. I'll get Doctor Schmitt. He'll know."

"My mind still works. Don't treat your father as an invalid," he complained as Elisabeth hopped down from the rear gate. "Wait, Elisabeth, wait."

ങ  ങ  ങ

From the near brush, brooding eyes from unimaginable logic and antiquity viewed the lass in her flannel gown as she raced the final feet. Queno allowed his mind to wallow in every debauchery as he watched the small form standing on the wagon step speaking to the occupants inside. He would be exalted above all warriors should he bring the scalp of an ocean people chief's daughter into the village. But he would made a chief if he brought her alive, as one of his wives. He contemplated the thirty-yard dash, sure he could carry the light framed girl back to cover before the confused white chiefs could act.

But Fleetaumountec would think it foolish, and it was not according to plan. Shots from the south increased in frequency. The raid was underway. Within minutes the white guard would charge in that direction and leave the circle of wagons with little protection. A bearded man and his squaw joined the young girl and moved toward the great wagon. The man carried a rifle. He turned, curious at the gunfire coming from the south. A white warrior chief with medals and a strange hat rode to the great wagon at the same time. His face and horse pointed exactly toward the brush where Queno lay hidden. Queno quickly took stock of his cover, fearing that his lust had allowed caution to waiver. If it had, darkness still covered him well.

Suddenly, Queno's felt his shaggy black hair seized from behind. A hand lifted him to his feet. Fleetaumountec twisted his son's face around and, in a voice that blended flat with the morning wind said, "Your tongue hangs from your mouth, coyote. Hide yourself. From here they can smell you."

Queno stumbled when his father let go of his hair. He recovered and scurried back into the cover. Fleetaumountec approached and thrust a finger downward – stay there until I say. Queno at twenty summers, had eight warriors to lead, all younger than he, one as young as twelve. None were short on courage, but he knew Fleetaumountec's disdain suggested they were short on brains, including Queno. Ordinarily, a twenty-year-old Comanche would have been considered a man, a warrior, for five years by now. His father, fourteen summers his senior, had exercised uncharacteristic patience, for, try as he might, he had produced only daughters so far.

The white warrior dismounted and spoke to the wagon briefly. He joined others dressed like him and disappeared into the twilight. Queno was sure it was the guard and all had ridden south, as his father had predicted. He heard the chatter of the ocean people come up the line of wagons like a wave moving on a lake. The noise, reminded him of the barking of a dog and meant nothing in particular. The chant, repeated from wagon to wagon, until it reached the great wagon, said, "Indians are attacking the rear. Arm yourselves. Pass it on."

Fleetaumountec told him, "Send two warriors at a time to kill the 'man who carries rifle' and set fire to the great wagon. Only squaws remain inside."

Queno sent Grasshopper and Little Wolf forward on their horses. When they leaped from their mounts onto the wagon's tongue, shots rang out from behind another close wagon. Both fell in their tracks. Fleetaumountec saw clearly what had happened and

72

told Queno to send two more. He ordered Cactus Grasses and Grows With Much Water to charge ahead. They refused. Fleetaumountec was accustomed to such refusal. Each warrior had his own code of discretion. But chiefs were always brave. Fleetaumountec said, "I go. Queno, follow close."

The two reluctant braves agreed they would follow behind their leaders. Fleetaumountec didn't charge straight for the great wagon as the earlier fools had done. He circled to steal in behind the wagon from where the shots came. He handed off his flintlock to Queno, notched an arrow to his bowstring as he rode silently, finding the two white men standing ready with their weapons, backs turned to his approach. His arrow sunk deeply into the broad back of the bearded white man on his left. The other, a man with a short beard, turned to face him, and he drew the bow again. The short beard fired at the same instant that the bow released its second shaft.

Fleetaumountec's powerful paint horse collapsed on its front legs causing the chief's arrow to slip low and stick in the muddy ground between the short beard's feet. The short beard snatched a long pistol from his belt. Fleetaumountec lived up to the reputation of his name in diving into the undergrowth, leaving his bow and dying horse behind. The distraction had worked, at great cost. Cactus Grasses and Grows With Much Water found their courage, charged, and ripped back the wagon flap, ready to kill Man Who Walks With Rifle and take the squaws. Their eyes saw *two* bearded white men, one with a rifle, the other, a short gun leveled. The belch of flame from the barrels was their last sights. Queno lighted an oil rag and flung it onto the wagon cover. He heard his father's voice from the trees and retreated. Another team of his warriors, Tail of Deer and the twelve year old, Wild Call, charged forward.

Fleetaumountec had ordered them to the wagon before the whites could reload. Tail of Deer leaped onto the wagon tongue like his earlier partners, and Wild Call stepped on a metal rung to gain rear entrance.

 og og og

Dawn broke fully. Wilhelm and Ernst sent half their guard to the skirmish at the rear and spread the others along the route. They alerted Felix Gossett and told him, to shoot to kill this time. Wilhelm charged back to the wagon circle with five guardsmen. He arrived in time to see a small, near naked figure tumble from the rear of Carl's wagon, and distinctly caught the glint of a steel blade pull backwards from its exit wound in the small man's back. A shot fired from in or near the wagon was followed by endless screaming as a Comanche warrior, holding his eyes, fled for the brush from the front of the wagon. Wilhelm thought his own eyes played tricks as he perceived the movement of an American bison in the brush directly in the path of the screaming figure. Could it be that the Indians had learned to ride buffalo as beasts of burden?

In a liquid movement, a guardsman scooped a leather bucket of water. He dashed the blazing top of Carl's wagon and snuffed the fire. Before Wilhelm could assess anyone's danger, a screeching whoop came from the woods. The buffalo head and three howling warriors charged toward him and his troops, at a slight angle. They passed before they could level any rifles. Wilhelm wheeled to aim and saw the four toss flaming rags on sticks into the beds and boots of the surrounding wagons.

"Fire!" he screamed. His four mounted lieutenants opened fire on the retreating figures. One slumped forward on his horse but held on. Wilhelm had meant the command as an alert to the wagon occupants against the flames. The occupants understood and quickly stemmed the flames. He ordered the guardsmen to circle the camp, then scrambled from his horse to Carl's wagon, leaping over one of the five Indian bodies on the ground.

Cg   Cg   Cg

Queno doubled in pain. His guts wouldn't quit wrenching. He hated himself for making such a display in front of anyone, much less his two surviving warriors and his father. Fleetaumountec stood with arms folded and displayed disgust. At last Queno panted. "Ocean people did not do as you said. They did not send all the guard to the rear. They had many more guns than you said. They understand Comanche ways. They did not give up squaws.

Five of my warriors are dead. One is blind. They ran a long knife through the belly of little Wild Call. You led us wrong."

Fleetaumountec smiled wickedly. "It was the greed of Queno for the young squaw. You sent your warriors to sure death. I stopped two of the white men with my bow because I did not act as a stupid child. It cost me my horse, Two Colors. You will pay me two squaws and two horses."

"I have but two squaws and one horse," Queno complained from his knees. "You ask too much. I will not give you both my squaws. You have other horses. I have one."

Fleetaumountec replied, "Take the horses of your dead warriors and the blind one. Give me your horse and one of them. You will find other squaws if you are brave. When we meet ocean people again, you will count coup and bring scalps or you will not be the son of Fleetaumountec."

Queno knew but one way he could cease to be the son of Fleetaumountec. He would have to be dead. The thump of unshod pony hooves disrupted the conversation as Horse Eyes entered the camp. He dropped from his mount before the beast slowed as did another twenty warriors. Fleetaumountec asked, "Where are the others? Where are the ocean people horses and cattle? Where are the squaws, scalps?"

Horse Eyes looked in all directions. There were no good words to choose. "The ocean people fight like Captain Jack. They have many rifles. All shoot true. One ocean man looks like Captain Jack. I think it is him."

Fleetaumountec stepped methodically the ten paces to Horse Eyes. Horse Eyes held his face firm as the sure, firm slap collided with his ear. "I told you where Captain Jack is. Does your chief lie?" Whack! His left hand put Horse Eyes on his knees.

Fleetaumountec continued. "You have loot? You have squaws? You have horses? Answer!"

"No loot, no squaws." He scurried backwards on his knees in defense before adding the most important item. "No horses."

"How many warriors killed?"

"Ten and six."

"Ten and ten did not come back. Where are the other four?"

Horse Eyes hesitated until Fleetaumountec drew back his hand. "The ocean people wounded and captured them. Put ropes on them."

"Fool!" Fleetaumountec began a merciless beating with his quirt as Horse Eyes doubled in a ball on the ground, his hands covering his head. "The ocean people torture the captives like Comanche torture enemy. You should have killed them and not let the ocean people capture them!"

When Fleetaumountec ceased with the quirt, Horse Eyes lay panting and groaning. He found his voice. "You told us wrong. The ocean people are brave, not stupid. They didn't send their guard to the rear. They have many rifles in the wagons. Where are the scalps of the ocean people that Fleetaumountec took? Where are the squaws Fleetaumountec captured?"

The Indian chief accepted the insults as he had from his son. He wouldn't react to scurrilous words, only failed deeds. With his own quirt he struck himself on each cheek. "We learned the ocean people way of war today. Now we follow, wait for a wagon to fall behind."

Fleetaumountec would kill the blinded brave. The warrior had failed. Besides, a man was better off dead than blind. He approached Tail of Deer, drawing his skinning knife. Tail of Deer rose from the ground holding a gray rag over his right eye. "Do not kill me! With one eye, I still see. I have things to tell you. I saw in the great wagon."

Fleetaumountec stopped. "Talk."

"Man Who Walks With Rifle shot me, my eye, with short gun. In the wagon was the young squaw and the squaw of Man Who Walks With Rifle."

Fleetaumountec suspected a lie. "A squaw stuck the long knife through Wild Call?"

"No, there was another chief inside. He had on his head a gold hat with the feather of a god bird on the top. He was sick on a soft bed until he saw Wild Call take the young squaw by the arm. Gold Hat moved as many lightnings. I think he is the main chief."

&#x6168; &#x6168; &#x6168;

76

Carl stood by his wagon for the first time in days as the committee, the guard, and Gossett gathered around. He clearly saw the wagons had not moved since he took sick. He fought against the demon cough, leaning on the front wheel. But he knew he must assess damages.

Wilhelm reported two men wounded, one wouldn't live. "Hagerdorn is still working over Krug, unable to remove the deep arrow. He does not believe Herr Krug will survive. The guard counted fourteen Indians dead near the rear, and believe two others died in flight. Gossett captured four warriors, all wounded beyond walking or they wouldn't have been captured. One continues to bleed from his chest and mouth."

Carl shivered in sadness as he and Schmitt pointed to five dead warriors. The one with a knife wound, front and back, appeared to be a boy. Carl explained, "He grabbed Elisabeth by the arm."

Elisabeth stood with her arms around her father, partly to support him, partly out of thankful devotion. She still trembled from the ordeal.

"Did we act correctly to capture the wounded enemy, Herr Carl?" asked Fritz Gossett.

"It was honorable of you. But I don't know how the Indians will react knowing we hold members of their band as prisoners in our wagons."

Ernst's reconnaissance of the train of immigrants showed all had returned to a nervous order. He said, "Wagons can be pulled from their bogs by yoking three or more teams to each wagon until it is free. Ahead is a well marked road wide enough that the we can avoid the old ruts."

Carl nodded. "I'll take charge of directing the teams. I'm much stronger now. Bring my horse."

When the horse arrived, Carl was sitting in the mud in a fit of coughing, declaring between each convulsion that it was a minor throat irritation. He needed but another moment.

At last Schmitt said, "Get him back in his wagon. There is no shortage of men who can direct the assembly of ox teams."

Carl didn't have the strength to lift his weight up the step and into the wagon. Inside, with Schmitt's help, he vomited the water he had drunk at dawn, and his fever returned.

Schmitt tried to cheer him. "I will send a rider to find the chief with the buffalo horns. He seems able to stimulate you to new strength, a better doctor than I."

Carl sputtered between coughs, "Schmitt, I will be well soon. I swear. But I must say to you, please understand, only as a contingency, you are to look after Elisabeth if I...but I will be well. I am able. I trust you with my life. I hope you know that, my friend. But I will be well. Pneumonia is a minor inconvenience. I am almost over it now."

"Herr Carl, I'm glad you are my director, my prince, and my friend. I will never fail Elisabeth. But if you don't close your mouth, I may fail you–or flog you."

Carl chuckled and started his coughing again. Schmitt's eyes misted at the rare words of praise, hard for the proud man to utter.

The wagons moved, camped, moved again. New cautions against Indians slowed progress. Three more children had died and were buried along the trail. As Ernst guarded the rear, he startled a handful of Indians who had dug open the small graves. He reported to Carl. Too weak to respond, Carl pointed to Schmitt to draw conclusions.

Schmitt called Doctor Hagerdorn and said, "The Indians are still with us. They follow night and day. What do you make of it?"

Hagerdorn stroked his beard. "They probably searched the graves for their members. Perhaps we could trade them back the captives in return for our safety."

"But once they get the captives, they could break their word, and attack anyway."

"We have nothing to lose unless they attack us while we're talking with them. Do you want me to try and lure them with Spanish?"

"It is your decision, Hagerdorn, and your danger. Are you willing?"

More serious than his colleague, Schmitt, Doctor Hagerdorn

carried the same courage. His short frame and stiff walk spoke of dignity, as did his neat, short beard and deep brown eyes. Now, a duty befell him that only he could carry out.

He called his wife, Pauline, and Schmitt's wife, Eva, together. "Ladies, fashion for me a banner using white and blue cloth. The lower, blue, half will represent scalloped waves on an ocean of water. The upper, white, half is the sky – the flag of the *ocean people*. Marshal Johnson at Victoria said it is the name that Indians use for people traveling from the coast. Sew it well, dear ones. It may save our lives."

He arranged for an armed guard of four to accompany him as he rode back and forth, ahead of the lead wagons, then lingered at the rear. The banner fluttered above as he shouted repeatedly in his best Spanish. "Fleetaumountec, Comanche chief. Ocean people will speak with you in peace. I have presents for your men and women."

After three days of calling, the worst wounded of the warriors lingered near death. Hagerdorn made a decision, to place the man on bedding by the side of the trail and announce his presence to the interlopers in the trees. Hagerdorn continued his jaunts to and fro, calling, "Fleetaumountec, Comanche Chief. We have released your wounded warrior. Our medicine cannot save him."

Ernst rode at a run from the rear. "Where is Hagerdorn? I must see him at once!" The doctor heard his name and met Ernst.

"Herr Hagerdorn. We may have serious trouble. First I witnessed the Comanches opening the graves of our dead. Now I have seen the most hideous sight of my life. The chief, Fleetaumountec, came upon the wounded brave we left behind. He raised the man's head by his hair, and calmly slit his throat with a knife. What does it mean?"

"We cannot guess. The Indian way is different, of course. I will still try to parley with them. Tell the people to gather every trinket, the jewelry they bought in New York, cloth, dried meats, corn meal. Have the meat cutters stand by."

Hagerdorn charged ahead of his guard, deep into the trees and brush, risking a lance or arrow at any moment. He called relentlessly, dropped behind the wagons and continued.

Toward evening, a week after the battle, Hargerdorn saw the buffalo skull ahead of him beyond the lead wagons. He commanded that half a steer be loaded on a wagon with the other presents.

Fleetaumountec held a tattered brown cloth on the end of a long pole. Hagerdorn and his guards rode forward, stopping fifty yards from the chief and warriors.

He shouted in Spanish, "Fleetaumountec! Do you know my words?"

"Peace," came the reply in Spanish. They rode closer. Hagerdorn sent a guardsman back to retrieve the wagonload of gifts, complete with the beef half.

The white chief raised his right hand in salute. Fleetaumountec kept his hands on his bow and on his horse's rope bridle. The chief recognized the short-bearded white man as the one who had killed his prized horse. He wanted to raise his bow and send a shaft at the man who had beaten him, but he respected the fact that it had been an act of war. He waited for the white chief to speak.

"We give presents. We return your three warriors. You give your word that we will be safe from harm."

Fleetaumountec replied as his warriors gathered. "See presents."

Hagerdorn told him a wagon would be coming, then waited. The wordless wait took half an hour. Hagerdorn hovered near apoplexy but could discern no change of expression on the chief's face. When the wagon arrived, the Indians tore into everything onboard. They giggled and showed items to one another, pointing and talking excitedly. They patted the side of beef, hide still on, and made smacking sounds.

Fleetaumountec watched patiently then grunted a word. The warriors moved away and mounted their horses. "Give wagon and horses?"

Hagerdorn hadn't figured on throwing in the valuable extras. At risk of his own life, he replied, "No." Then an inspiration hit him. "The wagon will return with your warriors. You agree?"

"See warriors." The expressionless face spoke of fearlessness.

The two teamsters driving the wagon seemed never so relieved to exit a scene as they whipped the ponies into a run. They returned another half hour later.

Teamster Conrad whispered, "The braves didn't want to come. They had to be tied hand and foot. One of them opened his leg wound in the struggle."

Panic seized Hagerdorn. "My God, what if Fleetaumountec kills them, too? That is what they feared. I must add another condition to the trade." To the chief, he said, "You won't kill your warriors. They fought bravely."

Fleetaumountec rode around the open wagon and observed the tense braves. Each kept a wary eye on his chief. He spoke. "They will live, fight again. No fight ocean people. Ocean people our friend. We not harm."

Relief washed over Hagerdorn's expression. He forced a smile and addressed the chief again. "We have made a treaty. May I shake the hand of my Comanche friend?"

To the surprise of the whites, Fleetaumountec dropped from his horse and strode forward extending his right hand, keeping his bow, with notched arrow, in his left. Hagerdorn dismounted and moved toward the approaching chief. The guards bristled in anticipation. If there was to be trick in this meeting it would happen now. Their hands clasped and held. Fleetaumountec said, "You brave chief. Chief with the gold hat. He lives?"

Hagerdorn started to ask him to repeat, then caught the meaning. "Yes, he lives, a great warrior like Fleetaumountec."

Without his war paint, Hagerdorn could see Fleetaumountec's broad, creased face clearly. He smiled briefly then the face from a thousand years of savagery returned to stone. He spoke his parting words. "Man Who Brings Cow is friend. I go."

Fleetaumountec mounted his pony in an easy bound. Beside him on an inferior animal sat a slumped younger warrior whose darting eyes watched every move. The words *silly looking* crossed Hagerdorn's mind as he watched the party turn. As the Indians neared the trees, balancing the beef half on a pony with braves on each side, other warriors emerged and joined them. They all disappeared into the live oaks pulling their wounded on travois.

Six harrowing water crossings and ten more days of slug-like progress brought the long string of wagons to the banks of a raging river where there was no place to go but across. Carl hadn't remembered seeing the sun since Schmitt put him back to bed after the Comanche raid.

"Where are we, Schmitt? Do I yet live? Are we ghosts from the carnage? Have we moved from the mud lake?" the prince asked.

"Carl, listen with all your strength. Hagerdorn negotiated a treaty with the Comanche chief. We haven't been molested in any way, though we see them at a distance each day. The 'Silly Looking' one, as Hagerdorn named him, calls out each evening that we are friends and he is much brave. I've told you this before, but each time you forget. This time you must remember because we sit on the banks of the Guadalupe waiting for low water to cross into the Promised Land."

"We are home. Elisabeth, we are home. Schmitt, send for Hagerdorn. I must decorate him."

"You already have, Carl. Twice."

# Chapter 10

Schmitt studied the landscape across the Guadalupe torrent daily and reported to Carl. He could see the few small structures of New Braunfels at a distance and its settlers approached the opposite bank and shouted across establishing a communication of sort.

"Carl, the Germans of New Braunfels send their greeting. They thought we were members of their own society, the stragglers from the coast, and welcomed us. I screamed myself hoarse that we are a different society. German, but not the Texas society but it didn't matter, they still wanted us to join. It may be a good deal. Each family gets ten acres to cultivate immediately."

"No. Do not encourage them. Tell them we are kindred souls but seek our own land, our own colony."

"But, Herr Carl, some have established blood relations with our people. They are most anxious for us to cross so they can shake hands with their cousins." Schmitt noticed he invoked the title *Herr* when he was pleading. So did Carl.

"Likely the Hanovers. Counsel them closely, Schmitt, that they do not bolt from us once we stand on the other side. Assure Herr Gossett of my fondness for him."

Schmitt and the committeemen visited the widows of Guard Wagner and Committeeman Krug daily, offering every personal and society support. The men had died agonizing deaths from their infected wounds before reaching the Guadalupe, a sight, Schmitt realized, which could have been an inspiration and cause for recovery. But, now, new hope existed.

He walked among the people constantly offering cheer, assuring that the Guadalupe couldn't run at such levels forever. He approached Carl's friend, Roth, who had all the wares of his fine wagon, purchased in Bremen, laid out in an orderly fashion.

"Roth, you have been quiet for the entire journey. I have seen you only at a distance. Are you well?"

"Yes, Herr Schmitt. I have been in a state of depression, but seeing the river in such a rampage cheers me. Is that water not a lovely sight?"

Schmitt knew the fun loving companion of Carl made a joke and scolded, "Of course, it is *not* a lovely sight, Perhaps you still suffer from sea delusions. Should I examine you?"

"I have not felt so well since I last entered the great beer hall in Altmann. Examine if you wish, but I could make better use of your services in helping me assemble my beer vats."

"Beer vats? The river could recede at any time. We must be ready to move."

"One must not rush a good thing." Roth hoisted a heavy iron pot. "This is the first time when pause permitted me to serve my society and my prince. I will hatch a barrel of beer soon and the people will enjoy Christmas."

As Roth spoke, folks continued to approach his layout, delivering corn meal, grain, scarce sugar and other ingredients. He had rallied a following. Schmitt told Roth to go visit Carl to cheer him. He chuckled as he continued his walk.

Light rain threatened to spoil the mood but it vanished and the river showed no effects. The guards took daily measurements at the bank, and reported to Schmitt that the surface had dropped a foot in three days. Then it dropped two feet in one day and held. A polka band from New Braunfels appeared on the far bank on Christmas Eve and struck up. The Society of Altmann Immigrants danced on the east shore as their cousins skipped happily on the west. Roth pulled his wagon close and served pewter mugs of dark ale to all who had furthered his cause. Schmitt laughed as every dancer claimed to be a major contributor. The barrel was drained.

When the dance ended shortly after daylight faded, a guard ran up from the river and excitedly announced that the waters had dropped five feet. A roar went up from the crowd. Children rushed the dark bank to see while mothers screamed for them to get back. Roth told Schmitt he wanted to give the news personally to Carl.

Carl heard the commotion and saw Roth approaching. "Herr Carl, you'll catch a draft in the night air. Please go inside."

Carl said, "I feel better when my body is upright. It's the royal blood in me. And the music has cheered me. Did your brew ripen in time for the festival?"

"Yes, I've spoiled your subjects, my prince. They will never be satisfied with New Braunfels brew." He handed Carl a half-full stein.

"Good, I trust they will find nothing about New Braunfels to their satisfaction, if we ever get there."

"You will get there tomorrow, Herr Carl, if the river is any indication. It has dropped another five feet. It lowers even as you watch it now."

Carl stood up. "Roth, I'm in no joking mood. Your ale has affected your mind."

"It is true. I swear. Tomorrow the committee will take you to the edge and ask for your decision."

Though the flood had washed out the moorings, the New Braunfels settlers had rescued a ferry. Carl watched as they crossed in small boats, dragging heavy ropes. Manpower adequate to the task on both banks lent muscle, and before noon, the men had secured lines for towing the ferry back and forth. Carl's heart raced with the first landing and silently joined in the celebration of his people as New Braunfelsers leaped ashore. On the ferry came the acting director for the New Braunfels colony, Hermann Spiess.

Spiess' party spotted Schmitt standing prominently in the crowd, slogged up the bank and exchanged greetings. "And, Herr Schmitt, you are the director?"

"No, our director has been quite ill. He recovers nicely at this time. There he's sitting in the seat of the fine wagon above. I'll introduce you."

"Tell me his name, if you please, Herr Schmitt."

"Kronprince Carl Franz von Altmann. He is a proud and able nobleman of Southern Bavaria."

Spiess' rosy-cheeked smile wilted to a frown as he slid backward down the slope muttering, "My God. Another prince. What will Meusebach say?"

Schmitt struggled to hear. "I beg your pardon, Herr Spiess. You made a statement?"

"I...well, yes, I saw his name when your advance guard came weeks ago. I hardly remembered that he was a prince, however. Please forgive my oversight."

Schmitt knew the colony had experienced financial problems which some blamed on Solms because of his arrogant disdain for fiscal matters. "Herr Spiess, you will be delighted with Herr Carl who makes light of his Old World titles. He is a most disarming and humble conversationalist among the common or the great, much beloved by his people."

Spiess relaxed his face. "I trust I have not offended you. Of course, the good prince is brilliant in his skills with all people. Our founder, Prince Solms, while well intentioned, had no such skills, I regret to say."

A cold breeze didn't prevent sweat from oozing from under Schmitt's wool shirt. He hoped Carl wouldn't put his boot in his mouth when he opened it. "Herr Carl, meet Herr Hermann Spiess, Acting Director for the colony of New Braunfels."

Carl remained seated on the wagon and reached out his hand. "And your permanent director, Solms. Is he about?"

Spiess answered, "Prince Solms has retired from the society. Our director is Baron Otfried Hans Frieherr von Meusebach. The colony is much impressed with his leadership."

"Herr Spiess, your news could not please me more. I knew Solms from the old country and I can tell you frankly, I did not like the man." Schmitt stood behind Spiess shaking his head as if to say, *shut your mouth, Carl.*

"Ah, it is as well. If you did not like the style of Solms, you will find von Meusebach quite the opposite. We will make good neighbors. Would you like for yours to be the first wagon to cross on the ferry? It will carry one wagon each trip."

Schmitt dragged a large handkerchief from his pocket and mopped his brow in relief. His director's wagon rolled toward the river's bank.

The Christmas day crossing on smooth water, consumed all daylight and several night hours. Spiess called another celebration the following day.

"Your Christmas was spoiled by the labor of crossing, Herr Carl. Look how our people take to one another. Cousins! No one will sleep cold this night."

Carl smiled and nodded, apprehensive that his colony may sleep too well.

Schmitt drove Carl's wagon down New Braunfels' San Antonio Street to its juncture with Seguin. "Smell the fresh cut cypress, Elisabeth. Just think, two hundred houses and businesses in the short months the settlement has existed."

"I am unimpressed with the architecture. Beneath German ability," Carl said, countering Schmitt's enthusiasm.

"Why, Carl? Look at the Zinkenburg. A stockade which would frustrate Fleetaumountec." The fortress glistened with new logs as the Comal River tumbled noisily behind it.

"We can do better. No, I shouldn't say that. New Braunfels started with money. We have determination." Carl's words rang hollow in his own ears. He knew when money ran out, fortitude may leave with it.

"Give our brothers the benefit of the doubt. They have only been here a short time. We will struggle, but their spirits will bolster our people for the future. Their proximity will give us every resource. We will help each other. Their offer for us to join them still stands."

"Schmitt, why do you spoil my jolly mood? We will become a colony. Our own colony. Does your fighting blood fail you before we even try?"

"Not at all. I'm most anxious for the tour Spiess has arranged tomorrow. We'll see lands which could become our own."

Carl was escorted in a one-horse carriage in deference to his weakness. Others rode horseback. The party, led by Spiess, proceeded first to the source of the Comal River, the seven "fountains" which burst forth with amazing volume and dropped along rippling falls to form the clear stream. The available land west of New Braunfels became hilly with frequent rock outcroppings. Spiess pointed out in general the patches of land still available for sale. The others, dispersed in between, were claimed by earlier grantees, title unknown.

"This tract contains about a square mile," Spiess said as he pointed, "from that hilltop to this lower ground and the creek."

Carl stared at the hill without speaking, then toward the creek, which resembled the Comal in miniature. "Where does the creek originate, Herr Speiss?"

They rode uphill for two miles as the passage along the creek and hillside narrowed. They entered a box canyon surrounded by fifty-foot cliffs. A single spring, like the seven on the Comal gushed from the limestone.

Carl inquired, "Would the fountain be available for purchase?"

Spiess replied, "Yes. Of course, it will command the higher value."

Carl knew Solms would take the best land, the best water. This area was like the Americans settle, scattered as a checkerboard. *And they plan to make a killing on the one runty spring.*

Heeding an adamant lecture from Schmitt, Carl behaved himself in the presence of Spiess and his council. They parted cordially for the evening. Carl's ambitions returned with his strength, and he resolved to assert his position that a minimum of land should be leased long enough to make a fall crop. Meantime, advance men could explore the western reaches of the Fisher-Miller grant for a permanent colony.

When he finished his half hour oratory on the glory that could be Altmann in the New World, he paused. "And now I would appreciate your comments if you have any."

Only Schulze spoke. "Herr Carl, I believe there is no comment. I move for a vote, if you please."

"Very well, all in favor of the lease proposal put forward raise your hand."

No hands rose. Carl's face flushed and his hands shook, forgivable in view of his long illness. "I said…"

"Herr Carl, you may call for the opposition vote," Schmitt said.

"Fine! All opposed to your director, all who have no

appreciation for the sacrifices I have made, all who have no respect for your leader, all who would defy what is right and decent as Germans, dare you have the nerve to raise your hands?"

All hands, including Schmitt's, shot skyward. "You have conspired against me while I was confined! You are criminals. Fleetaumountec has more honor." He stalked from the circle and opened the tent flap.

"Wait, Carl! You misunderstood the vote." Schmitt rushed to his friend and laid a hand on his shoulder. Carl jerked away. The committee could override Carl but would risk losing his leadership and his resources. "Carl, you must listen."

"I cannot imagine an explanation I will accept. Please speak quickly," he said, turning back to face the committee.

"The committee feels that we should offer to *buy* the larger parcel as a townsite, and the spring before someone else beats us. The properties will gain in value. And, who knows, we might have a change of heart when the fall harvest is done."

"I won't have a change of heart! This place has too many imperfections. Besides, the New Braunfelsers want to get rich on us."

Schmitt's hands worked. "The townsite has a high knoll suitable for a castle which could be seen to Indian Point. We could harness the spring for waterpower. If our people had the incentive of knowing this as their home, we could complete the dam by summer. The castle's foundation could be laid."

"You're trying to lure me, Schmitt! Don't be so smug. The agriculture land is scattered and not suitable for a close German colony. The price would be too high. There are many reasons why the place it is not suited. One spring! Humph. New Braunfels has seven. They call them Comal Fountains. We could call ours Comal Fountain – one! Pugh."

Carl tromped to his tent. Elisabeth had long since bedded down with her aunt. He blamed his recent illness for his lack of sleep. His back hurt, his side hurt, his head hurt. He thought his cough was coming back. Perhaps he would die in the night. It would serve them right. They could not deny he had led them this far. Would they build a small monument? Not likely.

89

At morning, Schmitt called from outside Carl's tent. "What is it, Schmitt? Have you come to insult me further?"

"Carl, there is news from Austin. Profound news. Texas no longer exists as a republic. She has joined the United States."

Carl emerged, squinting. "What? I had counted on the republic. We could sway its simple government to German ways. This changes everything. Damn you, Schmitt, why did you not tell me this would happen?"

Schmitt ignored the rebuke. "Just think, Carl. Ours would be on record for all time as the first city founded under the new state government. Also, it would be the last community founded in the year 1845. And one more thing..."

"Your mouth is running fast, Schmitt. Finish!"

"As a state, Texas could attract American immigrants more rapidly. How much do you suppose the spring will cost," he motioned to the east, "when ten thousand Americans arrive here in a few weeks, their wagons stuffed with greenbacks?"

"I am a man of will." Carl turned toward his tent. "You cannot persuade me with a few flowery words. The committee put you up to this. Tell the truth."

"Yes."

Carl turned back, into Schmitt's face. "Stop being so damned honest, Schmitt. Have you no sense of negotiation? If we would make an offer on the spring, we have to be clever."

Two days remained in the year. Carl felt panic that the papers may not be drawn in time to be presented and a response received before midnight, the thirty-first.

"So, we agree," he concluded to the committee. "The spring and the townsite are worth 50,000 guilder, or about 20,000 dollars. We will offer the New Braunfels council 30,000 guilder and negotiate upward to 60,000 if necessary."

Elated, the committeemen rushed to New Braunfels to present their first offer. When they accepted, Carl's mouth dropped.

Spiess signed the final paper and said, "Herr Carl, we could not be more pleased to have you for neighbors. And we had hardly expected to get 20,000 guilder for the package."

Privately, Carl told Schmitt, "Solms. He rapes his German

cousins from across the Atlantic. This fellow Meusebach is likely no better. I have made up my mind to dislike him."

On December 31, 1845, Carl stood at the pinnacle of the planned townsite, surrounded by 850 countrymen brought on his voyage and another 200 from nearby New Braunfels.

"I declare this day the Colony of New Altmann is established on this spot. I claim all privileges due The Society of Altmann Immigrants as rightful owners under the laws of the great Repub...State of Texas. Let go of my sleeve, Schmitt. I said it right."

# Chapter 11

Carl's strength rebounded daily, claiming that conflicts gave him new resolve. Schmitt swore that he saw a glow of happiness in Carl's face.

"Happiness? With a town site, we have every opportunity to incur debt on public structures, but not one acre of arable land. Please come forth with another brilliant idea and solve this problem."

They stood in chilly January wind, watching Carl's carpenters peg cut lumber to frame his spacious private home. He planned a front meeting room large enough to accommodate official gatherings, thus sparing the cost of a town hall.

"But the outline of your foundation suggests that this structure will serve as a courthouse, jail, library and church," Schmitt chided. "Who needs debt when we have a rich director? All princes are rich."

Carl mused on the chest of coinage and gold bar he had stolen from Julius, not daring to mention it. "If you wanted a wealthy prince, you should have solicited Streib as your director. Seriously, Schmitt, we need land for gardens immediately. Cheap land."

"A stockman, Covington, west of here, owns a number of scattered parcels close to us. Would you contact him and offer to buy? In fact, I will join you."

"You do it, Schmitt. My English is poor. Right now, I'm going to New Braunfels and hire Nicholaus Zink, their engineer, to plat the townsite for streets, public places, businesses, and residential lots." He pulled his horse close. "Covington, you say? Watch his negotiations. You know how the English are."

Zink, a stout, dark bearded man, wearing coveralls and a black cloth hat, spoke with a ringing Prussian accent. He accepted the job immediately and appeared the next day at Carl's tent with a wagon loaded with survey gear and two assistants.

"Herr Carl, I see that you have stakes set near the creek. I suppose that is the business district. You would want a street to run from your quarters directly to the stakes. Correct?"

Carl had recovered from learning that Prince Solms had hired the man to lay out New Braunfels. *Not Zink's fault*, he reasoned. "Yes, Herr Zink. Come out of the wind. I will show you my sketches."

As they studied the notes, Zink's quick take impressed Carl. The man easily grasped Carl's intent, and rambled about the businesses of New Braunfels. "We need wheelwrights and carpenters. I know you built some of your own wagons on the coast."

Carl pointed to his map. "Reserve this spot for a fountain. Um, yes, wheelwrights. What other skills are short in New Braunfels?"

"We need saddle makers, bakers, tent makers and weavers." Zink drew a stubby pencil from his bib, marking an F on the paper. He chuckled, "And if you can manufacture pencils, you'll become rich."

As Zink set up his transit, Carl contacted each of the skilled laborers daily, offering extra compensation from the society to work on shops to house their trades, never mind their need for a warm hearth against the wind.

"We must sell what New Braunfelsers cannot sell, and cannot buy from their own. The society will pay carpenters to build your house while you concentrate on starting your shop." He wrapped arms around shoulders as he spoke to each, warm, reassuring.

Carl turned his horse from the town square, careful to avoid Zink's stretched strings, exhausted for the day. He spotted Roth's wagon where three men unloaded hewn logs.

"Roth, the survey is incomplete. You may be building your house in the middle of the street. Lots will be assigned by drawings. Besides, you should concentrate on…"

"I anticipated your orders. Word gets around. This fachwerk frame will house the finest brewery in Texas. House? Pahh! I spent most of my time at the taverns in Altmann. I will be even more content to live in my own brewery." Pointing to a covered barrel, he added, "Our neighbors have already placed an order. Tell Zink to bend his road."

A week passed with Carl scribbling letters of encouragement to members back home, huddling with Zink, and riding to the fountain to determine the best spot for a dam. He hated the brooding feeling that now replaced his euphoria at progress. The committee's cash to the colonists couldn't last forever. How much longer could he hold out without detailing the dilemma to the committee? He wished for a confidante to share his concerns.

"Oh, hell. I have one. But I dread to tell Schmitt, too."

He heard the rumble and clatter of hooves, pulled himself straight, then stood to greet the gathering committeemen.

"Gentlemen, my main question is, how many families have registered for the town lot drawings?" He dreaded the answer.

Wilhelm, who had taken the census, dropped a tablet on Carl's table without looking up. "One hundred, sixty-two families. A total of six hundred persons."

Carl thumped the paper disgustedly. "Eight hundred fifty people survived the sea and land voyage. Defectors! Just as I feared. The Hanovers? I knew that Gossett could not be trusted."

Schmitt rescued Wilhelm. "Herr Gossett was the first to come forward for his land. But most of the departed were Hanovers, I'm sure. Remember, Carl, the society profited by their departure. They put up substantial funds to board our ships."

"About time something showed a profit," Carl said, his tone mellowing. "The wench, Berta. She had no husband to claim land. Where did she go?"

"It seems she has endeared herself to the brewmeister, Roth. They sing as they work on his fine building. Dancing breaks out around his wagon each night."

Carl leaned back in a hearty laugh. "What a pair! They richly deserve each other."

When Schmitt reported the purchase of multiple parcels,

though scattered, from Covington, at ridiculously cheap prices, Carl dismissed the committee with new joy in his heart and he wrote updates to his financiers in the old country.

Elisabeth appeared in the tent passage. "There is a man here to see you, Father."

"What's new? There is always a man to see me. What does this whiner want?"

"Ask him yourself. He introduced himself as John O. Meusebach, Commissioner-General of the Texas society."

"What? Elisabeth, you must delay him. I'm not dressed in uniform."

"Herr Meusebach is clothed much as a Texas native, and he speaks without ceremony."

Carl stood and straightened his tie and brushed his coat. He dusted his boots and ducked through the tent flap. Meusebach stood straight and tall a few feet away. His deep eyes, muscular neck and reddish hair and beard gave an impression of confidence. A long coat lent little disguise to his thick chest and waist but gave him an agelessness, a dignity well beyond his thirty-three years.

"Baron von Meusebach, I'm Prince Carl von Altmann. It is my pleasure to welcome you to our humble colony. My people are most industrious and I trust you will see daily the fruits of their labor. How may I help you?"

"It is my pleasure to meet you, Prince Carl. Their hands met, strong and sure. "I've discontinued proper German titles for myself. Please call me John."

"Herr Meusebach, a certain decorum must be maintained. The German people expect it. We are German above all else, would you not agree?"

"May I come inside your quarters, Herr Prince?"

"As my honored guest." Carl held open the flap and followed Meusebach inside. "Forgive my surroundings, improper housing for a director."

"Please, don't apologize. It's understood on the Texas frontier. German above all else? My predecessor, Prince Solms would certainly agree with you. But tell me about your colony. You succeeded in a fantastic journey from the coast. I understand you lost very few."

The man was drawing a parallel between Carl and Prince Solms, the last impression Carl wanted to give. "Please call me Carl. We lost fifty-one people overland. Some say it was very few, yet I agonized over each soul. Two we lost to a Comanche attack."

"I understand your grief well." The soft baritone voice spoke with disarming sadness. "My greatest concern is in the present members of our colony. Famine, disease, and lack of means could prove even more disastrous than the voyages."

"At least, Herr John, your society won't face financial difficulty." Carl turned a wooden chair, feeling surprising warmth toward the man. "I must tell you that we must find monies in the next few months or we will be destitute. I'm sorry, I shouldn't vent on my guest, and I'm not seeking charity. Please understand."

"Herr Carl, do you mean to tell me that you made the voyage, the overland journey, and bought this land, and you yet have means to last a few months?"

"You must understand, Herr John, our colony was not conceived with the same great finesse, organization, and backing as yours. We assembled only last summer. Poor but most determined. I'm sorry I caused you grief by revealing our dismal state."

"Heavens, you find yourselves far from a dismal state. When I arrived earlier last year, I found that the society owed tens of thousands of American dollars. I have spent my entire time scurrying to shore up our walls." He pulled a clay pipe from his coat and offered Carl tobacco from his pouch. "We hold our creditors at bay for now, but we still stand to lose all we have gained. I have opened many doors to bring Texas trade into our colony, and I will strike out soon to the west to find suitable sites for new settlements. I prefer the colonial approach, but survival is more important. I have been greatly impressed with the kind reception of Texans. Our people mingle with them more easily than I ever thought possible."

The man showed no personal arrogance. "I see. But at least you have a year behind you and all farmers will have a fine crop next fall."

"Again, you are ahead of the Texas society. You mentioned earlier the finesse, the planning. Perhaps too much. The society promised the immigrants that it would provide for them for the first two years. We still have those who have not turned a spade of soil. If your people know at the outset that they must work, you are far better off."

Carl's own pride grew as Meusebach advised him on men he could trust in Texas and New Orleans when he went to exercise his letters of credit. "Herr John, I can never repay you for the advice. The errors of the past will benefit us both in the future. Is there anything I can do for you?"

"I would seek your advice in dealing with the Comanche. I have been told you had a measure of success?"

"Yes, first, if possible, you should negotiate from a position of strength. We gave them a sound thrashing when they attacked. Then our Doctor Hagerdorn used Spanish to call them out and offer presents. Eventually they came out of the trees. When they asked for more than we offered he told them 'no.' We kept it simple. We gave them gifts in return for their word not to molest our wagons, our stock, or our women. I regret that I had to run through a young brave with my sword. My pistol was empty and he came aboard the wagon and took my daughter by the arm."

"And your daughter is lovely and precious. What sort of presents did you offer?"

Carl poured tea. "We had no idea what to offer, but the people took up a collection of trinkets, toys, simple jewelry and colored cloth. We added food and half a beef. It worked. We saw them almost every day afterwards but they caused us no more grief."

"Did you learn the name of their chief?" Meusebach scribbled notes.

"Fleetaumountec. An impressive, tall warrior with a buffalo skull head dress. It seems he gave me the name, *Gold Hat*." Carl reached behind and lifted his black and brass helmet, freshly cleaned and polished.

Meusebach said, "I've requested the assistance of the Texas Rangers to set a line beyond our western boundaries on the Llano for defense. With these fierce Texas warriors we can claim strength without ourselves becoming enemies of the Indians. Thank you, Herr Carl, I will heed your advice on negotiations. I would like to meet your Doctor Hagerdorn."

Carl couldn't refuse but he worried that Meusebach would seduce Hagerdorn to join him permanently. "If you wish, we will stroll and survey the work. Hagerdorn may have traveled to San Antonio with Schulz." He hoped.

Meusebach spoke openly and enthusiastically of each business in process. Before Carl could address the fact, Meusebach noted that the first merchants would be those in shortest supply in New Braunfels. He added, "And you should cultivate the trade of your Texas neighbors. They, too, have need of all that you can make. Have you had the good fortune of making acquaintances with their number?"

Carl had not. He had turned fiercely inward in establishing his German colony. "My time has been so short."

"You must meet the Texans, Herr Carl. They hold the key to our success. I perceive you as a man of strong will. But if I may render of a word of advice, give this issue priority."

"Thank you. I'll consider your advice. I've spoken at length to the marshal in Victoria, a most accommodating man. His warnings of Indians in the area doubtless saved our hides." Carl had a question. "Tell me, does the English language give you grief in dealing with the white natives?"

Meusebach lead his horse as they moved around scrub cedar and cactus, making their way toward the square. "Yes, but the struggle becomes less all the time. Texans speak with an ease that defies the knowledge of one who learned English only in schools. It requires careful listening. And I must say, do not misjudge their intelligence from their style of speech."

"Good advice again, Herr John. I particularly want to meet the Texas Ranger, Captain Hays. I understand he is a relentless warrior with a most novel approach. Have you made his acquaintance?"

"I have indeed. Yes, you need to meet Captain Hays. Do not allow your people to venture beyond a line of safety until you seek his advice."

"There is one more merchant I would wish you to meet. Our

brewmeister, Herr Roth. He has chosen not to wait until proper structure covers his vats. He has orders arriving daily from von Coll and von Wedermeyer in New Braunfels."

The thirty year old Roth spoke and smiled graciously through short facial stubble when he shook hands with the commissioner-general. He lost no time drawing frothy mugs from his new crock vat fresh in from San Antonio.

Meusebach lifted the stein to his lips and drank deeply. "Ah, Herr Carl, I've been thinking for a while on a proposition. Herr Roth has given me the confidence to ask. Would your society join forces with mine in a common effort to succeed in Texas?"

Carl didn't want to answer. "Surely, there could be a potential in such a thought. Herr Hargerdorn's tent is close."

Carl hastened to Hagerdorn's tent, this time hoping the man would be there. He was. Meusebach inquired politely of Hagerdorn's impressions of the Indians, their attitudes, their likes and dislikes.

Hagerdorn said, "I believe the Indians prize bravery above all else. They are honest to the extent that their word goes. A chief rules only a small band and his word will not carry beyond them.

"They love bright ornaments and cloth. They will eat anything. Their crude culture is not wrong in their own eyes – killing their own wounded, taking female captives."

Meusebach said, "I plan an excursion into the Llano and San Saba River areas soon. Our success depends on a negotiated peace with the natives."

Carl gasped when Hagerdorn answered. "I will join you, Herr John, if you so desire."

Meusbach mounted and rode eastward after cordial good-byes to Carl and Hagerdorn.

Fuming, Carl demanded, "What are your intentions, Herr Hagerdorn? Will you join the opposition society? Do we not need your services?"

"Not at all, Herr Carl. The man was so disarming I was saying things before I thought. But I sensed from his soulful eyes that he needs the few skills I have developed by sheer circumstance. For some reason, I fear that the Llano holds ten times the dangers we

99

faced on the Guadalupe."

"So now you read minds, Hagerdorn. Surely, you must be catching some sense of the anger that one of us feels at this moment."

I apologize, Herr Carl. If you wish, I'll seek Schmitt to calm you down."

"Do not bring that damned Schmitt into this! He will not allow me to enjoy my anger for five minutes."

C3   C3   C3

Barely settled inside his tent, Carl sensed it. Distant whooping and thunder of hooves grew to a grating roar, a vibrato of screams and trembling ground. Carl lurched and grabbed his long horse pistol from its hanging belt. How had attacking Indians gotten past his guard to the west? But the hoard was upon him.

"Indian attack!" He screamed as he saw uncountable mounted warriors charging directly for his and a dozen other defenseless tents. He raised the pistol to fire. The horsemen skidded to a halt as Carl saw that not all were Indians. Dust clouded his vision and doubt entered his brain. The brigand proceeded forward at a walk. A white man, with black hair and shaven face, held his hand at right angle to his shoulder.

"Slow it down, boys. A kid could run out under the horses." The blowing animals pranced nervously under the tight rein of their masters as they approached.

Several riders were, indeed, dark skinned, hatless, wearing crude leggings, carrying muskets above their heads, and in every facial feature, resembled the Comanches of the overland journey. But they were lead by this white man, a man who obviously respected life and property. Not the first sojourners to pass through the encampment, Carl lowered his pistol and breathed out.

The troop walked their mounts past Carl as the leader tipped his ridiculously broad-brimmed hat. "How'd do, sir. Just passing through."

Holstered revolving handguns and Bowie knives hung from his belt. Slung under either side of his saddle Carl spied short

100

rifles. The other whites were similarly equipped. The Indians rode coarse wooden saddles with scant padding. Their feet were covered by moccasins that joined their cloth leggings.

Carl nodded a greeting, watching closely where hands and eyes played. They rode on. As their images grew small to the east, he heard a single horse approach from behind. His pistol jerked upward by instinct as he whirled. Had he been tricked?

"Carl! For God's sake, don't shoot. Do you know who you just saw?"

"Schmitt, for once, I'm glad to see you." He stuffed the gun in his belt. "No, I don't know, but if you've seen one rabble, you've seen them all. That, I can do without."

"He is Captain Jack Hays of the Texas Rangers. They will stop in New Braunfels for a day or two. They rush to get at the coffee in Ferguson and Hessler's variety store."

"Whiskey, more likely. Jack Hays, did you say? Seriously, Schmitt, you must think I'm simple minded."

"I am serious. The Indians are Tonkawa scouts, the best in the world. They love nothing more than fighting Comanches."

Carl shuddered. "I can see how they would put fear into any enemy. Schmitt, you must take me to New Braunfels. I must meet Hays. Right now!"

At Ferguson and Hessler's store, Carl and Schmitt found the motley assortment sitting on kegs and counters, leaning, talking, and sipping coffee from tin cups. The Indians stood with their cups outside the main circle. Owner Hessler leaned in the center of the bearded men enjoying each exchange, responding in broken English as though to spur them further. Carl recognized the company's leader. He asked Schmitt to approach.

Schmitt entered the circle, careful not to interrupt the ongoing story. Hessler saw Schmitt and spoke to him cordially, then glanced at Carl and spoke formally.

Carl noticed the difference in the greeting and felt envy. But he knew that Schmitt had gone about methodically building public relations while he, Carl, had cloistered himself with his troubles. He also felt uneasy because he understood so few of the English words exchanged. *Even the Indians understand Texas English better than I.*

"Herr Hessler, the director of New Altman wishes to meet the Texas hero, Captain Hays, if he is among your guests." Schmitt spoke in English to prevent any apprehension on the part of the natives. He smiled, looking among them, fixating on the clean shaven one.

Jack Hays, a short but wiry man, dropped from his barrel and faced Schmitt and Carl, two revolving pistols at his hips. Other rangers had similar weapons thrust into their belts. His face revealed neither pleasure nor concern. He stepped forward.

Hessler said, "Captain Hays, please meet Doctor Schmitt and his able director, Prince Carl von Altmann, the founder of the New Altmann colony."

Hays took each hand politely and spoke English slowly, deliberately, and correctly. "It is my pleasure to meet you. May I apologize for the disruption of your peaceful colony an hour ago?" He smiled, adding, "The boys smelled Hessler's coffee. My men are impressed with the stories of your travel from the coast."

"It is my pleasure," Carl said in broken English. "We are likewise impressed with the credits of your forces." Carl felt joyous that he understood the man from the first word, and saw from Hays' response that Hays likewise understood. *Perhaps Meusebach misunderstands because he is deaf.*

Hays continued, "Prince Carl, I understand that you made a treaty with Fleetaumountec. Any man who would face him on the open plain is braver than any ranger I have ever known. You have my admiration."

Carl would not lie to bring himself glory. "I fear the main credit is not mine. Our own Doctor Hagerdorn took the lead. We have decorated him."

Hays misunderstood for a moment. "Oh, your companion here is the hero." He took Schmitt's hand again.

Schmitt laughed. "No, I am Schmitt. I cowered in the wagon with Carl when the Indians struck. Hagerdorn is another doctor."

The rangers and the Indians roared at Schmitt's words. The gaff seemed to disarm all present as Carl and Hays exchanged remarks.

Hays said, "Your success with Fleetaumountec exceeds anything the Texans have accomplished. His own tribe considers him an outsider and his treaty will not carry over to them, nor will his words of peace apply to *Texas* travelers wherever he may ride. Tell me, Mr. Carl, do your people plan to join the New Braunfels colony, or will you push west?"

"It seems the people are content to stay where we have settled. We are a separate society, though we have much in common. Adequate land is a serious issue. We have purchased tracts from a stockman to our west, somewhat scattered. The German custom requires living in proximity to the land we farm."

"From whom did you purchase the tracts, Mr. Carl?"

Schmitt answered. "Isaack Covington."

"A true Texas gentleman, Mr. Carl. I'm sure you agree."

"I regret to say that my duties have kept me from meeting him."

"You're correct, Captain Hays." Schmitt injected. "Covington is a prince." Hays smiled and sipped his coffee.

"Yes, get acquainted with the Texas natives. Understand, of course, they're brave men, and women, but a little crazy. They'll go anywhere, far out from settlements, far out from protection, in order to own land. The Texans believe that the only way to conquer the land is to live on it."

Hays' lieutenant, Ben McCulloch, spoke up. "They's some damn good fellars up thuh San Antonyee River and on up yonder on the Gawd-a-loop, ye know. Ye oughta go palaver with them, too. Lemme see, they's Ole Gene Nance and Curly Monfort. Look 'em up."

Carl stood stone faced and tense as the discourse ended. He hadn't understood a single word. Meusebach's meaning came back.

Hays rescued him. "Ben, when are you gonna learn to talk German, or English for that matter? Mr. Carl, what my ignorant friend said was there are other ranchers. The two he named, Nance on the San Antonio River and Monfort on the Guadalupe could be helpful."

Carl changed the subject. "Captain Hays, I am happy to see

103

your company in our area. I trust you will continue here and on the western frontier."

"War with Mexico is stirring. Seems General Santa Anna didn't like Texas joining the United States. He never accepted the Rio Grande as our border. He must assert his claim now or never. My company may be called into service if war breaks out. That could work a hardship on settlers. I recommend that you do all you can to protect yourselves. Train your men in the use of weapons and learn the habits of the Indians."

They exchanged conversation for an hour. As Carl and Schmitt prepared to leave, Hays asked a question. "Mr. Carl, out of curiosity, was Fleetaumountec accompanied by a warrior who looked different from the others? That is to say, he looked out of place from his choice of dress and the way he sat a horse."

"Yes, a young warrior. Hagerdorn christened him *The Silly Looking One*."

The ranger company laughed and nodded. Hays said, "That was Queno, Fleetaumountec's son. The prince. You are fortunate that he wasn't among those killed in the raid. There would have been no peace."

Carl and Schmitt rode westward, comforted by the new friendship, worried about war. Schmitt complimented Carl. "I'm proud of you, my prince. Not once did you reveal the usual arrogance and alienate this valued friend."

"I started to swat you over the head when you suggested that we cowered in the wagon. Princes do not cower. Perhaps doctors. And you never corrected yourself."

"But, Carl, they knew the story already. Did you see how our humility disarmed them?"

"Humility? Humph!"

# Chapter 12

"Hagerdorn has been gone for months. Are you sure he said nothing that would give away his intent to join Meusebach permanently?" Carl drummed his oak desktop as his nostrils breathed fresh-cut wood in his yet unfinished home.

"Nothing, Carl. And I still refuse to believe it. He will return to us. His family is still here," Schmitt said. "Of course, he may have been killed in the wilderness…"

"And that walrus, Meusebach, has not the courage to come forth and tell me." He paced again.

"Meusebach is large, yes, Carl, but take care in your choice of words. The man's mission with the Indians will benefit us, too." Schmitt joined Carl's pacing, crossing paths.

When Schmitt left, Carl kissed Elisabeth on the forehead before she skipped happily to her new room and pallet. His love for his daughter had no boundaries. The Comanche warrior who would have killed her, or worse, taken her captive, crossed his mind. He felt a surge of energy, thanking the stars that he could now draw his sword without strangling coughs and stagnant muscle reflexes. He would gladly die for her, but he swore he would live to see her grown.

At daybreak, Hagerdorn appeared at his door, drawn and weary. So glad to see him, Carl forgot to chastise him. "Oh, thank God, you are alive, Hagerdorn. Why has the wal.. Meusebach kept you so long?"

"He dragged me into the wilderness twice, Carl. The numbers of Indians you would not believe. I was so worn a Comanche arrow would have seemed welcome. I stopped twice to cut longer poles to hold my Ocean People banner higher. I could not tell that it had any effect, but it was my only hope had they attacked."

Carl felt the old mixture of adventure and fear in times of war as he motioned Hagerdorn to a chair. "And how did Herr Meusebach fair?"

"I worry that the man is daft. He showed no fear on any occasion. He often shouted out to the Indians, fired his rifle from his hip, and sent scouts ahead who could speak the language. The Indians always pulled away."

Carl smiled. "Did he not call for you and your great skills of negotiation?"

"He said he was 'saving me.' I felt like a pig fattened against a better day. He sent seemingly ignorant Mexican peasants. They obeyed every command. Like their commander, they showed no fear."

"Why did he fire his rifle if not to provoke the natives?" Carl examined the tea pot, which was cold.

"I think it was to show that he had discharged his weapon harmlessly. Thus, if they would talk, he would be approaching them without threat, an unloaded weapon. Not all of his companions agreed that it was a good idea. I was among the dissenters."

Carl asked, "Did you ever hold counsel with the Indians?"

Hagerdorn stood and removed his heavy coat in the warmth. "Yes, but without major success. Meusebach seemed greatly depressed, and came back to a spot he had earlier studied and set his surveyors to work forming a townsite not far from the Pedernales River. He will call it Fredericksburg. He is Prussian to the core, you know."

"A poor spot for a colony, if I know Meusebach's mentality," Carl concluded, thumping into his chair.

"No, quite beautiful, Carl, and it will fill quickly. He has many new immigrants on the way."

"Hmph. Hard work and dedication count more than money, and my people have it. Our colony will show more beauty through the will of the people than all the waters and trees of the Pedernales." A vision of his castle gave a glimmer of hope. "I'm off to New Orleans to exercise my letters of credit."

Though he collected on his scant credit in New Orleans, Carl found no new credit there. Mentally, he thanked Meusebach for the advice given on whom to contact. With Elisabeth at his side, Wilhelm, Ernst and five other guards, he returned from the arduous journey to find his colony prospering. Families harvested corn in every tract. He found the dam at Comal Fountain full. Canals flowed from its font and coursed past the construction sites of a sawmill and grist mill as they watched.

"I should leave more often," Carl told Schmitt while feeling a certain pain. "The people do well without me. Surely, it was your good direction."

"My chief direction was in telling the workers daily that their prince would return. They should make him proud. Such energy I've never seen." Schmitt sat on his horse watching water pour over the dam.

Carl brightened. "I told you we would succeed. I predict we see continued prosperity. Our economic dilemma may lessen."

"Economic? Maybe." Schmitt slumped in the saddle. "But a mad fever has taken hold in New Braunfels and the new town of Fredericksburg. Hundreds have died. Some of our people are sick. Hagerdorn and I have quarantined New Altmann. I think it will help."

"What? What is the disease, Schmitt?" Carl's mind raced to find another excuse to get Elisabeth out of danger.

"There is a doctor, an idiot, I should say, in Fredericksburg, who has diagnosed petechial fevers." Schmitt's face flushed in anger. "It is cholera. Hagerdorn agrees. We must boil all water and keep people away from each other as much as possible."

✂ ✂ ✂

The people arranged a harvest festival to be held outside Carl and Elisabeth's new house, which lacked but a few interior amenities. Helga's piano had been unloaded from its year-long stay on the wagon. Melancholy tears streamed from Elisabeth's eyes as she fingered the keys for the first time since Southern Bavaria. Carl instantly recognized the need to re-start her music lessons and resume her schooling.

Except for posted and mounted guards around the village, and those sick in bed, every person in New Altmann attended the fest as did a hundred from New Braunfels. Carl never felt better about the future, and he let his pleasure show by dancing with frauleins and fraus from ages fifteen to sixty. He even whirled the ever light-hearted Berta as Roth escorted Elisabeth graciously onto the hardened earth floor.

When he danced with Katheryn he took note of how much she resembled her dead sister, his wife, Helga. He forced the thought from his mind, determined to make the most of a happy evening.

Katheryn asked, "Carl, have you given thought to Doctor Schmitt's proposition that you consider remarriage?"

Instead of recoiling in horror as he may have with Schmitt, he said disarmingly, "My dear Katheryn, who could I marry of noble blood in this motley assortment? Perhaps Berta?" He thought it a good joke. "A prince must maintain his aplomb, you know."

Katheryn smiled. "Some women in Southern Bavaria would qualify. I could send letters if you allow it. For example, Baroness Wilhelmine von Schoener, the widow of von Dieselhorst. What a beautiful lady, and still young enough to give you a few sons, and daughters."

He knew he should have treated her overture as he would have Schmitt, cut her off the moment she started. Now, he must address the ridiculous idea. "Katheryn, I cannot entertain such notions. I'm too busy. Besides, my grief for Helga will never end."

"Baroness Wilhelmine would understand your busy schedule. She was born to nobility. And, Carl, my sister told me many times she would want such a thing for you and your lineage. Also, I know men well enough to know that though the flame grows weary in such times, a spark remains forever."

Katheryn spoke the truth, but Carl couldn't respond to a single statement. He escorted her to the standing observers including her husband, Christian Linnartz, bowed graciously and turned away.

At last alone in the comfort of his own bed under his own roof for the first time in over a year, Carl couldn't shake the conversation from his mind. Nor could he dislodge the image of the devastating Baroness Wilhelmine as her chiffon shawl swirled over the formal dance floor amid classical music. *Katheryn was simply giving an example. If I were ever to consider such a thing, and I will not, I must do so in a broad and general way, not specific to one woman... I wonder if she has remarried. She certainly would have suitors. Most likely...what am I asking? No more, no more thoughts! ...How old would she be now?*

At home, Katheryn spoke to her husband, Christian, of her conversation with Carl. "And how did he react?" he asked.

"Quite well, I thought. Doctor Schmitt said he typically went into a rage when he brought it up. But he answered me politely and gave the usual excuses."

"Darling, why not write a letter to Baroness Wilhelmine and describe New Altmann to her in detail. You know her well enough that she would not think you forward. And, of course, you'll casually mention the prince's loneliness, and implore that she reply promptly."

# Chapter 13

The new year's winter gave way to grass sprigs and crabapple blossoms as Carl and Schmitt rode the creek bottoms.

"Ah, 1847 will prove a fine year, Schmitt. We must steer a true course, watch the budget, and control our growth." As their horses pulled them in view of the main road, Carl added. "Look at the new arrivals. How did those wagons ever make it through the coastal mud?"

"How did ours?" Schmitt said. "Determination. By my count, half the new pilgrims come from Southern Bavaria, therefore ours by rights. The other half hail from scattered provinces, but they want to join us. Some say because we are more progressive than Meusebach's colony. A compliment. Do you agree? And, Carl, we must make a decision soon. Their ragtag camp numbers around three hundred now."

Carl frowned at Schmitt and glanced toward the motley assortment of weary travelers camped in tents. "Call a committee meeting for morning. Remember what I said about caution."

ଔ  ଔ  ଔ

Carl began. "While the Texas society has an insatiable appetite for bodies to fill the empty grant lands, we have no such ambitions. For us to take on endless numbers will simply burden our treasury. I say 'no,' and I expect my committee to support me."

Schmitt said, "Let's not act hastily, Herr Carl. We have succeeded thus far because our people have worked hard close to home. We could use the additional sixty men on our mill, road and canal projects. And their arrival time is perfect for breaking new ten-acre gardens for summer and fall harvest."

"Aughhh! Schmitt, you suggest we should buy more land to accommodate these freeloaders? Finance is our greatest worry. You know that."

"Finance is not our greatest worry. It is *your* greatest worry. Do you not see what Meusebach fails to see? He constantly worries about shoring up the fiscal walls of the Texas society. But even if they take bankruptcy tomorrow, their colonies will live. Individual determination will cause the individual German to survive. Our people have that determination and that determination will rub off on the new arrivals. The people will survive…and it is in large measure a reflection of your fine leadership."

Carl wanted to lash out. How could he ever have his castle if he didn't concern himself with finances? The working class may muddle along like the Texans, but German pride would die. But he pondered the compliment and gained control. "Perhaps we could take a census. We would take those who could pay."

"No!" Schmitt snapped. "We take them all or none. Most are agrarians. One is a vintner of some renown. Another the maker of iron forging equipment. They have an architect. These men will not come if you exclude the others."

"Schmitt, since when do you have the right to blurt 'no' in my face? Have you once again conspired with the committee behind my back?" When Schmitt hesitated, Carl continued. "A vintner? A forger? An architect? Are you sure?"

CB   CB   CB

Another festival immediately erupted when word went out that the new arrivals were accepted. Carl met with the three specialists and detained them for hours while their families frolicked to the music, dance and food outside. Vintner Young, Forger Triesch, and Architect Adrian enjoyed the personal attention of the prince and his promises of support if they put their trades into practice. But their faces cast longingly toward the door and the music as Carl's enthusiasm held them in check.

Meusebach learned that sixty of his families had opted to join New Altmann and laughed in pleasure. "Let Carl take some of the poor. He will learn to appreciate my dilemma. Perhaps I can send another two or three thousand his way when they arrive."

Hermann Spiess replied, "There were a few professionals among the defectors, I'm told. A vintner, a forger, and an architect. Prince Carl is courting them heavily."

Meusebach leaped to his six-foot-three-inch height. "What? How dare that seductive excuse of forgotten royalty rob my colony of its best. I'll have his head." He lifted the lid of a sea trunk and scooped out his Colt revolving pistol, in holster and belt.

"Herr John, are you going to kill the prince? Some should go with you. There is strength in numbers."

"I'll either kill him and bring back the professionals or he will give them up willingly and live. I don't need your help." He marched to his small, saddled horse.

He paid no attention to staring Altmanners as he entered the village. He walked his exhausted horse to Carl's house and committee hall where he pounded the door and screamed for attention. He proceeded methodically to stalk the village – head held low, jaw thrust outward, leading his jaded animal – in search of its director.

Lieutenant Ernst reached Carl at the dam on Comal Fountain. He told Carl graphically of Meusebach's demeanor and tone. Carl guessed his intentions. Ernst said, "Without doubt, he will learn your whereabouts. Shall I stand just out of view and drop him with a musket ball the moment he flinches?"

Carl stood dressed in his public regalia of uniform, helmet, sword and horse pistol. With depressing sadness, he pulled the pistol from his belt, checked the percussion cap, and returned the weapon cocked. "Give him more than a flinch before you fire. I'm sorry that it comes to this. I thought him a reasonable man, but that temper will be his undoing. I'll try to talk to him. It's all right if he kills me. But if he does, see to it that he doesn't ride away."

When the large framed, red bearded man entered the narrow canyon, riding the uphill grade, Carl noticed the animal's efforts. *Gad, the man needs to watch his girth. The poor horse... Wait, what am I thinking? He's coming to kill me!*

Carl positioned himself behind a boulder so that his body from the chest down was hidden to the view of the oncoming rider. When Meusebach closed to fifty meters, Carl called clearly. "Herr Meusebach, will you state your intentions?"

The rider and horse stopped. The horse appeared dwarfed by its awesome rider. Its head darted toward the ground as the animal blew audibly from fifty paces. Meusebach glanced hurriedly around. The creek flowed on his right; the canyon wall braced his left. Ahead stood Carl, half hidden where the canyon widened near the dam, and huge boulders dotted his background. "I seek a conference, Herr Carl. Are you alone?"

"If your conference seeks to drain my colony of its skilled workers, you should resort to the fine American weapon at your side now. Whether I am alone, you will see."

"My God, Carl. Surely, you don't think I come to do you harm."

"Herr John, I would respect your desire to kill me more than I would respect a lying tongue. Which is it?"

Meusebach lowered his face then raised it slowly. He reached and pulled his revolver by thumb and forefinger, and held it aloft, then threw it forward onto the hard road. With both hands he wiped his face and beard. "Carl, I-I-I made a mistake. I lost my temper. You are correct. I was near to false pretenses. Can you ever accept my apology?"

"Come close and state your business." Carl loved the man and dreaded the thought that now their friendship would die.

Meusebach dismounted and paced the slightly uphill grade. He extended his hand.

"Please forgive me, Herr Carl. I was so wrong."

Carl didn't offer his hand as he spoke. "At the request of sixty Texas Society families, we accepted them into our ranks. Three of them are highly skilled. They came as a package. I'm glad to have them. For this I have no remorse. But I won't kill to keep them. I was born to royalty but I don't believe in slavery. Do you, John?"

"Carl, must I get on my knees and beg your forgiveness? I will. I readily admit my mistake in coming to you in a menacing manner. I was wrong! I was wrong!" Meusebach exuded a single sob before he could prevent it. He couldn't hide his tear rimmed eyes.

When Carl continued to glare without speaking, Meusebach pleaded. "I don't think I would have killed you. But I was still wrong to come in this manner."

Carl interrupted, "I don't think you would have killed me, my friend, because I would have beaten you to the draw with this outdated single shot." Carl pulled the old pistol from his belt, lowered the hammer and handed it to Meusebach. Meusebach touched the handle then pushed it back toward Carl.

"Carl, we are friends. I have always intended to respect your independence and avoid competition. But, a vintner, a forger, and an architect? All in one group? I coveted those skills, even for my own future use. My jealousy knew no bounds."

"I will forgive you on one condition." Carl's face held firm.

"And that is?"

"You'll sell us lands to provide our new arrivals with garden tracts, and at most reasonable prices."

"Done!" Meusebach opened his arms. Carl stepped into the embrace as Ernst emerged from the rocks near the canyon wall.

When Meusebach's horse had rested they rode back to Carl's house. Carl poured schnapps and they drank to friendship. Meusebach revealed that the matter of parlay with the Indians was foremost on his mind.

He said, "I will meet with them this spring or die trying."

"And I'll be at your side. Hagerdorn has tantalized me with tales of the wild land. I must see for myself."

"No, Carl. Do not put your colony at risk by going there. Your loan of Herr Hagerdorn has been more than I should ask. It is enough." His face showed serious concern.

"I insist." Carl felt that he had the upper hand. Meusebach would agree to anything.

"Herr Carl, that was not a condition of our returned friendship. It is still my right to decide."

"Good, then you have decided I will go as an indisputable aid in military affairs should that become necessary." Carl's hand rested on the big man's shoulder.

Meusebach sighed. "You must keep your party small."

Carl told Schmitt of his intentions, mentally prepared for the argument. Schmitt said, "I will permit it provided I'm with you. You will need a personal physician if a battle breaks out."

Carl grinned. "Permit it? You have an audacity." Carl allowed that since the man hadn't fought him on the venture, he, too, wouldn't fight.

In February, Carl, Schmitt, Hagerdorn, Wilhelm and Ernst rode into the Texas Society's quarters at Fredericksburg. They were told the direction taken by Meusebach and his company of negotiators: Dr. Shubbert, Jean J. von Coll, Felix von Blucher, John Torrey, and Delaware Indian Chief, Jim Shaw. Additionally, they employed some twenty Mexican and Indian scouts as guides and negotiators.

Texas and U.S. Indian Agent, Major Richard Neighbors along with Dr. Ferdinand Roemer entered the headquarters compound.

With the briefest of introductions, Neighbors said, "Whatever you do, do not follow Meusebach. His party will not likely return alive. The governor has sent me with the message that the Indians are on the warpath."

Carl felt a rush of blood crawl up his neck. "I promised Meusebach military protection. I'm more determined to go than ever."

Neighbors, a diminutive, sincere man, lowered his face. "Then I must go. I know the Comanche perhaps better than any living Texan. I won't fear for my own life, and maybe I can help spare yours. Dr. Roemer, you need not endanger yourself."

Roemer made a fist and shook it in Neighbors' face. "Now, you two have my fighting blood up. I shall go, too."

Hagerdorn unfurled his *Ocean People* flag and the seven men rode into the wilderness to the north leading four pack mules and

115

three horses.

They slept little and built no fires at night, pushing their horses to make up time. Neighbors had no difficulty following the trail, knowing essentially Meusebach's direction. Carl and his companions stood amazed at the man's tracking skills over rock terrain where they saw not the scantiest evidence of a trail. Neighbors insisted that he was a poor tracker compared to the Delaware and Tonkawa Indian scouts who often got down on their faces and smelled and tasted the ground, the insects and the feces.

On the third morning, Indians appeared on the high ground ahead. Neighbors spurred forward and disappeared over the rise to the alarm of the others. Minutes later he loped back to the party. "It's Chief Matasane's band. I think they will tell him to come to the parley now that they know it's me. We will likely have company at night. Keep your guns out of sight."

Hagerdorn asked Neighbors, "Do you know Fleetaumountec? Will he come?"

"I know him only by name and reputation. He is difficult to deal with. He avoids white contact. But the Germans need his cooperation if there is any chance for peace."

No sooner than blankets were spread and saddles deposited as pillows, bare skinned warriors appeared on all sides. Some stayed mounted with bows and arrows held low while others tied their horses to the brush and entered the camp. Neighbors scurried to bring cornbread and dried meat from his packs to give them. With no change of expression, they grunted their appreciation while snatching the food from his hand. They plopped their rumps on the ground and ate voraciously. The mounted warriors dropped from their slender ponies and eased forward eyeing the odd clothes of the white warriors, Carl, Wilhelm and Ernst.

Hagerdorn spoke Spanish to the closest. The warrior continued to chew and gulp as though he were alone. Minutes later the Indian answered. "Man Who Brings Cow has food for women?"

Hagerdorn leaped. "They know my name! My fame has grown. Major Neighbors, may I ask him if he can find my friend, Fleetaumountec?"

"Yes, please do. But be prepared to give him some provisions for his women."

Hagerdorn made up a cloth sack of items estimated to feed four people at least two meals. He handed it to the warrior and spoke Spanish. "I am friend of Fleetaumountec. You can show me his lodge?"

The warrior inspected the sack's content, extracted a large piece of dried beef and began tearing at it with his teeth. In crude Spanish, he said, "Fleetaumountec no come to peace. Many suns away. No trust white man."

"Fleetaumountec trusts Man Who Brings Cow. You learned my name from Fleetaumountec. Man Who Brings Cow is Ocean People. Ocean People are true. Go, and tell him Man Who Brings Cow wants him at the peace talk. We will give presents."

Hagerdorn got no response from his subject but they noticed the next day that that particular warrior didn't ride with the others who continued to dog their tracks and mooch food.

Neighbors often charged ahead of the men and stayed out of sight for hours. Drs. Roemer, Schmitt and Hagerdorn used the occasions to catch up on medical news of mutual interest. They passed a great domed granite outcropping which Neighbors identified as Enchanted Rock, a holy place to the Indians, and a place of death for many, according to a legend spawned from Captain Jack Hays' men. The Germans marveled at the pristine streams and oak covered bottom lands where they were sure no white man had ever set foot. Carl pondered the possibilities that would never be his, only Meusebach's, if the commissioner-general succeeded. *The ox wants it all. He is worse than his predecessor, Solms.*

A day later, the party crossed the crystalline Llano River on its great flat blocks of pink granite, and camped. Riding fast before the next sunset, they encountered a rear guard of Meusebach's party. The forces joyously joined and charged onward to reach Meusbach's main body.

Indians camped openly under live oak canopies in a radius of from one hundred yards to a half mile from the Germans. Hundreds of mounted warriors rode to and from their own camps.

Carl broke into a cold sweat. He had brought two white soldiers besides himself.

*Meusebach is a madman whose ambitions have overpowered judgment. His last clear thoughts were when he implored me not to come. We are both crazy.*

Meusebach screamed in delight when he saw Carl. "Herr Carl, I would have waited had I known you were so close behind. I need badly the services of Doctor Hagerdorn and the Indian specialist, Captain Neighbors."

Carl dropped from his mount. "Herr John, you are insane to remain in this danger. I'll outline a plan of escape, proper guards, a signal. In late evening we will run for cover."

Meusebach patted the men's backs reassuringly. "Fear not, my feathered friend. One sub chief has already asked if Gold Hat and Man Who Brings Cow are among us. And Schmitt, you have a name, also. You are Man Who Walks With Rifle. I used the term *ocean people*, and they seemed to understand. I can tell them you're here. I must get Neighbors to seek Chief Santa Anna. He is suspected of causing the latest troubles with the Texans. He remains remote, aloof.

"None have threatened harm. I believe if they know we are a different people from the Texans they will talk peace. Herr Hagerdorn, come with me."

Meusebach called to a Mexican interpreter and saddled his horse. Carl insisted on joining them. They walked their horses to a distant Indian encampment. The Indian leaders immediately gathered in a giant circle. Mexican linguist, Lorenzo de la Rosa, spoke to the seated Indians according to Meusebach's instructions as a hundred women and children stood outside the seated circle of men. Carl felt a cautious pride that he could participate.

"The one with the Gold Hat is among us. The Man Who Brings Cow is among us, and the Man Who Walks With Rifle is among us. They are fellow ocean people. They are brave as the north wind. They want our people to live in peace. They want Fleetaumountec to come and receive presents. Go and tell Fleetaumountec."

At the same time, Neighbors and Roemer rode to the camp

designated as that of Santa Anna's band. Neighbors reported back that he got no reaction from Santa Anna's lieutenants when he urged the chief to attend the meeting, but such word usually reached a chief once delivered.

The white camp settled into an uneasy rest for the night. At daylight, the guards rushed to Meusebach and told him the Indians had broken camp and were leaving. Meusebach screamed in rage. "They gave me their word! They cannot ride out now. The conference is days away. See to your rifles, men. We will give them a proper punishment."

Neighbors stepped in front of Meusebach. "No, Mr. Meusebach. Calm down. They ride to find the other chiefs. Indian ways are strange. If they all choose to go, they go. They will come back."

"How long?"

"I estimate a week."

Meusebach's usual calm demeanor returned immediately. "Good, it gives me time to explore the Spanish Fort area and search for the silver mines."

Carl asked, "Silver mines?"

"There have been rumors for a hundred years. Even Bowie, who died in the Alamo, came here in search. His secrets died with him."

"And his secrets may well die with us, Herr John." Carl said it without conviction because he knew he would ride west with Meusebach to the site and hope to discover riches hidden for ages.

ଔ  ଔ  ଔ

The Spanish fort ruins consisted of a crumbling adobe wall. Doctor Roemer, also schooled in geology, offered no encouragement that the limestone formations could bear silver ore. Meusebach wouldn't give up the notion and cajoled Roemer into agreeing that *somewhere* within the gigantic Fisher-Miller grant, there *may* be minerals which *could* bear silver. When Roemer grunted a reluctant "possibly" Meusebach took on a new look of optimism and scribbled in his notebooks.

119

They marveled that no Indians appeared during their round trip odyssey. But Neighbors' theory allowed no relaxation. He said the greatest danger lurks when no natives are seen because they planned an attack. The party could only hope that the Indians were riding to their other chiefs and weren't in the area.

Then a party of three mounted warriors appeared on a knoll a half-mile to their north as they rode east, back to the peace rendezvous. Neighbors turned left and charged ahead. Meusebach wouldn't be denied and followed closely. The warriors spread themselves apart by ten yards as the two white men approached.

Neighbors, who normally used an interpreter, spoke Spanish to the rider in the middle. "We come in peace. At the fork of the San Saba and Brady Creek a council of peace begins. We will give presents to the Indians."

"No peace with Texas warriors! All liars! Fleetaumountec kill you all. You lie. Told Indian ocean people come to make peace." He spat, "You Texas!"

When Neighbors interpreted the statement, Meusebach exclaimed, "I am ocean people! I am ocean people!" His German speech was ignored by the strange warrior who wore layers of cloth shirts with rawhide tied around his chest in lieu of buttons. His slouched posture was in stark contrast to the usual Comanche form – ramrod straight.

Neighbors interpreted. "Ocean people hold the conference. I am Indian agent for Tex...for all tribes."

The warrior's eyes darted from one man to the other, also not a Comanche trait.

From the low ground, Carl and the others heard Meusebach's powerful voice. "Carl, come forward! All of you! They want to see Gold Hat and his companions!"

When Carl's party drew near, Hagerdorn exclaimed, "Silly Looking!"

As the white men rode abreast of Neighbors and Meusebach, Hagerdorn continued. "It is the son of Fleetaumountec. The one we called Silly Looking."

Queno smiled widely when he saw Carl and Dr. Hagerdorn.

He knew Hagerdorn by sight and he easily recognized Carl by his feather decked, brass trimmed helmet. He said, "Man Who Brings Cow, friend. Trust Man Who Brings Cow. Important chief. Talk to him. No other."

Hagerdorn interpreted the words before Neighbors could make the mental translation. Meusebach, Neighbors and Carl began talking at once in their native tongues each protesting that *he* was the important chief. Queno watched in alarm and pulled his horse backwards, drawing his bow into position. His warriors acted likewise.

Hagerdorn shouted, "Will you all be quiet? He thinks you want to kill him. Silly Looking, do not fear. They play as children." *They may kill each other out of jealously but not you. Too stupid,* he thought to himself.

Queno lowered his bow. "Man Who Brings Cow give white name to Queno?"

Hagerdorn was trapped. He had spilled the insult in the heat of excitement. He was sure the warrior, who never missed anything, understood the words. He turned to Neighbors. "Now we're in trouble. I gave him an insulting name and I just revealed it to him."

Carl and Meusebach quickly agreed that they had no choice but to kill the warrior and his companions before they rode back to Fleetaumountec.

Neighbors raised his hand. "Indians seldom feel insulted by mere words. Did you see how he lowered his bow when you spoke it? He is proud. Tell him his new name again."

Hagerdorn argued but Neighbors insisted. Hagerdorn addressed the brave. "Ocean people give Queno new name because they find his dress strange. The name is 'Silly Looking.' No other warrior, no other white man, no other ocean people have the name."

Queno smiled and spoke proudly to his companions, then wheeled his horse northward and raised his bow high. "I am Silly Looking! Tell Fleetaumountec!"

Slumped, Hagerdorn watched the trio vanish into the trees and sighed, "Oh, shit."

CR CR CR

The bands were gathering in even larger numbers at the designated meeting place when the exploring party returned. Neighbors immediately rode among the clan of Santa Anna to see if the chief had arrived. Meusebach took the New Altmann contingent to seek out Fleetaumountec. Neither chief was present and no Indian would confirm their expected arrival. Meusebach was determined to start without them. Neighbors warned against it.

Various bands wouldn't enter the circle with other Comanches. Santa Anna's people shunned all groups. No Comanche pretended to speak for Fleetaumountee, forcing Meusebach to hold three conferences: one general session; one for Santa Anna's band; and another for those he hoped would carry the message to Fleetaumountec.

He spoke long of the beauty of the land, the benefits of peace and his admiration for Indian bravery. He even suggested that as whites and Indians become friends, the white men will want to marry the beautiful Indian women. He said such marriages will assure the lasting friendships between their people. But he kept the treaty terms simple: no hostilities between the Germans and the Indians within the confines of the Fisher-Miller Grant; surveyors would be allowed to work unmolested; and presents for the Indians now and later.

After two days of shifting himself and his translators among the factions, he concluded that he could do nothing else to bring in the reluctant chiefs. But the Delaware Indian guide, Jim Shaw, primary interpreter and himself a chief, assured Meusebach that everyone in attendance would willingly accept the terms conditioned upon their satisfaction with the presents offered.

True to his word, Meusebach ordered goods taken from his pack animals and a third of the presents delivered immediately. The other two thirds would be delivered at Fredericksburg "when the disc of the moon has rounded twice," Meusebach's words describing when the treaty would be signed.

As far as the Indians were concerned the treaty was in effect immediately and they tore into the packed goods with appalling vigor. After efforts at hand delivering the goods to individual

122

chiefs with specific instructions, "This good for squaw; make fine clothes; carry water; cook meat; hold horse," Meusebach stepped back and wrung his hands.

Hagerdorn said, "Herr Meusebach, I could have told you of the futility of playing Saint Nicholaus. Let's relax and enjoy the scene. One of the chiefs is approaching."

Comanche Chief Ketemoczy approached Meusebach holding a large pendant of cut yellow glass on a string, obviously from the booty of presents. Behind him followed a twelve-year-old boy. The chief held the string open and placed it around Meusebach's thick neck and over his flowing reddish beard. He spoke softly to the lad behind him.

The boy said in perfect English, "The Comanches give you the name *El Sol Colorado.*"

Neighbors and the Germans gasped in surprise. The Indians had had an interpreter among them all along. They looked, wide-eyed at one another. In English, Meusebach asked the boy, "Where did you learn English?"

The lad looked downcast and touched the glittering stone around Meusebach's neck. He repeated, "The Comanches, the Indians, give you the name *El Sol Colorado.*"

Meusebach saw his error and fondled the necklace and roared with laughter. "You make two presents. The shining jewel and the great name, *El Sol Colorado.*"

He reached and took Ketemoczy's hand firmly, then the boy's. Laughter and chatter among the Indians continued for several minutes as Meusebach showed the stone to all the whites and continued to speak warmly of it.

As the wonderment over the necklace subsided, Meusebach asked, "My son, tell me where you learned English."

"My father was killed in the Council House fight at San Antonio. The Texans held me prisoner until I learned their language. Then they gave me back to my people."

Meusebach's curiosity continued. "Were the Texans kind to you?"

"Young Texans made fun of me, threatened me. But a white squaw cared for me with great love. She cried when they gave me back. I call her my white mother. Now, you are my white father."

Meusebach hugged the young man warmly as tears welled. "What is your name, my son?"

"Potrunnucha. The Texans called me Potra. I like that name."

Meusebach used his great baritone voice. "From this day forward, Potra will be known as the son of El Sol Colorado." De la Rosa interpreted and the Indians roared in approval.

Carl, Schmitt, Hagerdorn and Meusebach chatted lightly in front of Meusebach's tent at the end of the long, gratifying day, ready to break up for their respective beds. A small party of warriors appeared. Carl knew he shared with each white man a surreal satisfaction that these wild men could approach without a choking fear seizing their throats. Hagerdorn addressed the Indian party in Spanish. "What may we do for our friends?"

A tall, proud warrior pulled a young maiden by the arm to his front. She dressed in soft buckskin. A beaded headband held her raven smooth locks in place and framed a perfect face. She was beautiful to behold. Each of the German men could see that she wasn't Comanche, obviously a captive to the tribe.

The warrior said, "Fleetaumountec will come to the second meeting. He sends a present of White Goose to the head chief of the ocean people."

With that, he thrust the girl into Meusebach's bosom forcing the large man to support her around the waist to keep her from falling. He held her there as her adoring eyes cast upward and Hagerdorn interpreted.

"No! Oh, my God. No. No. Hagerdorn, you must tell them. I cannot accept. Tell them. Tell them." Great droplets of sweat leaped onto Meusebach's forehead.

White Goose curled her arms around Meusebach's considerable girth and continued to hold tight while uttering a soft coo. Carl and Schmitt began to giggle, then chuckle, then erupt into mindless laughter.

Hagerdorn couldn't find the Spanish words to translate.

"You three have gone insane! Stop it! You must help me!" the commissioner-general begged in panic.

Hagerdorn stumbled through the words in attempting the explanation but the Indians showed no sign of comprehension. They turned and walked into the darkness leaving their present in the white chief's arms.

Carl, Schmitt and Hagerdorn watched in hysterical laughter as the young woman pushed the large man into his tent. They heard a definite thump as the pair collapsed in a heap on his wooden cot. They could still hear Meusebach's gentle protests as they walked to their own camp, leaving him to his own devices.

# Chapter 14

Carl, Schmitt and Hagerdorn chuckled for weeks over the incident, never learning for sure how Muesebach disposed of his unsolicited gift, or if he did. They laughed also at the newspaper accounts of the treaty which, depending on the source of the news – Meusebach or Neighbors – varied as to who had contributed the most to its success. The three knew with certainty that the treaty would never have been made had it not been for both. They agreed that both men were helpless without the Mexican and Indian guides and interpreters. Neither did the articles give credit to the Altmann men, the only link to a critical element – Fleetaumountec. They roared again that it had been their friend, Fleetaumountec, who had gifted the girl to Meusebach.

The venture with the Indians had given each man a renewed and different confidence which spilled over into their charges. Many had left property unsold in the German states and they directed entrusted kin and assigns to handle the sales and send the money to Texas. Carl did likewise, instructing his administrator to sell some of his farmlands and vineyard.

No month passed without the arrival of tired but optimistic new immigrants, encouraged by letters and the new treaty. The committee brought each family to Carl for a personal introduction. Carl welcomed them with backslaps and assurances, lifting each infant and toddler, bending low to shake hands with each child. When they left he felt a creeping anxiety. *Too many people, not enough land.*

Calling together Schmitt, Hagerdorn, Wilhelm and Ernst, he said, "We must visit the stockman, Isaack Covington. Why have you four not insisted that I meet him sooner?"

Schmitt snapped, "Do not press your luck, Herr Carl. Until

126

now, your reputation for honesty is unmolested. Always, you have excuses – the upcoming fest, letters of credit, the construction…"

"All true." Carl feigned hurt at the rebuke, redirecting the conversation. "Would this Covington know of available lands for sale near us?"

"He has sold us all his available lots. His own ranch and the free grazing he occupies lies half a day's ride from here. But he would know." Schmitt's eyes took on a glow. "Yes, yes, Carl. If you're ready to travel, finally, I'll introduce you."

Carl closed his ledger and rose. "As though I must make excuses to you, I'll tell you, I have been uncomfortable with my command of the English language."

Carl was amazed at the man's youth, no more than thirty. His young wife stood at the door of their two-part log cabin with an infant son in her arms. Covington recognized the Germans from the new colony and marched forward to greet them. His broad-brimmed straw hat spoke of Mexican origin; his gray clothes, homespun. Though the man commanded more acres of land than many German principalities, Carl read no pretense about him, though he did note confidence in the way he carried his tall, slender frame.

"Howdy, gentlemen. Git down and git in the shade. Shore hot for October." He extended his hand as the men dismounted. "I believe I've met some of you. Doctor Schmitt, ain't it? And I'd know this soldier anywhere," thumbing toward Wilhelm.

Schmitt took Covington's hand as they dismounted. "Herr…Mr. Covington, I want you to meet the director of our colony, Prince Carl von Altmann. He much regretted that he missed meeting you when we were trading."

"Mr. Carl, pleased to meet you. Ya'll come on up on the porch outa this sun." Covington immediately turned from Carl to Ernst. "Ike Covington's the name. I didn't get yours."

Ernst spoke politely as they moved to the shade. Carl noted the lack of special attention paid him but forced the thought from his mind.

Covington introduced them to his wife, June. Carl took note

that her beauty was still intact after giving birth. Her brown hair, pulled straight back, offered a few loose curls above her dark eyebrows, giving her an appearance of working but never failing to care for her appearance.

Covington said, "This youngun is John. He's gonna make me a fine horseman one of these days. Need him now, though." June smiled and spoke collectively to the visitors, adding that her husband was already taking the baby on long horseback rides.

Covington's only deference to rank was to offer the community water dipper to Carl first. He took it, drained it, dipped again before handing it to Schmitt. Covington said he would bring chairs out to the porch "where it's cooler," and told June to "fix some vittles for the company."

June said, "Ike, remember what Captain Hays told you. Do not use contractions when you speak to the German people. Say every word full out."

The visitors didn't follow her words until Covington responded. "Contractions? What's a contraction. Ain't I talkin' right?"

She faced her husband, babe in arms. "You say 'what is,' and do not use the word 'ain't' now or ever. And add the 'g's on every word. These are educated men and they know good English. Do not show your ignorance."

Covington's brow knotted for a second. "Oh, yeah. Now I got it." He grinned, a hand on her shoulder as his wife explained that the word is "yes," not "yeah."

Carl, often insensitive to the personal relationships of married couples, noticed the easy rapport between the pair and felt admiration, if not envy. These frontier people with little start had found land, happiness, and love in a hostile world. With any luck, they would raise a fine son, maybe a half dozen, to carry on their name and their pride. Carl, born a prince, had no wife, no love, no son and no land.

With effort, Ike Covington improved his English as they got on with business at hand. Was there land available not too distant from New Altmann, larger tracts, much larger tracts?

"Yeah...yes, there is some land. Two owners, I believe. Joins you on the north. As you know, the hills crop up startin'...starting there. But when you get above the slope, the land is real good. I would like to have it myself, but it is a little too far east for me. Besides, I am looking to the west to add to mine. One of the owners is an heir to the Veramendi estate and the other is an old woman in San Antonio. The Veramendis have about twelve hundred acres and Old Lady Snodgrass must own around ten thousand acres. How much was you lookin'...Uh, how much land were you seeking?"

"I would be pleased to add all of it to the holdings. The price would be the determining factor, of course. Does the land have water and fertile soil for farming?" Carl asked as he glanced toward Schmitt, noticing a frown.

"There is a good creek and the valleys spread out in a number of places for farming. What you cannot farm, you can graze cattle."

They ate a frontier supper with the settlers – beans, cornbread, pork, and pumpkin. Carl offered to pay and feared he had incurred the scorn of his Texas neighbor forever when he received a sound rebuke. But Covington slapped the prince on the back as he explained frontier hospitality on the way to their horses.

A week later, Carl and his party met Covington on an appointed hill and they rode into the Veramendi and Snodgrass lands to explore. When the day ended Carl was frantic to travel to San Antonio to negotiate the purchases. They walked their tired horses as white-tailed deer looked up and moved gracefully to cover.

Schmitt opened up. "Carl, by what magic have you come forth with funds for such a purchase? Had I suggested it, you would have dressed me severely because of our financial plight."

"Very simple, my dear doctor. You sign papers saying you will pay, take the land, settle on it, then, at a later date, you claim it by adverse possession, a common practice among crooked princes in the old country. It's time I invoked it here."

"Prince or not, law or not, I wouldn't wish to face the likes of these determined Texans if I tried to steal their land." Schmitt smiled knowingly at Carl's humor, but he still wanted an answer.

129

Carl watched a cardinal flit among the overhead live oak branches. "It may surprise you to learn that I am not so miserly with my own means that I cannot do a magnanimous thing from time to time. Perhaps you could take a lesson. How much do you have hidden in a sock some place?"

The other riders moved close to hear Schmitt's reply. "The fees of a colonial doctor will keep him humble indefinitely. Perhaps in your generosity, you would like to make up some of the medical charges that your subjects have skipped paying me."

"I need work on my toenail, I'll pay in cash, provided you don't cause me pain. Now listen, Schmitt, if my farms and vineyard sell at a good price, I could buy one or both of the parcels and put our people to work immediately at breaking ground for crops, solving a major problem. We badly need more space for our growing population, and I would become a Texas land baron in the process."

"And, with time, you would become wealthy from the rents you charge our farmers."

"Schmitt!" he scolded. "You disappoint me. I wouldn't charge them rents at all. Perhaps a small levy from the society of one tenth of their crops."

"Carl, I know you would not cheat in a land deal. And I know you have the best intentions for the people. They'll praise your name for all times. It will be your legacy."

Carl's smile turned serious as their mounts blew and stepped from a hoof-deep, gravel stream. "I want more than idle praise for a legacy."

"What? What did you say, Herr Prince?"

"I keep certain things even from you, my curious friend, though I find it difficult with your constant inquisitions."

"But you brought up the subject. Now, I'll toss all night unless you tell me."

"I have allowed Frau Kathcryn to invite the Baroness Wilhelmine von Schoener for my courtship."

His companions awed in harmony. He glanced toward Schmitt. "I shall examine her, in intellectual matters, of course, and determine her suitability as a bride. Yes, Herr Schmitt, you've driven me to the brink of insanity with your constant harassment to have a family again. I'm considering it for one reason only – to get you off my back."

Schmitt smiled and gazed toward the cloud-fleeced sky, as though envisioning the gorgeous baroness. "I should think she may wish to examine *you*. Be careful that your royal pomp does not dampen her ardor. Many noblemen would petition for polygamy to gain opportunity with the baroness."

Carl's property in Altmann sold better than expected And he negotiated down payments for purchase of all the acreage with the owners in San Antonio, saving enough cash for improvements and stocking. On return from San Antonio in late winter, a letter, sent in care of Katheryn, awaited him. The baroness would arrive at Galveston in the spring with her lady-in-waiting, Greta von Gotlieb, famous for her long nose and short patience. The timing was perfect. He would have his land, his plans, his dreams in order. He could show her the accomplishments of the colony and tell her tales of intrigue among the Indians, taking care not to frighten her.

His daughter, Elisabeth, now turned fourteen, shocked him by agreeing warmly with his plans. He hid tears and a certain shame at the thought of procreating a son to carry on his name. Maybe he would live long enough to see Elisabeth's own son grow to manhood and assume the title. But though he worshipped his lovely daughter, he couldn't deny his own desire to see once again the stunning Baroness Wilhelmine, and under conditions most favorable to him. The two and a half month wait would be excruciating.

He commissioned the building of a cottage near his own home for the indefinite use of the baroness and her escort, von Gotlieb. Youthful energy drove him to ride the new land daily, overseeing the subdivision of lowlands – 60-acre farm plots, wood cutting crews to lay in posts and rails to fence livestock out of the fields. He remained on horseback most times, directing. Creek waters would flow in common, open to all. Live oak, elm, hackberry, mesquite and pecan along the slopes and highlands charged his ambitions for filling the great voids with native cattle, sheep and goats.

CB CB CB

Only in that first visit had Ike Covington noticed a stiff formality about the prince. His frequent visits, alone, seeking advice, had become commonplace since that time. Covington enjoyed the company and the feeling seemed mutual. Covington knew that foreign royalty didn't use surnames, so he had simply called the prince Mr. Carl, whose ready smile spoke approval. And the prince didn't hesitate to ask Covington to repeat a statement when he misunderstood. Covington chuckled lightly that Mr. Carl had taken to using contractions in his own English speech. *Got a quick mind*, he thought, as he looked up to see the uniformed German prince charging his way, ostrich plume twisting furiously in the wind.

"Here comes Old Feather Head," he said to his Mexican hired hands. "Guess I won't git any more work done today,"

As Carl's glistening chestnut stallion pulled up, Covington admonished, "Mr. Carl, you oughtn't be ridin' out here by yourself. Indians shore would like to have that feathered hat, and what's just below it."

Carl gave a familiar reply. "I have so much to do. No time for an escort." This day, he added, "Once again, I seek your advice. I need cattle, sheep, goats and swine, and men with experience to drive them. Where can I find stock and herdsmen?"

"Well, you can go into San Antonio and hire… No, I tell you what." Covington mopped his brow. "Why don't I sell you some stock and drive 'em over there for you. Now, what you want is straight breeding stock. I'll loan you some male animals until you git 'em all bred. No use wastin' good money on bulls and billies. Ride with me a while and I'll show you what I've got."

Covington drew the reins to his saddle horn and leaped aboard, ignoring Carl's protests that the offer was too magnanimous. He grunted a few Spanish phrases and gestured to his hired hands. He carefully surveyed the western horizon before moving the horse and caught Carl's scrutiny.

"Herr Isaack, tell me specifically what methods of defense you use against Indian attacks."

"Call me Ike. Please. And leave off that *hair* part."

They grinned mutually as they moved out. Carl said, "All right, as you wish, Ike. My question was…"

"Oh, yeah. Well, I guess we ought to take a lesson from your people. Stay close to home and travel in bunches. My Mexcin boys know how to use their guns and that helps. But the truth is we don't have a lot of defense. I got burned out once but me and the mizziz made it to the neighbors before they got us. We bunch up when there's a scare. That's why I don't understand you ridin' out here alone. Ain't…It is not German style."

"I took courage from you and the Texans. Captain Hays said you're fearless. I thought I too was unafraid until I came to this land. I don't want the Texans to think they're ahead of us in conquering the wilderness."

Covington led the pair into a lope to cover ground. "Hays prob'ly said we wuz crazy."

As the horses walked their riders to Covington's cabin near sundown, the prince had placed an order for two hundred cows, three hundred goats, four hundred sheep, and as many sows and pigs as the rancher would part with. Covington knew a bond of lasting friendship had developed in that Carl hadn't even asked the price. Trust. On the frontier, you have nothing if not that.

Although Covington could easily have driven the hundreds of mixed animals across the rugged hills with his caballeros, three dozen ill equipped Altmann men and boys anxious to enter a Texas trail drive joined the effort.

They wouldn't allow the animals to drift more than a few feet from one another inside their tight circles. Covington gave practical roping lessons to the younger participants and laughed in admiration at their faltering efforts but undying enthusiasm. They chattered in awe of Covington's saddle, joking that their own caused their missed loops.

Carl placed herdsmen over the animals to keep them from returning home while a fury of work went on to build fences around fields for plowing and planting. In this period, the time grew near for Baroness Wilhelmine's ship to arrive at Galveston.

Carl knew the laborious trip to the coast would require a sizeable escort, including wagons adequate to bring back the wares of the baroness and Greta von Gotlieb. But he dreaded taking his close friends for fear of some embarrassing incident. Suppose his charm should fail him. Suppose the baroness abruptly changed her mind and decided to return to Europe. Other immigrants had done as much.

The land voyage was only days from starting, and Carl still hadn't named his escort when John Meusebach rode into the village, and Carl noticed Meusebach's somber countenance immediately.

"Herr John, surely you don't regret your decision to step down as commissioner-general." He slapped the thick shoulder.

Meusebach wrapped the bridle reins around a hitching rail. "If you refer to my strained expression, I should tell you that my intended bride has passed away in the homeland." He raised and drew a quick sigh. "I see the future as a bleak and forbidding place. There are a few projects I must force myself to complete, then, I don't know, Carl. I just don't know."

Carl felt an old ache in his heart as he wrapped arms around the man. "John, not you, too. And just as I had found the courage to risk pain again myself."

Meusebach's eyes brightened as he gripped Carl by the elbows. "Tell me, Carl. Tell me. It will help my own grief."

Carl told him of his plans, including the eminent trip to Galveston. Meusebach's tears dried. "Oh, Carl, you've saved my life. I shall join you on the voyage. One of my projects... I have a pair of caged cougars and a dozen marsupials ready to ship to the university in Berlin. I trust no one to see them onto the ship in good order."

Carl mused, *No wonder the man does well in Texas. He shows all the symptoms of geographic insanity so characteristic of Texans.*

Meusebach's entourage was more than adequate to assure

safety, and Carl recruited only four teamsters from his own colony to join. He kissed Elisabeth with sadness on his face and joy in his heart as he left New Altmann. He met Meusebach at his Comanche Springs home. He had loaded his vehicles with potted plants of Texas flora and fauna. From two covered wagons, the scowl of caged animals continued unabated as the caravan moved toward the coast.

Carl couldn't bear the thought of a late arrival, so he planned the trip to precede the unpredictable ship by two weeks. He and Meusebach took lodging at the Galveston Buccaneer Hotel where he ordered his uniforms cleaned and pressed. Meusebach failed to persuade him to dress more casually.

Each day, Carl's brass telescope searched the gray horizon, spotting playful dolphins leaping close in, gulls crying and soaring above, but saw only waves where sea met sky. Until the tenth day. Anxiety attacked every part of his body as the great sailing ship appeared magically where he had just scanned.

A gale wind whipped up and the air burst into raindrops. Within an hour, it became obvious that the ship couldn't risk docking this day. He returned to the hotel where he found Meusebach in the tavern surrounded by a dozen admirers whom he had charmed from the first day. Carl joined them and ordered wine.

"Already, I worry for her safety. What if the ship wrecks this near to shore? What would I ever do?"

In a mellow mood, Meusebach replied, "Herr Carl, I have looked into your future and have seen it filled with the joys of family. I know with certainty that your bride and your happiness await you on that ship. Tomorrow they will land. You will see. Drink your wine while I order you a flounder."

When Carl left the hotel the next morning at sunrise, he looked toward the docks and saw the tall sailing vessel towing to shore. His heart leaped. He raced to the planks. He felt more calm this morning, glad the ship hadn't landed the night before.

When the ship docked an hour later, Meusebach and his assistants as well as Carl's teamsters had arrived to watch the passengers disembark. Everyone had heard of the baroness' beauty and nothing could keep them away. Carl wished they would step on a rotten board and take an unwanted bath before his potential bride stepped down.

Almost a hundred passengers descended the gangplank and the procession began to wan. Carl was ready to ask Meusebach to seek the captain and review the list to see if the baroness had come, when he saw Greta von Gotlieb followed a step behind and to her right by a young fraulein. Carl painted the ship's deck with his vision in search of the baroness. For some reason she must have remained in her berth. Perhaps she was ill.

"My God, that hag is going to ruin everything," he said aloud. "Does she not know that the baroness is to come ahead of her assistant? And who, and why is there a child with her? Now, I'll have to board the ship and find Lady Wilhelmine in her sick bed. How base!"

Von Gotlieb spotted Carl and his group standing away from the press of passengers and greeters at the dock. She marched straight to him. Her razor sharp nose glistened in the sunlight as she lifted it high and extended her hand, palm down. Her tight, gray streaked, blonde braids swept from behind her ears to her waist. The fraulein stood smiling to her right. Carl was determined to get past the formality of kissing the hand, but before he could bob low, he caught a haunting similarity in appearance between the girl and his intended, Baronness Wilhelmine. For a split second, he thought his eyes had been mistaken and the baroness stood before him. His heart surged.

Von Gotlieb's eyes narrowed as though insulted that Carl was gazing at the lass instead of kissing her crusty hand, as princes should do. Still he hesitated.

"Ba-Baroness... I...where is the baroness?"

Gotlieb jerked her hand away in disgust. "You're *staring* at the young Baroness Maria Elisabeth von Schoener. Sister of the *late* Baroness Wilhelmine von Schoener, I regret to inform you." Harshness of tone was an understatement.

Carl felt his head swim and his knees sway as though he were on the ship. Surely, he had misunderstood. Meusebach caught him from behind in time to prevent an embarrassing fall.

"I did not hear you, Frau Greta. I thought you said…"

Meusebach, who had recently suffered the same emotional plunge, understood the statement as he cradled Carl from behind. He said, "Herr Carl, I fear you heard correctly. The baroness is gone. Can you stand?"

"Yes… Frau Greta, it was not necessary to make the long and dangerous ocean voyage to bring me this news, although I accept it as a token of the respect her family feels for me. On your return, please extend my deepest…"

"Prince Carl, you have not allowed me to finish!" Gotlieb's words were curt and unbelievable in the face of the grief Carl felt. Again he swayed. She continued, "Young Baroness Maria Elisabeth has come in the stead of Wilhelmine. She will entertain your courtship, and at the proper time, consider your proposal."

Carl's full weight fainted backward into Meusebach's ready arms while his eyes remained as round and open as his mouth.

The young baroness stepped forward and extended her hand. "Your Highness, I have seen you at the royal balls and always wished to dance with you. I must admit I was but a child then."

"Child, indeed." Carl found his trembling voice. "You are still a child, my child…" He knew he had said it wrong. He was glad Schmitt and others weren't along, glad he hadn't offered to bring Elisabeth.

Meusebach spoke quietly from above. "Carl, pull yourself together. The offer is completely valid. Tell her you will see her safely to New Altmann and extend every courtesy."

Like a parrot, Carl repeated, "I will see you safely to New Altmann and extend every courtesy. It is out of the question…"

"Enough, Carl," Meusebach intoned. "Frau Greta, Baroness Maria, your prince is overcome with gratitude, a characteristic of his superior breeding. You are most honored to have witnessed it."

Carl regained his footing as ship stewards began depositing trunks and baggage at the ladies' sides until a complete wagonload stood in a vertical stack. Carl watched each piece placed on the other until he felt a cramp in his neck, yet no words came.

Meusebach chuckled. "Do I recall a time when I was distressed by a young female to your great amusement? Ladies, our men will deliver your grips to the prince's ample wagons. Save back the few pieces you will need for your stay tonight in the Galveston Buccaneer."

The grinning assistants quickly advanced to the luggage and managed to carry it away in one trip. Meusebach extended his elbow to Frau Greta and motioned with his face for Carl to do the same for Baroness Maria.

Carl's breathing came rapidly as he observed the beautiful lass closely for the first time. Her features were nearly identical to her older, deceased sister. Thick auburn hair framed her face, small but chiseled, showing a mature sadness when angled away. Her blue-green eyes radiated good health, and her smile projected happiness and comfort when she looked at Carl. Her flared skirt hid none of the curves of her body, nor the narrow waist. Her skin glowed a flawless ivory, slightly transparent, yet firm. He thought her perhaps an inch shorter than Wilhelmine and lighter of weight. *But she cannot be more than twenty years of age. If she were at least twenty-five, I wouldn't feel like a criminal in her presence.*

They paced slowly to the hotel, the women insisting that they didn't want a carriage. Carl rushed to the desk and secured the best suite available while Meusebach chatted comfortably with their charges. Carl returned and said, "My ladies, you have endured an exhausting journey and your health depends upon rest. The attendants will see you to your suite right away. There is no rush tomorrow. Sleep late if you wish. We will meet you in the lobby at your pleasure." He forced a smile and a bow hoping they would depart instantly.

Baroness Maria placed her hands on his shoulders. Before he could react, she tiptoed and kissed him on the cheek, her breath in his ear.

"Good night, my prince."

He whipped his helmet from his head and replied, "G-Good night, Elisabeth," confusing her second Christian name with that of his daughter. He felt foolish but didn't try to correct himself by adding that she reminded him of his daughter.

When they moved out of sight, he turned to Meusebach. "John, you must save me. You have great persuasive powers.

Mighty Indian war chiefs heed your words. I'll be making a mistake to move them to the colony. Tomorrow, I'll disappear, and when they come down you will greet them with words of regret and send them with your tigers back to the old country…caged, if necessary."

"I have great powers of persuasion with Indian chiefs, so you say, my friend. But I'm as a bowl of jelly in the presence of females, as you well know. No, Carl, if you must be rude to them, it will be after a proper courtship… I should say, after a platonic visit to your happy colony." Meusebach took on a serious expression and wrapped his arm around Carl's shoulder. "If you wish, simply avoid the central issue of courtship and marriage. Show them the country. Wear them out. Be enthusiastic. And if you still wish to be rid of the lass, introduce her to the handsome young men of your colony, perhaps even some young Texas men."

Carl fell into a chair. "You are no more help than Schmitt. Now I have no chance to court other women until this ordeal ends. But you have one good idea. I'll wear them down with travel through the countryside. With your help, I can arrange to frighten the wits out of them with an Indian raid. This could even be fun."

*Maria*

# Chapter 15

Formal words and small talk marked breakfast among the four. Carl immediately pulled Meusebach outside and persuaded him to carry the pair on his wagon to portend proper social graces and avoid discussions advancing to courtship or marriage during the trip.

Meusebach had one more order of business before departure – the delivery of his animals to the ship. Greta and Maria walked to the wagons where Meusebach threw back the covers to reveal two tawny, pacing felines with long tails. The male released a wail to chill the blood and the women cringed. Then Maria stepped forward for a closer look.

She said, "Herr Meusebach, I find it appalling that you would trap these lovely wild creatures and commit them to prison thousands of miles away. You have no heart."

"My dear fraulein, it is in the interest of science. Many things will be learned in Berlin from their study. I have instructed all attendants on their proper care. They are to be fed a dozen live rats each day.."

"Herr Meusebach! Indeed! Surely they had a better diet than rats when they were free. But the studies could be done in Texas by learned men such as you. I shall always feel a hurt for the cats."

When Carl announced that the proper ladies would ride in the company of Meusebach, Maria refused. "I will not accompany a slave merchant. I shall sit at the side of my espoused."

Carl sputtered when she said that word, but he knew German formality. The fraulein wouldn't be permitted to speak of courtship unless chaperoned by her lady-in-waiting.

He said, "As you wish, Baroness Maria. And for the comfort of all, Frau Greta will ride with the commissioner-general."

Greta spoke sharply, "My duty requires me to escort the baroness at all times. I shall assume my place in the middle of your wagon seat."

Carl cast a longing glance toward Meusebach who ignored him and moved his wagons and animals toward the dock. Carl decided to take charge.

"Ladies, as soon as my teamsters have tended to their weapons to ward off Indian attacks, we will be underway. You must keep a close watch at all times on the near and far horizons. At the least movement, you are to dive into the bed of the wagon, cover your head, and scream 'Savages!' at the top of your lungs. With luck, we won't be attacked. If we are, we'll all fight bravely to prevent either of you from being kidnapped into a fate worse than death."

*Damn, the fraulein is not turning pale in fear. She continues a childlike grin.* But he felt a glee when he saw Gotlieb's lips disappear as her mouth pulled her nose ever skinnier.

Meusebach took the lead and Carl's wagons followed, with him and the females situated as the third vehicle for safety. The wagons not filled with the travelers' trunks, contained goods bought at Houston and Galveston – a copper bath tub, free standing schranks for clothing, tables, hand carved chairs – to grace the cabin of the visitors. Carl felt troubled that he hadn't been able to deliver an expensive sapphire and gold necklace he had selected to adorn the lovely neck of Baroness Wilhemine and accent her striking blue eyes. *I should have bought green jewels. No! There is no relationship here. Any gift would have been inappropriate. I am not a molester of children.*

Greta spoke rapidly as soon as the creak of wheels began. "Herr Prince, you are to keep your hands to yourself at all times. I will tolerate no overtures or mischief. You will address the baroness when I give permission. She will address you when I give permission. You will not discuss indiscreet subjects such as body functions or sexual activity. This includes the possibility of future child bearing and breast feeding. Do you understand me so far?"

Carl formed his words, fuming. "I am not accustomed to taking orders from females, dear frau. But I assure you my intentions are entirely honorable. And *you*, my dear lady, have nothing to fear, now or ever, from my roving hands!"

"I was speaking of the baroness."

"How could I possibly, with your scrawn...body...yourself thrust between us? I see no reason our conversation cannot be open to all. When I speak to one, I speak to both. I shall not seek your permission when I open my mouth."

Greta turned to Maria. "The man is as crude as Meusebach. Are you sure you wish to go through with this?"

Unperturbed, Maria said, "The prince comes with impeccable credentials. He has my permission to address me directly. Never fear, dear Greta, he shall treat me with respect."

"Hmp."

Few words passed between them for days after the clumsy start. At Columbus, Carl found lodging with a German nobleman. Count von Holz, his wife and house servants set a glorious old world table evening and morning. He took copious notes on Meusebach as did Meusebach on von Holz. Each picked the other's brain for information on plants and wildlife, supposing to claim one another's discoveries later on, they joked.

Out of Columbus, the road ahead disappeared under the hooves of several hundred longhorn cattle which loomed as an ominous shadow on the horizon.

Greta leaped from her seat and dived for the wagon bed screaming, "Savages! Savages!" as though she were the first to see them. Her narrow rump pointed skyward as she grabbed a blanket to cover her head. Carl resisted a chuckle as he glanced backwards. His hands shot almost from their hold on the reins as the thump of Maria's form landed against his right side.

"Prince Carl, I see strange men on horses surrounding the beasts. Are they savages?"

"No, Baroness," he replied as he felt the squirming of her warm body along his side from hip to shoulder. These are Texas cowmen..."

"Savages! Savages! Maria, take cover!" Greta screeched.

"Watch their form and style. You'll learn much of Texas."

"Savages! Savages! Maria, in the wagon, quickly."

"No need for alarm, fraulein. The animals are Longhorn cattle. Aptly named, would you agree?"

"Savages! Savages! Maria, save yourself. Why are the men not shooting?"

Maria slid her arm around Carl's back. "Are the cattle treated with respect by the cowmen?"

"Certainly, until the day they are placed on your dining table as fine beef."

"Savages! Maria!" With the last shriek, Maria's light form vanished behind Carl. His glance caught only white logo losing their covering as her body went end-over into the wagon bed with her lady-in-waiting. The wagon stopped.

Meusebach and the other lead wagon had pulled off the road to allow the herd to pass as Carl stepped down amid the cattle herd which now surrounded the caravan. His experiences with Covington had given him courage. He walked forward, moving and ducking gracefully to avoid horns as he approached the man he presumed to be the trail boss.

Greta and her charge peered over the wagon seat as Carl approach the rider, spoke, and extended his hand. The cattle ceased to move forward, milling about the wagons. Carl visited with the rider, trying to give a reassuring appearance.

He turned toward the wagon just in time to see the younger woman climb down along the step. He shouted. "No, Maria!" He forced himself to subdue his powerful voice for fear of panicking the horned creatures. "Don't get on the ground. No."

Maria seemed not to hear, and bounced to the ground. Carl called again, but she already stood among the cows who jerked their heads randomly tossing six foot racks of horns. A great horn swung from behind, struck her across the back at the shoulders, and knocked her flat. Hooves pounded nervously around the spot where she went down.

Trail boss and cattle owner, Samuel Maverick, saw precisely what had happened, dismounted and motioned for Carl to take his horse. Carl vaulted into the saddle like a Comanche warrior. A bitter acid stung his throat and tongue. His mouth tightened. Sweat broke from every pore in his body. His military training told him to charge forward. Good sense told him why Maverick hadn't done that very thing. He had no choice but to leave Maria on the ground until he could push through the herd twenty yards, and only hope that he could get there and move the animals away before they trampled her. She may already lay mortally wounded.

He entered the circle of beasts whose heads were lowered and facing the prostrate form on the ground. Their nostrils flared and blew. Steel hooves pawed the ground. Carl dismounted slowly. Maria pushed from the ground on hands and knees as he reached for her.

Greta's voice, throaty and coarse, came from the wagon. "Get her out of there! Why are you so slow?"

Carl's terror turned to killing anger for a split second as he subdued the urge to respond. He lifted Maria by the shoulders, placed her left foot in the saddle stirrup, and helped her by the waist to straddle the horse.

From the wagon came another scream. "That is improper riding style for a lady! Take her down this instant."

Carl vaulted onto the horse's back behind Maria, reached around her on each side and took the reins. He walked the horse toward Maverick who had not moved a whisker from his stand.

Maria cried gently, "I am so sorry, Herr Carl. I made a fool of myself. Now, I know you were trying to warn me. But your courage had inspired me. I was sure the cattle were harmless. I am so sorry. Will you forgive me?"

Carl would forgive her but he might yet kill her lady-in-waiting. He said, "You're not to be blamed, meine Feinheit, my gentle one. Your innocence caused the error. Fortunately, the cattle are somewhat tame."

Samuel Maverick said, "That was a fancy piece of maneuvering, Mr. Altmann. That crazy woman in the wagon will get you all killed. I hope you're on the way to an asylum with her."

Maria said, "What did he say of the lady in the wagon?"

"He said all the credit for your rescue goes to Frau Greta for her expert directions."

She blushed. "You jest. All the credit goes to you. I want to get down and hug your neck."

145

When Carl eased her to the ground, she rushed to the rustic trail driver, Maverick, and hugged him, declaring in German, "Your forethought saved me. You are a wonderful man."

Maverick laughed as she moved back to Carl and clung to his neck. "Mighty purty daughter you got there, Altmann. Now, I'd thank sump'm of that hug that I shouldn't thank if she wuz a little older than seventeen."

Carl enjoyed every measure of relief as he answered. "She is not my daughter, Herr Maverick. It's almost a joke that she was sent from Southern Bavaria as my fiancée, a misunderstanding. And she is twenty years of age."

"Looks about seventeen to me," Maverick said grinning. "Plain to see she's stuck on you. I'd say you're a goner, Altmann." He muffled a rolling laughter.

"Thank you for the loan of your horse, Herr Maverick. Come to New Altmann as my honored guest when time permits." Carl called to his teamsters to move his wagon forward. Maverick waited until a driver had come on board before beginning to move his herd out. Meusebach wisely remained on his wagon in odd amazement as the scene unfolded.

As they waited for the wagon, Maria said, "You gave me a new title, Herr Carl. One I shall cherish all our years."

"All our...uh, what was the name?"

"Meine Feinheit. It is lovely, and I shall always try to deserve it."

Carl smiled, remembering the offhand remark. "And what *is* your age, meine Feinheit?"

"Seventeen years."

"Sev...? I...I have a daughter but 3 years younger! You must know there is no..."

"I should hope you have a daughter. What a pity to know a man of your splendor and courage had remained stag throughout his youth."

Her blunt mature speech stunned Carl. "Frau Greta would not approve of such talk." He pointed. "On the wagon. We must roll."

Greta began a berating onslaught as the caravan moved. Carl would have blasted her into silence but his preoccupation with the

146

last conversation had humbled him. He convinced himself that the sadness, seen only when her face angled away, had caused him to think her older. Surely, it was a natural mistake.

He rolled the thought around, then forced it from his mind to assess the drama. *What a man that fellow Maverick must be. Equal in valor and intelligence to Covington. As Meusebach has said, don't mistake their brilliance by their clumsy use of English.* Carl found pleasure that he had come to understand these unpolished characters. They seemed also to understand his improved English.

Carl found himself plotting travel with Maria, taking her to the Covington ranch, introducing her to the arts of ranching. Surely she was older than seventeen. The sadness. But she had lost a beloved sister. It could account for the look. Then Carl realized he was confusing her with the dead sister. He vowed to grieve more, express it convincingly.

His thought processes dashed from business to adventures to the task at hand, then returned to the mental image of the fraulein at his side, once removed by the rickety body of another woman between the two. He could not, would not glance toward Maria out of respect, but also because he would have to view the hatchet nose first. He almost laughed at the thought.

Greta broke the silence. "Herr Carl, the baroness suffers great discomfort at the seating of this oaken slat. You must appropriate a cushion for her. Two, if you please."

"Hooo!" Carl called to his mules as he pulled the reins. He used the Texas English language for draft stock instead of the German word *Halten.* It alerted the other drivers to his intentions. He moved quickly to his rear wagon and pulled out two tightly stuffed pillows.

Mischief overcame him as he approached. "Baroness Maria, I regret that I didn't hear your plea. If the bouncing wagon has caused agony to your lower posterior, I am grieved."

Maria laughed, flashing her dimpled cheeks and tossing her face upward. "My posterior? I think it is Frau Greta who suffers. She lacks a certain natural padding."

"Fraulein! This is the sort of base conversation from which I

147

seek to protect you. Do not indulge the man's perversions. Give me that pillow!" Greta ripped the sham from Carl's hands, rose and thrust it under her body in a single motion.

Carl's side ached as he subdued tumultuous laughter. He didn't dare look into Maria's eyes as he said, "Allow me, Baroness."

Maria rose and Carl plopped the second cushion on the wagon seat, barely retrieving his hands before Maria's backside returned firmly to it.

"The hands, Herr Carl! The hands! You have already been told!"

"But, Frau Greta, does it count against me if the lovely young baroness is the aggressor?"

"Enough! I will not tolerate another word of this mockery." Greta's demand was lost on the odd couple who released all control over their amusement.

For the rest of the trip Carl subdued a giggle as he sensed the tall thin woman towering above him on her high pillow staring steadfastly at the horizon. They avoided camping by seeking shelter with settlers and in villages except for one night. Greta demanded that Carl post guard and remain awake himself. Once, they met a band of friendly Tonkawa Indians and Greta again dived for the wagon floor despite all assurances. At stream crossings she held her nose and mumbled prayers. Maria looked always to Carl's lead in matters of safety. If he appeared confident, so did she.

When the ferry delivered them into New Braunfels, colonists emerged from doorways and cheered the procession. Meusebach stopped his wagons there and bid Carl farewell but dispatched a rider on a fast horse to New Altmann.

When the four remaining wagons trundled into Carl's colony, a band met them in the street. The crowd rushed around them. Dancing started among the cheering throng. Schmitt, Hagerdorn, Schulz, Wilhelm, Ernst and Roth stood in the gathering with arms folded, grinning mischievously. Greta's rigid face broke into a smile as she waved and blew kisses as though she were the attraction.

Maria watched in awe. She asked Carl, "Where is your daughter?"

"I haven't seen her yet. There she is." He pointed to his left and motioned for Elisabeth to come. He dropped from the wagon seat to receive his dark haired daughter and crush her to his chest. Katheryn Linnartz stood waiting with a perplexed expression.

Carl tensely assured Elisabeth and Katheryn that he would explain as soon as conditions permitted. The well-wishers accepted the arrival without question.

Roth approached Carl, smiling, "Welcome home, my prince. Tell me, which of the fair ladies will be your bride?"

"Shut your face, Roth, and bring the ladies schooners of your beverage. Conversation is not your forte."

Schmitt and the other committeemen blurted their greetings and questions all at once which he ignored, using the music as an excuse for poor hearing. Those who now perceived a mistake no longer enjoyed the festive atmosphere but milled around the wagon worriedly. At last the music stopped and Carl felt he must address the people. It was the first time that Greta and Maria would witness the power of his speaking voice.

"My fellow New Altmanners, I return with much news of the fatherland, both good and bad. I will address the good news only. It is with delight that I introduce you to the fair Baroness Maria Elisabeth von Schoener." He motioned directly to her so there would be no mistake. "And her able lady-in-waiting, Greta von Gotlieb. They shall be my honored guests as long as they choose."

The close audience appeared worried. The more distant ones cheered the introduction. One cried out, "Prince Carl, when is the wedding?" A thunderous cheer rose amid lifted beer mugs. Carl curled his hands to restart the music.

The cabin built for Baroness Wilhelmine was completed and surrounded by a yard decorated with native plants, a birdbath and heavy trees which had been uprooted and transplanted. As the party drew near, Maria broke into sobs, knowing the intended use. Carl, seized by sorrow, stammered through a statement of respect and regret. Carl had invited the committeemen along with

Katheryn and Christian Linnartz to join them in his home so that he could explain to everyone at once.

Carl spoke briefly to the point. They stood or sat silently for a bit.

Elisabeth responded first. "Father, and Baroness Maria, the tragedy can now be turned into an occasion of joy. Not only will I get a stepmother, I will gain a sister."

Her words answered the question on the minds of the committeemen. Would Carl go through with the wedding? They suppressed nervous laughter

"My child, the baroness is too young to wed. I'm too old...for her. But they made the hazardous journey. They will enjoy the hospitality of our colony and learn much of Texas and her freedoms. The lands of our ancestors are in revolutionary turmoil. We will extend all options to the baroness and her escort, even the decision to remain and become citizens."

Greta said, "Herr Carl, you eliminated an important option. The wedding. The baroness is not too young. Neither are you too old. It is with the greatest dignity that a young bride receives an older bridegroom."

Schmitt injected. "I have never seen our people so ecstatic. Carl, you will be thrilled to see the progress made on the dam, the mills, the merchants' buildings, the farms. Corn is planted on your bottomlands. Homes are going up. I shudder to tell them the wedding is off."

Maria sat with a rigid sadness returning to her eyes and mouth.

Carl refused to engage anyone in an argument. He directed that the women's goods be delivered to their cabin and dismissed the committeemen. Elisabeth spent the night with her father rather than return to Katheryn's but she said no more.

The women of the colony organized a formal reception for Maria to be held in Carl's parlor, the only room approaching adequate size, but still too small. Many saw the young baroness up close for the first time and were confused. But the news of the switch soon swept the hall, fazing no one as they lavished Maria with gifts; homemade clothes, household decorations, bonnets, stockings, food as nearly to German authenticity as their goods and equipment would permit, embroidery, bedding, underwear with lace, presented with giggling. The girls around Elisabeth's age showed the greatest enchantment with the young noblewoman.

Within days, Carl sent word that he wished to take them on tours of the country with the dam below the spring first. Carl explained the construction and boasted that it had been built in less time than any dam of its size in history which didn't employ slave labor. The colonists had cut and graded adequate carriage roads throughout the creek bottoms of the range land. When the farmers saw Carl's new gilded coach on the road they stopped work and rushed forward to see the "princess." Maria was gracious to all but reserved in conversation.

A field of spotted goats caught Maria's eye as they played carefree in tall grass among scattered live oaks.

"Herr Carl," she exclaimed. "Please stop." She dropped from the coach's door and moved gracefully toward the curious animals. Obviously hand tended, the goats showed no fear of man. Maria easily caught a black and white infant which cried lightly as she clutched it, turning its feet upward. Carl identified it as a female, a nanny, and Maria said, "This Zicklein shall be my child. Herr Carl, may we take it to our quarters?"

Greta interrupted, "Maria, you must not. The animal could have fleas." Maria ignored her.

Carl realized for the first time that he was unable to refuse anything to his guest. "Yes, but like a baroness, she must have a lady-in-waiting. You must find her mother to take as an escort."

"How do I determine the mother? Does it matter which of the mothers we take?"

"It matters to the goats," Carl said, smiling. "Walk away from the herd with the kid in your arms."

When Maria had done so, a black nanny followed bleating her plea for the infant's release. Carl told the caretakers to hold the nanny and kid for a wagon to come the next day.

On the way in, Carl pointed to the high knoll at the north edge of the townsite and mumbled that he would construct his castle on that spot.

He drove her to San Antonio where she shopped for ready

made clothing, passed by a wedding dress displayed behind a tailor's window, looked at elegant glassware for table settings but didn't buy. They traveled to Austin in an entourage of seventy colonists who, along with Carl, Elisabeth, and the committeemen and families placed applications for naturalization in Texas. Also, Carl filed for a charter of Altmann County.

When he took Maria and Greta to the home of Isaack and June Covington, Maria took the Covington infant, John, from his mother and held him past departure time. Greta and Carl had to team with each other to get her to leave.

Headed home, Maria said, "Carl, you and Mr. Covington conversed without ceasing. And you often looked toward me. What did you discuss?"

"What you might expect. He knew I was expecting an arrival. He expressed his disappointment at…"

"At me?" Maria asked as tears welled.

"No, no, my dear. At the death of your beloved sister and my chance for happiness…" Maria broke into wails. "Please, meine Feinheit, what I meant to say was that Mr. Covington was most grieved to know that I would not go through with the wedding because you are too young."

"Did he think I am too young?"

"I…suppose not. How did you like Frau Covington…and the child? Need I ask?" His effort to change the subject failed.

"Prince Carl, if we should marry, I mean if you should ever marry, would you want to again have children?"

Greta interceded, "Maria, this talk is inappropriate."

Carl hadn't wanted to discuss the subject, it seeming too presumptuous to seek a bride for the sole purpose of giving him a male heir. But the fact was he had been willing to consider marrying the girl's sister for just that reason, with or without love. He agreed with Greta and terminated the conversation.

The summer of 1848 passed with the visitors showing no inclination to depart. Carl worked long hours and traveled often between calls on Maria. She was lavished with food and gifts, all the villagers anxious to please her and win favor with Carl. Each visit, each festival, each outdoor adventure with Maria had brought greater indecision to Carl.

Maria expressed fear that she was gaining weight. Uncomfortable with the subject, Carl simply gave a dismissing "Of course not." If she was gaining, her youth carried it in splendid attraction, making her appear more mature to Carl. He watched from his window as the baroness fed a simple Texas goat that was growing as large as its mother from constant indulgence. At last he sent for Roth.

"Roth, Schmitt is of no use to me in this quandary. He wants to give a political answer to my personal dilemma. Likewise, my own daughter sees Maria as a potential sister. That offers me no help. Tell me in all honesty, what do the people think? What would they think if an old goat such as I should marry such a...a child?"

"Herr Carl, is there any question?" He looked serious for a moment. "The people expect you to marry her and expect you to set a date."

Carl collapsed into a chair facing away from Roth. "But she is so young. I was appalled at the behavior of Prince Streib who cavorted with young frauleins. I laughed hysterically when the Indians delivered a young Indian woman to Meusebach. I'm torn with shame when my own thoughts switch from the similarity of Maria and my own daughter, then back to the idea of marriage. In Altmann, I would have hanged a man for improper behavior with a child. How can I reconcile that difference? If only her sister had lived." He rose and paced. "How did I let myself get talked into this? Better that I had taken an Indian bride. At least I would know what I was getting instead of sending six thousand miles across the sea, and being delivered green merchandise."

Roth's round eyes stared at Carl. "Streib was an old fart; Meusebach was not the perpetrator; Maria in no way resembles your daughter...no more than any woman. And she is not a child. She is of age, intelligent, refined, educated, fully aware." He tugged Carl's lapel. "You want a son, do you not? There is every possibility that Baroness Wilhelmine would have been too old to deliver you an heir."

Carl frowned, "Of course, she was not too old! She was but

153

thirty years. How dare you say…"

"Then why did she not bear a son for von Dieselhorst, her husband?"

Carl made a rolling motion with hand. "It was because, well, it was because Dieselhorst was a…"

"Carl, please! You must not defame the dead. In any case that will not be a contention for you. You are tried and proven breeding stock."

"Bite your tongue. If I marry, I shall not marry a brood mare." Carl brushed Roth's hand aside and turned. "How did you lead me into this forbidden subject? My question was, what do the people expect? Are there whispers, chuckles, eye rolls? I could stand it myself but I would not bring such disrespect upon one I care about as I do Mar…" He faced Roth abruptly. "Forget that last remark, Roth. You never heard it."

With great tenderness, Roth said, "Would you rather the people think *you* do not respect and care for her? Carl, open your eyes. Listen to your heart and to the people at the same time. Everyone wants the wedding. You want it, too. Only Maria wants it more." Roth lowered his face and raised his eyes. "And Carl! You will get a fine governess in the deal – Gotlieb!"

# Chapter 16

In San Antonio Carl bought a gold wedding band and traded in the sapphire necklace on one set with emeralds. He also bought two mirrors each a foot wide and three feet tall, framed in mahogany, one to replace his own which gave him a squat appearance, the other for Maria. He blushed when his daughter caught him for the fifth time gazing at his own image in the new reflector. He couldn't help it. The improved image gave him courage.

In front of the new mirror he rehearsed his proposal for days. It had to be perfect. If he lost confidence in that moment, he may never regain it. While he planned, he saw Maria daily if but briefly.

From her own small mirror, Maria told Greta, "It's time we prepare for departure. The prince grows more distant. His speech holds a tension. We have no time alone. We...I pushed him too fast. His mind is set on having an older bride. I'm sorry, Greta, our best efforts have failed."

In a rare display of warmth, the tall, thin woman wrapped a bony arm around her charge and consoled, "Your conduct has been exemplary, dear Maria. Do not blame yourself in any way. Only Prince Carl can blame himself for this colossal failure. He is such an ass."

"Greta! I have every respect for the prince. At our next meeting I shall express my admiration and announce our departure."

Greta was half pleased at the decision as she watched Maria rehearse her speech. She gladly obeyed Maria's request to summon the prince. She found him dressed in a fresh uniform, his hair and beard immaculately groomed, his polished helmet on the table in front of a new mahogany framed mirror. A large flat object, wrapped in brown paper, leaned against the wall. Two smaller wrapped articles lay on the table with the helmet.

From his mirror, Carl turned to the tall lady. "Greta, there is a matter of the most grave urgency which I must address. Please tell the baroness I would seek an audience with her at her earliest pleasure."

Greta saw the carriage and fresh horses parked in front of his house. Doubtless, the wrapped items were gifts for an unknown object of Carl's affections, his grooming for the same, and the carriage was to whisk him to his rendezvous. He sought only to make one of his million excuses to the baroness for another absence. Without answering Carl, she rushed back to the cottage.

"Maria, the prince will not be available for a conference. He is groomed to a shine, and his carriage awaits departure. He...he even has gifts for the object of his affect...Well, I'll give him the benefit of the doubt. I do not know what the packages hold."

"Did you ask him where he's going?"

"I fear you will not want to know that fact. It would only bring you sadness, fair Maria."

Though Maria seldom gave Greta direct orders, she turned from her hand-sized round mirror and creased her brow. "Greta, you will not make unfounded accusations against the prince. You will return and ask him precisely where he is traveling. Or, I will do it myself."

When Prince Carl told Greta that he was preparing in hope of a visit to the young baroness, her face reddened. "Well, I, really...It was just that she lives some ten meters away. Your carriage is prepared for traveling..."

Carl entered the immaculate log cabin, holding a flat wrapped parcel in one hand and two smaller ones in the other, Maria curtsied and smiled nervously, spreading her full skirt with her hands.

*I've never seen a woman so beautiful,* he thought.

*I'm not sure I can go through with my speech...but I must,* she thought.

Carl began tentatively. "Meine Feinheit, I have brought you a present. A small token of my great esteem." He held the wrapped mirror forward, then swirled the paper away.

Maria clutched her hands in front of her breasts and subdued a childlike squeal in delight, smiling radiantly. "Oh, Carl, you have read my mind. How often I've wanted a mirror. I've feared that my appearance is inadequate. Yes, this will help me so much." She rushed to see herself where Carl leaned the mirror against the wall. "Now, I can resolve to watch my eating. I know my body has responded to the great feasts given me constantly. Even my bosom has..."

"Please, dear," Greta's voice broke in as her nose lifted.

Carl smiled. "Your bos...body...your person has never looked so ravishing, my baroness."

Greta stood suspiciously, arms folded. "If you two must carry on in this despicable fashion I shall remove myself to the bedchamber."

Neither would bet a florin on her continued absence, but pleasure showed as they spoke to one another with their eyes and bade her goodnight. Prepared for the occasion, Carl produced a small hammer and two nails. "Select a spot. I'll afix the mirror to your wall."

When he stepped back, Maria moved forward into the reflection. She ruffled her full sleeves and smoothed her hair. "How can I ever thank you? Carl, I must tell you now why I called this conference. Would you take a seat?"

"Not yet, my dear. Please continue looking at your lovely countenance in the mirror." He leaped to the table where the larger of the small parcels lay. When he approached her from behind, they both saw for the first time their combined images in the flawless mirror. Maria gasped.

She allowed him to move close enough that she could feel his breath on her neck, and he could smell her hair. "Carl, I must not...I must tell you..."

"Quiet, meine Feinheit. I have something else for you...for

your lovely neck."

Though she wanted it with every fiber of her womanly being, she couldn't allow him to continue through the kiss which she felt was sure to come. "No, Carl, you must not."

Before she could turn, he took her shoulders in his strong hands and said, "Fear not, Maria, I think you will like the other gift. It adds to your sparkling eyes." He unfurled the gold and emerald necklace, reached around her neck, and fastened it from behind.

*My dear...lovely neck...sparkling eyes, He has never said such words. Is he guilty as Greta thought, trying to make up for something? Should I try to win him back with charm or challenge him?* Her tears came unannounced. She would do neither, but go back to her earlier plan. She wanted to be in full control.

"Carl, we must talk." She turned to face him. She was in his arms. Her will failed as their mouths joined perfectly, passionately. No weight bore on her feet as his steel arms held her breathlessly against his body. Her head was not thinking but her arms knew to circle his neck. Neither wanted the moment to end. She couldn't believe herself as she pulled away trembling, feeling her valiant warrior prince do likewise.

"C-Carl, the, the last thing I want is to bring embarrassment on your name and your people. I have decided that Greta and I will prepare our depart...mmm." The lingering passion from the first kiss broke into full flame. When he released her the second time she had forgotten names, titles, embarrassment, and Greta. She was positive he had no other plans for the evening.

"Do...do you want me to go away?" she asked breathlessly. It was a failed attempt to get back to the subject.

Carl was slow in forcing himself to let go of her waist. "I have yet another gift for my love. If you would allow me."

"No, Carl, two gifts so lovely in one evening are too much. Save it for another time. What did you call me?"

"My love. Sit."

She sat, wiped tears, and looked perplexed. Carl turned his back to open the packet containing the ring in a carved wooden box. Turning to face Maria, he bent his knees to kneel and caught the handle of his sword in his stomach. He whipped the weapon away causing a clatter. The bedroom door swung open. When Greta saw the baroness seated peacefully in a chair and the prince on his knee making a fool of himself, she smiled and retreated. The philanderer was begging her forgiveness.

"Maria Elisabeth von Schoener, I once knew love, and I thought it could never happen to me again. But it has…with you. Will you consent to become my bride?" As he spoke, he opened the box to reveal the decoratively carved gold band.

"Oh, Carl!" she shouted. The bedroom door sprung open.

Greta rushed to her charge. "What has he done to you, my child? Have you told him of our departure? If there was any doubt before, this should convince…" Greta's eyes beheld the gorgeous necklace, then the gold ring on Maria's left hand. "I…I, well, I suppose you do not seek my presence. If there is anything I can do, I will be but a shout away." She scurried back to her sanctuary.

"Carl, are you sure? My presence has made you uncomfortable since the first day. Your people are more important. I barely know English."

Carl thought she was refusing. "I'll make up to you all the discomforts of your visit. I'll cause the people to love you even more. I will give the largest wedding Texas has ever seen. I'll build the castle just for you, my goddess."

"You need not do all those things…but you can call me your goddess again." She was smiling.

Carl saw no humor as he waited for her answer. He said, "If you don't feel love for me, I'll cause you to love me in time. I'll bathe you with luxury. The castle will bear your name…"

"Love holds more importance than luxury. I came to Texas not knowing that. Now I do. I know what a woman really wants now. I didn't understand before. I've grown up."

Carl was sure she was concerned about their age difference. "I am still a man in every respect, my darling. I'll prove it to you. My active life and healthy eating habits have caused me to retain the vigor of youth. I've never been sick. Well, once."

"I believe every word you speak, Carl, dear. I have no concern that you are not healthy."

"It's my appearance, then. How would you wish me to dress, cut my hair and beard? Should I, yes, I'll get rid of this damned sword."

Maria reached and steadied his erratic hands, then turned them to place her palms in his. "It is not anything, my love. I love you, and I will accept your proposal…if you're serious." But she only said the last to get him to grovel a bit more.

"Greta, the prince and I are going for a short carriage ride. He wants to show me the bats when they fly from the cave beyond the hill."

Greta's voice came from behind her closed door. "Are you sure, my dear? The man is not himself this evening." They giggled.

As the carriage rounded the hill, the Mexican free-tailed bats already darted above by the thousands. They watched amazed as the line continued to rise and disappear into the sky in a snaking pattern, seemingly forever.

As daylight faded, Maria said, "I want another trip to San Antonio where I can view wedding dresses without sadness. And I want to shop for wedding decor of all kinds. Several trips may be necessary."

Carl said, "Let's go inside the carriage. This wind must be chilling to you, my dear. Maria gathered her full skirt and leaped the four feet from the driver's bench. "Maria, never do that again! You could…"

She looked up, beaming, as Carl slid down in front of her. "Please don't treat me as such a delicate flower, darling. You are like Greta."

Carl pulled her close. "Agreed, if you will never again compare me to Greta." He kissed her gently and ushered her into the glass windowed carriage amid rustling skirt and petticoats.

"The wedding will be expensive, I know. And another thing I want, immediately, is a tutor for my English, and…"

"Costs will be no object, my love. I would pay a king's ransom. Well, a prince's ransom, I'm so happy…"

"No, Carl. No." She touched his cheek, then took his waxed mustache between her thumbs and forefingers and twirled the

160

ends. "You will not pay for everything. I have a substantial inheritance from my father's estate. And half of sister Wilhelmine's goods fall to me. I'll send to Southern Bavaria for an advance."

Carl resisted. "No, my love, it is my place…"

"And I want to apply for citizenship immediately." She planted a playful kiss on his lips. "Don't argue with your fiancée."

Carl found no words or heart for an argument as they cuddled, alternately kissing and talking. Respectful of her youth and vulnerability Carl kissed her gently, often and passionately, curious that she seemed to have such a knack. But he made no improper advances feeling that she would do as he commanded. He wouldn't command what was to be his soon anyway.

As light dimmed on the horizon, Maria sighed, "This has been the greatest evening of my life. Your gifts were perfect. Your manner superb, well, except for the sword. And it was the sword's fault. And my surprise at your proposal! I could hardly catch my breath. You have made me so happy. Even the bats were wonderful tonight."

Carl said, "Speaking of bats, I suppose you should see to the well being of your lady-in-waiting."

# Chapter 17

Schmitt and Hagerdorn rode in from the west on nearly dead horses, raced into Carl's house and saw Elisabeth. Schmitt exclaimed, "Daughter, where is your father? We must prepare at once. The treaty has fallen apart. Indians are swarming Fredericksburg, Bettina and Castell. The villagers are in terror. Where is he, quickly?"

"My father is in Maria's cabin, proposing marriage at this very moment."

"What!? There is no time. We must form a militia. He must lead... Marriage, did you say? Are you sure?"

"He was never more determined."

"In that case, the Indians can wait."

Weeks would pass before everyone learned that the report was partially true. The Indians had become so chummy with the settlers they had turned into pests. Other than an occasional braining by an irate Hausfrau with a fireplace poker, the Indians enjoyed the food and wares of the colonists in peace.

Carl lost no time in seeking out the architect, Adrian, who was bored stiff with trivial advice-giving to the carpenters and construction oversight of his own modest but decorated residence. "Herr Adrian, I must engage you in a most urgent project. The happiness of my bride depends upon it."

Adrian replied, "If you seek to enlist me to fight Indians, Herr Carl, forget it, I am a peace loving man."

"No, no, no. I wish to enlist you to design a castle, a castle grand enough for the Baroness Maria Elisabeth. I made it a condition of our marriage. She will be disappointed, or refuse altogether, if I fail."

"A castle? Where? Are you returning to Altmann with your bride?"

No! Here! On the hill. With adequate labor, how long do you think it would take?" Carl had thought a year.

"A minimum of forty years. Most castles along the Rhine and Danube took a hundred years. Princes, even kings, had to spend their fortunes over several lifetimes to complete them. Oh, perhaps we could draw plans and study the bedrock before the end of our days."

"Adrian, don't attempt to scuttle my determination." As Carl spoke, he felt his enthusiasm slipping. "Could we start small? The outer walls?"

Adrian shook his head.

"The foundation?"

Adrian's head wagged.

"Dig the trench?"

No.

"Turn a few stones. Damn, man, there must be something."

"A castle is built from the inside out. Not like any other structure. You'll need a castle engineer. Let me see. No, there's no place in North America. We will have to send to the German provinces. I know one if we can get him. Are you prepared to spend money?"

" Yes, I am." Carl thought the overture of sending overseas for an engineer might satisfy Maria. He hadn't given a whisper of thought to the outlandish cost of such a project. And despite Adrian's negative answers, Carl determined that he would hire workmen to excavate a ten foot wide, ten foot deep ditch around the general outline of his envisioned castle wall.

He rushed to Maria. "My love, your dream will be a reality, not entirely in my lifetime, but at least in yours. Already, I have put the plans in motion."

"Darling, would you explain my dream. Whatever are you speaking of?"

"The castle, Maria, the castle. I won't fail you."

She marched to him and kissed him firmly on the lips. Greta frowned from behind. "My prince, the most pressing dream is our wedding. If you'll lend an escort, I'll travel to San Antonio tomorrow. I'll marry you in the lowly hovels of the poor, in an Indian lodge, on the creek bank, in the bat cave. I don't need a castle to have an elegant wedding."

"I regret that Herr Adrian is so negative on the time required to build your castle. At least we'll have the thrill of seeing progress. I've hired workers – Mexicans. They are superior excavators. Second only to the Negroes owned by the Texans. I could contract for their services."

"Carl, I know you jest," She brushed his uniform front, her long eyelashes almost helping with the dusting. "You are of high principle, far above slavery. Of course, you will rent no Negroes from their owners."

"Of course, my dear." He subdued his shame. "You read me so clearly."

Carl called on Schmitt at home on the cool September morning. He needed the advice of his longtime confidant. Few individuals were privy to Carl's plans for a castle on American soil, much less the location of the building site. The two rode to the hillside overlooking the townsite of New Altmann. Carl spoke with the enthusiasm of youth and the wisdom of age.

"As I have stated before, I desire to establish a safe haven for any and all German emigrants here. Symbolism plays a big role in these people's lives for many were raised under the remnants of feudalism. Our folks can identify with a castle on the hill overlooking the town of New Altmann. They look to me to provide leadership and to give them the sense of stability and security they need. Good luck has allowed us to survive these two first years in the open without Indian attack. But our luck, and my presence is temporary. Am I making sense, Herr Schmitt?"

"Yes. Is there more?"

He spoke with formality. "Not only do our people need the castle for physical protection and their sense of security, they need it for the eternity of time after my life, and yours. And that is my plan, to give them a good life beyond ours. The idea of individual freedom in America intrigues me. You know, Schmitt, the only real difference between me and many of the leaders is not the 'Divine right of the monarchy' but the level of education. We have depended on New Braunfels long enough for schools and other institutions. We must build our own school and educate our youth. They will grow into tomorrow's leaders in this land of freedom. I must now provide a secure environment. With security and education, the store keepers, the millers, the farmers will find their niche in this new land. That is the will of God, if in fact there is a God."

Schmitt was sure he had just heard Carl's first rehearsal for a future grand speech either at his wedding or at a groundbreaking ceremony for the castle. Though his prince was driven more by his newfound enthusiasm for Maria than by nobility, he was talking good sense and he did not doubt his sincerity.

Carl didn't want to take Adrian to the castle site and share his plans for fear that the meticulous architect would again dampen his enthusiasm. But he didn't want to make a serious mistake. The thirty Mexican laborers busied themselves stretching strings and planting stakes for the outside perimeters. Oxen, carts, boring bits and tools arrived daily. Carl was amazed at the seemingly simple people's ways of organizing a project with the least direction.

"No, no, no, Herr Carl. You are going about it all wrong. Backwards, in fact. These outer walls will be built by your great grandchildren. A castle starts with the 'keep,' the strongest and most permanent structure, usually a thick walled tower."

"But I must show progress."

"Then show progress on the keep."

Carl huddled with Adrian and turned away most callers for weeks. He could be found in dire emergencies on the castle hill or on the valley floor below, a two-hundred foot, nearly perpendicular drop above the cave exit of the bats. Adrian told him of a Swedish physicist living in St. Petersburg, Russia, who was performing miracles with new explosives, though his experimentation had resulted in dismissal from two universities. Carl dispatched a request for advice, along with an invitation, to Immanuel Nobel, the eccentric genius, when it became obvious that hand labor on the *keep* excavation would take forever in the flinty limestone.

Months later, Nobel's son, Alfred, arrived, intrigued by Carl's letter and the promise of unrestricted experimentation. It seemed that authorities followed him and his father everywhere in Sweden. Carl was shocked to see how young he was – hardly older than Maria or Elisabeth, though his face bore several ruddy scars and his mouth was set in a permanent frown. His command of the German language was poor, his English worse. But, like the Mexicans, he needed few instructions. Carl put him with the Mexican laborers under Vicente Azul and directed that they begin where the hand picks and iron bars had given out in digging a shaft below the intended keep.

Carl's request for a tunnel from the limestone hilltop to the valley below puzzled the young Nobel. But his job was cutting rock, and he claimed he could do it if he could perfect the formulae on which his father had despaired in Sweden. Carl understood that Nobel's work would be experimental and provided him with every conceivable raw ingredient and tool.

Schmitt, who loved all science, wanted to meet him.

"Herr Nobel, may I introduce my friend, Herr Heinrich Schmitt, physician and vice director of the society."

Nobel looked up from his long benches which held tubs, vats, buckets, and glass tubes, some of which held black powder. The iron vat contained a thick, clear liquid. He acknowledged the greeting with a cursory bow and motioned for the men to step outside of his patchwork tent. He carried in his hand a glass test tube containing a half ounce of liquid.

In mixed German and English he said, "Step to the bluff and I will demonstrate my explosive." They understood the word *explosive* and his hand motions directed them to the precipice of the cliff. He looked below to assure no person stood there, then pitched the test tube into the oblivion. Carl and Schmitt had time to glance at one another then back to the cliff when a thud shook the ground as a cannon roar rushed their ears from below followed by a billow of dust. Rock and sand particles peppered their hats.

"Too unstable," said Nobel, "but this open site in the wilderness is perfect for my experimentation. I must find forgiveness for the University in Stockholm which dismissed my father after a small accident." In fact, Adrian revealed, the senior Nobel had virtually destroyed the campus thinking the thick rock wall was more than adequate to absorb his detonation.

Nobel said, "Return tomorrow morning. The holes are drilled for the first blast. We will perform the first experiment." They did.

"It is a mixture of nitroglycerin, like you saw yesterday," Nobel explained, "and powdered coal to stabilize it. Each of the six-foot deep drill holes is firmly packed. A total of thirty holes make the circle you see, six feet in diameter."

"How did you drill the holes, Herr Nobel?" Carl asked, impressed with the outline of the intended opening to his tunnel under the keep.

Nobel's frown deepened. "Labor and time. Your Mexican workers cut them using star bits which they tap with a hammer, twists lightly, then tap again. That is not science."

Schmitt tried to return the conversation to Nobel's achievements. "Surely there is a science in your method of ignition for the charges, Herr Nobel."

Nobel smiled, though the men barely saw it. "Not yet. I am using the crudest of ordinance, a small charge of gunpowder ignited by a fuse."

Carl and Schmitt sought cover behind a large bolder. Following a chain-like roar, they knew something had gone wrong when they heard a string of Swedish expletives, and guessed at their meanings. A spectacular display of fire, exploding sparks and smoke spewed from each drill hole.

"Herr Alfred, what happened?" Carl asked.

"Mixture is wrong. Need more nitro or less coal. Come back tomorrow."

They did.

Positioned behind their bolder as before, Carl and Schmitt waited comfortably for a firm blast. They chuckled as the Mexican workers scurried down the hill. Nobel lit his fuses and ran like an antelope after them. Carl and Schmitt hardly had time to get nervous when their eardrums crashed against their brains and the earth leaped a foot sending their grand boulder toward them like a bullet. In unison, they dropped beside the smaller stone where they sat. The huge meteor ground to rest on the smaller, rendering total darkness and scant breathing room underneath.

"Schmitt, are you killed?" Groping hands found one another's faces.

"I saw my life flash before me," Schmitt coughed. "I feel no pain. With a certainty, I'm dead. Good-bye, my friend."

"No pain? I'm hurting all over my body. My legs are crushed. I can't breath. I can't see. But...the pain is leaving. Yes, I too, am dead."

"Carl, do you suppose we feel no pain because we're not hurt? Here, let me pinch your nose. See if you react."

"Let go of my nose, you idiot, and help me get out of here!"

From outside their trap came the voice of Nobel. "Prince! Doctor! Did you survive?"

"Yes, if you set but one more charge to dislodge a twenty ton rock from our heads," Carl shouted.

It took a few minutes of thrusting ropes into the crevasse for the two to grapple and be towed free. They emerged, lumps of white limestone powder.

In perfect German, Nobel exclaimed, "Ah, you are beautiful to behold! Come with me."

They tried to dust their clothes and raised an impossible cloud, but followed. The site of the explosion still yielded smoke. They could see a perfect, six-foot round hole, six feet deep in the previously unyielding stone. Carl reached to touch the edge. He jerked back his hand from the searing heat.

Nobel began a Swedish folk song as he hopped in circles slapping his legs. The laborers returned and chattered happily in Spanish. Minutes later they scooped rock into hand carts to store for later fill in the keep wall; the larger pieces would be shaped for the wall itself. Nobel continued his dance as Carl and Schmitt retreated downhill to retrieve their horses. They enjoyed an adrenaline driven walk home when they found that the animals had stampeded.

Each visit with Maria became a conflict with what Carl

described to Schmitt as a competition with an army of over-excited women. Each transaction called for greater complications in making the wedding perfect, more delays, less importance for men, especially the groom. To offset his frustration, he poured himself into the first phase of the castle – the tunnel. With Nobel's daily blasts, he grew confident that his tunnel would become reality.

The shaft would enter the hill on the flat, top surface area and descend at approximately 30 degrees in a large semicircle before exiting on the valley floor at the base of the tall cliff. The tunnel's exit below began a few days after the entrance. In this manner, the laborers cleared the debris from the previous blast at alternating locations.

Nobel found it a challenge to make the tunnel large enough for a man to walk upright after the stonemasons had completed the staircase. Work progressed until it became obvious to Adrian that the upper and lower tunnels were past the point where they should intersect.

Carl's depression lasted one day, then Adrian's German castle engineer, Albert Fuessel, arrived. Carl wanted to charge through the village heralding the arrival, but when he suggested it, both Elisabeth and Schmitt blocked his path. Fuessel calculated that the tunnels lay twenty feet apart but at the right elevations. Nobel shifted his charges. His next detonation left a gaping hole in the tunnel's floor. He sent for Carl.

Prince, engineer, scientist, doctor, and a dozen excited Mexican laborers peered into a chasm of indeterminable depth. They dropped a stone, then another.

"We have broken into a subterranean cavern," Nobel said. The torches gave them a momentary, awesome view of the abyss.

Nobel brought a rope, attached a lantern and lowered it into the abyss. At the end of its fifty-foot length it still hovered above the cavern floor. He tied another rope to the first and measured the extension at ten additional feet before he plumbed bottom.

When he drew the rope back, he said, "This rope is adequate. I shall tie myself about my waist and legs. Vicente, your men will lower me into the cavern."

"No, Herr Alfred, I won't allow it," Carl demanded. "Too

dangerous. I will go."

"Ridiculous, Herr Carl," said Nobel. "You could die. I would never forgive myself."

"Nor would I," Carl protested. "Give me the rope."

The two began a childlike tugging match, ending with Schmitt arbitrating a compromise. Both men would go. Nobel first.

As the stout rope slowly lowered Carl and another lantern, he marveled at the array of stalactites hanging from the cave's ceiling and the crystalline sparkle of the walls. At the flat floor, he untied himself and held his lantern high. A four-foot-wide, one-foot-deep stream of cold water flowed gracefully from a large pool on one end with no visible entrance and exited through a man-sized passage a hundred feet away. Though Carl lost all sense of direction in the flickering shadows, he reveled in the fact that he had found a fresh water source within his future abode.

Nobel perfected his formula and packing techniques more with each blast so that hardly a dust plume occurred with the detonations. The stubborn limestone absorbed all the explosive energy. He curved the final connection upward to avoid another collapse into the cavern.

On December 10, 1848, the two tunnels merged into one. Carl called for a celebration of Alfred Nobel Day in New Altmann and sent out couriers to invite every dignitary he knew. To honor the young scientist, Carl invited from New Braunfels: Nicolaus Zink, engineer and surveyor; Ferdinand Roemer, doctor and geologist; Ferdinand Lindheimer, columnist and, in Carl's opinion, general loud mouth; L.C. Ervendberg, protestant minister admired as a non-fanatic by Carl; Hermann Seele, Elisabeth's teacher; all the councilmen and merchants. He also sent a special dispatch to Meusebach, not wanting to miss the opportunity to rub in the fact that he had done something first. He told all couriers to get messages to Jack Hays and Samuel Maverick if possible. He personally drove to the modest home of Isaack and June Covington, an excuse to ride in the country with Maria, and without Greta. And, he contracted the popular San Antonio restaurateur, J.L. Kincaid, to cater the occasion with his famous mesquite roasted veal and pork.

Satisfied that he had covered all bases Carl waited for the day. He was jolted awake by a nightmare of royal terror. He had forgotten to commission the engraving of a medallion for the brilliant Swede, Nobel, the whole purpose of the occasion. He lit every lamp in his house and dug through trunks and boxes. He found a heavy silver medal, three inches in diameter and a quarter inch thick. One side held a bas-relief of a spread-winged eagle, on the other, the image of a clean shaven man of fair countenance. The medal had a hole near the top edge of the figures where a ribbon once ran. Where and when had he been given the medal, and for what occasion? Since neither side had any inscription whatever, he decided it would do. Even the man's image could pass for Nobel if one didn't look too long and critically.

Schmitt stood in the crowd smiling as he listened to the more refined version of Carl's earlier speech, then watched the prince place the medallion over the neck of the budding young physicist. Nobel's permanent frown vanished temporarily as he admired the likeness of Julius Caesar on the grand coin, thinking it his own.

He rose to the occasion to say, though few understood him, "All good and noble deeds should be justly rewarded, whether reward is sought or not. Should I be successful in the future with the marketing of my inventions, I vow to you I will see that the greatest scientists, the greatest statesmen, the greatest proponents of peace on the earth are justly rewarded as long as my means will permit. Even beyond my own life, if possible."

Nobel left New Altmann the following day. Carl and Schmitt laughed, watching Meusebach fawn over him begging that he stay and come to his Comanche Springs home for further experimentation.

# *Chapter 18*

Elisabeth entered the cottage of her future stepmother as Greta pushed the spotted kid goat, Frauka, away from the door and groaned, "Ewww." Baroness Maria greeted her with a warm hug, a slight blush on her cheeks in anticipation of the pending conversation.

"Maria, tell me true. Did my father propose to you as he said? And did you accept? There seems no gracious way to ask, yet I must know."

"Yes, Elisabeth. He proposed and I accepted. Of course, I accepted! Did he not tell you?"

"He told me, but my father sometimes tells things in advance, positive that it will come about exactly as he has said. Oh, I would have died of embarrassment had it not been true. If I'm to host your wedding, I must know for sure." Elisabeth smiled.

Maria was overcome. "Oh, Elisabeth, would you be my hostess? You've been so wonderful about all of this since the beginning. May we always be friends? I shall avoid in every way to seem superior to you. I know I can never replace your mother."

Elisabeth refused to get melancholy. "I laughed so hard my side hurt when Father told me what you said when he told you he had children. I knew then that I would love you."

"What did I say?" Maria asked as they held shoulders and blinked tears.

"Something to the effect that it would have been a pity had he remained stag all his life."

Greta said, "Elisabeth, you must forgive the baroness for such coarse talk. She was in nervous ruin when we first arrived. Not her cultured self. Never will such words proceed from her lips again."

The seventeen year-old baroness and the fifteen year-old

princess broke into laughter. Elisabeth regained composure first. "But, Greta, it was a sweet thing to say. It showed that the baroness held no bitterness that her suitor had a previous family."

Greta's narrow eyes darted from one young lady to the other, obviously struggling to see the humor. "Well, there will be no time for further discussion of baser instincts. We must all work at full speed to assure a proper wedding. Maria, have you and the pompous a... the prince set the date?"

"Alas, Carl has been preoccupied and we haven't discussed a date."

"Yes, it is those silly rocks on the hill that occupy all his time." She lifted her nose. "Dare I say, he loves them more than he does either of you."

Maria turned to Elisabeth. "Is there a kind way to tell your father that the castle is of secondary importance? He seems to be building it for me, Elisabeth. Yet I have never asked for a castle. I only want to be his frau, an American and a Texan."

"Maria, please understand my father. He must have a grand project at all times. In the fatherland, he sought out wars to fight. My grandfather once told me the schoolmasters thought my father was demon possessed because his energies knew no bounds. They even had him examined by a specialist. The doctor said if he is learning his studies, be thankful he has so much energy, do not discourage him. And now, we should be thankful he has found a local undertaking. He's close to home."

The women reviewed samples of cloth and pictures of modern dresses. They agonized over the apparel the bride would wear, the right dress for the departure, clothes for the wedding trip, the number of bridesmaids. Maria put Greta in charge of decorations – candles, lamps, flowers, and layouts for musicians and food service. She took on a rare radiance with the responsibilities. She sought out every sheet of unmarked paper in the cottage to write plans. Soon, she returned with a question.

"Where, may I ask, will the wedding be held? Maria, you must set the location. Carl will surely spoil everything with some bazaar notion such as the bat dwelling."

"Already my head swims with the number of decisions I must make. I'll confer with Carl on that and other points. Yes, I'll ask him to set aside a day when we can conclude a million questions." Maria felt a tug of discomfort, knowing an even more important question was not settled. When?

A week passed before Maria found a moment alone with Carl, though he paid morning respects each day when he was home and before he departed to his business. She could tell when he was going to the castle hill because of his work clothes.

This morning she held his hand as he tried to break away. She followed him to his horse and, when he kissed her gently on the cheek, she encircled his back with her arms, tiptoed, and kissed his lips firmly.

Surprise and pleasure showed in his eyes but again he tried to ease from her grasp. She planted her right hand behind his head and pulled his mouth to hers. When she released slightly, he had dropped the bridle reins and she felt the nervousness of his hands on her back.

"Carl, my darling, is it so painful to spend a little time with me? I'm a lonely woman, you know." She kissed him again.

"Herr Fuessel is expecting me at the site of your castle, my love. Though you tempt me greatly to spend the day with you, just you."

"I should hope I tempt you greatly, my darling. I was beginning to wonder. We must confer on wedding plans. There is so much to do. Would you set aside a day in the near future when we can settle all matters?"

Carl glanced left and right, fidgeting with the reins. "A day? My dear, women are so much better at wedding decisions. Gather Elisabeth, Katheryn, Eva, Pricilla, and, let's see, yes, Sophia. Of course, Greta is a gold mine of sophisticated aplomb. Whatever colors you decide, I will accept. You have my complete confidence in carrying out all duties. My time is consumed with the grand wedding gift." Carl motioned toward the hill where a white line rose above the irregular horizon.

Maria massaged his back with her strong fingers. "There are matters that only a man can decide. The bridegroom, in fact. Will

174

you give me an audience or must I beg?" She pursed her lips. His melting eyes surveyed hers. Before he found words, Maria purred, "Besides, I want to spend a day in your arms, feel your strength, your muscles. Think of what it will be like…" She pressed her form tightly to his.

"Maria, please! We must… I'll be here in the morning. Have your list ready. And Greta should be present to take notes, of course. Do you think?"

Maria could only guess that Carl wanted Greta present as a chaperone. "I knew you would agree. We'll have meals prepared. Plan to make a day of it."

Maria allowed Carl to wriggle from her closeness, though she knew she could have held him. He bent to pick up the reins again. "I doubt that my duties will allow the whole morning, my love. If your list is prepared, I should be able to agree with your superior plans in an hour."

"Not an hour, not the morning, Prince Carl Franz von Altmann. The entire day. When you see the myriad of detail, you'll know why it requires time. And I can send Greta on a buying expedition if you wish."

"Yes, I wish!" he said excitedly, then added, "No. Greta will be fine. Greta will…be…fine."

Carl dreaded the morning meeting. He dreaded the mixture of passion, love, and hostility toward Greta. The conflicts would cause him to misstate himself at any moment. He hated being cowered by women – Maria on one hand and Greta on the other. He hated the lost self-control in their presence. He was no longer the sole authority, the last word on anything. But he loved the presence and the scent of the gorgeous young baroness.

The next day, Maria finally released him after the noon meal, remarking with pity in her voice, of the beads of sweat that continued to erupt on his forehead. When he staggered from the cottage and stumbled over the bleating Frauka, Maria had a location, a date, and a minister for the wedding. Carl couldn't remember where, when or who.

Carl caught himself on the palms of his hands and pushed the spoiled pet goat from under his feet. He straightened and glanced toward the cottage, feeling childish. If they had seen, no humiliating giggles exuded from behind the door. Regaining balance, he tried to walk normally, a slight march in his step, toward his horse. Frauka beat him to the yard fence, ready to exit ahead of him. He seized the goat by the hair on her back to throw her ten feet from the gate, then changed his grasp to a gentle patting. He turned the animal's face from the opening, stepped outside, and closed the gate quickly. This time he avoided looking toward the cottage.

Astride his stallion, he sensed a return to control. "At the castle site, I'm a prince. In Maria's presence, I'm a servant. I should have chosen a bride for convenience instead of love. I did. It just didn't turn out that way. I must be more firm with her. She forgets that I was a prince in Southern Bavaria. No, I'm still a prince. The castle proves it. The people respect that. Even American democracy will prove it. I'll run for election to the office of my choice when our charter is complete. No one will dare run against me. Now on to more important things…"

He dragged his mind from the scents and sounds of his bride, though he knew he would drift back, especially in the evening hours when alone. He had grown tired of sleeping alone. But he vowed to concentrate on his public work, the castle underway, and keep the pending wedding in proper perspective. With a self-assurance born of royalty he spurred his horse to a gallop and took comfort in the progress on the castle just ahead. He recalled young Nobel's success in blasting the first tunnel. Now, the foundation construction was proving a marvel of engineering to him.

German Engineer, Albert Fuessel, had accepted Carl's invitation to stay, pouring himself into supervising the construction of the foundation of the castle *keep*, the main tower. The man worked with a vengeance, setting the site over the Nobel tunnel based on drawings presented him by Carl and the architect, Adrian. The circular site, some 80 feet in diameter, stood not at the crest of the hill but some two thirds of the way up. Carl envisioned the four levels, double walls of cut, three-foot square blocks of limestone

176

with earth and rock fill inside the ten-foot space between them. Fuessel hadn't flinched at the enormity of the task.

He told Carl, "This will take some time to design but I can take care of that during the removal of the brush and rocks. I'll spare those large live oaks just below and preserve the drainage that makes their growth possible."

He had set about clearing and leveling the ground up to a twenty-foot bluff which overlooked the village of New Altmann. A grassy slope from the live oaks to the village promised a breathtaking view to the south.

Carl formed a guard to accompany a caravan of wagons to the Llano area. They retrieved two pink granite stones already cut by the Fredericksburg colonists to the specified size of six by four feet on the face, and four feet deep. The two-week round trip moved at one mile per hour giving Carl's small militia ample time to scout for danger fore, aft and flanks. From the west, tree cutters brought in the largest straight tree trunks they could carry. Fuessel set a huge oak timber in the center of the intended castle keep as Carl watched.

Though mesmerized by the progress, Carl felt control slipping from his grasp as Fuessel labored, uncommunicative. He'd had enough. He slid from his saddle on the windy hillside.

"Herr Fuessel, like an obedient child I braved Indian threats and the terrors of the wilderness to bring you two cut stones of granite. Yet, you offered no explanation for their purpose. Do you harbor secrets from your client?"

"Herr Carl, I thought you knew. Adrian suggested it. Perhaps your worthy architect conspires against you."

"I'll speak to Adrian, but at the moment, you are near. I tire of your game, Herr Fuessel. What is the purpose?"

"Herr Prince, there should be no secrets between us. Therefore, I'll trade my information for the secret you have withheld from me."

"What secret have I withheld?" Carl tamped tobacco into his clay pipe. "I speak openly and honestly with you at all times."

"Come now, Herr Carl. The shaft. The awesome tunnel which Nobel blasted, and joined with my help. Why did you want such a

thing? One can cut a trail down the cliff. Surely you know that."
Fuessel drew his own pipe from his coat.

"Oh, the tunnel. You didn't know? It's for…wait a moment. I
am the client. You are the person of service. You must tell me your
secret first."

"For a pipe load of your fine smoking tobacco, I'll tell you the
purpose of the granite." He gripped his hat against the wind.

Carl, brought forth a tobacco pouch from his coat pocket.
"You've played the tobacco games with the laborers until it has
affected your judgment. Now, *out with your secret*, you damned
German!"

"Carl, calm yourself. Let me light up first." Three matches
failed before the fourth lit the pipe. "All right, all right. I'll tell you
first." Fuessel stepped backward against Carl's advance and
blazing eyes, smiling. "They will serve as grand cornerstones on
either side of the entrance arch. You must think of a suitable
inscription for your children and grandchildren to read long after
you're gone."

Carl relaxed and gazed skyward. "Yes, an inscription.
Something profound and eternal. Something that joins the old
country with the new. Something that shows my wisdom for future
generations. It will take time to write a suitable maxim. Fuessel,
you and Adrian are genius. Surely God has smiled on me when he
sent you to me. I must go at once and write my first draft."

Carl swung into the saddle and wheeled his horse. "I'll see
you in a week."

Fuessel panicked. "Carl, you haven't told me your secret. Why
did you dig the tunnel? We had a deal!"

Carl spurred the horse into a gallop. "It's a riddle! You have a
week to solve it. Enjoy your tobacco. Try to make it last."

The tunnel was the first of several escape routes Carl
envisioned. Old country castles held passages known only to the
owners and designers long since dead. If word of mouth had not
transmitted the knowledge to the next generation, then the routes
were lost to history only to be uncovered by archaeologists when
last stones were separated. Carl's childhood dream required that
his castle have the same. And, on the edge of the Texas wilderness,

he knew a day could come when such may be needed.

With the agreement of Engineer Fuessel and Quarrymaster (Steinbruchmeister) Fritz Braun, Carl selected a limestone quarry site a quarter mile north of the castle hill where a vast supply of white, semi-hard limestone, called Austin chalk would furnish an easier-to-cut material for walls. The site was out of view of the New Altmann residents although the farmers in the valley would see the constant caravan of heavy laden oxen wagons winding slug-like toward the hill.

When Christmas, 1848, arrived, Carl issued a proclamation of ceremony for celebration of completion of the first level of the castle keep and the southern, outer wall. According to German tradition, an evergreen tree – western juniper, out of necessity – was placed atop the thirty foot wall. Saint Nicholas appeared in a red and black suit, driving a buggy from behind the castle and distributed hard candy to the children. Young children were completely taken in by the charade. To Carl's chagrin, older children guessed that the three-hundred pound man was "actually Prince Carl." Families went home to their own Tannenbaums decorated with ribbons and candles. Small toys, jewelry, or homemade dolls were the usual gifts along with an apple, a handful of pecans and hard candy, or, for the wealthier children, chocolate.

Groundbreaking had begun on Saint Joseph's Catholic Church under the leadership of Missionary Claudius Dubuis. A small Lutheran church, called Saint John's, served both the Catholic and Protestant congregations. L.C. Ervendberg served as supply pastor although he titled himself Protestant rather than Lutheran.

Tavern owner and brewmeister Roth complained to Carl that the recent mass wedding and the erection of churches had cut heavily into his business.

"Carl, assure me that when you are elected judge of the new Altmann County, you'll pass a law requiring all good Germans to drink voraciously, whether they are religious or not. It would restore the smile to my once happy face and provide a jolly jingle to my money box. I would even contribute heavily to the churches if they are not my enemy."

"Roth, first let me congratulate you again on making an honest woman of Frau Berta." He spoke with his usual reserved hand motions. "You, too, should join one of the churches and take regular communion. Your future children will revere you more highly. Second, look about you and see the great accomplishments of this small principality. Work is good. Drunkenness is bad. If I pass a law at all, it will forbid drunkenness. Your former clients are happy men. They go home to their fraus each night." He turned Roth toward the window. "Look at my cas...our castle on the hill. Does it not give you pleasure?"

"It gives me pleasure thinking of the festivals I'll cater there." When Carl didn't get the joke, Roth hurried to add, "Of course, it gives me pleasure, my friend. How could it not? A finer prince the people could never have. And a finer castle doesn't exist on the Rhine or the Danube. But tell me, Carl, why do I sense that the great walls harbor secrets that only you and Adrian and Fuessel know?"

Carl slapped Roth on the back and retreated toward the tavern door. "A few bodies are buried in the walls. Mostly the over-curious."

As Good Friday of 1849 approached, Carl's excitement grew because it was to be his wedding day. The completion of the rock frame of the castle's first floor so overjoyed Carl that he decided to move the event to that site. He would combine the wedding with a dedication ceremony. It would attract every member of the colony and most from New Braunfels. In fact, he reasoned, no other structure would hold such an audience. He told Engineer Fuessel.

"What will keep out rain? A few dozen sheets of..."

Carl spurred his horse and shouted, "No time for small talk. Must see the minister."

Reverend L.C. Ervendberg stood outside the small Lutheran chapel with the newly arrived permanent pastor, Edward Clemens. When Carl dismounted, Ervendberg introduced him. Clemens, cordial and respectful, expressed pleasure at meeting the prince, congratulated Carl on his bride, and expressed God's blessing for them both.

The young, dark-haired man's strong voice took Carl by surprise. Ervendberg's voice held a vibrato that seemed to revere all things holy and reinforced his genuine sincerity. But, without doubt, Clemens was a better speaker.

Carl didn't linger. He informed Ervendberg of the change of locations and added, "Since you are the new pastor, Reverend Clemens, you should officiate the ceremony."

As Carl straightened to ride away, he saw Ervendberg lift his wire frame glasses from his downcast face.

On his gallop to Maria's cottage, two dates collided violently in his mind. He was to be in Austin for the final chartering of the County of Altmann on the Friday of the wedding. He kissed Maria gently on the cheek as she greeted him at the cottage door.

"My darling, I've made minor adjustments in our plans. And I'm in a hurry to dispatch a letter to J.L. Kincaid in San Antonio, so I'll tell you briefly. You'll be thrilled to know the first level of your castle is complete with a ceiling. We'll hold the wedding there."

Maria stood with her lips slightly parted. "Darling, much planning has already gone into the location. The food will be cooked and delivered hot from the local ovens. It can't be transported to the castle. The cakes will fall, the meats will cool. Decorations are already going in place."

"But, my love, the chapel is too small to hold all our guests. Not a person in New Altmann will want to miss the radiance of the bride." Long arms circled her waist. "You are a realistic woman, the reason I adore you. I've already informed Pastor Ervendberg. Oh, and another small item, we will use the new minister, uh, what is his name?" Carl regretted that in his haste, he had forgotten.

"Clemens. Edward Clemens," Maria said as her face turned to stone.

"Yes, of course. Clemens. A fine man. Fine voice. A good switch, do you agree?"

Maria pushed from his strangling waist-hold. "Reverend Ervenberg and Reverend Clemens were here yesterday. Reverend

181

Clemens said that his mentor, Ervendberg, has been floating on a cloud for weeks from the honor we have paid in selecting him. Are you sure they have agreed?"

"Yes, I told them when they were together."

"Carl, darling, did you tell them or ask them?"

"I…is there a difference? Told them, I suppose."

"What message must you send to the caterer, Kincaid, on the eve of our wedding?" Green eyes glistened under studied brows. "Are you planning another festival near the same time?"

"My dear Maria, as your bridegroom, I must not appear to be worthless. I'm ordering our banquet."

"Our banquet is arranged! Your daughter has worked day and night assigning food orders to every frau in the village. She has looked after every detail. Germans in the old country have never eaten so well."

Carl sought retreat. "Well, I'm pleased that we communicate so well. Had I not stopped by for this small chat, I would have made a grave error on the food order. Ha, ha. Come close, my lovely. Let me feel your hair. Where is Greta?"

Maria didn't come close. Her dark eyebrows tightened. "Are there other surprises?"

"No, no." He said nervously. "Just those minor items. I could almost believe you aren't pleased, my dear. May I hold you in my arms while the witch is out?"

Maria screamed, "The 'witch' has worked herself into rheumatism preparing the decorations for your wedding! I won't hear of you using that term. I will agree to your changes only after I've spoken to the two reverends and to Herr Fuessel. You spent one morning with me and I let you go early because you assured me that my plans would suite you in every detail. Now, nothing suits you. Perhaps Greta is right. Elisabeth warned me."

Her attack stunned Carl into slience. Maria held her ground until he recovered. "What, what did Greta say? No, I don't want to know. What did my daughter say? Can I no longer trust the ones I love?" he groped.

"Trust must work both ways." Maria turned her back, arms folded. "You agreed to the location, the minister, and the date.

Now, you change everything without consulting me or anyone. Have you changed the date, also?" Tears blurred her emerald eyes when she turned forward again. Their first fight.

"Actually," he spoke meekly, "I was going to ask you, out of love and respect, if we could alter the date but one day? You see, I have this conflict…"

"Get out of my cottage! I cannot stand in your presence another second without learning to despise you. Out! Out!" Maria's fists clinched close to her sides.

Carl couldn't summon anger. Even when angry she was beautiful beyond compare. The trickle of tears that glossed her lips gave her a new appeal. He wanted to say so. He didn't dare. He fought against an emotion he thought foreign to him – fear. Fear that she would cancel the wedding.

*What damned difference does the location, the minister, and the food make. I want this woman more than I ever wanted anything. Why did I act with such haste? Even that was because I was preoccupied with thoughts of her.*

Carl held up his hand. "Maria, my love. I will…"

"Get out, Carl! I cannot abide your presence for the rest of this evening. Go tell your daughter what you have done. Greta is there. You'll take delight in telling her."

He backed through the door, aided by Maria's push. She slammed it as his face cleared the frame. He turned and tripped over Frauka but paid her no mind. He spun back to the door and knocked lightly.

"Maria, I can't leave like this. I'll undo all the mischief I've caused. Will you forgive me?" He waited. "Maria?"

At last the door latch clicked open. "And what about the date? What is the great conflict?"

"It's the date at the capital for completing the charter of Altmann County. I can change that, too." His voice was subdued.

Maria emerged in the fading sunlight. "Carl, I know how important the charter is to you and to all the people." She put her hand on his chest. "But did you have to set that date for Good Friday?"

The purr was back. Carl felt a surge of relief, passion and

silliness as he reached for her shoulders. "My darling, the people in Austin set the date. I would never change what we had agreed too… Well, not anymore."

"The charter is important. If you change the date, the state officials may not reschedule it for six months." She wrapped her arms around his neck and smiled. "Darling, you simply must not go around changing dates."

Forcing her to step backwards into the cottage, he released her from a smothering kiss. "When do you expect Frau Greta back?"

"Too soon, silly boy. If you'll fix the other items, I'll agree that we will marry on the Saturday before Easter."

The weather for the two o'clock ceremony held to more than a perfect spring day. An overcast sky dulled the heat and the wind cooperated with the outdoor affair. As expected, all the citizens had gathered, standing in a circle a hundred yards wide along with guests from as far away as Southern Bavaria, including Maria's brother, Hermann von Schoener.

Reverend Ervendberg lauded the couple as examples for all citizens and Christians, a match that only God could make. They glanced at one another when he pronounced a blessing of children from the marriage. The music, food and dancing forbade their departure until sundown.

When the gilded carriage took them out of sight toward San Antonio, the party went on until total exhaustion and depletion of food and drink forced the guests home. A few hours later, the new Reverend Clemens expressed disappointment with attendance for his first Easter service.

# Chapter 19

Initially, Carl had planned to leave New Altmann with only his bride. He wanted time alone with her. But Schmitt, Elisabeth, and others who noticed the lack of a planned escort, confronted him, and persuaded him to take a guard. He relented, and even included Greta in the party for Maria's needs. They would spend one night at the fortified home of Merchant Viktor Wetzel, halfway to San Antonio, and enter the city the next day where a private suite awaited the honeymooning couple at the Veramendi Inn.

Carl ordered a traveling party of two wagons and drivers, his carriage and another driver. Wilhelm and Ernst rode as a mounted guard. He and Maria sat comfortably in the carriage. Greta sat outside with the driver to "enjoy the view."

They left New Altmann at dusk amid ecstatic cheers. Dark overtook them and Greta began to complain. "I told Carl this wouldn't work. 'Enjoy the view?' Hmp! I cannot see my hands, and we've just left town," she groused to the driver Berge. "Stop the carriage. I shall give him my mind and adjourn to one of the wagons."

When the carriage halted, Carl and Maria surrendered their close embrace and Carl said, "Now what? We need to make time."

Greta's face appeared inches from Carl's as he swung open the window. His wonder turned to disgust. "Oh, you! Is your seat comfortable, Frau Greta? Do you need a pillow?"

"I need a wagon, if you please. Had this voyage been better planned, we would not..."

Carl snapped, "Had this voyage been better planned, there would be fewer stops..."

Maria touched his face. "Please, you two. Please!"

Carl said, "Darling, see to the needs of your lady-in-waiting. Whatever you tell the guards, they'll hasten to your command."

Maria hopped to the ground as Wilhelm rode close. "Willi, please see Greta to a wagon and make her seating comfortable. She is not amused by the darkness."

Wilhelm directed the rear wagon driver to rearrange materials inside his wagon. Greta took a hand valise and followed Maria to the wagon. As Maria boosted her onto the wagon step, Greta reminded, "Now, Maria, you must remember your promise. The drafty upstairs of Herr Wetzel is no place to begin a marriage. You must wait until San Antonio. The city, too, is inadequate for your dignity, but I will consent under the primitive circumstances."

"Greta, I made no such promise. My husband has waited long enough. Frau Wetzel was greatly honored that we would spend our first night in her chambers."

"*If,* young fraulein, *if* we arrive at all. Savages could come upon us at any time. Your husband's impatience could cost our lives. We should never have left New Altmann at night."

"My title is Frau, dear Greta. And please be kind to Carl."

Greta managed a brittle smile in the lantern light, kissed Maria on the cheek and vanished into the covered wagon.

The entourage moved quickly under Carl's orders to make up lost time. Wetzel's trading post was four hours away. Carl and Maria took the front seat of the carriage to avoid being thrown forward again.

Maria pulled close, seeming to seek Carl's strength. "Greta is not herself for fear of an Indian attack. Carl, do you think there is danger from savages?"

"Nothing for my princess to fear. Meusebach's treaty will protect us. And we brought a guard." He believed what he said but had no confidence in either. New Altmann was not a part of the Indian treaty, though he felt that it would apply to all Germans, provided the Indians *knew* they were German. If that failed, the guard of two professional soldiers and three teamsters would fall with the first volley of arrows. Passion had caused his poor planning, and he had hoped the subject wouldn't come up. But, Greta!

In minutes, the conversation drifted to future plans. Their dreams returned to self indulgence as the padded coach rocked them gently. Clothes grew loose as they found themselves on the floor, positive of the four hours of uninterrupted freedom. Maria giggled, muttering that Greta wouldn't be pleased. Carl joined her as his own mind raced through princely decorum so absent on the trail at this moment. The clop of hooves and the rumble of wheels on gravel made the only sound except for the breathing of two people much in love. The world belonged to Carl and Maria. Nothing else mattered.

Their cramped sprawl didn't change until both knew that most of the four hours had past. Reluctantly, they released each other, and clumsily buttoned clothes. The darkness prevented awkward embarrassment but added tantalizing desire to see each other's bodies in better light. There would always be another time, and another. The hour neared midnight.

Wilhelm's low voice broke the silence. "Herr Carl, we have visitors. I know not who."

Carl unlatched the window.

"Many riders are following on both sides."

Carl's heart leaped to his throat. They could be nothing but Indians, riding off the road, at this hour. "Keep moving forward if you can, Willi. I'll hail them."

Carl took a deep breath, seeking his voice. With a bellow that split the late night air, he let go. "Greetings, visitors! We are friendly Germans – ocean people – traveling to Fort Wetzel."

No answer came as he groped in the floor for his new revolver amid masses of unclaimed clothing. He fought against the dread of colossal failure in the face of his greatest triumph. Energy surged through his body. *As long as I'm alive, I'll fight for Maria. I won't fail her.*

A Comanche war scream interrupted his thoughts as he pushed Maria to a sitting position on the floor. Then he knew the scream was no Comanche, but Greta, awakened by Carl's own speech.

"Willi, silence that woman one way or the other. Quickly." He

187

ripped the pistol from under Maria's posterior, and heard a yelp.

Wilhelm rode quickly to Greta's wagon to the rear and instructed Teamster Bruns, ending with, "gently if you can." Carl repeated his salute to the mysterious riders as Wilhelm moved ahead, even with Ernst.

Moments later, he called back to Carl. "Definitely Indians. We cannot go forward. We are surrounded. Shall we shoot?"

Carl envisioned the naked chests and legs, the stone faces. "No, pull the wagons as close together as possible. I'll try again."

In seconds, Carl's carriage pulled close, but the rear wagon and Greta didn't move forward though the thump of feet and subdued cries came from within.

Ernst said, "Bruns is struggling with the lady." Wheeling to ride, he added, "I'll lead his team forward."

The wagon pulled alongside Carl's carriage and stopped. Its bed continued to sway amid flashing arms and heads. Carl started to tell Maria to go calm Greta but thought better of letting her leave the carriage and exposing her to the Indians.

Instead, he stepped to the wagon. "Greta, you will not cry out! Bruns, render her unconscious."

Bruns pulled the wheel brake while holding her with one strong arm. Greta relaxed her struggle.

"I must see to Maria," she pled meekly. Carl motioned for Bruns to let her go.

"Get in the carriage," he ordered curtly. "Another outburst and I'll deliver you to the Indians."

Greta held her tongue. She leaped from the wagon, and in a single bound opened the carriage door. Her hands felt the clothes scattered and piled on the floor.

"Oh, no," she exclaimed, then caught Carl's silhouette towering over her. She jumped inside. Though Maria was outwardly fully clothed, sans petticoats and bloomers, Greta found Maria's outer cloak and wrapped it around her charge, as though ashamed to find her naked. "Has he hurt you? He threatened to kill me. You heard him."

Carl didn't wait for Maria's reply. He called out, "Germans are friends to Indians! We mean no harm. Who are our guests?" He wished he had brought Doctor Hagerdorn, the interpreter.

Still, the darkness yielded no sound. The threatening horde stood their ground in front of them. Hooves drew closer in the side trees. Guards leveled their rifles. Carl started to climb onto his carriage driver's seat. Wilhelm urged him not to do so. He dropped to the ground and allowed eternal minutes to pass before called again, still without result.

He spoke to the men. "Hold your fire unless they fire first. If that happens, empty every weapon you have into the nearest target." Awful, conflicting solutions coursed his mind. Would he kill Maria and Greta to prevent their capture? The thought brought a chest cramp akin to a childhood dream of drowning. He had never felt so helpless. He doubted every decision. He despaired, then rallied. But he kept trying to communicate. Hours passed.

Carl couldn't count the number of times he called into the darkness before dawn. He tried again as faint light appeared to the east. "Ocean people chief, Gold Hat, is your friend. Come forward and talk." He knew there was no use because they held no common language.

As a gray light illuminated the visible riders in front, they began marching their horses backwards, removing themselves from rifle range. He heard voices from the brush on the left. They grew clearer. He caught the Spanish inflection and the words "Sombrero de Oro."

"What did they say?" he asked anyone who could answer. Ernst said, "I believe they heard 'Gold Hat' in your last call."

Carl took no comfort in the revelation. Comanches had honored the treaty because there was strength in German numbers who seldom traveled in small groups. Now, if they found Gold Hat isolated, traveling with a beautiful young woman, their passions would get the better of them. When a band of riders thundered from the brush on the left riding away from the wagons, Carl thought surely they had seen the women in the carriage and went to make a report. The band came in view a hundred yards to the left of the road as they turned to join their comrades out front.

Moments later, a warrior walked his horse forward holding a white cloth on a pole. He closed the two hundred yard distance by half, waving the flag left and right overhead. Light of the breaking sun clearly identified the rider as Comanche.

To give his people hope, Carl said, "We may live to see another day." He walked briskly forward to meet the rider. Suddenly, he turned and charged back toward the carriage.

The eyes of the guards as well as Maria and Greta reflected terror. He had seen something they had not. Rifles drew into position.

"Don't fire," he said calmly. "Maria, hand out my helmet." The brass and feathered headdress appeared in her hand out the carriage window.

With his hands held at his sides, Carl walked calmly toward the naked warrior. The warrior held Carl firmly in his sights as the horse turned to the right when they stood only four feet apart.

Carl said, "Gold Hat is friend to Comanche." The warrior didn't change expression. "Speak English?" He knew the German language held no hope for communication.

The warrior handed the flagged stick to Carl and muttered in his native tongue. He wheeled and rode back to his companions. Carl stood still with the pole resting on the ground and in his hand. Without looking back, he called gently, "Lower your rifles, men." He heard the thud and slap of wood and steel being lowered instantly.

Carl knew enough of the Indian way to know they didn't act as European warriors, on or off the battlefield. They didn't respond to direct orders or requests. One could seldom tell if they even understood. Days could pass, if ever, in determining their response or intent. He waited. He wanted to console Maria. He could do nothing but stand and stare straight ahead.

Half an hour passed when four spotted ponies with riders abreast moved forward. Suddenly, all four horses shifted to their right, and, without losing a step, pranced sideways, oncoming, in a cadence that brought chills to Carl's spine. Each bow and arrow was rigidly aligned to release into his torso with the least pull. He would die now, or he would learn that they all would live. He pressed his arm against the pistol on his right. *They will pay a price if they take her.*

The party stopped ten feet away. One spoke in English. "If you are Gold Hat, where is your long knife?"

"Short gun better than long knife." No sooner had he said it, he regretted it.

When the young brave chuckled, Carl recognized Potra, who claimed the title, Son of El Sol Colorado – Meusebach.

"Potra! My friend. It is good to see you. Why did the brave warriors frighten my people all night?"

"Not know who you are until you call 'Gold Hat.' Fleetaumountec not believe until he see your long knife."

Fleetaumountec was here! Carl had never seen him. Now this wild chief whom Carl's people had injured severely on the road demanded to see the long knife for proof. Carl had given it up out of love for Maria. He would tell the truth.

"Gold Hat has a new bride. New bride told me to leave the long knife at home."

Potra replied, "I remember you from the peace talk. I will tell Fleetaumountec it is you." He raced back to the band while the other three warriors stood guard over Carl.

When Potra approached again, another warrior rode at his side. The tall Indian wore a horned buffalo headdress. His body was covered by a faded red shirt. His left hand held a thick long bow. Above his shoulder protruded the feathers of a dozen arrows. Naked leg muscles rippled above glossy new English boots. His broad face was split in half by red coloring from the bridge of his nose and to the left. On the right side, black.

His thick mouth was frozen in a perpetual frown. His long hair was fixed in two braids which swept forward over his shoulders, tied with colorful seashells.

Carl felt disadvantaged on the ground. Another oversight. He should have brought his horse. Fleetaumountec walked his black and white stallion the final ten yards. He rode so close to Carl, he seemed to sniff him as he leaned forward from his saddle. He straightened and spoke to Potra.

Potra interpreted. "Fleetaumountec say your long knife made you brave. He asks if a woman has made you a coward."

"Tell Fleetaumountec that if my woman has made me a

191

coward, the coward will kill all who try to harm her. And he'll gladly die to defend her."

Potra spoke in the non-syllabic grunt and the mighty warrior responded. Potra said, "Fleetaumountec wants to see your squaw. See if you treat her well."

Carl hadn't wanted the Indians to even glimpse Maria. But he was sure they had already done so during their hiding in the brush. Despite arm motions to the contrary, she and Greta had kept popping up above the carriage windows as daylight broke. He could refuse and offend the chief, or he could try to limit the visit.

He played the Indians' waiting game by holding back his reply for several minutes. "Fleetaumountec and Potra come to the wagon with me. No other. You will meet my woman."

Carl watched as Potra interpreted. Fleetaumountec's nod was barely perceptible. With great trepidation, he turned his back to the chief and his warriors and paced toward the wagons. He saw the rifles of his own guard rise from their resting positions.

When he entered voice range, Carl called, "Chief Fleetaumountec and his interpreter, Potra, want to meet my wife. Maria, please calmly step from the carriage. Do not be afraid. These men are of the treaty."

When the two Comanches entered the line of guard, Wilhelm lowered his rifle and spoke politely, "Buenas tardes, hombres." Fleetaumountec would have understood the Spanish greeting but didn't respond. His narrow eyes took in Wilhelm and Ernst, then the others, showing no fear in riding past them.

"Maria, did you hear me? Come and meet the nice Comanche chief. We would not want to offend him, would we?" Carl could hear subdued objections coming from Greta who seemed to still acknowledge house arrest.

Maria bounced to the ground and looked up. Terror showed clearly in her eyes. Greta had restored all underwear, even brushed her auburn hair which caught the sun's early rays. Her eyes glistened green as she stared into the black eyes of the curious savage. She couldn't hold her gaze against his.

While watching Fleetaumountec, Carl said for Potra's translation, "This is my frau...my wife...my squaw. She radiates good health and happiness. She is a contented woman."

As Potra spoke to the chief, Greta's long nose exited the carriage window. Fleetaumountec's eyes diverted there for a split second and spoke through Potra, "Gold Hat has three squaws."

When Potra translated, Carl was confused. *Oh, he must think Greta is another wife. I'll correct him with certainty. But he said three. Would he somehow know of Helga?*

"I have only one wife. Her name is Maria." He motioned. "She stands before you."

Potra translated, "You not like present Fleetaumountec sent?"

Carl's puzzlement grew. "I am sorry. I have received no present from the great chief."

Following a quick exchange, Potra said, "Where is White Goose, the Caddo Fleetaumountec gave you at the peace meeting?"

Carl failed to understand the question, thinking a gift of a bird had been proffered and he had forgotten. "All food was consumed on the trail. Why does he ask?"

When Potra translated, Fleetoumountec spat words through his clenched teeth and backed his horse away. His bow raised as though to receive an arrow. The rifles leaped.

Potra said, "The chief believes you ate the girl. You Tonkawa. You not live."

"The girl? The girl? *Oh, my God. He sent Meusebach a girl. He meant the gift for me, the head chief of the ocean people.* "No, Fleetaumountec. Herr...Mr. Meusebach received the girl. Not I. Tell him, Potra. Quickly."

Potra translated. Fleetaumountec didn't relax. He shouted at Potra.

Potra said, "Why did you give the squaw to the minor chief? You not like?"

Carl resisted the urge to go for his pistol and end this discourse. The reason he didn't stood by his side. Paralyzing fear showed in her eyes. Diplomacy would have to do. Avoiding hand gestures which could seem threatening, Carl said, "Your warriors gave the squaw to Meusebach, not me."

Fleetaumountec spoke a single word, and Potra translated it

into three. "You not like?"

Carl said, "I liked her fine. She was fair of face and form. Meusebach liked her as well. He..." Potra had already started the translation, and Carl didn't know how he was going to finish the sentence.

Potra said, "How you know you like? You try her?"

"No, I liked her beauty. That is all. White men have only one wife." Aggravation, fear and caution conflicted in Carl's mind.

Potra exchanged words with Fleetaumountec again, then said, "One wife or not. Man is still man. Why did you not try her?"

"God, Potra, you must help me. Tell him the choice was Meusebach's. I am sorry there was a misunderstanding."

"El Sol Colorado, the fat man who is my white father?" Potra asked without consulting the chief.

"Yes, he is quite large." It sounded clumsy.

Fleetaumountec lowered his bow as Potra translated his words. "Fleetaumountec will go to El Sol Colorado. If he not treat White Goose well, Fleetaumountec take her. Bring her to you."

Carl was trapped. He could refuse and catch an arrow in his gut. He could say Meusebach no longer has the girl, and the ex commissioner-general would be in trouble. He could agree to the deal in Maria's hearing.

He searched his mind. *Change the subject.*

"Wife of Gold Hat has presents for Fleetaumountec's wives. How many wives does Fleetaumountec have?"

Potra translated then said, "Six."

Carl said, "Maria, darling, you must do exactly as I say. Do not argue, and do not allow Greta to argue. Do you understand the importance?" Maria nodded, her mouth too dry to speak.

"Take off all your petticoats, and all of Greta's. Go into your luggage if necessary. But come up with six petticoats in the next five minutes. Do you understand?"

Maria reached to comply in full view. Carl stopped her and pointed to the wagon. He said, "Greta, go with Maria. She will tell you how to spare your life."

As Greta hastened from carriage to wagon, Fleetaumountec followed her with his eyes. He spoke again to Potra.

Potra said, "You sell skinny wife? Fleetaumountec has horses."

Carl involuntarily glanced at Greta before answering. She had turned and was listening. "She is not my wife. She is not for sale. She is a servant, a slave for my wife."

Potra spoke to Fleetaumountec, then said, "Your squaw whip?"

"No," Carl said.

"Slave no good unless you whip," the young brave said for his chief.

"White man...ocean people ways are different."

Maria jumped from the wagon and handed a bundle of petticoats to Carl, her skirt hanging limp around her slender hips. Fleetaumountec reached, clutching the underwear in one hand as he spoke again to Potra who translated, "Both wives skinny. Maybe White Goose more jolly now. You like her better when Fleetaumountec bring."

They pulled their horses backward for ten yards before wheeling them, then scattered dirt in a speedy departure.

"She is not my wife! Not the skinny ...!" Carl shouted, though sure they didn't hear.

Carl's party watched in awe as sixty or more warriors joined forces from the woods and moved to the west. All sight and sound vanished the instant the first trees surrounded their path.

Carl avoided the questioning stares, especially Maria's and Greta's, as he ordered everyone aboard, and the caravan to move forward. Greta perched herself on the carriage driver's seat as Carl and Maria took refuge inside. Maria clung to him and said nothing as he sought words of comfort. "It's over, my love. Don't be afraid." He held her close and patted her shoulders.


Frau Emelie Wetzel emerged from the two-story rock structure to greet the guests. Her German speech was fresh and reassuring. "Herr Carl, Frau Maria, Frau Greta! Climb down! We expected you last evening. Was the wedding delayed?"

Maria spoke the first words since the encounter. "Travel was delayed by Indians who held us captive all night. They…" A burst of tears cut her words short.

"My darling child! I pray they didn't harm you. Come with me. I'll make you comfortable. Greta, come." She guided the women to the house as Viktor Wetzel greeted the men. He ushered them inside and seated them at a long table. He poured homemade liquor into clay mugs and insisted they drink heartily. Though the hour was early, none refused.

Upstairs in Frau Wetzel's chambers, the hostess brought water basins for her guests and sent outside for their personal effects. "How dreadful that your wedding night was spoiled by the Indians, my dear. Are you sure you are not harmed? Savages seldom allow a white female captive to escape a fate worse than death."

Greta replied. "The chief wanted me badly. I must give Carl credit for refusing to sell. He was making so many compromises, I was sure I would be swept away on that wonderful painted horse into a life of primitive love slavery."

Maria and Frau Wetzel stared open-mouthed at Greta whose face took on an easy radiance. Maria added, "Yes, well, they settled for our underwear."

"Your underwear?" Frau Wetzel screamed in horror. "I will replace the garments for you. What did you lose?"

"Six petticoats," said Maria.

"Seven," returned Greta. "Who knows when the chief will get another wife?" She still smiled.

"Greta!" Maria said, aghast.

Frau Wetzel said, "I can't provide seven petticoats, but at least I can give you one each, so that you'll not feel naked before the men."

"Yes," Greta said. "I never felt more naked in my life."

When they had washed their hands and donned the new undergarments, they turned to descend the stairs. Greta said, "I wonder how many horses Herr Fleetaumountec would have traded."

Wetzel had already placed a feast of meats, sausages and

German pastries on the table and his guests laughed and joked at their ordeal. Carl leaped up at the sight of his bride in a golden, full-length satin dress which accented her narrow waist and gave rise to her bosom.

"Never have you looked so ravishing, my bride. Please, seat yourself and partake of the feast. What marvelous hosts. Do you agree?"

"Carl, are you drinking schnapps at this hour? Where will you be at sunset?"

"It was prescribed by Herr Wetzel. A finer doctor of Indian trauma recovery the frontier has never known. I promise. No more before I take you to a proper bed."

When the polite chuckles died, Maria said, "You are in a mood. Herr Wetzel's remedy seems to have erased all fears. I'm still trembling."

"Then you must take the cure!" Carl handed her his tumbler. She sipped it lightly and sat down. As her platter was heaped with samples of all foods, she once again sought Carl's cup as Frau Wetzel poured Greta's drink. As Maria's appetite abated, she reached more often for Carl's cup. She laughed at the least statement, intended to be funny or not.

"Maria, it's my turn to admonish." Carl smiled as he said it, knowing he wouldn't bar her from anything she desired.

Frau Wetzel said, "Indeed. The day is young and you two will complete your partnership in that most important way in the comfort of our home. We are so honored that it should happen here."

"Frau Wetzel," replied the relaxed bride, "Not to detract from your honor in the least, but I fear the first glory goes to the carriage floor." Hosts and guests broke into noisy laughter. Greta's cheeks glowed red as she howled in glee.

Bone tired from their all-night ordeal, the weary travelers sought refuge in an early afternoon sleep. Frau Wetzel placed the honeymooning couple in a prepared suite and guaranteed their privacy. Carl told Maria that he understood women far better than she supposed. He wouldn't expect a response from her after all she had been through. She needed to relax and recover. She kissed him and thanked him for his understanding as they retired to bed.

After an hour, Maria turned to her ever-close bridegroom and whispered, "Darling, I'm relaxed…and recovered."

In San Antonio, to the couple's delight, Greta gave them ample privacy by seeking out German stores. She ate alone at the inn's café because their long absences went past her rigid schedule for meals.

Carl and Maria glowed as the lazy days took them from everything except their own pleasures. On the morning set for departure, they lay in bed rambling over major and minor topics, plans and dreams, the narrow brush with the Indians. They had grown comfortable with each other. As Maria stretched to see the wall clock on her side of the bed, Carl jumped in alarm.

"Darling, you have a severe scratch across your…your buttocks. It shows on both …well, both cheeks. Did you fall? When did this happen?"

"Let's say that my buttocks were the first casualty of your new revolving pistol. I hope it will prove equally deadly when you confront an enemy."

New passion followed the laughter. When it was over, they lay apart for a long period. Carl dreaded getting out of bed but finally tossed his legs toward the bed's edge.

Maria asked, "Carl, who is White Goose?"

# Chapter 20

Maria sat on the edge of the bed listening. Carl couldn't tell whether the strain on her brow suggested concentration or doubt as he struggled to explain White Goose. He asked often if she understood. She nodded but didn't change expression. She refused to speak, thus giving him no opportunity to end the one-sided conversation.

At last, Carl said, "There, you have the story, my love. No greater joke could have been played on Meusebach. He wanted always to seem so proper."

"But, White Goose was given to you. Do I understand that you passed her on to Herr Meusebach?"

"Maria, please, White Goose was given to me or so Fleetaumountec says now! I think he was attempting to make me uncomfortable in the presence of my bride. Indians have a sense of humor, you know."

"No, I'm glad you enlightened me." She scooted to the edge of the bed and stood. "Tell me as you told the chief, without a trace of humor in your tone, why you found the maiden so fair of face and form."

"I was trying to please the chief. I wouldn't want him to think I found her homely."

"So, she was homely, in reality?"

Musing the question, Carl watched Maria throw a crimson robe over her shoulders. This could bring an end to the discourse. He could lie. But pride precluded it. "Compared to you, my love, all females are unattractive. That shall always be true."

"But, was she homely or not?"

"Maria, that was long before I beheld your beauty. You could ask Meusebach the question. He's a single man, and his words

199

would need no modification."

"Good, I will. We'll go to his residence on our return. I must have answers. My darling, I don't doubt your sincerity. But since I heard of White Goose, I wonder what became of her."

Carl was anxious to start home, get back to his castle and the colony's business, add to his house a lavish bedroom and manipulate Greta to remain in the cottage. But, he, too, had wondered what Meusebach did with the girl, how long he had kept her, and if he had tried her, as Potra called it. He doubted if he would learn the latter, but he could draw his own conclusions from whatever else Meusebach said.

Their entourage turned in at the Comanche Springs estate of John Meusebach in early evening. Riders were returning to the pens from the north and west on tired horses. Meusebach talked with men standing by the corral. When he spotted Carl's carriage, he set his milk bucket down and rushed forward.

"Prince Carl, and Lady Maria, you both look radiant. I trust that frontier travel has not dampened your love. Step down and be my guests for a long while. Excuse my state of affairs. We had a bit of trouble with Indians last evening."

Carl grew alarmed. Of all places, Meusebach's stone homestead should be safe. He set the wheel brake. "Herr John, trouble with Indians? Tribes outside your treaty? What happened?"

"It was your friend, Fleetaumountec," he said, receiving Carl's hand. "I fear the treaty has fallen apart. He threatened my life, then drove off fifty of my horses during the night."

Carl said, "What did you do to offend him? White Goose?"

Meusebach's troubled smiled turned to a frown. "Yes, Carl, it was. How did you know?"

"We had an encounter with the chief ourselves on the road to San Antonio. He mentioned White Goose."

Meusebach directed the vehicles and horses stabled, then guided the visitors inside where he ordered supper. He scurried about the log and stone house for half an hour. His size and energy always seemed in amusing conflict to Carl. Finally, settled by the fireplace with Carl, the two women, Wilhelm and Ernst. "I'm sorry to delay our visit, but I was helping the maid to arrange your quarters."

As he spoke, a dark skinned, lovely young woman, carrying an armload of bedding, passed the chairs.

Maria leaped. "It's White Goose. Herr Meusebach, I must meet her. Why do you call her a maid? Can you not afford domestic help?"

"Oh, God, Maria, please! She's not White Goose. This woman is Mexican. She is paid for her services. White Goose was not..." He glanced about as he seemed to gasp for breath, adding hurriedly, "was not a maid. She was... Carl, does your lovely bride tie you in knots as she does me?"

"When it comes to White Goose, yes. Maria, please allow John to explain, that is, if he can."

Meusebach stretched into his soft chair, weighing his words. "As soon as I could, I transported White Goose back to her people who live in the Indian Territory. She didn't want to stay there but, for some reason, which I will never understand, wanted to remain here as my bride. Finally, she agreed to stay with her people, though she broke my heart with her wilting eyes. Even so, I sneaked out during the night for my departure, fearing that she would follow.

"Now that you know that story, please tell me, Carl and Maria, what troubles did you have with Fleetaumountec?"

Greta answered. "He wanted to buy me as his bride, and he wanted to find White Goose and give her back to Carl."

Meusebach leaned back and laughed. Greta tightened her brow.

"My dear Frau Greta, I can see he would want you as his bride. I laugh because this explains his argument with me. He demanded to see White Goose. When I told him she wasn't here, he asked me if I ate her. Carl, surely you didn't tell him something absurd such as that."

"I..."

"Then, if I understood Potra correctly, Fleetaumountec said if I didn't keep the girl, I owe him for her. I suppose he collected payment last evening when my horses disappeared. Oh, Carl, I am beside myself with concern that the treaty may unravel."

Carl said, "I suppose Indian gifts always have strings attached with which the giver can pull back the gift. No, John, I think the treaty is intact, or you and I both would be dead. They could have easily killed my party on the road, or you at your own house."

Greta offered her advice. "Keep plenty of petticoats about. They seem to love them for their women."

Meusebach smiled, rolling his eyes to Carl and Maria. "Tell me of your honeymoon. Well, not every detail. You seem delirious with happiness. I hope that such can be mine someday."

Carl looked to Maria, still stifling a snicker from Greta's remark. She said, "This has been the greatest time of my life. Carl and I have suffered grievous losses in our past but God has put us together to make up for it."

Meusebach's lips curled. "Does that mean that the old coot should put you with child soon?"

Maria reached for Carl's hand. "If he is old he has done a magnificent job of chicanery. But it's funny that you should ask. Carl and I have hardly spoken of children. Darling, do you want children?"

Though Carl seldom showed embarrassment and had grown accustomed to the good-natured honeymoon jokes, he blushed as he answered. "Only if you do, my dear. Only if you do."

Maria scooted close and reached around his neck. "That is the real reason you married me, true?"

It was, and it wasn't. Oh, how she had ways of making the truth seem unimportant. "There was a time when I thought of remarrying only for more children. Then I met you, mein Feinheit, and you became the reason for life itself." Their lips met instinctively.

Meusebach said, "We must let the love birds find their nest, Greta, or we shall suffer untold embarrassment."

"We, yes, but not them. They have acted without shame since the first night in the carriage." Greta slapped her hand to her mouth as her cheeks reddened.

As they retired to their rooms, Carl told Meusebach, "There's a matter of grave concern to me. Could we discuss it in the morning before the ladies rise?"

"Now, Carl, I've told you before, I'm no expert on the fairer sex."

"No, it's not a matter of women this time. It has to do with Indians, Germans, and Texans."

The two men rose early, as agreed, but the women were stirring, so they left the house and walked toward the barns. "John, don't get the wrong impression. My honeymoon was most rewarding. But there's been a burden on my mind since I met Fleetaumountec. He was wearing a new pair of English style boots."

Meusebach said, "Yes, I saw them. Ah, Carl, it is a pity that the Texans cannot band together to gain some understanding with the Indians as we have done. I know what you're thinking, that he killed the owner of those boots and took them. Possibly. I don't want to know. I don't know what I could do about it. The Texans are such an independent lot."

"John, below my matrimonial passions, I have a dread. I may not live long enough to become a father again. If Fleetaumountec has killed my Texan friend, Isaack Covington, I'll kill him or die trying. The boots looked to be Covington's."

# *Chapter 21*

As the chill of winter settled over New Altmann in late 1849, influenza broke out and took its toll, Progress came to a halt on the castle and commerce slowed to a crawl. Doctors Schmitt and Hagerdorn put out bulletins warning people to limit contact to close family members as much as possible. They advised married couples not to sleep together if either had been exposed to the afflicted. School was suspended from the first of December until year's end. Carl brooded.

Maria tried to cheer him. "Darling, the plague will pass. You'll see. I know Dr. Schmitt told you not to sleep with me because of your continual contacts with your subjects, but it matters little. Our child will be born in a few weeks, and the bed could only mean frustration at this time."

Carl took comfort. "Women have…what do you call it? A way of knowing the future. What has your body told you of the sex of our unborn?"

"Intuition. I've listened to most of the fraus in the colony. Half of them guessed correctly from their intuition. Half didn't."

"But what does your intuition tell you?"

"I see a five-year-old boy standing, smiling at me. Behind him, a little girl tries to look beyond him and find me, or you. Do you suppose it means twins?"

"I think not. Otherwise your belly would be much bigger." He patted the growing middle. "But it could mean we will have one of each, sooner or later. When do think this one will come?"

"Today is December fourteenth. I think you'll again be a father in one month. Can you wait?"

"Of course, my love. Is there any reason for you to believe I'm short on patience?" Carl knew he was short on patience, always had been. But it never stopped the passage of time or assured that he got what he wanted after waiting.

He left the house and rode to the dwelling of his young brother-in-law, Baron Hermann von Schoener, who had elected to spend a year in Texas following the wedding. Carl had at first regretted his insincere invitation, fearing that the young man would be too protective of his sister, Maria, or usurp influence with his pleasant personality and good looks. However, as the summer had passed, Carl lost his trepidation and came to like the man. He felt the family tie would be a basis of trust, and von Schoener could be useful to him in business and public affairs.

"Hermann, ride with me to the west. The plague is not bad there. I've neglected an old friend. An English Texan. One of the few I trust. Get your rifle and pistol."

Hermann saddled a horse and collected his guns. When they arrived at the modest cabin of Isaack Covington, no animals stood in the pens. The ashes of a barn, only one corner still upright, told that a fire had swept the structure. Carl was surprised that the work-driven Covington hadn't torn down the rubble, or replaced it. Then, coldness crept up Carl's spine. The ranch had been a hubbub of activity every time he had come before. He dismounted and charged across the porch.

Carl looked through the single, glass windowpane. The boarding normally put in place after dark or when the owners were gone had fallen inside the house. Rough-hewn furniture lay in disarray on the floor. He turned the door handle to find it unbarred. He entered with pounding heart and furiously sorted through torn cloth and papers.

"Carl, what is it?" Hermann asked.

"Why have I ignored my friends? I knew this in my heart." Carl couldn't hide his concern. "Let's go to the barns, the pens. They may hold a clue."

As they marched to the pens, Carl's voice trembled. "Livestock is always present in these pens. Workers are about, like a beehive."

They rounded the first barn when Carl saw it. Old blood stained the pole fence to his right. He looked left and saw more blood and gore strewn over the barn's wall. Under the eve of the roof, a gallon of black blood saturated the ground. The pool trailed off toward the fence to the southwest. More splatters showed on the sides of the rails, where rain hadn't washed it away. The line played out as it entered the open range.

A blinding flash of horrible visions drove Carl's chin against his chest. He wheeled and fell into Hermann's arms who caught Carl before his knees buckled. Carl clung to his brother-in-law's shoulders. His breath came strained as he sucked air hard between clenched teeth.

"Carl, what are you thinking?" Hermann asked as he kept Carl from falling.

"I think murder. I know who did it." As he spoke, winter's first snow flakes melted against his face. The wind rose.

"Who do you believe did this, Carl? I'll help you in any way I can. Though I'm untrained in matters of tracking, it's obvious to me that the blood trail is quite old. We'll need to think."

"Yes, we must think. But we'll act when the thinking is done." Carl wanted to lash out. He hadn't felt such hatred since he ran his sword through a warrior who would molest his daughter Elisabeth. He couldn't vent his rage this time. It turned into grief. He broke into wailing sobs. His body shook. He didn't care that Hermann saw his vulnerability.

The snow turned to cold rain and the wind caused the sudden temperature drop to feel double in intensity. Hermann's comforting tone let Carl know the young baron would back him any way he asked. But he couldn't speak.

Hermann said, "Let's mount and ride. We think more clearly on horseback."

Carl followed the younger man like an obedient child. When Hermann asked him if they should head home Carl didn't answer. Mounted, Hermann waited briefly, then led off to the east, homeward. Several times Hermann tried to slow and pull alongside Carl to give his senior the opportunity to lead or speak. Carl held his horse back and pulled his hat low.

In front of Carl's house, Hermann stopped. "Carl, go inside. I'll put away your horse."

Carl pulled beside Hermann. "Please don't tell Maria or anyone what we saw back there. This matter must be handled in secret."

"As you wish. Are you all right?"

"I'm fine, Hermann. Thank you for coming with me and preventing me from charging like a juvenile in pursuit of ghosts."

"Carl, could you tell me who committed this crime?"

"Indians I thought were our friends." The strain returned to his voice. He stood at the gate and watched his brother-in-law lead his horse away. Carl wiped his face discovering frozen tears on his pointed beard. He picked at the ice until he thought it was gone. He straightened his coat and hat, took a deep breath and entered. Maria was not in sight.

He called, "My love, I'm home. Are you here?" He knew his voice cracked and hoped Maria wouldn't notice, or was visiting Greta or someone else.

From the bedroom, Maria called. "Carl, Sweetheart. I'm in bed. Come in." He detected a sigh at the end of her words. A glance in the mirror told him his face was still grim. He had to go in.

When he saw her lying on her side looking toward the wall instead of the door, he gasped. "Maria, are you well?" He felt her forehead. "Do you hurt?" He knelt beside her.

"The pain comes in waves. Dr. Schmitt told me it would be like this when the baby is due. Carl, it's not time." Her face turned toward his and her eyes dashed shut with another stab of agony. "I'm sure I became pregnant on our trip. I know the exact moment. It could not have been sooner. You know that."

As Carl raced to Greta's cabin his thoughts rambled. *At least she didn't notice my appearance. Even if the baby comes now, it's not so early that the child couldn't live, I hope. Greta will probably make some accusatory remark. She must come quickly while I get Schmitt. Where is daughter Elisabeth when I need her? But, what if something is seriously wrong? What if I lose Maria?*

A few words into his report, Greta lunged from her cabin without a winter wrap. She shot ahead of him to reach Maria. As

207

soon as she entered, Carl said, "I'll bring Schmitt."

As he closed the door, he remembered that Hermann had taken his saddled horse. He ran the quarter mile and worried that Schmitt wouldn't be home. He swung open the door of the Schmitt house without knocking.

Eva Schmitt, used to the panicked patient, turned slowly from her iron cook stove. "Heinrich, the prince is here to see you. Heinrich, wake up, lazy man."

Schmitt, Carl knew, had worked over his flu patients twenty of the last twenty-four hours and had fallen asleep, upright in his cushioned chair. His head bobbed up lazily.

"What is it, Carl? You look a mess. Could you not have sent someone? You are a prince, you know."

"Don't start with me, Schmitt. It's Maria. The baby wants to come into the world tonight. Come."

Schmitt dropped the frivolity. "I'll go, but, please take your rest. Stay here and enjoy Eva's dinner. You wouldn't be permitted in during my examination, anyway."

Carl argued but Eva took his arm and pleaded. "Stay at least for a few minutes. I can see you're starved."

The aroma of kraut and sausage combined with her pleas, plus the absence of a horse to ride, convinced him. Schmitt shouldered his coat, gripped a black bag, and shot from the house. He shot back inside. "Carl, where is your horse?"

"I walked."

"Damn, man. Has the whole world gone crazy as the birth of a prince grows near? I hope the child doesn't inherit the trait." Schmitt struck out afoot.

As Carl settled before Eva's platter of steaming foods, she told him about the warm friendship between her daughters and his. She revealed that Elisabeth had found infatuation with a young Texas man, Samuel Smathers.

*I'll nip that silliness quickly*, Carl thought as he sipped hot coffee over potato salad and slices of tender sausage. Eva continued to describe the young suitor, assuring Carl that Elisabeth had shown good judgment in her selection.

He slowed eating. "Yes, yes, but you said Texan. It won't do.

208

She *is* my daughter, you know. What will the colony think? Besides, one eventually marries according to whom she courts. No, I'll not have it. Elisabeth is wise for a mere sixteen years of age, but still much a child. I'll persuade her, gently, of course."

Eva said, "Elisabeth is no child, Herr Carl. She's near the age of Maria when you wed her last spring. Have you taken time to look at your daughter lately, much less talk to her? She is the image of Helga at that age." Her voice quivered.

"Frau Eva, are you implying that I married a child or that Elisabeth is a woman? Quite the opposite is true, you know. Maria is far more mature in every way."

"They are both fine women, Carl. Women!"

The Schmitt girls, Elisabeth, and their friends, Magdalene and Christine bounded through the door and closed it quickly. Carl greeted them with gentle hugs, taking note that they were no longer shapeless children.

He admonished, "Are you running about after dark? The sun has set while Frau Eva and I have chatted endlessly. Children should be home at this hour."

Elisabeth clung to his waist and said lovingly, "Father, your distractions have gone on forever. I haven't had a private conversation with you in most of a year. We're not children. What is Maria going to name the baby?"

"I shall choose the proper name for the child. It's not fitting that a mere female should name a future prince."

"Are you holding to the prince theory? New Altmann is a city. Altmann Colony is a Texas County. We don't have princes in the new world. And if so, I claim my inheritance as a princess. But I will gladly surrender it to please Sammy."

"Sammy! Indeed. And what has this base young ruffian said concerning princes and princesses? What does he know? Does he work in the stables?" Dark eyes glared into dark eyes.

Elisabeth frowned upward at her father. "Sammy is not base." Then she smiled, "He understands that hard work and intelligence determines success in Texas. Besides, he's handsome and strong. Father, you have never seen such a rider and handler of cattle. He can swing an ax with the best of men. He *is* a man."

Cupping his daughter's firm face, Carl said with a twinkle, "I could use him in rock demolition on the hill. Sit to the fine dinner Frau Schmitt has prepared. We'll talk later of your childish infatuation. I must be off to see to Maria. It's possible that your new brother will be born this night. I've stayed too long."

Carl entered his house to see it filled with women – Katheryn, his first wife's sister; Pricilla and Sophia, mothers of Elisabeth's friends; Hagerdorn's and Wilhelm's wives, and Greta. Except for the most casual greetings as each saw Carl, they ignored him and talked in a hum among themselves. Since he couldn't single out one to demand a report, he stalked to Maria's room.

Schmitt leaned by the bed carefully packing his bag. Maria sat bolt upright, smiling. "Darling, I have the best news."

*Has my son been born and those wenches outside didn't tell me? Elisabeth is right. Princedom is dead. We are all commoners.* He said, "What is it, Maria? Schmitt? For God's sake, will someone answer a former prince?"

Maria winced, reaching for her stomach. "Tell him, Dr. Schmitt."

"I've advised your wife that she shall refrain from liverwurst and fresh apples until the baby arrives. When she told me the quantities she ate earlier, I almost gave birth myself. Carl, the good news is that Maria shows no sign of premature delivery. But I'm confining her to bed for the duration. You are to stay close."

Maria said, "But I had such cravings for those two foods."

"My dear, never give me such a fright again. Thank you, Schmitt. Please report your findings to the self-indulgent women in the outer room. I am unable to hold their attention. Such gratitude after all I've done!"

Schmitt said, buckling his case, "Please understand women, Carl. If men could band together for self protection as women do at a time like this, we would have a better world. I'll speak to them as I go."

"Speaking of banding together, we need a meeting of the committee. Could you call them for tomorrow? Bring them here, I suppose, since you've quarantined me as well as Maria."

Committeemen Schulz and Mueller reported sick and didn't come to the meeting. Carl seated the others around his long table and asked Maria to adjourn to Greta's cabin. Maria asked Carl if it was a good idea to call a meeting in the face of the epidemic. Carl mumbled that some things are too important to wait. She left.

Carl opened the meeting. "Gentlemen, the Indians have taken our best Texas friend and his family. The English rancher, Covington, is missing and his ranch covered in blood. Baron von Schoener and I saw it clearly." The agony displayed by the men dragged Carl's spirits low. He drew a deep breath. "Here's our dilemma. Meusebach's treaty with the Indians precludes Germans from carrying out a campaign against the savages. The Texans have no protection from the German treaty. They have only the threat of force. Obviously, the Indians have no fear of that threat until they look down a gun barrel. But I cannot abide the destruction of this family who has aided us so greatly. I want your ideas on what we should do, and when."

The questions came. "Herr Carl, when did this happen?"

"I estimate the time as early as last spring. I regret that I haven't tried to contact Herr Covington in that time period."

"Herr Carl, who, what Indians do you believe committed this atrocity? Perhaps they were not of the treaty. We would have the right to act."

"When we met Fleetaumountec in the spring, he was wearing a new pair of English boots, the exact style that Covington wears…wore." His voice choked.

Dr. Hagerdorn groaned, "We had come so far with the chief. I thought he was our friend. How could he do this thing?"

"He sees the Texans differently. He doesn't understand that we should be upset with the killings. It's a flaw in Meusebach's treaty. There can be no peace with the Indians if half of the whites are fair game for their ravaging and the other half are safe. I told Meusebach this, but he said he didn't know what he could do. Are we so helpless?"

The committeemen seemed to catch Carl's fire, instantly knowing that the director meant to act. "When could we form a

211

militia? Not this winter, for sure. Many are sick. The trail is old. Where would we start? But you are right, Carl. We have to take action..."

Hagerdorn spoke again. "Carl, let me try again in the spring to negotiate with Fleetaumountec. He still doesn't view us as his enemy. We can also try to involve Meusebach."

Carl shouted, "How do you negotiate murder? Meusebach is so comfortable with his hobbies and self-indulgence, I doubt that he would be interested."

"Still he may have some ideas."

Carl calmed. "We can talk with him in the meantime; see if his brain is working. But the Indians, Fleetaumountec, have taken to raiding Meusebach's own property. I have one other idea. We could contact Captain Jack Hays. See what he would propose."

Hagerdorn's face flushed. "Hays will propose one thing, and you know it. When word gets out that the ocean people put Hays on Fleetaumountec's trail, there will be no treaty for anyone, ever again."

The meeting ended in stalemate, each determined to find the right solution, each supportive of Carl. Carl's heart ached as he envisioned his young friend, Covington, strong, alert, smiling, advising, hugging shoulders. How he grieved for one more visit to that enchanted household; for just one more word of advice from that mighty ally on stocking, ranching, and land.

Carl wouldn't tell Maria of the loss. He knew she'd question him about June Covington and the child, and he wished to spare her any trauma in this very sensitive time. He fought his own mind to avoid pictures of the bodies that lay out there, maybe closer than he dared think. Too, he had believed June Covington to be pregnant again when he last saw her not long before the wedding. He pushed the agony from his mind as best he could, determined to hide his feelings during Maria's final month.

The month ended. Maria's labors began in earnest exactly as she had predicted. Carl again ran the quarter mile to Schmitt's house, forgetting that his saddled horse awaited him in the stable. This time, Schmitt's carriage was ready. They returned to Carl's house together. The town women entered Carl's house just ahead of him and Schmitt. Carl remained outwardly calm, claiming to be a veteran of such affairs, until the labor went an hour beyond his reckoned deadline.

He burst into the bedroom with only Schmitt, Maria and Greta. Schmitt and Greta looked up, and in unison, said, "No men in the delivery room. Out! Out!"

Maria's weak voice said, "Carl, come to me. Your child is almost here." He ignored Schmitt and Greta long enough to approach the bed and kiss his wife gently on her wet forehead.

"Are you all right? I will leave. Would you like for one of the others to leave with me?"

"Greta has been a great comfort. It won't be…long. Oh!" She reached for her sides.

Schmitt looked at Carl as Carl rose from the bedside and gave a gentle head motion as if to say, "Carl, get yourself out of here." Carl smiled and strode out the door.

He had hardly poured his coffee when he heard a child's cry from the bedroom. He set the cup down and moved toward the door. The women blocked his way. Katheryn said, "Give them about a half hour to be presentable. Maria will be proud of your patience."

The infant's cries gained strength. At the risk of being wrong, Carl burst forth with a prediction. "It's a male child! The cry is the same as Hans when he was born."

Katheryn put a hand on his shoulder. "And would the world quit spinning if it is a female? You and Maria will have more children."

"Oh, it's a boy, I can tell. Fathers know these things. Of course, the world wouldn't stop spinning, Katheryn. I adore girls. But I had looked forward…that is, I need a male heir while I am… Never mind."

After several tries, they succeeded in forcing Carl to sit with his coffee. Katheryn approached the door and called, "Is there anything we can do?"

Schmitt's cheerful chirp came through the thick door. "Keep Carl under house arrest." Elisabeth hugged her father in tearful joy.

Greta burst from the room with the precious, wrapped bundle. They gathered close.

She beamed. "It's a boy. He is beautiful beyond compare, blonde, and good tempered. He doesn't resemble you in the least, Carl."

Carl hardly heard the intended insult as he pulled the soft blanket back and declared, "Prince Johann Mathias von Altmann is born this day, January 14, 1850."

# *Chapter 22*

Ecstasy carried the new parents through the winter. He hardly wanted to leave the house to view the stalled castle construction or talk with the farmers about irrigation projects. He dismissed petitioners as rapidly as possible, and as soon as his office was cleared of people, he dashed into Maria's quarters and continued to coo over his blond haired son. Often, Maria was nursing the infant or Greta was changing a diaper.

When little Johann Mathias was sleeping, one or the other of the women blocked Carl's path to prevent awakening the infant, as he had often done. When Johann cried out from his sleep, Carl used it as an excuse to pick him up and carry him about the room. At night, Maria drew the youngster into their bed for his final feeding and Carl left the lamps on long beyond their need to admire the child. He chatted endlessly of his ambitions for the young Texas prince, raving of his fine nose, his curls, his strength, his wisdom.

Maria's joy turned to fear that Carl had lapsed into a form of doting grandfatherhood from which he would never recover. The thought occurred to her, time and again, that maybe Carl *was* too old to become a father again. He had held tenaciously to his youth to achieve this one goal. Now, he was letting it all go. She didn't want that. She wanted Carl to be the husband and lover she had known. She wanted him to be an energetic father, not a grandfather to their child.

With the lights blown, finally, and the babe tucked into his own crib, Maria kissed Carl and said, tomorrow, she wanted to speak of religious training for their son. It was just the excuse Carl needed to continue his prattle.

"Will you want him christened a good Catholic like all his

ancestors? Or shall we have Reverend Clemens induct him as a Lutheran? I'll let you decide on religious matters. You're much better at it than me."

"A good question, Carl. Why haven't we spoken of spiritual matters more often? As infants, we were both baptized in the Holy Roman Catholic Church, but you showed no interest in being wed in the Catholic Church when the question came up. Why was that?"

"I'm not sure. Oh, yes, I am! I had a hideous experience with Father Gaspar in Altmann. He supported my worthless brother in seizing my principality, and over a trivial contribution to the repair of his roof. The man even rebuked me after I gave the greatest confession of my life. You could ask any of the witnesses. But you haven't answered my question."

"You gave a confession in the presence of witnesses? Carl, are you sure the confession was genuine?"

"Of course, it was genuine. I rehearsed for days."

"A confession is to be from the heart, not rehearsed." She cuddled close. She couldn't see his face in the dark, warm room. "But in your case, I'm sure God forgave you, even for *that* sin."

"God…yes. I'm sure. Now, what about Mathias?"

"Mathias? Do you intend to use his second Christian name?" Before Carl could answer, Maria went on. "I've grown fond of Reverend Clemens. I would want his advice on any approach we take."

"And, is he likely to advise that you have your son baptized a Catholic?"

"No, but Reverend Clemens has persuaded me that true religion is of the heart. One is religious because he believes what God has taught, not because he observes certain rituals for public show, such as confes… Well, you know what I mean. Do you agree, Carl?"

"I, too, am fond of the reverend. Whatever he says, I'm sure he's sincere."

"You missed the point, darling. All my life, I thought religion was doing what you are taught, or told. I suspect you did, too. The idea is that each individual makes a decision for God in his heart.

And no public show can fool God. Now, that's a unique idea. Reverend Clemens showed me scriptures that plainly say this, too."

Carl was slow in answering. She felt and heard him draw a breath. "My grandfather believed that God placed certain families in positions of rule over their subjects. God did this because he had given these special families skills and wisdom which the common people didn't have. It was for their own good. The English called it The Divine Right of Kings. I suppose, in a smaller sense, the same would hold true for princes. And if that's true, I've been ordained of God to lead my people. Whatever I decide has a blessing from above. Am I making sense?

"What's your point?" She squeezed his arm.

"God is naturally in my heart because he caused me to be born a prince. Do you agree, my loyal subject?"

"No."

"No!"

"Being born a prince doesn't exempt you from seeking God in your own heart. Besides, did God leave you and go to your brother's heart when you abdicated?"

"Hell, no! How could God be in the heart of scoundrel like Julius? He'd be a poor excuse for a God."

"Carl, giving up your principality was not an easy thing, I know. But you did it because you wanted something more, America and its challenges. The castle proves that. Reverend Clemens says forgiveness is the mark of a true Christian." Emerging moonlight enabled her to study his face. "Do you think, with the passage of time, you could ever forgive Julius?"

"You're speaking of more religion than I'm capable of. The Bible says 'an eye for an eye,' doesn't it?"

"In the old days, before Christ, they used that law, but it didn't apply to the individual, not even then. It was meant as a tool of justice."

"My point, exactly. I'm a prince. It's my divine…my right to pass judgment on the likes of Julius."

"Sweetheart, you're not a prince on a throne in Texas. You left the past behind, and I'm glad. Like all men, common or great,

217

you'll some day give an account of your heart to God."

"All right, if my beloved wife doesn't believe I'm a prince, then I must concede." He ran a finger down the length of Maria's nose. "But Mathias is a prince. You can see it in his noble little brow."

"You still haven't answered my question. Are we going to call him Mathias?"

"Yes, although when he grows up among Texans, they'll likely corrupt the beautiful German name to Math-Yewwww."

"I'll speak to Reverend Clemens tomorrow. Now can we sleep?"

"I doubt it. I'll lie awake in terror of my mortal soul after your sermon. Darling, I've never been an evil man. Perhaps a bit mischievous along the way. And speaking of mischief, how long has it been since Mathias' birth? Six months?"

"Go to sleep, husband. It's been thirty days. Mischief will have to wait a bit longer."

Maria turned away seeking sleep. As consciousness vanished she was pleased to see Carl show the old fire. But she remained troubled that she hadn't made a dent in his arrogant system of beliefs.

At the same time, in Carl's fading moments, his eyelids fluttered in thought that Maria had challenged the comfort level he had achieved in his agnosticism. Was there really something to this faith question? Was it worth reversing a lifetime of philosophy over a mere child? Yes...

Mischief didn't wait much longer because, by summer, Maria recognized the symptoms and told Carl that she was again with child. Carl beamed and went about the colony ensuring that everyone knew it. This was against German custom which would have allowed the women to whisper the word among themselves until the news had spread to everyone. When he told Roth, the brewmeister drew mugs for Carl and himself, and turned to the tavern patrons and announced a toast.

"Countrymen, lend me your attention. The prince and duchess of New Altmann will present their noble colony with another heir to the throne in the near future. Lift your mugs. Here is to the most virile of living princes, or the dirtiest of old men, as you choose."

The tavern burst in laughter and applause.

Carl couldn't suppress his smile as he scolded his friend. He forced the corners of his mouth downward and said, "Roth, how dare you! You assured me they approved of the wedding. Is this what my subjects are saying behind my back?"

"This is what I am saying to your front, friend. Drink your brew." Roth upended his mug in example. "Learn to take a joke. You're much more pleasant when under the influence."

"You've not seen me under the influence since my torment in Altmann. And heaven forbid that I should ever be that unhappy again." He sipped lightly.

"You *are* happy, Carl. That pleases me. You finally realized that the grand castle was but a childish pipe dream. Fatherhood is your real forte." He pointed through his window. "Look at the lazy rock wall on the hill. No workmen in sight. No clouds of limestone dust smelling up my air. My brew no longer tastes like liquid rock. Your insane quarrymen are not exploding my windows. Thank you for giving up the silly project, Carl."

Carl knew he was being chided, but this time he didn't see the humor. Roth had always been a barometer to Carl's outside world. And although Roth was rubbing salt into a wound, Carl knew that the citizens of New Altmann must be thinking somewhat along the same lines.

"Construction slowed through the winter for a number of obvious reasons, Herr Big Mouth. It will resume at full tilt soon. In the meantime I've established Triesch in building his iron forge. Herr Young set out eight hundred grape cuttings on the hillside. Architect Adrian is so caught up that I loaned his services to Meusebach for a while. And you know well, my full attentions and energies have been devoted…"

"The entire colony knows where your full attentions and energies have been devoted," Roth said with an easy smile and an eye roll.

Carl drew in his eyebrows and pulled close. "Don't play ignorant with me, my friend. All the things I've mentioned are toward the ultimate and correct completion of the castle. And if there is no peace with the Indians on our countryside, or as we travel, then we'll all fail. I'm not procreating children to see them slaughtered by savages. I have a plan."

Roth looked puzzled. "Herr Carl, I know of no Indian atrocities against Germans. Of what are you speaking?"

In a brash attempt to avoid criticism or scorn, Carl had revealed more than he intended. "We found a family of English Texans slaughtered not far from us. If we allow it, how soon until the savages decide that we are fair game?"

"Herr Meusebach has made a treaty with the Indians for the protection of Germans." Roth put on a look of contrived innocence. "You trust the former commissioner-general in his wisdom to do the right thing, don't you?"

"Your statement is an oxymoron, Roth. Do not use trust, wisdom and Meusebach in the same sentence. He's promised to make inquiries among the savages to learn who committed this crime. I trust him to do that. But his wisdom was lacking in excluding the native Texans from his treaty. If he doesn't find the guilty parties, I will!"

Roth looked at his long-time friend. "You use the term 'savages' without reservation."

"Ah, yes. Indians, Indians. Don't speak of this to others. You'll know all you need in due time. Are you still proficient with a rifle?"

"Never was. My oak club has served me well in this peaceful place."

Carl formed a minor militia – the usual travelers, Wilhelm, Ernst, Arnold, Schmitt and Hagerdorn, and the leader of the Hanover contingent, Felix Gossett. Now he added Baron Hermann von Schoener, his brother-in-law. They rode first to John Meusebach's place where they found Meusebach busily laying out foundation lines with Carl's architect, Adrian. Carl felt heat rise in his ears. *The man hasn't done a damned thing to find the guilty parties.*

His words came without formal greeting. "Herr Meusebach, do you have news on the perpetrators?"

The rotund former leader of the German Society rose from his stoop and smiled. "Greeting, Herr Carl. Dismount and come into my humble abode. I'll order a feast. We have much to discuss."

Carl leaped from his mount and ran the few steps toward Meusebach. "We have little to discuss if no progress has been made." Both men bore revolvers.

Meusebach dropped the string line in his hand and eyed the guard behind Carl. "Progress? If you infer that I should be out in the wilderness in a personal search, perhaps your troops would join me. Word has gone out by Indians, Carl. Friendly Indians. The inquiries are being made. It is the only effective way I know. What have your own inquiries produced?"

Carl's temper subsided. He realized that he was accusing Meusebach of inaction when he, Carl, had done no more than wait for others to act. "You're right, John. Accept my apology. We are on a mission of fact gathering at this time. Your home seemed the logical first stop."

The two reached and gave one another a brief bear hug followed by a long handshake. The usual courtesies followed and Carl's party enjoyed Meusebach's superb hospitality and a restful night's sleep.

They left early for the ranch headquarters of Gene Nance, the stockman on the San Antonio River. Again, Carl regretted not having cultivated the friendship of this man recommended to him by Ranger Jack Hays.

Nance stood on the covered porch of his log house as the riders approached. He was bent at the waist, and his fifty or so years could have passed for sixty-five as the German company rode close enough to note his white hair and beard. The Texan removed his felt hat, revealing a nearly bald pate. He adjusted the hat's crease nervously, seeking a reason to keep his hands away from the gun. Carl had seen this gesture before. The man didn't trust strangers, but didn't want to seem deliberately unfriendly.

"Mr. Nance, I presume? I am Carl von Altmann of the German

colony, New Altmann. These are my men."

"Germans, eh?" said Nance. "Never had any trouble from the Germans. Git off yer horses and set a while. Mabel, we got company. See if there's any coffee left."

"Mr. Nance, I regret that I have not sooner made your acquaintance. Captain Jack Hays recommended you to me as a Texan worthy of trust. We won't stay long."

"That dadgum rattlesnake Hays better say ye can trust me. I bailed him outa a few pinches with thuh Indins. Huh, huh. But I won't git in tuh that. My own kids er tired o' hearin' my war stories. What kin I do fer you fellers?"

The party dismounted and Nance handed the traditional water ladle to Carl. When they had all drunk, Carl started. "Mr. Nance…"

"Call me Gene, if ye don't mind."

"Of course. You're acquainted with your ranching neighbors, the Covingtons, near Cibolo Creek, are you not?"

"Yeah, fine fellar. We see each other ever few years. Been a while. How's Ike gittin' along?"

"The entire family has disappeared from their ranch. I was the first to discover it. We found a great deal of blood. I fear the worst. Have you heard nothing?"

"Doggone, hadn't heard that. Mabel, git out here and listen to what this German fellar is sayin.' Mabel, git on out here."

Mabel Nance emerged drying her hands. Her stout shoulders, graying strands and sad brow told Carl he was looking at an enduring frontier woman, unafraid of the future but the pain of the past would never leave.

"Mama, this here is Mr. Carl from the New Altmann colony of Germans. He says that the Covingtons has disappeared. Mr. Carl, are you thinkin' it was Indins that done this?"

Mrs. Nance said, "Just shut up a minute, Gene, and let me speak to the man. How'd do, Mr. Carl. Did Gene git your name right? He seldom does."

"Carl von Altmann, Madam. It's my pleasure." He bowed slightly.

"Mr. von Altmann, do you think the Covingtons was killed or

222

just moved away?"

"I believe they were murdered by savages. There was too much to move, and nothing had been moved. I had hoped you could tell me something. Has the word of their disappearance not reached you? It happened as much as a year ago."

Mabel Nance's face cast downward, and more sadness entered the lines around her eyes. "Folks that live out like we do don't get much chance to visit. Too much work to do. I sure thought the world of young June. Oh, I pray to God…"

She turned and ran back into her house as though running back into her own sad past.

Carl thought how right Meusebach was. The Texans are such an independent lot they didn't even know for a year when a whole family of neighbors has been wiped out.

Carl continued the conversation with Gene Nance, asking if Indians came around. They did. Most were friendly. A band came through recently asking if warring Indians had been in the area in the last year.

*Probably Meusebach's men*, Carl thought.

Warriors had ridden through and Nance wasn't able to identify them. Carl asked if he knew anything of Covington's kin before he came to Texas. Tennessee. Carl asked if Nance was acquainted with Curly Monfort on the Guadalupe. The two had fought Indians with Hays on the upper Colorado and Brazos some years back.

When the visitors showed signs of departure, Nance asked if they were going after the Indians that killed the Covingtons. He would get a bedroll, and a grub sack, and go with them.

Carl said, "That time will come. When it does, we'll seek your assistance. Right now, I want to see your friend, Monfort."

"Aw. Mr. All Man, I don't know as how ye ought to go over there. Old Curly's got a lot of rage in 'eem. Don't like outsiders comin' into Texas. Might not take kindly to Germans. Not that I have anythang agin ye, ye understand."

Carl felt disgust. He was out to avenge the death of a Texas family, and he was likely to be attacked by the one man who could help him, a Texan, a friend of Covington. He said, as they turned their mounts, "I'll take your words under advisement, Mr. Nance.

Thank you for your help."

In camp, the team talked about the strange conversation. They had encountered little evidence of resentment or prejudice against Germans among the native Texans, although they knew it existed. Most Texans accepted the Germans as an amusing curiosity with their strange dress and speech. Others welcomed them with open arms as a means of settling the wild frontier. The state, and previously, the republic, had encouraged their immigration for just that reason. Still there were those with the Anglo arrogance who thought they were superior to all other life forms. And there was always a core of first-arrivals who believed no one else had a right to come. They didn't know which category Curly Monfort fell into. They would find out.

Expecting to find a man Nance's age, they hailed the tumble-down ranch house. A woman the age of June Covington, about twenty-five, emerged.

"Good day, Miss Monfort. Would your father be home at this hour?"

"Mrs. Monfort to you, Mister. No, my husband is not home. He works for a living. If you'd like to get off them fancy horses and cut some wood, I'll fix you something to eat while you wait. Course, if you're afraid of work, you can just sit there 'til he gets in about dark. Take your choice."

Carl expected some form of coolness although not from a woman. He turned to his company and said in German, "If anything, Germans are good neighbors. Let's fall from our horses and cut this woman enough wood to last through winter. Then, we'll repair those fence rails, and patch her roof. By the time her husband gets home, he won't recognize the place, he has let it lapse into such a state. We'll shame her with kindness."

When the third and fourth cords of wood were deposited atop the armload that had lain under the kitchen window when they started, they could see Mrs. Monfort's eyes peering out in astonishment. They found a second, dull ax without a handle, whittled one from oak, located a file, and laid in another cord. Then they cut a dozen trees and split them into fence rails. While

224

four men mended the fence, Carl, Schmitt, von Schoener and Gossett, felled a Cypress from the river bottom and shaved it into shingles. They attacked the roof.

The aroma of meat and bread cooking in the small house became incentive to finish the chores. Near sundown, Mrs. Monfort shot from the house without a word and ran down the faint road toward nothing. Then Carl realized she had spotted a rider approaching. Carl checked his revolver for proper loads. The others followed suit. He ordered them to put the weapons away before the rider drew close.

Curly Monfort rode slowly toward the house, his wife walked alongside. Across his saddle, he held a rifle, standard fare in this country. He bent forward in the saddle straining to see the visitors against the setting sun in his face. A broad hat hid the detail of his features. But Carl could see that he was tall and slender, similar in build to Isaack Covington – not nearly as handsome. The same could be said of their respective wives.

Carl told the men to hold under the live oak while he approached Monfort.

Before Carl could speak, Monfort said, "My wife says a bunch o' lazy square heads chopped some wood."

"How do you do, Mr. Monfort, I'm Carl von Altmann of Altmann County, newest county in Texas." Carl approached extending his hand.

Monfort didn't extend his. "She had you figgered right. Krauts. Fer frum your own kind, ain't ye? Germans generally afraid to go off by theirselves."

"I beg your pardon, Mr. Monfort? I missed the descriptive and colorful word you used."

"Square heads! Krauts! Ya'll deaf, too? I guess you cain't understand English too good."

Carl fought every instinct to prevent an instantaneous, head on challenge. Roth could call him any name. Schmitt could label him insane. But this ignorant Texan who hardly knew the English language himself was insulting the men who had done his chores for him, supplied his wife with her needs, protected her from the weather, made it possible for him to keep livestock. And it was the

225

'krauts' who were lazy, cowardly, and the Texans who would work?

"I know a few lazy Germans. Do you know any lazy Texans who leave their wives without firewood? We built you a new ax, cleaned your old one." Then his rage would hold no longer. "If you care to step off your horse, Mr. Monfort, I'll be happy to clean your plow."

"Talk's cheap when ye got seven men to back you up, kraut."

Monfort's wife interrupted. "Curly, I told you they are nice men. I met you out there to keep you from pullin' some stunt like this. Now, stop it! Stop it!"

Monfort sat starring for a long moment. "Aw, I'm jest havin' a little fun." He leaned back in the saddle. "Surely, you been called a kraut before. Like callin' a Englishman a limey. No harm done." He laughed nervously.

"I've been called that and worse names. But not by strangers. And none of the men with me have ever been termed lazy or cowardly. You'll retract those words or your eyes will be too swollen to see your dinner."

Mrs. Monfort burst into sobs. "For God's sake, Curly! See, see what you done. Now, you're gonna have to take a whoopin', and it's fittin'."

"I don't believe that slick lookin' kraut could take me in a fair fight. But I'll take back what I said about lazy, if it'll make you feel any better."

Mrs. Monfort added, "Go ahead and whoop 'eem, Mr. Altmann. He don't mean it about takin' back his words."

"Oh, good gosh, Idabel! I mean it as good as I know how! Whose side you on, anyhow?" Then Monfort added, "Did you say Altmann? Are you the German prince that brought that colony across the country and built a castle and a dam?"

Carl said, "It was lazy, cowardly Germans who did those things. But, yes, I'm their leader. Allow me to introduce my party."

Monfort hoisted his right leg over the front of the saddle and handed the rifle to his wife. He extended his hand. "I *am* sorry for sayin' them thangs, Altmann. I'm jest a little suspicious of foreigners movin' in to take over Texas, that's all."

"I will try to convince you that we're not all bad. These men are Doctors Schmitt and Hagerdorn. This is Gossett who held off an Indian attack on our overland voyage. These men in uniform fought bravely by my side in the old country – Wilhelm, Ernst, and Arnold. This is my young brother-in-law, Baron von Schoener. He learned the English language in six months."

Monfort's blue eyes glanced back and forth, a sense of awe came over his face, sensing the magnitude of their credentials. "And...and you...you rode all the way out here to see me?"

"Yes, you may hold the key to a mystery. A fine Texas family has been massacred by savages. Did you know the Covingtons near Cibolo Creek?"

Idabel Monfort's face streamed tears. "Oh, no! Oh, no. Did any of 'em get away? Did June get out? Where is she? What about the baby? Oh, God..." She doubled over not waiting for answers.

"The entire family vanished. Blood was the only trace. It couldn't be tracked in the winter. No one has been able to help us yet. What can you tell us?"

Monfort said, "Le's move to the house. Idabel's got some good grub fixed." He waved his arm toward the door. "Ike was supposed to be here over a year ago drivin' a few hunnerd head of beeves to me. When he didn't show up, I figgered he changed his mind about sellin' to me on credit. Made me mad, so I didn't go lookin' for 'eem. Now, I wished I had."

As they pulled a homemade bench to the table, Carl said, "Von Schoener and I went there in the winter. We found the situation. It appeared to us that it could have happened as early as the spring before. Like you, I regret not calling on my friend, Isaack, sooner. He was a great hero to the colony of New Altmann. We have friendly Indians making inquiries among the tribes as to who was in the area at that time. I'm not sure I have the patience to wait for their conclusions."

Monfort said, "Hate to say it, Altmann, but I have to disagree with you. Ain't no such thang as a friendly Indian. I know you Germans got some so-called treaties with 'em, but that don't help us white folks, us Texans, any."

"I have had the same discussion with John Meusebach, the architect of the treaties," Carl explained. "Doctor Hagerdorn was his interpreter on the San Saba. Several of us were there."

"Took a lot o' grit what Meusebach did. I'll say that. If you was there, I guess I better re-thank what I said about bein' able to whoop ye."

Carl took careful notes on all that Monfort could tell him about roaming Indians in the area, their directions, their numbers, their tribes, during the period in question. The company camped under the live oaks, prepared to leave when morning came.

Idabel Monfort scurried from the house and asked for the doctors. Schmitt and Hagerdorn walked back to the house with her.

As the troop rode away, Carl said to von Schoener and Schmitt, who were in earshot, "I believe we created some goodwill with these obstinate Texans, though they were no help. I dread to think we'll have such a confrontation with each new native we meet."

Schmitt said, "We may have created more goodwill than you imagine, Herr Carl. Not from your threats of violence, but by the good medicine administered by Hagerdorn and me."

Carl said, "Schmitt, my tactics worked. And what healing miracle did you perform in ten minutes?"

"I don't speak to outsiders of the private medical conditions of my patients, Carl. You know that."

"I'm only asking in the interest of public relations. And where do you get that I'm an outsider?"

"If you must know, Frau Monfort had a private, intensely private, infectious condition. I believe the medication we provided will cure her, and she will be able to conceive a child, if she isn't too stubborn to use it."

"Who would want a child by the likes of Curly Monfort? Heaven forbid."

"Carl, a child changed even you. When we meet the Monforts again, if she is with child, you'll see a change in him. Never again will he call you a square-headed kraut, although you are one."

"I'll surely get you for that, Schmitt. You should sweat day and night in terror of my revenge."

By letter, courier, or in person, Carl pestered Meusebach every week for news from the Indian inquiries. Meusebach advised patience. Indian ways are different, he preached. Carl got a crew of stonemasons working on the castle again. He attended the christening of his infant son by Reverend Clemens. As winter approached, Carl and Maria turned full attention to the impending birth of their second child. He resolved to quit brooding but knew that after the baby was born, he would wait no longer. He would pierce the wilderness with his forces, and personally seek out Fleetaumountec.

Friedericke Anna von Altmann was born on February 1, 1851. Greeters said she was the image of her beautiful mother. Greta was delirious with relief.

# Chapter 23

Greta sat before her mirror, the one handed down by Carl after he bought himself and Maria new ones. When it had been offered six years earlier, she immediately suspected Carl's motives. He brought her gifts occasionally but he either made a sarcastic remark, or one she took as sarcasm, when he handed it to her, or he said nothing. Even if his gesture seemed kind, she knew he was trying to make up for some bizarre slight he had already inflicted. He gave her the mirror because, he said, it gave him a squat appearance which he always hated. "But you, fair Greta, look superb in it."

She even thanked him without adding, "And what have you done that you need penance?"

Her face did take on width. Her narrow lips took on broadness. And her nose looked less skinny. She used the mirror every day for grooming. She brushed out her hip length ashen hair and carefully reset the braids which would flow forward over her shoulders. It was those braids, she thought, that Fleetaumountec had seen when he offered to trade Carl horses for her. The Comanche chief wore his black hair in a primitively similar fashion. She regretted, ever so slightly, that she had revealed her inner glee to the others over the offer. But, she had feeling! She was a woman after all. *Well, no one in Texas knows my age, and I'm not about to tell them now."*

Greta believed she had an ageless appearance about her flawless skin. Only when she smiled did fine lines appear around her eyes. So she tried not to smile so often. And if remaining slender helped preserve a youthful appearance, she had certainly done that. As she rose from the dressing stool she marveled that Carl had given her the *good* mirror. A thought had been occurring to her for a year. She wanted to visit the old country, see her relatives, tell tales of the west, and tell them of the chief's offer. And she studied inviting Maria and the children to go along. Maria still had cousins, uncles and aunts and she wrote to them all the time. The children needed to see Southern Bavaria and old Altmann before industrial changes swept the past away. Greta worshipped young Mathias, now five, and his little sister, Anna, four, continuing in pleasure that they didn't resemble Carl.

In Maria's dressing room the young mother finished penning a letter to her aunt. As always, she said a prayer over the envelope that it would get through. Carl told her that if the mail reached the coast where it would board a ship, it usually got to the addressee overseas. But coach mail to the coast got raided, robbed, burned, rained out, drowned or broken down, enroute about every third try, it seemed to him. Maria's stories of Texas and the children had been written before, at length, only to never get a reply, thus she didn't know if they reached her family there. She, too, had begun longing for a visit to the old home.

Other than distant cousins of royalty, such as Prince Carl von Solm-Braunfels and Prince Streib, both of whom he despised, the only relative Carl had in the provinces was his despicable brother, Julius. He wouldn't cross a cobblestone Texas street to see that man. But Carl still owned property in Southern Bavaria which he wanted to sell, and he thought he could pick up some credits, or cash, from the committeemen who remained there when the colony emigrated. He would travel alone, trusting his friends, such as Schmitt, and, of course, Greta, to look after Maria's needs as well as the children.

Carl regretted the lack of progress in locating Fleetaumountec and meting out just punishment for the slaughter of the Covington family. His expanded militia ventured far into the western wilderness twice but without results. He felt a tinge of shame that his castle wasn't operational. Ranching duties in the hills, building his herds and expanding his land claims had milked time and money. He reviewed his decision to run for the office of judge of

Altmann County, knowing that the duties had consumed what remained of his time. But having handed Lutz a defeat in the polls of 447 votes to Lutz' 88 had been gratifying. It proved he was still a prince. But it also cost him more than the salary paid; and personal time was all but nonexistent anymore. Anyway, he would show his magnanimity by appointing Lutz as acting judge while he traveled to old Altmann, in Southern Bavaria. Traveling light and alone, he could return in a hundred days.

He left his house that morning to give final instructions to Engineer Fuessel on the second floor construction work at the castle. He glanced into the yard where Maria had lived for most of a year before they married. He shook his head when a dozen black, white, and black-white spotted goats of all sizes rounded the house where Greta still lived. Slightly to their lead was Frauka, their mother, Maria's first pet when she came to the new world. *Another reason Maria should not go. She would miss the damned goats more than she'll miss me. Of course, I'll miss Mathias and Anna.*


When Carl, Maria, Mathias, Anna and Greta boarded the ship at Indian Point, Carl held Anna in his arms as they walked the gangplank. Afoot, she had screamed to return home to Frauka for fear of the lapping waves. But in her father's arms she looked down at the water and said, "Will we see snow in Southern Bavaria?"

"On the high mountains, my darling," Carl assured her.

She said, "I was born in Texas but you were born in Southern Bavaria. Will I get to meet my grandfather?"

Maria answered the question. "Anna, I've already told you, your grandfather has gone to be with Jesus."

Mathias addressed his father as they neared their cabin. "I want to meet Uncle Julius. He's a prince, like you used to be, Father."

Carl bristled. He had already told the boy that they wouldn't be meeting Julius, and he had never referred to Julius as *prince* or *uncle*. "Where, does he get the *uncle* title, Maria? Have you been filling the boy's head with notions?"

"I've told him everything of the old country. Sometimes he asks questions. Other times, he seems uninterested. Carl, you *do* intend to seek audience with Julius, don't you? When we were baptized by Reverend Clemens, you seemed sincere in trying to exercise all Christian virtues. Even forgiveness." Maria set her valise inside the cabin.

"If Julius had earnestly implored me to write to him or to visit him, I would have considered it. But I've heard no word from him since I left Altmann ten years ago. I owe him nothing." *Except a saber lash.*

As Carl lowered the heavier grips, Maria said, "I'll say no more about it. But you heard your son. For him, and for the sake of your soul, Carl, think about it while we're there."

Carl hoped there was a heaven because, the day before sailing, he had directed the setting of a Texas pink granite monument at the grave of Helga, his wife who had died just before the initial immigrants landed at Indian Point. He believed Helga deserved heaven if any person on earth ever deserved it. *Well, of course, Maria deserves heaven…and Mathias…and Anna.* Though his heart had waxed heavy after the massive stone was set, now, as he thought of those who should go to heaven, he chuckled silently that he had excluded himself and Greta.

The voyage would take over a month with brief landings at New Orleans, then New York. The travelers took turns at sea sickness, little Anna suffering the most. The ship entered the English Channel without docking on the English coast. Although the travelers could have used a break, they were anxious to harbor at Bremen on the Weser River inside the German state of Hanover. They would take the first train to get them within striking distance of Altmann village in Southern Bavaria, old home to the adults.

Aboard the steam locomotive, Mathias noticed and commented that the grass was greener in Hanover, the trees taller, and the air cooler.

Carl asked him, "Would you like to live here?"

Mathias said, "Could you be county judge here?"

Carl replied, "No. Officials are not elected exactly as they are in Texas."

Mathias watched the hills roll away as the train moved south. He said in English, "Aw, I think I like Texas best."

Carl took pleasure that his son's schooling successfully taught him English as he grew. He also found pride in the boy's intelligence. *Why is being elected county judge more important to him than the idea that I was a prince? Hmm, even if I don't agree with his logic, he shows obvious brilliance, like his father.*

He turned to Maria, "Did you hear the lad, dear? Was that not an ingenious answer?"

Maria stopped her needlepoint and formed a sarcastic smile. "Like his father."

"All right, Maria, I don't deny that you're an intelligent woman, and your people were bright, also. The children get good brains from both sides...and good looks."

Little Anna heard the last remark and chirped, "I look like my mother!"

"You are correct, fraulein," Greta put in.

At Munich, Carl rented a carriage pulled by two sleek bays. He knew many along the rail and horse route none of whom he cared for enough to stop and visit. None with a measure of wealth with which they would depart. He knew the carriage ride would take days, he was in a hurry, and his family was tired. He cursed silently in frustration that his principality was removed farther from a seaport than almost any of the Germanic lands.

Letters had gone out ahead to the homebound committeemen, all of whom would welcome him: Eisenlohr, Kloss, and Trenckmann, and especially Jacob Beigel who seemed most open to further financial assistance, though he had seen no profit on his earlier investment. Carl had kept the lines of communication alive to all, made small payments along the way, and always urged them that if other businessmen would join, the Society of Altmann Immigrants would show a return sooner.

When the carriage rolled into the village of Altmann, Carl wore his military uniform without the usual feathered helmet, which he feared was out of date, even in the old country. Also missing was his sword, but his coat held every ribbon and medal collected in a dozen conflicts and ceremonies. The American revolving pistol was placed out of sight under the seat. He entered the Altmann Inn, once owned by his father.

The clerk turned the register back to himself, looked up and shouted, "Prince Carl! It is really you."

Ten years had passed and Carl didn't recognize the young man, and before he could speak in return, a hum of voices began in the lobby. People moved toward the counter. The press of a dozen bodies prevented him from exiting to retrieve his family in the carriage, but the princely acknowledgments were too gratifying to ignore. After fifteen minutes of handshakes and smiles, Maria, Greta, and the children entered, disgustedly, through the door. Carl spotted them and called them close.

A man said, "Baroness Maria! You are so lovely. Your children?" Hands reached down to greet Mathias and Anna. A female voice said, "No, it is Princess Maria. They will reclaim the principality. It will be like the old days."

Questions and statements poured from every mouth overrunning each other. At last Carl called order by waving his hands above his head. "Fellow Altmanners, may I please speak?"

The peel of his piercing voice hushed the lobby. They waited, grinning. Some wept.

"The baroness…princess, if you please, our children, and I have come for a visit on business to Altmann. We will see all our friends as time permits. But our home is Texas in North America. I trust that all is well in this principality under the able leadership of my former…my brother, Julius…"

"No, all is not well, Prince Carl. We want you back," came a male voice from the crowd. "He taxes without fairness, and he acts as a coward in the council. His toad of a wife rules Altmann. Please, come back to us."

Carl had no desire to seek details with this largely working class group. He would learn from the committeemen. "I'll provide the newspaper with a summary of our activities. I'll tell tales of the New World, its people and its commerce. Thank you for your kind words tonight. And now my family needs rest."

The throng would not be easily dismissed, but when the *royal* family turned to disappear at the top of the staircase, the respectful crowd didn't pursue or continue their noise.

The meeting had been bittersweet for Carl. As sitting prince, he could have never been so popular. How he wished he could. He would have never left. As the director of the Society of Altmann Immigrants, and as county judge of Altmann County in Texas, he knew he had the admiration, the respect, of the people – the polls proved it – but the public never expressed it so worshipfully.

Committeeman Jacob Beigel and wife, Sophie, had purchased Carl's fine home in the shadow of the alpine peak. It stood in readiness to receive its prior owner the following morning as Beigel led Carl's carriage with his family through the brick streets. Beigel's children were grown, married, and had children older than Mathias and Anna. The women planned a party to welcome the visiting American-Altmann children. Carl thought, *Good, that rids me of the need for childish chit-chat with women and children while Jacob and I get down to business.*

But Beigel wasn't so anxious to talk business. He fussed endlessly over Carl's comforts. Carl found himself put off by all the pomp, the stuff that regal provincial life was made of when he lived here. Now, a Texas impatience beset him. Never mind the view of the lake versus the mountain, never mind the correct wine, never mind the comfort of his chair. Finally, Beigel seated himself seeming ready for a briefing on society ventures to date, excited of the future.

Carl's patience had all but terminated when his friend said, "Herr Carl, may I delay society business a bit further while you update my knowledge of the great troubles that beset the United States of America. We read of it constantly in our newspapers. Will that great nation burst forth in war as the European writers suggest? If not, what will be the outcome of the agony?"

Carl's blankness of stare must have disturbed Beigel. He continued, "Slavery, Herr Carl. For all we read of the issue here, surely, your mind must be surging with worry over the eventual consequences in that land. The news there must carry nothing else."

"Yes, there is talk. And, yes, there is news." Carl adjusted his

236

seating. *Damn, the man knows more than I on the subject.* He crossed his legs. "What...what do you read here, Herr Jacob? I would be interested to know of reports here. I could learn from it. Almost everything one reads in American newspapers on the subject carries a bias of one sort or the other.

"Our newspapers carry complete transcripts of the debates in Congress as well as long commentaries from high officials in both the Southern and Northern states. One can easily discern the biases." Beigel's stare was intense. "The authors try not at all to hide them. But what troubles me, and I want your view, is whether war will come, and when. Which side will you take, Herr Carl?"

"I have always opposed slavery. You know that, Herr Jacob." Carl rebuked himself for being so poorly read on the subject, though he had heard rumblings on every hand in Texas. He hoped his answer would satisfy Beigel.

"But, Carl, you speak so warmly of your adopted state of Texas. It is a slave holding state, is it not? How could you fight against slavery there?"

"Slavery in modern times is an institution peculiar only to the Americans. It is one American oddity I have not adopted, one way or the other. I would remain neutral politically while maintaining my personal conviction."

Beigel packed his pipe. "My readings tell me that would be most difficult to do. Each side will carefully ferret out the views of citizens, demanding loyalty to the region where you live, seeking out its best military men for the war. And, Carl, do not withhold from me, your true German friend. I know too well you have never remained politically neutral in such a conflict. And your military skills could be in great demand." Beigel narrowed his eyebrows. "And another thing. You speak of conviction as though religion would play a part in your stance. I know better than that." He laughed.

"Herr Jacob, could we move on to business and economics. I don't believe the Americans will go to war against each other. They have life too good to throw it away. I'm living proof. And for your information, I joined Maria in vows to the Lutheran faith. I am a changed man."

"Right, Carl. I regret troubling you. Business at hand. Tell me of your successes, your failures. What do you want me to do with your remaining properties here? We have but an hour before that roaring lion, Eisenlohr, arrives. Only your lungs could put him down."

"Business! My favorite subject. Now, Jacob, you will forgive me if I go lightly on the failures. I was never proficient at explaining such." Carl wanted to bring levity back to the talk. He would struggle to forget what had been said more that Beigel.

Carl asked Beigel to sell his meadow lands and the two water powered mills – flour and lumber – and their surrounding acreage. He told Beigel that the Altmann colony was producing leather goods, heavy carriages, cloth, ginned cotton, beef, cottonseed oil, corn and building stone. Soon they would have capacity to export wine and iron tools. They could use more labor and he would welcome further immigration from those who could pay their own way. Additional funding would accelerate expansion of the iron forge. He believed they could enter firearms manufacture in another year, a solid source of revenue for repaying debt.

Beigel commented that firearms manufacture would be a welcome enterprise if war broke out, then apologized for saying it. Carl pretended he hadn't heard and continued his accolades of Texas, the reasons why Beigel should invest further.

Eisenlohr's rasping screams irritated Carl. Maybe because he could reach volumes equal to Carl, but more because Carl didn't like to talk of war in America, a subject in which he was too ignorant. As each committeeman arrived they wouldn't start the business conversation until they had asked Carl's view on the growing turmoil. For subsequent visitors, he contrived a response. "I assure you, the talk of war will subside in America. You are far more interested in it than Americans. Americans have life too sweet to let it slip away." That response not only squelched further questions but emphasized Carl's confidence in the economy of Texas, and, he hoped, loosened the purse strings of would-be investors.

At the grand festival given the visitors by the Biegels, Carl met young Wolfgang Kloss, twenty-one year old son of the home committeeman. The bright young man was university educated as an engineer, a good listener, and showed astounding interest and knowledge of America. In appearance, he reminded Carl of himself thirty years ago.

Carl turned abruptly to Maria. "Darling, I want Elisabeth to meet young Wolfgang."

Maria asked, "Is Wolfgang going home with us?"

Only then did it come back to Carl. They hadn't brought Elisabeth with them because she was again infatuated with that Texas ragamuffin, Smathers. Maria had even made the mistake of suggesting that the pair would likely be engaged when they returned to Texas. He had ranted so violently, both to Maria and Elisabeth, that Maria didn't dare bring up the subject again. And Elisabeth had, more or less, made a promise that she wouldn't accept an offer of marriage without her father's blessing.

Carl didn't admit it at that moment, but he had forgotten that Elisabeth wasn't with them. He slid out of the trap by saying, "Yes, if I can persuade him."

The reception included guests of all rank of society. In earlier days, Carl wouldn't have thought of inviting commoners. Now, he understood the value of the craftsmen – tanners, weavers, shoemakers, millers, stonemasons, even the unemployed who truly sought work. Beigel and the other committeemen commented glowingly of the obvious effort the peasants made to clean and dress decently for the occasion. They also expressed delight at the commoners' faces from the music, the dance, the food. Carl watched, grinning, with Texas-gained knowledge that the destitute have more fun than the opulent.

In addition to the continued questions about turmoil in America, guests asked if Carl would reclaim his principality. Others asked simply if he had visited, or would visit, Julius during this time. Carl didn't give direct answers but made clear that he had no respect for the reigning prince, or his *toad of a wife*.

The next day, Carl noticed processions of mounted castle guards following his carriage from place to place, always at a distance. Once, the guard entered from a side street and met him face on. Their captain pulled up quickly, looking slightly embarrassed, spurred his platoon to the right and sped away. A day later, a letter came to the Beigel house addressed to Carl. Below the Altmann family crest, the paper read:

*Prince Julius Christian von Altmann*
*Supreme Ruler of the Principality of Altmann*
*Of Southern Bavaria*

*Requests of:*
*Carl Franz von Altmann of Texas*

*An explanation for your presence in the Principality of Altmann, and a statement of your intentions toward actions regarding prior claims to heirship in this principality.*

*Your reply should be made by express mail.*

Carl showed the letter to Beigel and swore he wouldn't dignify his estranged brother by giving a reply. Beigel said he would send a courier, Philip, to the castle and find out why Julius was concerned. It took another day to get inside the castle, but when Philip returned he reported that Julius lay seriously ill. And without saying so, Julius' attendant caused Philip to believe that Julius was in fear for his life because of Carl's return.

"What illness?" Carl asked.

"He wouldn't say, Herr Carl. I tried several ways to get further information. I think Lucille had forbidden the man to speak openly."

"Did you see Lucille? Is she as rotund as I've heard?"

"I'm positive she was in the next room monitoring the conversation but she didn't show herself. Be assured, Herr Carl, that Lucille is in robust good health. Altmanners see her in the royal carriage often. God help the small fur bearing animal population whose numbers now cover her hide."

"I still have no intention of responding to his, or Lucille's, ridiculous inquisition. Let them sweat," Carl said, raising a finger.

"If you learn the nature of the illness, I would like to know."

The next day, for the first time since they arrived, Carl left Maria in the Beigel house at dusk to negotiate with Beigel's purchaser of the meadows. Half a kilometer from the house, four castle guards appeared, mounted, facing his carriage. He pulled the horses to a stop inches from the nervous breaths of the guards' animals, testing whether they would give way. They didn't. Carl's right hand reached across his waist for his sword. *Silly.* He bent and felt for the pistol under the seat. *Back at the house.* As he started to speak he heard more horses thundering from the rear, closing.

# *Chapter 24*

Carl shouted at the top of his lungs, "Move out of my way. Do you know whom you delay?" He stepped from the carriage holding his arms crouched about his body as though a weapon was about to emerge.

The troop from behind roared to a halt, one horse skidding to its rump on the cobblestones. Carl refused to look back.

"I know full well whom I have detained, Prince Carl. You have long held my respect. I am Captain Ludwig Kroesche. I once fought the Slavs beside you."

Carl appreciated the respect, remembered the name. "And why do you detain me now?"

"Prince Julius wishes a response to the query he sent. You received it?"

"I received it and I chose not to answer it."

Kroesche spaced his words, "Prince Carl, in all respect, would you give me a verbal answer I can carry back to the prince?"

"I will not." Carl dropped his crouch, revealing no weapons. "The coward can live with his fear. He brought it on himself years ago. I have no respect for him. I remember you as a brave warrior. You should understand what I'm saying."

Kroesche sat easily in the saddle. "I take your statement to mean you have no designs on regaining the principality."

"Don't be so sure. I have found wide support among the people for my return, and with just cause."

"Prince Carl, you make my duties most difficult." Kroesche steadied his mount. "There are others who wish to know your answer. Also, you should know, Prince Julius is dying. He wants to see you, but he dared not to ask."

*Others.* "Lucille, no doubt. You do your past an injustice in serving a craven dictator." He felt, more than heard, the dismounted men approaching from behind.

Kroesche stepped down as did his men to the fore. He said, "I respect you, Prince Carl. And, like you, I respect loyalty. I act under orders. I am loyal to Altmann. Can you say the same?"

The question enraged Carl, the idea that he was disloyal to Altmann, repugnant. "As *your* captain, I apparently didn't teach you enough lessons about loyalty. Drop your weapon and I'll graduate you from the course!"

The struggle was brief. A strong arm from behind encircled Carl's neck. Two men clawed for his arms. He broke free briefly but the beefy arm again tightened about his throat. Down was the only direction he could go. Light of day disappeared.

The guard used Carl's own carriage to transport him to the castle. Kroesche sat on one side of him, and the attacker from the rear, the one with the *arms*, sat on his right.

Kroeche said, "Prince Carl, you will never lose my respect, no matter how hard you try. Your honor is fully intact because you refuse the inquiry. You will see Prince Julius because your arrest forces it. No other reason."

Carl's labored breathing from the strangle-hold on his throat subsided. He knew, without weapon, it was useless to fight. Was he afraid to see Julius? *Hell, no! God, how the Texans have influenced my speech, even my thoughts.*

When they reached the castle, Kroesche eased his tight proximity, seemingly convinced that Carl wouldn't resist further. He allowed Carl to walk freely through the door and into the chambers. Down a hallway and into the old office where he had often talked with his kind and loving father, he was escorted on both sides. He expected to see Julius seated behind the carved mahogany desk.

Lucille!

Masked behind the layer of flesh that had accumulated over ten years, was still the beauty that had seduced his simple brother. Her face, her skin, her black hair, her hard black eyes still held an enchantment that he could understand. He controlled the impulse to rage against her. As a princess in a chair behind a desk, she appeared proper. As a wife in bed, *I pity Julius.*

"Carl, thank you for coming. I trust you have no motive for attacking me as you have in times past." Her lips formed an insincere smile.

"Frau Lucille, I left Altmann of my own accord. I don't come back after ten years to attack you. If you will recall, you attacked me first. But never mind that. Why do you call me here?" He avoided the word *arrest.*

"Julius is frightened. He believed you would never return. His loan of money, you will recall, specified that you wouldn't. You owe him an explanation. He has not tried to collect." Then Carl perceived, not sure, that a tear appeared at the corner of one eye. "He loves you, Carl. He has never stopped loving you. You are everything he ever wanted to be. If you would not come to him, he would die in sorrow. He would never force the meeting. But I would. I would!" She stopped abruptly and daubed the one eye.

Carl saw her scheme for extracting pity. He said, simply, "So, what now?"

"Will you see him?"

In his wildest dream he would not have expected a gush of sorrow from within as Kroesche's ignored words came back. His brother was dying. He had to let it subside before he could answer.

"Of course, Lucille, of course. I'll see him. Is he awake at this hour?"

"Good! I dreaded to have you dragged before him resisting armed guards. Come with me."

Carl entered the upper bed chamber behind his rotund sister-in-law. Lamps were lit though Julius appeared to sleep. Lucille spoke firmly, "Julius, your brother is here to see you. Julius!"

The blonde head rolled from left to right on an elevated pillow. Then Carl saw it! He hated it. His son, Mathias, resembled Julius more than he did Carl. He should have never returned to Altmann.

Julius pushed himself upward and asked, "Who?"

"Your brother, Carl. You wanted to see him. I brought him. Can you speak with him?"

"My broth… by brother? Carl, is it you? Is it really you?" Then fear seemed to consume his otherwise gaunt expression. He shot upright. "Lucille, does he mean to harm us?"

"I think not, Julius." Her voice sunk in disgust. "He came of his own accord."

Julius reached out his hands. Carl took them, surprising himself. "Brother, they told me you're sick. You look the picture of health. Surely, a small swamp fever cannot fell a prince." Carl couldn't believe the comforting lie he told to one he despised so deeply. But a compelling pity took hold, a family loyalty, even a love, that he had long forgotten existed. He saw his own son in that pallid face, and sensed the sorrow he would know should that son ever fall ill.

Julius spoke. "You have a family. A beautiful family. Something I will never have." He glanced at Lucille who looked away. "I read of you in our own papers. Now, I hear first hand, that your wife and children are as lovely as all the written descriptions which come from America. I must see them, Carl. I must see them. Would you grant me that last wish? Carl?"

Carl was willing to see his brother, once he entered the castle. He had no desire to involve Maria and the children. But his lips said, "If you will trust your brother to bring them here, without threat of arrest, and if you will quit speaking of last wishes, I will bring them."

In wilting voice, Julius said, "Please, Carl. Please, Carl. Lucille, leave him alone. He is a man of his word."

When Carl entered his bedroom at Beigel's hours later, Maria sat up in bed. The children were long asleep. She asked, "Has the popular ex-prince found such pleasure in his old home that he can't come to bed with his wife? Please explain."

"Maria, there's no pleasure in what I've done."

"Is that not the statement of every philandering husband in the world? I've seen the women of Altmann look at you and shed tears for your return." Her voice broke. "I want to go home to Texas, and reclaim what is rightfully mine. My husband."

"Oh, good Lord, Maria!" he scolded. "The only woman I've

seen is Lucille. I stood in pity of my poor brother thinking of… Darling, tomorrow, we'll go to the castle and visit Julius. You've won the argument."

She smiled, melting Carl. "What persuaded you to relent?"

"The strong arm of a professional wrestler."

By appointment arranged through Beigel, Carl's carriage pulled up to the old Altmann castle entrance at precisely three o'clock. Ludwig Kroesche stepped from the archway, bowed deeply and extended his hands to Maria. She smiled brilliantly as her light frame bounced to the ground. She turned to lower her children, but Kroesche stepped ahead of her with, "Allow me, Baroness," and missed Mathias' hand as the lad leaped the distance. Anna allowed him to hold one hand as she poured from the carriage before Carl could round the vehicle to help.

Kroesche extended his hand to Carl who took it. Carl spoke to Kroesche and joked lightly that the guard from the night before wasn't present. Kroesche chuckled and apologized for the arrest. He invited Carl and family to proceed to the door. As they did so, Carl sensed Kroesche's eyes from behind surveying his attractive family, especially his wife.

He leaned toward Maria. "I must say, your suitor today is more attractive than mine last evening. May I compliment the smile you paid him?"

"Hush, Carl. Children, remember what you've been told of manners."

The young ones looked up with serious expressions. Anna said, "Father, does Uncle Julius look like you?" Mathias appeared to have a lump in his throat.

As the huge wooden doors swung open, Carl expected old Gustav to appear, regretting that he had not thought, or asked, of him the night before. Instead, a formally dressed butler, about Carl's age, distinguished gray hair and sad, sincere eyes greeted the family. The man curtsied before Maria, speaking softly. He bowed to Carl and extended his hand while still slightly bend. "Prince Carl, welcome home. I shall strive to make your visit comfortable."

The butler introduced himself as Louis Mann, successor to Gustav who was buried with dignity in the Altmann plot near Prince Christian.

Lucille entered the receiving chamber, managing a smile, though Carl and Maria could easily detect nervousness. She extended both hands to Maria who responded, each bending a knee in formal greeting.

She turned her attention to Mathias with a gasp. "The lad! The lad bears a strong family resemblance...to...his father." She glanced at Anna as though she would continue, then straightened. "The prince will see you in his chambers. If you will follow me."

Throughout the introduction, Carl remained silent, hoping that his face revealed only neutrality. Nostalgia had hit him hard when he learned of Gustav's death, although he should have known. He followed behind Lucille, Mathias, Anna and Maria.

Julius was seated in old Prince Christian's ornate chair, padded under and about with gleaming satin pillows. Daylight made it possible now to see the extent that the illness had wasted his body. His bejeweled collar gaped open about his white neck, slightly hidden by his short blonde beard. His pale hands were skin stretched over bone, long, unsure. Ample leather armchairs formed a circle in front of Julius' chair. The old desk looked, and smelled, lonely ten feet behind.

Julius grasped the arms of his chair with both hands, tried to rise, failed, tried again and succeeded. He seemed breathless as he spoke. "Carl...Maria. And it is Johann Mathias and little Fredericke Anna, I believe." A smile broke over his slack cheeks as he dropped back to the chair and said, "Will my nephew and niece come and meet their uncle?"

The children glanced to their parents, and seeing no objection there, trotted to each side of their uncle. With tremulous hands, Julius reached to encircle their shoulders. Tears streamed immediately from his eyes as Carl and Maria drew close to one another and found hands, as natural as rain, without speaking.

Julius retrieved his voice, looked left and right at the gorgeous boy and girl, and said, "I hold you dear in my heart, though this is the first time we have met. You have wonderful parents, and you

247

are blessed of God. For that I am thankful."

Young Mathias said, "I'm glad to meet you, too, Uncle Julius. My mother has told me much about you and Aunt Lucille, and Altmann."

Julius lowered his arms back to the chair and pushed himself upward. He smiled again. "Good, my son. You should listen to your mother, and not your father in matters of Altmann."

Anna brightened. "Are you as tall as my father?"

"Yes, my child. Perhaps taller. I regret that my strength is lacking today, or I would stand before your father and show you."

Carl injected, "You seem stronger than last night, Julius. You're up and about. Do you feel better today?"

"Much better, brother. The excitement of your visit has stimulated me. Please forgive that I've ignored greeting your lovely bride. Baroness Maria, though we must have met in years past, allow me to re-introduce myself."

Maria stepped forward and extended her hands. "We need no formal introductions among family. We already know each other, Julius." When she had taken both his hands she reached, pulled his face close and kissed his wrinkled cheek. Tears coursed his face again and a subdued groan, a sob, came from deep within.

Knowing his brother was suffering great emotional pain, Carl tried to break the spell. "May we take seats, Julius, if you feel you can talk?"

Julius straightened and said, "Please do. Children, would you sit on my left and right. You give me great comfort."

Lucille took a chair aside from the circle. Carl and Maria positioned themselves directly in front of Julius. "Carl, the duties of prince have been excruciating these ten years. The peasants are poor. The land has been in various states of revolution ever since you left. Lucille says the principality is more stable now. But much of our time has been spent in the castle, virtual prisoners of the land we rule. There have been repeated threats on our lives. How often I've longed for your counsel."

Lucille stopped him. "Julius, you know I've solved every crisis. You had all the counsel you needed."

"But, Lucille, you simply don't understand the bond between

248

men…brothers."

Carl sensed an argument brewing. At other times he would have taken delight in it. Even now, he could think of clever words to put his power-stealing brother in his place.

But the old anger had gone and he joked, "But, brother, you'll recall that I emigrated half way around the world because there was not room for both of us here." He smiled.

Julius nodded. "And you've come again, successful in the new world, a beautiful family, a wife who has given you heirs. I would gladly give you back the principality for such wealth. Alas, I'll never have heirs. Altmann is lost to our family unless, unless you, or young Mathias will someday return…"

The old hate and rage burst in Lucille's voice. "That you have no heirs is your own fault, Julius. You know that!"

"I beg your pardon, frau, it was in no way my fault in the early years. It was your own inability to con…."

She raged, "And in recent years? Whose fault is it now? Can you not take responsibility for anything?"

"Lucille, I am a sick man. Must you attack me so?" His tone begged pity.

"You haven't been sick for five years. Where has that time gone?"

Carl broke into the lull after Lucille's outrage. "To suggest that I, or Mathias, could ever again come to Altmann to rule the principality is out of the question. Yes, Julius, years ago, I left here in depression. It got worse. I lost my beloved Helga, but God was kind and gave me Maria and a new family." Carl tried to lift the conversation from gloom. "Texas has become our home in ways you would never believe. I'm building a castle there, far more grand than this drab…the old one. My son has even said he loves Texas better because government officials are elected by popular vote. I serve as judge in the county our colony established. I was elected by a vast majority. There is less rainfall, but there is far less winter, too. And the wild land is unlimited. People are free there, Julius. Free. Altmanners continue to cross the Atlantic to join us. Few come back this way."

Julius placed his hand on Mathias' head. "A little Texan. If you stayed with your Uncle Julius, I would decree that you should be Prince von Altmann when I'm gone. I declare that your fair hair is that of your Uncle Julius. Your eyes, too. Oh, how I would love to have you for my son."

Mathias' furrowed brow turned to his father in fear as though Carl might give him to Julius. Carl said, "Mathias could be tempted by your offer had he been born in Altmann twenty years ago. But he is a Texan through and through. When we leave in a week he will be the first on board the steamer."

Anna asked, "Could I be princess...if we stayed?"

Lucille scowled. The question brought another gush of tears from Julius. He turned to the fair face of Maria in miniature, touched it, and said, "Of course, my child. I would love nothing more..." He sucked back a moan.

Julius changed the subject and asked about economic conditions. Carl and Maria explained the hardships and opportunities. No unemployment existed in Texas because any resourceful person could seek land to homestead or buy, eke out a living, use his family for chores, harvest wild game for food, grow enough to live on. Julius expressed interest in the slave questions as did everyone else in Altmann. He wanted to know how that system worked and where it would end.

Maria graphically illustrated the hardships of daily life for the average frontier family, the shortages that even she and Carl endured. Lucille brightened and expressed pleasure that she wasn't there. Julius inquired of Indians. Carl told him the Germans had a treaty but didn't refrain from telling him that troubles didn't disappear because of it.

When they rose to leave, Julius asked that Carl remain alone with him. Maria and the children found themselves seated in the carriage for half an hour before Carl emerged. Sure that Carl would tell her and the children everything they discussed, he waved her questions away, stating that they talked of family heirlooms. Maria's eyes said she doubted his answer. Something had happened in the old castle that Carl intended to keep secret and she wondered if she'd ever know.

# *Chapter 25*

Carl disagreed with John Meusebach that Texas sentiment was growing against European immigrants who opposed slavery, secession, and war with the North. He disagreed with everyone. Each time Schmitt, Hagerdorn, Roth, or Maria brought up the subject, he looked up the hill at the limestone dust drifting from the cutters' tools where great stones continued to raise the skyline of his castle.

"Look what Texas has permitted me to do. Never was the old country so free." The family's visit to Altmann in Southern Bavaria six years earlier remained ever fresh on his mind. How sure he'd become of the rightness of his decision to immigrate. How positive the future!

When word swept through New Braunfels, then New Altmann, that Abraham Lincoln had won the election, Carl remained unmoved. When Meusebach rode in to personally tell Carl that Texas had seceded from the Union, he declared, "The people are still the same. Democracy will prevail. And there is less reason than ever for war with the North. John, you know I couldn't go to war against the Union. Now that we stand as a separate nation, war is spared. Right?"

"Wrong, Herr Carl. The Union won't lightly allow its great experiment in democracy to crumble into a dozen disjointed states. It will strike with all its industrial might with the least provocation."

"Please, John, pessimism doesn't become you." Carl wrapped an arm around his tall, stout friend and directed him toward the front door, determined to use the castle's ramparts as a point of persuasion.

Meusebach froze, refusing to be ushered from his resolve. He

251

turned to face Carl. "Carl, listen to me for once. Perhaps most American Texans would wish to avoid war, though much talk is spun among the young hotheads. Farther east, where the seceding states border the Union, some minor dispute over territory could light the fuse. If that happens, watch how rapidly all Southern states rally with those where the clash occurs. And, my friend, then watch how quickly the amiable Mr. Lincoln seizes the opportunity to force the sovereignty of the Union Constitution over all states."

Carl blinked, shaken by the strength of Meusebach's thought-out position. "The Constitution is good. Are you sure it couldn't be adopted, at least its essential parts, by Texas apart from the Union?" He knew his question groped, but he wanted more of Meusebach's wisdom. *Damn, once again I've failed to give attention to important matters.*

Meusebach yielded to Carl's arm pressure, urging him toward the door again, to move out of the family's hearing. They finished the few steps outdoors on the cool February afternoon. A tear welled in the corner of Meusebach's eye, in profile, then drained quickly into his red beard. "Whether Texas adopts its own version of the Constitution, or whether the North imposes theirs on us again, either document will be drenched in red before its effect will reach us again."

Carl had already fixed his eyes on the castle, ready to find an optimism to share, when the word *red* caught him off guard. A lump came quickly to his throat. It was Meusebach's turn to see shining eyes, blinking rapidly. "There must be a way. We must not act hastily. This could pass more easily than you suggest."

Meusebach nodded, now looking toward the castle himself as if to find hope. "Even so, what of the Germanic people? Already sentiment runs strongly against us because the American Texans perceive us as Unionist, opposed to their..." The great man's voice choked, "to their precious, goddamned slavery."

Though Meusebach never seemed to need others, now he appeared vulnerable. Carl struggled to console him. "We are opposed to slavery...for ourselves. You and I know that. But we've lived with it, beside our Texas friends for years. Can we not grant them their beliefs? Certainly, we oppose cruelty to slaves.

And I would like to strangle your friend of the New Braunfelser Zeitung. Ferdinand Lindheimer constantly runs articles declaring Germans unopposed to slavery but opposed to secession. At this point, he talks from both sides of his mouth. You should use your powers to throttle the man."

Meusebach chuckled through his strained voice. "He's not the radical that Douai in San Antonio is. But, Carl, it little becomes you to sound so silently neutral. I know there is nothing cowardly about you. If war should come, which side would you take? Or, could you stay at home without your sword?"

Carl shook his head while holding firm his stare at the hill, the rising wall. "Chief Fleetaumountec once said that the absence of my sword and the presence of my squaw made me a coward. Maybe he's right. I shall never touch the sword again if to lay it down means I can defend Maria and my children. No politic is so important to me." He sighed. "But a personal matter remains. Fleetaumountec will surely pay for what he's done to my friend, Covington. May God will that I should live long enough to render such justice."

Meusebach laid a hand on Carl's shoulder. "Obviously, we can settle nothing tonight, but, Carl, remember, there is politic in dealing with the Indians. We still have a treaty, though ragged after thirteen years. Promise that you'll talk to me before you act out of vengeance, no matter how long away that date should be."

"I'll promise. But you won't persuade me otherwise when the time becomes right."

When John Meusebach rode away without re-entering the house or taking dinner with the family, Carl knew that worry hung heavy over the wise and usually gentle man. Carl had carried envy for years that his own subjects, while respecting his courage and forcefulness, had not perceived him as brilliant as Meusebach's people saw that man. *I must not let the winds of war catch me unaware. I must take the threats seriously, even if it means another delay on my castle.*

Privately, Carl admitted to himself that the castle had become an obsession, an object he no longer possessed but one that possessed him. He knew the ancient rule. *A castle is never finished in the lifetime of a single man – seldom in two lifetimes.* Though his health showed no waning, he still felt a need to rush construction. The great monument must come to a stage of completion where he could move his young wife and their children; yes, even Greta, at the far end on a different floor. The castle vindicated his decision, fifteen years earlier, to give up his principality without a fight and come to America. It proved he hadn't played the fool. It rallied his people.

Now, the threat of war could destroy all he had gained. If Texas itself turned against him, they could isolate the German settlers, discriminate against them at every turn, starve them out, even imprison or kill them. He wondered how he could keep it from happening.

With melancholy, he recalled how his brother, Julius, had died within weeks after his visit to Altmann in Southern Bavaria six years ago. Easily, he could have returned there and reclaimed his lost principality. He cared nothing for it in the old country, but longed, oddly, to recreate it in the democracy of Texas. His fellow Altmanners had expressed great concern over possible American civil war. Carl had put them off. If war were to come, it would come soon. Even if it didn't, he saw oppression of his people as eminent. He may have already lost his life gamble by immigrating.

"Darling, did you have a pleasant visit with Herr John?" Maria asked, walking toward the kitchen. Carl settled into his favorite stuffed chair as Mathias, eleven, and Anna, ten, rushed to his arms.

Carl hugged and kissed both children while groping for the San Antonio newspapers he had ignored for weeks. "Please, children, would you let your father read?"

Maria called, "Carl, why are you short with the children? Are you going to answer my question?"

He whopped the stack of papers onto the near service table. Anna jumped. "If you must know, I didn't enjoy my visit with John... And I'm not short with the children." He reached out for Anna. She approached reluctantly.

Maria entered from the kitchen. "Carl, if you lost your temper and refused to invite him to dinner, neither he nor I should ever

254

forgive you. We roasted an extra hen. Herr John enjoys them so much."

"It's not that I lost my temper. The man is in a quandary over possible war and other problems. He had no appetite. And I fear his pessimism has spread to me."

Carl wanted to change the subject before dinner. Even if he didn't eat much, he would appear at the dinner table for the children's sake. "Will Elisabeth and what-is-his-name join us tonight?"

He knew full well the name of his grown daughter's husband – Samuel Smathers, who insisted on being called "Sammy." And for all the trouble he incurred bringing Wolfgang Kloss to Texas from Altmann, the lad turned into a dud. He and Elisabeth instantly hated each other. She continued her relationship with the rough cut Texan. But did Kloss pack up and go home, as Carl had offered? No! He roamed the countryside as though he were born here, promptly met a Texas girl of plain countenance but strong character and married her. In Carl's view the boy could have tried harder to compete for Elisabeth's affections. They called it courtship, personal selection. *Humph!*

Maria smiled as she and Greta finished setting the table. Carl enjoyed watching his young wife move gracefully about the huge oaken table, strained to look around Greta who usually found some detail to complain of, usually with implications that the problem was Carl's fault. A favorite was the worn finish on the table which would likely develop "splinters and harm the children...if something is not done soon."

Maria said to Mathias, "Run to your older sister's house and see if she and Sammy will take dinner with us. We have too much since Herr Meusebach left early."

Mathias shot to the door and stopped. "Father, may I ride your horse?"

Though the jaunt was less than a quarter mile, Carl knew how the boy loved to ride. "Of course, son."

"May I take your custom rifle?" When Carl didn't answer immediately, Mathias tried to justify. "It looks so pristine in the ornate scabbard. I look like a prince when I ride with the rifle."

Carl knew the lad was weaving words, but they worked. "Very well, but have mercy on the enemy." He watched with pride as Mathias thrust the rifle into the scabbard, vaulted aboard the tall stallion and lunged toward Elisabeth's cottage. "I have it! Maria, I have it. Why didn't that idiot, Meusebach, think of it? I have it."

"Have what, darling? I thought you didn't quarrel with Herr John." She motioned for him to sit at the table.

He sat quickly, scooping up a bib to thrust into his collar. He grabbed a knife and fork.

"Manufactured goods! Our village produces saddles, guns, wagons and carriages. All manner of leather tack and wheels. We even make gunpowder and primer caps. The Texas armies cannot do without our goods. That's how we will endear ourselves to them. And we'll turn a tidy profit in the process."

Embarrassed, Carl lowered his knife and fork, stood and took the carving knife. He leaned forward to slice the chickens into plate sized portions.

Greta, who had remained pleasingly silent during the evening, said, "I wondered when we might get a bit of participation from you."

Carl ignored the remark and continued listing the manufactured items New Altmann could deliver, the increased production it could expect. Aloud, he calculated the present versus the future numbers of rifles, saddles and carriages the village could turn out. Elisabeth and Sammy Smathers entered. Since he considered Smathers near to a half wit, and a Texan besides, he hushed his dissertation but fussed happily over his two grandchildren.

When word of Fort Sumter reached New Altmann, Carl and his small entourage of guard, Wilhelm, Ernst, Schmitt and Harderdorn, rode to Fredericksburg, where Muesebach now operated a mercantile. The former director of the German Society praised Carl's manufacturing scheme highly, slapping his back repeatedly.

Carl loved the accolades. Though the cause was looming war, it put him in a pleasant mood. "And judging from your indulgence in garlic, Herr John, the cook has prepared wurst in celebration of my arrival."

Surely Carl hadn't offended the overstuffed egghead. Surely there must be some other reason for the frown on his face. "Oh, and John, you deserve every praise for correctly predicting the course of events."

"My table is always set for special friends." Meusebach released Carl's shoulders and moved away. "If I appear strained it's the news from San Antonio. Shooting has erupted in the city. Shooting from rooftops between Germans and the native born."

Carl felt a sinking weakness. War may break out before he could execute his plan. He stiffened. "If it's war they want, war they shall have. We must call to arms to defend our brothers and sisters. We have no choice. I won't stay for dinner."

"Stay for dinner, Carl. You must hear the rest. Often the Unionists among the Germans take potshots at the Texans from rooftops. Not all Germans are perfect, you know. Our people are scattered throughout the city during the day, mingled in every establishment. I pray the victims, in their retaliation, can discern the radical element from the innocent German population."

Carl picked at the wurst, which had lost its flavor, while thinking of Douai and Lindheimer's provocative editorials. But he knew neutrality couldn't continue. Sooner or later Carl would have to face his conscience.

# Chapter 26

An uneasy year passed and Carl should have been proud. His colony doubled, then tripled, its production of manufactured goods. Prices increased for the finished products – long rifles and ammunition, saddles and tack, wagons and wheels – as raw materials became scarce and their prices skyrocketed. The craftsmen carefully sought the exchange rates for Confederate currency before setting the prices of their goods to assure they could replace raw materials and still profit.

Altmann streets looked deserted with the absence of young men. The women's faces bore the mark of awesome secrets and grief. But Carl knew the reason. Many men had vanished into the wilderness. Others had drained family coffers to travel far to the east and join the Union army, hoping they'd never fight close enough to Texas to harm their own. Still others submitted to the conscription, loyal to Texas, ignoring politics. The hubbub of stone cutting and raising on the hill ground unceremoniously to a halt.

Carl's gut never gave him complete peace, knowing he and his people walked a tight rope of neutrality which could snap at any moment. Neutrality grated on his nature. He had never needed much cause, in one direction or the other, to take sides and enter the battle. Now, at age sixty-three, he gazed at his beautiful family and told himself he must ride out this wave and hope for a peaceful end. But he didn't want to. He wanted to fight. But who?

Word from Fredericksburg burned a fury into Carl's mind. He would have taken the matter into his own hand, acting with his personal militia, had he believed half the news coming from that quarter. The Texas Volunteers, it was said, had established provost marshals in all the counties where draft evasion ran rampant. These included Gillespie at Fredericksburg, Kerr, Kendall, Medina,

Comal which encompassed his neighbors at New Braunfels, and Bexar where open riots broke out daily. All these counties were home to the vast German population of Texas. But at Fredericksburg, a monster and his deputy were said to be hanging citizens arbitrarily to intimidate the populace into submitting to the draft. Their names: Captain James Duff and Lieutenant C.D. McRae.

So far, the lesser populated county of Altmann, producer of firearms for the Confederacy and free of any domestic rebellion against the new government, had escaped marshal law. Carl believed his plan of neutrality had worked and hoped it would hold.

Roth dismounted his winded horse and charged through the gate at Carl's home. Carl stood inside his window, amused at seeing his old brewmeister friend in such a sweat. He had seen it before. Roth's excitability was always a source of pleasure for Carl's teasing. But all fun drained from Carl's face when he saw blood coating Roth's forehead and mouth. Something was wrong. Terribly wrong.

Carl swung the heavy oaken door back to receive Roth. "Carl, they've come. They've taken my brewery, my pub, my home," he panted. "They're playing cruel games with Frau Berta. I escaped from the back room where they made me prisoner."

Roth's breath failed him, and his knees gave way in Carl's arms. He broke into open sobs.

Carl braced his friend. "Calm down, Roth. Let me get you into a chair. You're not making sense." The two moved clumsily in mutual embrace to the nearest seat. "Greta, Maria! Come quickly. Roth needs attention."

As soon as he said it, Carl wondered why he had called Greta's name first. But the way Roth had used the word *they* caused him to shiver in realization that what had happened came directly from the ugliness of war. And he didn't want Maria to see it. Also, he knew Greta, despite their differences, would minister well to the needs of the injured man. He had seen it with the children.

259

Immediately the women entered, then Greta fled to a back room to fetch cloth, water, and medicine. Maria rushed to Roth and took him by the shoulders to examine his head wounds.

"What happened, Herr Roth? Did you fall from your horse?" Her eyes went to Carl who could offer no comfort.

"It's Duff and McRae, the butchers from Fredericksburg. They took over my business, and they...Berta..." He rolled his face in unspoken horror. His voice calmed somewhat as Maria stroked his bearded face. "They aim to establish a conscription office in New Altmann."

Carl felt that the top of his head would explode with rage when the impact hit him as Greta laid out her cloths and water. He kept his silence while the women cleaned the distraught man's face, gradually improving his appearance.

Seeking a calm voice, Carl finally spoke although he knew his tone betrayed his fury. "Tell me everything. I must know all that's happened. Then I'll act." When he added the next sentence, he knew he hid nothing from Roth or the women. "They won't find an easy time in New Altmann as they did in Fredericksburg, I assure you."

Maria began to weep as Roth described how the troops had entered his establishment, demanded beer, and then demanded the premises. They had laughed and joked about the great barrels of beer that would make their stay more palatable. At first, Roth had thought another rowdy troop of Confederates had come for a good time and would leave. He had served Confederate soldiers and Texas volunteers many times. Though rough in language and behavior, they paid for their food and drink, offered cursing compliments on the beer, then left. When Lieutenant McRae rudely shoved Roth aside and groped at Berta's bosom, he saw it was no sham. Roth backhanded McRae who reeled ten feet, then fell with blood pouring from his lip.

"Git 'eem!" McRae had cried. In less than a minute, Roth found himself, semi-conscious, being dragged to the back room of his beer hall. Faintly, he heard Berta's screams of terror but couldn't see what the soldiers were doing to her. The troops thrust Roth roughly into the locker where stores of beer barrels lined the thick log walls. Fortunately, they hadn't seen the tiny lower window behind a barrel which offered Roth an escape route. He lost no time thundering to Carl's quarters on horseback.

Carl sent Mathias to tell Wilhelm to place the "small militia" in readiness. Wilhelm would know. They had ridden in pursuit of Fleetaumountec, without success, but they had developed military skills second to none, thanks to the training and drill of Wilhelm and Ernst. Guard and sniper positions had been established on the rooftops surrounding the town's business square, primarily against Indian attacks that never came. On the streets, members of the team could fade into the crowd or behind a building with no notice. Revolving handguns had replaced the old horse pistols of previous days. Home manufactured, rifled long guns had replaced the muskets that most Confederate soldiers carried. The new rifles shot accurately for over two hundred meters. The old muskets were lucky to hit a cow at fifty paces. The "small militia" could swell to fifty men when needed.

Carl met Wilhelm at the gate, not allowing him to dismount. "Place four sharpshooters on the roofs. Surround the beer hall with another six pistoleers who can watch through the windows to make sure Duff and McRae don't try to shoot from inside without revealing themselves. You, Ernst, Arnold, and I – choose four others – will approach the front of the hall and call out the invaders. No shots to be fired unless the enemy fires first."

As Wilhelm swung into action, Carl reentered his house and told Roth his plan. Roth wailed pleas for speed, mumbling "Berta." Carl's heart cried inside him with impatience. But Wilhelm was gone most of an hour.

"At least," Carl thought, "the beer hall patrons will be well drunk inside by now." After all, thirty barrels of Roth's finest would temp a priest. These ruffians would offer no contest in willpower.

Carl's mounted guard of eight approached the front of the beer hall and aligned themselves ten feet apart. They could hear the commotion inside and Berta's piteous groans. Carl looked up and down his row of soldiers. He called in his famous tenor scream which only the dead could ignore. "Captain Duff! Lieutenant McRae! You will come out and state your intentions."

Townspeople, huddled near the corners of buildings across the street, drew back as though Carl's voice intimidated them. Inside the hall, silence took hold. Carl allowed a minute, and called again. "Captain Duff. Come forward and state your business."

Minutes passed with the hall remaining silent. Carl started to call again but a soldier emerged, then another and another. Carl scanned carefully for bars on the shoulders of their uniforms. He saw none. A fourth soldier emerged, staggered and moved to the left of the front doorway. Carl smiled nervously within, knowing, now, that he had been right. They were all drunk. Two took positions to the right of the door, two to the left. According to Roth, about twenty men had taken command of the hall. Duff, McRae, and maybe fourteen more remained inside.

Then, Duff stepped into view. Carl recognized the man by Roth's description – light colored, short beard on his wide jowls. His broad, hunched shoulders and plodding gate resembled a bull frog. He was fairly well dressed; his wide set eyes were partially hidden below a black fedora pulled low on his jutting brow. No unsteadiness revealed itself in his walk. Obviously, he had paced his drinking, unlike his vulgar troops. He moved alongside his men to the right of the door – Carl's left.

McRae emerged. His cloth lieutenant bars dangled as though they would fall from his shoulders. He lurched but caught himself before the step seemed clumsy. His black hair and beard appeared unkempt. His hollow eyes showed a cold courage, possibly born of alcohol, possibly not. He moved to the left of the door as two more soldiers appeared in the doorway and stopped. No soldier held a weapon in his hand, but each rested a fist above a Colt revolver in his waistband.

When Carl's hand moved within easy reach of his holstered revolver, all his guard did likewise. Duff glanced up and down the line nervously. When he saw the guns were not to be drawn, he growled in a British accent, "So! It's the famous prince of New Altmann. The man himself. Are you here to defy the authority of marshal law?"

Carl said, in paced, clear, loud voice, "Marshal law does not allow abuse of women. Send Frau Berta out. And be quick about it."

"Do you really think you can bluff me, Altmann? I'll have a rope around your neck before dark."

Carl raised his left hand, pointed a finger skyward, then lowered it to point exactly at Duff's face. Instantly, a rifle bullet from a near roof ripped Duff's hat from his head and sent splinters flying in the face of soldiers standing next to the door post. Carl saw a tuft of hair flick from Duff's head as the man ducked and groaned from the bullet's close encounter.

"The woman, Captain Duff! Now!" Carl's voice slammed into the nearby buildings, ran down the street and returned as if spoken a second time. Before the reverberation ceased, the line of Texas Volunteers wobbled and broke formation as though a second shot had been fired.

Duff held his crouch momentarily, then straightened. He said to the troops in the doorway. "Send the woman out. This man's crazy."

His hands moved nervously about his pistol as though he would pull it. Carl raised a finger again. Duff dropped his hands to his sides. McRae stood in a drunken slump, seeming unable to make any decision, but wise enough to hold his hands wide from his sides.

From inside the hall, a voice called out, "Give the word, Cap'n, and we'll open up." Obviously, those inside held more courage than those in full view.

Carl said, "Tell your men inside to look to the windows if they care to open up." Each window stood covered by Carl's guard, easily visible now to the insiders. He added, "You have sixty seconds to free the woman."

Duff screamed to his troops behind him. "Get the goddamned woman out here! I told you he's crazy."

Berta stumbled through the front door, clutching her full skirt and blouse, badly ripped, as best she could in two hands. Obviously, the soldiers had thrown her torn clothes back on her following the command, but they couldn't repair the damage done.

Her lip dripped blood. Her eyes showed pain and horror. She rushed to Carl's side causing his stallion to shuffle. Never looking down, Carl pointed across the street to the waiting civilians. She scurried toward them.

"Marshal Law does not apply in New Altmann. You and your troops will mount and ride. I know the law and you are the one violating it. I won't repeat this order. Move to your horses at once."

Duff looked to his left, then his right. He started to speak. Carl split the air with his mighty lungs. "No threats from you! Not one! Ride now or die!" His left hand shot into the air.

Duff scrambled, mumbling, toward the horses around the side of the building. His troops followed, including McRae, whose bloodshot eyes kept a wary stare on Carl.

For the next hour, Carl and his militia followed the Volunteers as they reeled in their saddles and trotted in a northwesterly direction, ostensibly toward Fredericksburg. He followed at a distance out of rifle range but close enough to keep an eye on the travel direction of the vanquished invaders.

Ready to turn back, convinced the raiders wouldn't return, at least not today, Carl reined in his stallion and raised his hand to halt his troops. Suddenly, they heard the thunder of hooves from the rear and turned in their saddles. Roth charged past the militia, bent forward in the saddle, a long rifle in his right hand. His face showed an uncharacteristic grimace and rage as his brown mare brushed Carl's stallion in a dead run and continued toward the disappearing soldiers out front.

"Roth! No! You cannot! Roth! Roth! Roth!" Carl screamed as the others sat mute in their saddles as though they hadn't recognized the crazed man. Rider and horse dropped over a slight cedarbrake rise within seconds. The others looked to Carl for leadership. Seconds passed, then they heard the distinctive bark of Roth's Altmann-made rifle, followed instantly by a volley of pistol and musket shots a quarter mile away.

Carl felt the white heat of panic rise in his chest. More than ever in his life he wanted to order an all-out charge against the volunteers. He raised his hand. Then his military training told him not to do it. They could hope for only limited success in the open country against a scattered enemy. And he would surely take heavy casualties. Furthermore, he would have declared open warfare against the Confederate States of America. *A good soldier picks his battles.*

"They have... they have killed Roth. What else could they do? We'll pick him up." Carl sobbed and allowed his men to see tears stream down his face as he nudged his stallion forward at a walk. Others joined him in crying for a beloved friend.

In minutes they approached the fallen horse and rider sprawled headlong on the rocky ground, in the shade of a giant live oak. Carl dropped from the saddle and turned Roth's face upward. Blood flowed freely from his chest and back, his right thigh and right arm.

He drew a strangling gasp and said, "For Berta, Carl." He coughed pathetically and exhaled his final breath in Carl's arms.

After Wilhelm worked a reconnoiter to the forward and determined that the retreating troops still moved to the northwest, they hoisted Roth's body across Carl's saddle, tied it securely, and turned toward home. Carl walked the entire distance, refusing the offer of all mounts.

Carl posted guards at strategic points on all sides of New Altmann as well as in town, but no hint of trouble showed itself for two months. Berta recovered from her injuries and hid her grief successfully as she set about reopening the business. She promoted Roth's apprentice to brewmeister and supervised his every move to assure the quality of Roth's product.

When John Meusebach rode into town at the end of the two months, Carl was ecstatic to talk with him. But, as the last time, Meusebach showed no humor on his face, and did not speak until he dismounted. He grabbed Carl in a bear hug and began sobbing. "Carl, it's much worse than you imagined. The butchers of Fredericksburg have gone mad. A band of anti-slave citizens, from Fredericksburg and Comfort, set out for Mexico to avoid the conscription. Duff sent McRae in pursuit. I have word that most of them were ambushed and murdered on the Nueces River." His groans broke Carl's will to keep a straight face.

Carl spoke through a strained throat. "How many, John?"

"Maybe thirty. Maybe more. What can we do?"

Carl gazed toward the sky, and took a deep breath. "I don't know what others will do, but I can no longer remain neutral. I'll enter the war and gladly die for the cause of freedom I've come to love."

When Maria heard the story of the Nueces massacre, she sobbed, "Carl, will I lose you now?"

Carl took his quaking wife in his arms, smothering her to his chest. Young Mathias and Anna looked on in stark alarm. Greta stood grimly at a respectful distance

"For a while, my love. For a while. You know I must act, or I'm not a man."

Totally unsure of how to proceed, or where to contact Union forces and offer his services, he settled on a dubious course of action. Maria, Greta, and domestic maids sewed gray flannel to make mock Confederate uniforms for Carl, Wilhelm, Ernst and Arnold to wear while traveling to Galveston. He would size up the situation there. If the Confederates held the port city, he would buy booking on an outgoing ship of any kind which stood a chance of landing on neutral soil where he could sail to a Union port. He hoped the casual disguise would overcome Rebel suspicions. Carl's three comrades wanted to join him but he only accepted their offer of escort to the coast.

In October, 1862, they neared Galveston, successful thus far in their simple guise. They learned from travelers that the city had been abandoned by the Confederates and occupied by Union forces, apparently without a fight. Rising from camp just out of view of the mainland Union garrison, they switched their clothes to neutral fair and approached the post, all except Carl. He donned his finest German uniform.

Carl felt as though ants were crawling in his belly when he hailed the suspicious guards and asked to speak to the officer in charge. If this patrol decided they were spies, they'd likely be shot on the spot. A Union lieutenant, gray and grizzled in appearance, exited his tent and walked to the travelers who dismounted quickly.

"Guten Morgen, Lieutenant. I am Prince Carl Franz von Altmann of the Texas county of Altmann. I am a Union loyalist seeking office in the Union forces to fight the enemies of America." He threw away all effort at cultivating his best English. He let his German show all over – his uniform, his rigid spine, his tone. If honesty didn't work here, it would never work again.

The lieutenant watched him through sun-narrowed eyes without speaking for more than a minute. "A prince, huh? That's a new one. What do you have to prove yourself? And what about your men? Are they joining the Union, too?"

"I have ample credentials in my case, if you care to examine them. The men traveling with me will return home once I have booked passage on a ship. They, too, are loyalists, in my service since before we immigrated to America. But I have insisted that their age precludes service in the Union armies."

"You don't look much younger yourself, sir. Exactly what could you offer to the army?" When the officer relaxed his rigid stance his troops lowered their weapons.

"I was a cavalry officer in various engagements in the old countries. My medals and documents will attest to those campaigns. Would you care to see?" Carl hoped that the low ranking officer would pass on examining the credentials. After all, Carl would have to go through the process time and again, in all likelihood.

The lieutenant stroked his gray beard. "Tell you what. You seem sincere enough. I'll send a guard with you to the island. He'll introduce you to Colonel Potts." The officer turned to his right. "Sedgley, go with Prince Carl and his men. Tell Potts that Lieutenant Ridgway examined him and says he's all right. I recommend him for service in the Union army."

The smooth-faced private snapped to attention, seeming delighted that the assignment fell to him. "Yessir! The ferry is on its way now, Sir!"

Ridgway dismissed them with a wave of his hand and a final

word to Sedgley. "And don't talk the prince's ear off, Sedgley."

Sedgley did talk incessantly, excitedly, on the ferry to the island. He asked questions about German royalties, where Carl wanted to go, what he expected to gain. Carl and the others found him amusing and answered his questions with generalities.

When Carl had disembarked his wagon and all horses, Sedgley led them directly to command headquarters, an ornate, three-story, stone Galveston home abandoned by the owners when the Yankees landed.

Sedgley unhesitatingly stated his business, to which the guard showed no objection. Within minutes, Carl, Wilhelm, Ernst and Arnold were escorted to Colonel Potts' office. No one had said – and signs were non-existent in the building – whether Potts was the commanding officer or an officer of rank whom Lieutenant Ridgway trusted to follow through on the request. Carl didn't care. If a higher ranking officer wished to see them, they would comply.

Sedgley exited the office and said the men could go in. When he followed them back into Potts' office, the officer told the young private he was dismissed, please leave. Carl almost chuckled, pleased that the process seemed to go so well. He clapped a hand on Sedgley's shoulder and thanked him.

Potts raised his eyebrows above a bushy beard and declared that he had heard of the prince and his successful colony in Texas. Carl wondered whether fame would now bring accomplishment or failure – fame with the Union could mean unfavorable attention from the Confederacy, and vice versa. But the officer quickly warmed to Carl's proposition and promised him passage on a soon-departing schooner bound for New Orleans. Potts wrote a letter of recommendation to officials on the Mississippi and upward to Tennessee. He said the services of a competent cavalry officer could be put to good use by his friend, General William Rosecrans. Carl beamed with pleasure.

಄ ಄ ಄

Engineer Fuessel and Architect Adrian saw the gloom settle over New Altmann. Their director, their county judge, and more importantly, their prince, had left them to the perils of a nation at war. They functioned, but without enthusiasm. They knew their leader had gone to war against the state in which they made their home. They knew that most of their manufactured products went to purchasers for the Confederacy. But they muddled along, surviving for a better day.

The two men approached Maria. Fuessel was delighted that Maria looked well and smiled brilliantly as she ushered them into her home. Carl and Maria's son, Mathias, now thirteen, followed the trio to the sitting room.

Fuessel saw the making of a fine specimen of manhood. The blond, blue eyed boy seated himself with the company, taking profound interest in everything said. When Fuessel told Maria he and Adrian wished to continue with castle plans, and even construction to the extent that manpower could be found, Maria hesitated. Carl had directed every decision – the thickness of walls, the routing of hallways, the height of bastions, the location of tunnels. They understood her reluctance to approve the work without his presence.

Mathias, tall for his age, solemn in his voice which showed signs of changing to a baritone, rose from his chair. "Mother, I think it a splendid idea that Herr Fuessel and Herr Adrian continue. Many times, Father has expressed to me his desire that I continue with the project after his time. I could oversee the plans and work in his absence. I know far more about the progress than you would believe. I know the direction father intended to take the project from here."

Maria's admiring smile faded. Her eyebrows knitted. She leaned forward. "Son, you're a child. Too young to understand engineering and architecture. Besides, Fritz Braun is ruthless in his demolition. If we should lose your father in war, it's imperative that you survive. No, Mathias, I must insist that you not put yourself in danger."

Mathias showed no change in facial expression. He continued standing. Pacing his words like an adult, he said, "I understand engineering and architecture. Most of that phase is completed, anyway. Herr Fritz is pleasantly insane but he hasn't killed a single

269

worker. These gentlemen need to go back to work or seek employment elsewhere. I know what father wanted. No one else does. I would let him down if I didn't act in his stead."

A tear appeared in each corner of Maria's eyes. "Oh, Mathias, you've always thought yourself a grown man. Is there anything you can't do?"

Fuessel saw Maria weakening. He believed the determined young man up to the task, and he knew how critical the passages and secrets had seemed to Carl. He wanted to do the job right. He wanted to please Carl, but he held scant hope that Carl would return from war. Word had been received that he was engaged with the bloody Army of the Cumberland in Eastern Tennessee. If Carl didn't return, Mathias would become the heir to please.

"Frau Maria, allow the lad a chance. We'll assure his safety. And he accurately states the immediate needs in the planning and construction process."

Within the week Mathias, had toured the castle with all the principals: Fuessel, Adrian, Fritz Braun, Vicente Azul, and Speck Vogel. He studied the drawings, amused that the men gasped in admiration when they saw his quick mastery of dimensions, columns, beams, and arches. While skipping the complicated calculations, Mathias grasped the principal of strength and spans. The fact was the engineer and architect skipped the calculations, too. There was no possibility of weighing the heavy limestone blocks, and without accurate weight, the equations went unfinished. Most column and span estimates were made based on an overkill of strength.

When Mathias suggested just that, Fuessel agreed. "The appearance of strength is what makes a castle a castle."

Soon, crusty, old Texanized Fritz Braun began calling the lad "Matthew," then shortened the name to "Matt." Mathias instantly loved the nickname – the American, the Texas ring it gave. He told his mother, sister, and Greta. More than anyone, Greta protested the corruption of his beautiful Christian name, particularly since such a vulgar man as Braun had rendered it. Finally, his mother, asked Mathias to use his authority to respectfully request that his full English name be used at the work site. 'Matt' ignored her request. Soon the entire village of New Altmann called the young male heir "Matt" or "Prince Matt." He never discouraged a soul. Eventually, Maria, Sister Anna, and even Greta, surrendered. Occasionally, they slipped and used the nickname themselves.

He traveled with Speck Vogel to the south and east and helped to recruit Mexican labor. At Seguin, he noticed an abundance of brown-skinned men who should have been swept into the draft. Vogel said the provost marshals didn't enforce the draft uniformly on the Mexican population, considering them inferior for military service. In a few weeks, Foreman Vicente Azul had twenty-four laborers, some of whom had worked the quarry before.

Matt divided his time between studies under a tutor at home and attention to the castle. He struggled to always give the appearance of confidence in both endeavors, turning down playful hunting trips and horse sports with friends. He practiced not changing expressions when the men at work wrapped arms over his shoulders, or when his schoolmaster complimented his studies of mathematics, languages, history and music. He favored the violin. But on occasion when he spoke with his mother alone, they both allowed tears to flow freely as they shared their fears for Father, wondered if he was alive, dreamed of his return along with a dread of his condition – the condition war could crush upon him.

# Chapter 27

Troubles rolled through Carl's mind like wildfire. Though he constantly chastised himself for leaving his family in Texas, he also regretted not having consulted Pastor Clemens to give a full confession before his departure. Never before, except for public consumption, had Carl cared for religious matters. Now, it burned deeply in his soul. He wondered if cowardice had crept in. Did he no longer have the stomach for battle which he was determined to join? Did he fear for his immortal soul should he not return from war? When the answer came back *yes*, he shuddered. Ever since he had met privately with his brother Julius, he knew that he must change his heart. He had tearfully forgiven Julius back in old Altmann, but lacked the courage to tell even his beloved Maria of this triumph over vengeance. His proud will still considered the act a weakness. *A warrior vanquishes his enemies. God forgives.*

He reflected on the bureaucracy in New Orleans, the eternal wait below Vicksburg before a Union boat sailed down river and told his party that the fortress had surrendered. Visions of the defeated soldiers, emaciated faces, and the arrogance of the Union victors, as he toured the captured point, still coursed through his mind. And that tortured Texan prisoner, a bound bloody nub for an arm, who knew of *Prince Carl* and his *fabulous colony*, looked up from his cot in glowing admiration. The enemy?

Now, near Chickamauga Creek in Northern Georgia, Carl took scant comfort that his long coveted Union commission as a cavalry captain had become reality. General William Rosecrans, commander of the Army of the Cumberland, seemed to enjoy a sound reputation as a tactician based on his West Virginia and Mississippi campaigns. But Carl grew dismayed when the general offered no organized battle plan when intense fighting opened in the woods. Carl saw meadows where Confederate soldiers had broken out of the trees. He requested permission to charge them with his mounted troops. Rosecrans didn't seem to understand the request and refused.

The enemy moved closer to Carl's vulnerable, mounted force. He ordered a retreat to move away from the action and organize an offensive. He heard Roscrans' scream as they pulled away, which he ignored. A reconnaissance officer rode to Carl minutes later and reported that the Confederate infantry stood in disarray all over the patch of cleared flatlands, having penetrated the Union infantry in the woods. He didn't hesitate.

With hand signals and his commanding voice, he ordered a charge. He knew scattered, victorious troops usually didn't know what to do with themselves for up to an hour after they had ceased their advance. Moreover, in the first few minutes, many troops wouldn't have reloaded their rifles, standing, relishing their victory.

Rosecrans eyes bulged when Carl, sword raised, thundered past him on his bay stallion, in a startling charge. Seconds later, Rebel troops glanced up from their huddles, seatings on logs, full prostrate positions, taking a well-earned rest, waiting for their commanders to give the next order.

When they saw the charging horses, the Rebels broke and ran. None turned and raised a Springfield. Many met the slash of a cavalry saber, others, the point of a bayonet. Even more caught a rifle ball or pistol shot in their backs. Mortar loads whistled above the charging horsemen, but all exploded behind Carl's line. As the new captain pulled to a halt inside the edge of the trees, he realized he had moved so fast the mortars couldn't adjust their range. In his element – battle – he laughed out loud.

The Confederates carried the bloody day as Rosecrans moved his army back. But everyone knew the battle wasn't over.

Rosecrans called Carl to his side as smoke cleared. "I'm promoting you to brevet full colonel as of right now."

Carl still held his sword low at his side. "I beg your indulgence, General. But you haven't assigned me enough troops to justify the grade. The grade is not important to me. I function well with the troops you've given me. Instead of promotion, I would request another hundred cavalry troops. Nothing more."

Rosecrans' voice drew grim. The pain of defeat showed on his face. He growled, "Don't argue with your commanding officer. You showed true military brilliance today. I'm assigning you four companies of infantry. And don't give me that crap about *cavalry officer*. You have a knack. You'll figure out what to do. I gotta do this now. I might not be in command tomorrow." He jerked his horse violently to his right. Mud clods from the retreating animal peppered Carl and put his horse in a frantic dance.

Carl knew he had no time to organize four companies of infantry. The battle loomed again with the rise of the sun. Neither side had driven the other from the field. He found and met the commanders of his four new infantry companies.

Captain Howard expressed the sentiment of all four. "You're a cavalry officer. What do you know about infantry?" The man's face still held the day's coat of dust and sweat, but disdain showed through.

Carl knew that all the companies had taken heavy losses that day. He controlled the impulse to feel pity or anger. "We'll see what *you* know of infantry with first morning light," he screamed in thundering tenor. Pointing to each captain, he added, "Make no mistake. You'll give account of your actions to me. You'll pitch your tents next to mine and meet me at six o'clock tomorrow morning. Earlier if artillery opens up."

Canon thundered at five that morning. Carl jumped from his tented cot. Having slept in his clothes, he quickly strapped on his sword and pistol and dashed outside. Darkness held the camp. No one moved, not even Roserans' large tent showed signs of life. He felt a lonely, helplessness akin to a trapped animal. *Cowardice!* Was it creeping in?

"To hell with it," he cried aloud. "Howard, Clark, Ford, Ainsworth! Out of your goddamned tents. There's a battle to fight." They may not like a German accent, but they would obey his command or play hell.

The officers complied quickly, to Carl's surprise. He saw the lamp glare in Rosecrans' quarters fifty yards away. "Wait here. I need a word with the general." He paced hurriedly to the tent.

Without the courtesy of a hail from outside, Carl ripped the loose ties of the tent and entered. Like Carl, Rosecrans stood fully dressed, strapping on his gear.

Carl saluted before the general looked up. "General, you know I'm not skilled in deployment of infantry. For your record, I appreciate the confidence you've shown in me. But, God knows we are in a battle for our lives." An artillery shell burst with alarming closeness. Rosecrans ducked, then seemed embarrassed. "If I fail today, remember me as a cavalry officer, not infantry."

The two rushed to the flap door. "Altmann, I'll remember you the best I can. My command here is doomed. In all likelihood, you'll be under General George Thomas by the end of the day." With trembling hand, the general stroked his hair. "Or some other son of a bitch that doesn't know any more than I do." He turned to face Carl. "Success in war is the luck of the draw. Mine has run out."

"I feel no better than you, General. But I am fit to fight one more day. That, I will do. Good morning, General." Carl rushed from the tent, knowing he would get no relief from infantry duty, but anxious to escape any further restrictive orders.

For lack of a better strategy, Carl deployed the four companies of infantry to the wooded areas which made up more than ninety percent of the battle zone. He took careful note of their points of entry. At the first sighting of Confederate troop movement, they should position themselves for battle. They should charge the enemy long before it seemed logical from the perspective of distance.

Carl held his cavalry ready, believing instinct would guide the correct moment to charge. He wouldn't wait for enemy troops to take the initiative. He wished for an opposing cavalry, but he was sure none existed, at least not in this southern sector of the battle of Chickamauga Creek.

Confederate shells burst on the open field ahead. No Union troops had yet moved there, so no harm was done. Infantry units entered the brush in an arc almost encircling Carl and a dozen other officers, including Rosecrans. Carl watched his four companies enter. They seemed coordinated with other companies. For now, he could do no more.

When no Rebels entered the open area during two hours of ineffective, but nerve rattling shell bursts, Carl tensed to the point of apoplexy. He had to fight. He couldn't sit on his horse and do nothing. Though frustrated, he still knew this was no cavalry battle, but the entire war was an insane process of mutual annihilation. The two sides simply ground one another down. The one hurting the worst would leave the field first. Except in isolated points of battle, neither side ever overran the other. Often, defeat was assigned when the two sides communicated through couriers as to who lost the most men.

Apparently, the infantry in the woods fought well. Carl wondered if he should seek another location for his horse troops. Where could the small cavalry fight? He turned his horse to find Rosecrans who had disappeared.

"Colonel!" cried Carl's Lieutenant Abernathy. "Straight ahead! That's gray coats bustin' outa the trees." The man lowered his spy glass and turned to Carl. "Should I order a charge?"

If the infantry units didn't trust Carl, at least his horsemen did. He felt an uneasy pride from the lieutenant's willingness. He answered, "Form two lines, twenty each. Yours in front. Mine to the rear. Space horses fifty feet apart. And prepare to charge."

Abernathy lost no time. When the lines formed, Carl clicked off his self-made list of prepardness. "Arms loaded; sabers at ready; saddle girths tight; eyes alert; space between horses. If any man is not ready, let him prepare now!"

One cavalryman jumped from his horse and rammed the rod down his Springfield. Satisfied, by the depth the stick entered, that his gun was loaded, he leaped back aboard and sheathed the weapon. Such actions never offended Carl. As most officers, he hated losing a single man. "Lieutenant Abernathy, charge at will. Second line hold for my order."

Carl raised his binoculars. The gray shirts now swarmed the far middle reaches of the open ground, a half mile away. It was no mistake. The Rebels had broken through the Union infantry in the brush near the mid-point. So far, no place else. Abernathy screamed, "Charge!"

Twenty horses sprang forward. Nostrils flared. Sweat glistened on man and beast in the morning sun, though the September morning held cool. The anxiety to follow was nearly irresistible to Carl. But he forced himself to allow the lead line to progress for half the distance. A shell burst near Abernathy, and Carl saw the man sprawl headlong from his stumbling horse. The charge continued.

Binoculars lowered, sword raised, Carl held as the remaining twenty men watched him. "Chaaaaarrrrge!" he yelled, simultaneously with putting spurs to his prancing mount.

A hundred yards out his line held even, no mishaps, no falls, no whizzing bullets yet. From over a rise, rifle fire from his first line broke forth in uneven sequence. Moments later, Carl topped the knoll and saw gray shirts. Some stood bravely. Others stumbled backwards, clumsily trying to reload in the face of oncoming horsemen.

"Full speed!" he screamed, whipping the point of his sword forward. The line took on a snake-like irregularity as stronger horses pulled ahead. Carl led. His men unsheathed rifles. The Confederates couldn't know how many more cavalry, spread across a thousand feet of flat ground, would appear from the rise. They broke for the trees.

Mortar shells burst on Carl's right and left, almost simultaneously. From his lead position, he couldn't see if any of his troops went down, and he was too close to the action to turn and look. He pointed his sword directly ahead. "Give them hell!"

The words barely escaped his mouth when a deafening explosion ahead tore him violently from his stallion, slamming him to the grass backwards. His first instinct was to open his eyes to see if he had vision. He struggled for breath, blinked against gunpowder and dirt, but he could see. At least one eye was intact. A horrible burning in his belly set in. He had never imagined such intense pain. His efforts to regain his breath failed. He'd rather suffocate than endure the pain caused by his convulsing chest and abdomen. The bright noon sun darkened. Sounds lightened, then intensified. A voice penetrated the din of horse's hooves, bullets, and bombs. Carl heard it clearly. *You are intelligent by the standards of man*. Everything went blank.

Consciousness returned. The throbbing, burning pain in his gut hadn't abated at all, but he breathed. Carl knew he was alive but seriously wounded, probably fatally. If only he could move, he could try to assess the battle in progress. He would even rise on his elbows, if his arms were intact, and try to see why his belly hurt so bad. Then he realized gunfire and cannon had ceased. Despite his pain a chill settled over him. Was he surrounded by the enemy or his chosen army? If the Rebs had him, he stood no chance for survival. He heard moving horses and scattered shouts. One came, more faintly this time, "You are intelligent by the standards of man."

*What a useless rambling of the mind. I've always been proud. Now my head is telling me I was right. So what? I lie dying on an enemy battlefield. I never felt more stupid.* Then involuntarily, he said aloud, "God forgive me."

A peace coursed through his body, alleviating the fire in his bowels. *All right! I've been wrong to ignore God and his precious son. Maria was right. Pastor Clemens was right. Take my life, my Lord. I give all to you.* Tears burned, then cooled, his swollen eyes, but the pain wouldn't allow his body to convulse in sobs which his heart so desired to do.

He lay still for an indeterminate time, wondering who would find him – friend or foe, and whether he would yet live when they did. Maybe he should pretend dead lest the Rebels come to torture, then kill him. *No, I care nothing for life. I want to see my wounds before I die.* He forced himself up on his elbows.

When he looked down his chest and saw, he wished he hadn't. His trousers were torn, or burned, away down to his pubic hair. Bloody intestines bulged skyward from the non-existent skin of his belly. Flies swarmed over the hideous wound. "Oh, God, have mercy," he cried and leaned back to the ground.

He continued staring at the darkening sky. How grating, how humiliating, for a man of pride now reduced to helplessness. Death was hell. Hell was death. Now he had to suffer it like many he'd seen do, in most cases without real compassion.

"He's not dead. Let's get him on the litter." The soft words came to Carl as if in a dream. He opened his eyes. It was no dream. Medical pickup personnel stood around him, ready to ease his body onto the canvas litter and into a buckboard. They wore blue.

"No, you'll kill me if you move me," he heard himself say. But he was the same as dead. It didn't matter what they did. He wouldn't fight. A junior officer fanned flies from Carl's stomach, then eased a linen cloth over the ugly wound. He gritted his teeth and groaned as several men lifted him onto the stretcher.

The buckboard ride to the temporary hospital seemed endless, bone jarring, unnecessarily fast. He felt the pinch in his guts with every roll of the wagon bed. He didn't remember being taken to a straw mattress bed, but recognized it when he regained conscious thought.

An army surgeon stood over him. "You are a lucky man, Colonel," the officer said, then repeated the statement as though Carl hadn't heard. "I'm Major Stanley Gilbert. You got no broken bones, and it looks to me like there's no major punctures in your intestines. Just the skin blown to hell. I'll do my best to pull it back together. You're through with combat, if that's any consolation. But, you'll endure much grief recovering from this wound…if you recover."

Carl wanted to ask a million questions but the doctor covered his face with a strong smelling cloth. Carl panicked and struck the cloth away. "What are trying to do?"

"It's anesthetic. Chloroform. I hope I have enough to keep you asleep during surgery. Poor rascals. The enlisted men get their limbs sawed off with nothing more than a slug to the jaw and four men holding them down."

"You mean, you mean, I'll sleep during the surgery? Will I awake alive? Does it really work?" Carl knew his inquiry sounded childish, but he felt himself slipping away, and nothing intelligent came to him. He remembered the strange words on the battlefield. "You are intelligent by the standards of man."

Drifting into painless sleep, he told himself, *I won't rely on the intelligence of man, but God.*

Three times, during surgery, they told him later, he woke and tried to rise. They pushed him down and slapped the smelly rag on his face again. Though no time seemed to have elapsed, he gained awareness of his surroundings.

Major Gilbert stood smiling at his bedside. "We pulled enough membrane together to cover your exposed guts. But there wasn't enough skin and muscle to completely close the gap. Damn, you took a hell of a shot out there. With time, we hope nature will take care of the skin. Your greatest danger now is infection. We'll keep the wound coated heavily with an antiseptic salve. You may have to continue with that treatment the rest of your life."

Carl listened passionately. "When may I rise to use the latrine? I feel near bursting."

"Go ahead and burst. You can't rise for at least a month. Even then, it's doubtful your sutures can stand the strain of defecation. The nurses will handle your needs."

Panic loomed. "Nurses? You mean females? Is there no male attendant? I could hardly allow a female to see to such personal needs." Even as he spoke he knew his bladder could wait no longer. Sweat beaded his forehead as warm relief covered his legs.

A small lady dressed in white, a blue collar and an embroidered cap approached. He moaned.

"It's all right, Colonel Altmann. Like the men I'm hardened by the tragedy of war. You have nothing that I haven't seen many times." She reached and pulled a flannel sheet from under him. Gilbert helped her gently lift his lower torso to replace the pad. "Now, let's get that wet gown off of you before you catch the grip."

He found her voice comforting. In a way she reminded him of Maria, about the same size, same hair color but not nearly so beautiful.

"Madam, if you'll turn your face away, I'll pull the nightshirt from my body."

She smiled and continued with her ministrations. "I'm Girlie Langston. For the next few weeks, I'll be your nurse." The gown came free over Carl's head. His black swirls of chest hair, his ugly wound and his privacy lay bare for the world to see.

She pulled a sheet over his nakedness. "Someone told me you were a prince in the old country. Is it true?"

"A crown prince. I left before it could come about. Until today, I've been glad I left." The stretching pains of the surgical repair had eased. The internal throbbing abated. "I have a beautiful family in Texas." *Stupid. This woman cares nothing for my personal life.*

Nurse Langston bundled a fresh nightshirt so that it would slip over Carl's head. He raised his arms to thrust them through the openings. "Tell me about your wife, your children, your grandchildren. I'm sure you have many."

"Only two grandchildren. My grown daughter married a Texas ruffian. Her mother died on the voyage to Texas. My new wife is thirty-one years of age. We have a fine son who is now…let me see. Yes, thirteen, and a daughter twelve." How speaking of his family to a woman warmed his heart. "I'll recover from this wound for two reasons. To see my Maria again and to see my children grow to adulthood." Tears squeezed from the corners of his eyes.

Nurse Langston bent low and kissed him on the cheek. It was quick, not romantic, but warm and sincere. "I'll help you get there, Prince Carl." She smiled and took his hand. Dashes of missing skin showed on the backs of his hands.

"Is there a mirror?" he asked, concerned over the appearance of his face.

"I'll get you a mirror. But vanity has no place here. Concentrate on healing."

The mirror revealed what he feared. Though now clean, tiny shrapnel lacerations, like on his hands, peppered his face from top to bottom. "How could my eyes have been spared?" he wondered aloud.

"God was with you. Do you believe in God, Prince Carl?"

"I do. More than ever before. He revealed himself to me on the field of battle in a way I can never deny. I regret that I haven't taken religion seriously."

Restless nights, little sleep, constant pain visited Carl for weeks. Officers reported to him the casualties in his cavalry. Generals seemed to drift in and out constantly. He accepted his plight by believing it meant he was healing. He came to accept, even look forward to Nurse Langston's services, even those he found embarrassing. He hurriedly hid his naked body at the earliest opportunities, finding his arms, grip, and upper mobility gaining as time marched on. He asked for a tablet and pencil to write a letter to Maria.

Temporary Camp,
Northern Georgia,
November 10, 1863

My dearest beloved Maria,

With heartfelt prayers, I ask God daily for your safety and that of our children. I am fine except for minor shrapnel wunds I received in combat. I can hardly wait to re-enter the action. My doctors, and Nurse Girlie Langston, have ministered my needs with great effect, though they declare me far more invailid than I am.

I am proud to tell you that though I was unable to complete my mission on the field, our forces went on to drive the enemy from Chatanooga, Tennessee. German soldiers under my friend, General August von Willich, lead the victory up Missionary Ridge. I could not be more proud. It is counted as a major victry by even General U. Grant. He gave me a medal, which I did not deserve, for my cavalry actions at Chichamauga Creek. I was embarrassed that I could not stand to receive the honor. But there was scarce honor because the battle took a best friend, Alpine, my beloved stallion.

Tell Elisabeth, Mathias, and Anna how much I love them. I can hardly wait to be reunited with you all. I ask God each day to make that possible. He has been kind to me in battle and in the healing of my wunds.

Will right as often as possible, hoping and praying

that the letters will get through. Warm regards to Greta.
Tell the colony of my well being.

    All love. May God keep you.

    Carl


Matt and Anna read the letter to Elisabeth and the children time and again during the year that passed after they received it. Their mother could never finish reading it. Someone always insisted on taking it from her to read aloud to avoid her emotional crush. A few letters had come through since then, but none meant as much. They said nothing more, except to leave off the part about re-entering battle, and with more emphasis on his return.

"Mother," Matt said, "We've read the letter and the others many times but we've not talked seriously of what Father means. I believe if we look more deeply into his words, we'll learn things he tries to hide from us."

"What?" Mother looked surprised. "Well, give me an example of what he's trying to hide. I'm not sure I like your tone, young man. Your father has never hidden anything from me."

"He's been gone over two years. He was wounded in battle more than a year ago. Yet, in a recent letter, he speaks vaguely of being unable to walk without assistance. His wounds were much graver than he told us. In fact, he has never said where the wounds are located."

"It was his legs, Mathias," resentment in her voice. "Do you not remember? That's why he struggles to walk."

Matt, always serious when he should be, said, "He never said it was his legs. You read that into the letters because you wanted to believe it. Furthermore, even a broken leg should have healed in a year. Father would never speak of assistance with walking if he could struggle simply to the latrine."

She grabbed up the small bundle of letters and read, shuffling through them. "I know it says someplace. Where is it?"

"Not there, Mother." He turned to Elisabeth and her husband, Sammy Smathers, and to his younger sister, Anna. "Sisters, help me. Mother, I'm not trying to be cruel. But Father was more seriously wounded. I fear his wounds may never fully heal. The good news I read from his writings is a true faith in God, which you know he never had."

His mother's mouth dropped open. "True faith? Of course he had true faith! He simply wasn't demonstrative with it."

Matt sat in his father's chair, regretting that he had brought it up, but he felt his father's spirit in his chest. He wouldn't back away. His mother must know the truth, and now. "Mother, I could give a dozen examples, but the fact was Father was virtually an atheist when he left home."

She broke into wailing tears and ran from the room. Matt pursued briefly, trying to console her. "It's good news, Mother, nothing to cry over."


In the weeks following, Maria wrote letters to Carl at his last given address. But each time she heard from him, he had moved again, never mentioning that he got her letter. She recovered from her anger at Matt and agreed with his interpretation of the "good news." The family talked again openly of Carl, but did not reread the letters. They spoke of finding ways to get him home, whether the war was over or not. And Matt was probably right about his never-healing wounds.

*Prince Carl as a Union Cavalry Colonel*

# Chapter 28

"If I wind my middle with wide strips of linen, tied high, I find that I can stand and walk without severe pain. It holds me together, one could say." Delighted at his discovery, Carl wondered why Girlie Langston hadn't thought of it. She stayed ahead of him on most techniques for easing his suffering. Now, in a drafty Atlanta building, a survivor of Sherman's inferno, he talked easily with his friend, the nurse who had cared for him from the first day.

"I feel I should seek release from Union services. Too long I've eaten and slept without earning my pay. With my new bindings, I can venture out and hire a coach, or even a wagon to drive me to Texas. I only regret that I couldn't serve more." Carl could speak to Girlie almost as freely as his internal thoughts would flow.

Hatred, temper, impatience hadn't consumed him since his encounter with God. Otherwise, he would have to hide his inner thoughts from most people, especially women, as he had often done with Maria. He added, "I'll also regret the loss of your fine services and moral support, my dear lady." He hugged her shoulders easily.

"Prince Carl, I'm afraid your homemade truss will last about as long as the Atlanta city limits, if you decide to ride by wagon to Texas." Girlie looked up into his eyes. "But I know you must try. I want to send a letter to your Maria, telling her of the interesting discussions we've held on the Bible, how you've studied on your own, and your million questions."

Carl's eyes twinkled. "Dare you say how we've fallen in love, and you wish to join us in Texas?"

Girlie blushed. So straight was her approach to matters of the opposite sex, she could hardly speak to it at all. "Carl, hush your mouth. Else I'll doubt the sincerity of your faith."

Chuckling, Carl said, "I would take you to my home, but not for me. A strong Texas cowman would whisk you away in no time. When the war ends, I hope you find a fine man, that is, if you would want one." Girlie would never admit it. "A minister, perhaps. What a fine wife you would make for a man of the cloth."

"Maybe," she said, retreating, pink faced.

Carl found no trouble in resigning his commission and offering to leave the first hospital with hard walls he'd seen since the wound. In Atlanta he found Guy Hunsacker, a humpbacked driver of some age, with a tattered freight wagon, who agreed to carry him to Little Rock, Arkansas. He would have to accompany the load. *God knows there are no rail lines left.*

He packed his spare clothing, his Colt revolver, and the two pieces of his gilded Damascus sword, broken near the hilt when he was blown from his horse. He set a goal of again squeezing into a pair of his tight trousers. But for now, he would wear the loose fitting Union blues. He made a bed of blankets and pillows among Hunsacker's freight boxes, to the quaint little man's disgust. With good-byes said to Girlie and a few of his cavalry, and to officers, he mounted the wagon seat and waved heartily. Sure that he was out of sight, he sighed heavily and retreated to the blankets.

Despite pain, he dozed for an hour, then lurched upward. He hadn't written to Maria. He wanted to give her his planned route in case there were delays, or in case.... Too late. He would likely get home before a letter traveling at the same speed, by some mysterious, circuitous route, arrived. He could write from Little Rock. No, the route from there was even more direct, and he would beat the letter. Oh, well, if there were delays in Little Rock, he could post a letter. Still he was satisfied that the overland plan was superior to sea. *Who knows who holds the Texas coast at this moment?*

Mail and freight horrors loomed all over Texas, Matt von Altmann knew. No payments from his father's or mother's holding in Southern Bavaria had arrived since early in the war. Money of

287

all kinds ran low. Texas and Confederate scrip and notes had suffered devaluation until there was almost no point in transacting commerce with the government. Brooding, he paced to his father's old log smokehouse and storage room to retrieve a ham. For the first time in years, he viewed the interior door to the storage compartment. A huge, crude padlock blocked the entrance and crinkled leather hinges appeared ready to snap. He'd never been inside. Using the house key, he tried the padlock. The entire rusting pad disintegrated in his hand. He pulled the door back, watching the hinges, which ripped instantly, and entered.

Flattop sea boxes and humpback trunks stood stacked on one another as though forgotten from the day his father, or mother, arrived. Opening one he examined the contents – tools of iron, including a hand turned gristmill for grinding corn. His father had bought a new one, apparently forgetting that he already had such a tool. Items of clothing, both men's and women's lay in various stages of rot below other lids. Shuffling the containers, Matt spotted a smaller trunk, similar in design, but much sturdier in construction. Metal straps wrapped around it in abundance. None showed deterioration like the iron belts of the others. He scratched the black metal with a butcher knife, discovering brass.

"Probably mother's prized possessions when she crossed the Atlantic." He shook his head, remembering the story of his reluctant father, chuckling at how young and innocent his mother must have been. Brave, too, to make such a voyage. How he loved her. Surely the little trunk was empty now.

Reaching for the hinged handle on one end, he lurched forward from the dead weight of resistance. *Maybe it's nailed to the floor.* No, its bulk scooted reluctantly once he gained an angle to apply his strength. A brass lock secured its hasp.

Matt unhooked a ham from the smokehouse ceiling and returned to the house. At dinner, he asked, "Mother, there's a small trunk in the storage room, full of something heavy. Is it yours or Father's?"

"I brought only large trunks from the old country. It must be your father's but I don't remember it. Why do you ask?"

"Curiosity."

288

Mother passed the platter of sliced ham to Matt. "Whatever was his, is yours now, son. If you wish to look inside, I'm positive your father would approve."

Matt caught the sadness of face and voice as she spoke. "I can wait until he returns. Maybe it won't be long, now." He was no more confident than Mother but felt duty as the man of the house to encourage her and his sisters. He would turn fifteen in a few days.

Hours later, Mother called to him from the bedroom. "Matt, are you preparing your studies? It's past bedtime."

"Yes, Mother. I'll retire soon." Studies? Yes, he studied the figures on his ledger wondering where money would come from for the castle construction. He dreaded the thought that he or Mother would have to seek credit from the merchants to subsist for the rest of winter. Or worse, sell most of their land at hideous losses under the Confederate economy. But mainly, he studied the desk for the location of a quaint, possibly brass, key.


From the low, south side of the castle, Matt looked down at his house every few minutes. After noon, he saw what he sought – Mother, Greta and Sister Anna, leaving the house by carriage headed for the village.

"Herr Fuessel, I have business to attend. I must leave now."

The engineer hardly looked up from his concentration on the rock leveling. "Take care, young prince."

Matt mounted and rode straight home. He entered the smokehouse and the storage room. Seconds later the old lock released. He tossed it aside, unlatched the hasp, and swung open the curved lid of the small chest. A faded oil cloth covered the mystery contents. Snatched away, Matt's eyes blurred, and stared in disbelief. His heart pounded like a hammer mill.

Bars of gold and silver glistened in the thin sun ray. Coins of every denomination, and national origin extruded from rotten canvas bags – gulden, guilders, thalers. The door creaked from behind. Terror seized the young man. He leaped, wheeling, from his squatted position. Frauka the goat nuzzled her way inside,

289

bleating.

"Frauka, you old goat. I should barbecue you." Relief and pleasure flooded his racing heart. He had left the inner door in shambles the day before and had no way to lock the outer smokehouse door. For the first time in his life, he felt the need for a gun, a handgun. He charged into the house, and scrambled back with a blanket. He covered the heavy trunk and dragged it into the house. Frauka rode atop the parcel to the door.

His breath and pulse caused him to stumble as the trunk crossed the threshold. Quickly, he closed the door, then sat on the trunk until his mind and chest cleared. *What do I do now? It was a safe secret in the smokehouse. Now, knowledge will create a threat. Mother and Greta and Anna can keep a secret. Hmm, well, I don't know about Anna. I'll give her a stern lecture.*

Don't? The English language often arose in his thoughts these days, crowding out the German on which he was raised.

*Should I tell Elisabeth and Sammy?"* He trusted his grown and married older half sister. *But Sammy may be as dense as Father has long suspected. I'll ask Mother, but I need a plan of my own.*

Thirteen-year-old Anna got the stern lecture from her brother, but couldn't hide the glee she found in the *buried treasure*. She danced through the house, returning to the chest, sifting the gold coins through her hand. The family took delight, but Matt held back an uneasy feeling. He said, "Anna, your pleasure is well received in this house. But you know you dare not tell a soul outside."

"Will I get the new dresses I've wanted since before the war? After all, I'm a young woman now." She continued a childlike skip-dance.

"We'll use the treasure sparingly. Never draw attention to new wealth. You'll get the dresses, but not tomorrow, not the next day. They will have to come gradually. For now, we can fund the castle and maintain our status as the ruling family. But no excess is to be shown. Do you understand, sister?"

She laughed, "You're the boss, or should I say *tyrant*, like Father. My clothes have been altered time and again as I've grown during the war. Must you have the final word on everything?"

Matt felt the blood vessels on his temples swell. "We are still at war! You'll listen to me and keep your mouth shut at school and elsewhere concerning the chest. Do you hear me?"

"Yes, Father!" She stuck out her tongue and retreated to Mother's bedroom for consolation. Shortly, she exited with tears in her eyes. Matt had heard his mother dress his little sister for making disparaging remarks about her father. She had found no ally.

Next morning, Matt watched with trepidation as his sister skipped to school the few blocks away for her Latin lessons. She was too old to skip. Indeed, she had taken on a womanly appearance this last year. *Why does she act so childlike over the find?*


A week passed, and Anna didn't return from school at exactly four o'clock. Maria left the house to watch down the muddy road for her. After ten minutes, she walked to the one-room schoolhouse where Professor Schumacher taught Latin to a dozen aristocratic children.

"Professor, where is my Anna? She didn't come home."

The teacher looked up from his desk and lowered his monocle. "Frau von Altmann, she left with the other children. Surely she went to a friend's house."

Maria felt cold panic. "Never has she done such a thing before coming home. Who was with her? Whose house? Professor, you must help me. Has she said anything unusual the last few days?"

"I'll help you look to your friends, Maria, but I'm positive there is no cause for alarm. She's of an age where she wants to act independently on occasion. Unusual, you say? No, nothing at all." He snapped his fingers. "There was one thing. I've never heard Anna brag of her heritage, and I was amused when I overheard her tell her friends that the family had found a new wealth, a great wealth. I presumed she spoke of a puppy or kitten."

They rushed from the schoolroom into the street. They charged to the Linnartz house, then the Renninger home, to Doctor

Schmitt, to Doctor Hagerdorn. They exhausted the list of friends. As they ran toward Maria's home, Matt met them halfway.

"Mother, you look in a panic. What is the...?"

"Anna!" Maria cried, then wailed. "Anna is missing. Oh, Mathias, what can we do?" She fell into her tall son's arms.


With the help of Wilhelm, Ernst, Schmitt, and Hagerdorn, they canvassed every house and business in town without success. Demolition expert, the smelly old German converted to Texan, Fritz Braun, charged out of Berta's beer hall, screaming, "Wait! I have something to tell you." Obviously, his deafness had precluded his hearing the story when they surveyed the tavern. When Berta had repeated the dilemma to him at close range, he leaped from his table, slamming a stein of beer on the oak top.

To Matt and the others, he said, "I saw Anna and another girl leave the school. The other girl turned like she wuz goin' home. Two horsemen rode up to Anna and she talked to 'em for a minute. I didn't pay any more 'tention except to thank how that kid has growed. But if she's really missin', and I hope yer wrong, look for two horseback men on a dun and bay stallion. They looked like Texans, but they could be tryin' to fool somebody."

Matt's heart sunk to unfathomable depths, blaming himself totally, but still hoping it wasn't true. As soon as his mother settled at home, surrounded by supportive friends, he turned to Wilhelm and Ernst. They rode the creek bottoms and the wooded areas south and west of town.

They returned to the path which Anna would have taken home. Horse tracks, where the abduction would have taken place were clearly visible in the moist soil. Though many other tracks surrounded the area, they agreed these were the ones of the culprits, if... Matt searched his mind for answers. Where would his father start? For a moment he hoped his father was dead so that he wouldn't have to witness the event, and he wouldn't see Matt's shame at failure. *But he lives in me. I won't give up until my body draws its last breath.*

He located plaster of Paris and used torches to dry the shod hoof imprints so he could pour the mixture without defacing the tracks.

At home, the vigil continued. Townspeople searched all night. Matt wanted to ride in the direction he thought the guilty prints trailed, but he resisted the temptation.

"Herr Wilhelm, can you obtain a pistol for me? One of the modern revolvers. I have gone too long without protection for the family. And I must have a weapon when we ride out with Blacky Ruggers, your tracker." Matt knew of no better source than Wilhelm, his father's long-time, faithful companion. The older man had fluttered over Matt since he had returned from delivering Father to Galveston. There was nothing he wouldn't do. Guns were scarce – non-existent on the open market.

"I'll inquire, but it's unlikely I can find one before we ride. I'll give you some advice on the use of my old horse pistol. More deadly for one shot than the modern arms. Seventy caliber."

They rode back toward the house now. How Matt burned to do something, anything, except sit still until Ruggers came up from San Antonio. But he knew if the kidnappers could be found, that black-eyed, half Tonkawa, half black, could do it. The man was the ugliest creature Matt had ever seen, but when he spoke, a kindness came forth that melted the fear, even in a boy like Matt. He saw his mother waving from the yard gate and spurred his sorrel gelding.

As he dismounted, Mother rushed to him with a scrap of brown paper. "They left a note." Her voice trembled. Tears flowed as she struggled to speak the next words. "It's a demand for ransom. They want ten thousand dollars in gold. The searchers found the note on the trees in the creek bottom."

Anger flared in Matt's chest such as he never knew he could possess. He had prided himself on his calm approach to most everything, glad that he didn't have the impulsive nature of his father, Carl. Now, he wondered. He snatched the paper from his mother's hand, hardly noticing her distress.

*To Allman famly,*

*We have your dughter. She will not be harmed if you pay tin thousand dllrs in three days. Send one rider to the dry creek above*

*the San Antonio river. No more riders or she will be killed. Call*
*the name Oscar three time rele loud. Do it til somebody answers.*
*No guns or she will git klled. All gold or she will kiled.*

Matt handed the note to Wilhelm. He took his mother in his
arms but could find no words of comfort. They stood trembling as
Wilhelm viewed the note slowly.

He spoke. "There's more hope than we had before, my friends.
This gives us evidence that little Anna is alive."

They looked to Wilhelm, suddenly relieved. But the relief
couldn't hold. Matt said, "But it says three days. One day has
passed. Ruggers won't come before tomorrow. We have little time.
Could we go without him?"

"Not wise, Matt. If I know Ruggers, he will arrive tomorrow
ready to travel. We must prepare. If you have ten thousand dollars
in gold, fetch it together to take along. If all else fails, prepare to
pay the ransom. We can track the villains afterwards."

"They say 'no guns.' How should we deal with that?"

"The man who makes the initial approach will have no gun."
Wilhelm's determination sounded through the gravel in his voice.
"But the rest, well hidden, will bear arms in our teeth." Matt loved
the man.

They turned to enter the house. A covered wagon and driver
approached from the direction of the village. Matt recognized
freighter Christian Damman, hunched in the seat, holding the reins
behind two mules. He felt frustration that the man, though a friend,
would approach the house at such a time. He continued toward the
door but Mother turned back. Matt stopped.

His mother rushed, it seemed to Matt, toward the wagon. His
impatience grew. Did he now need to chastise *her* for deferring to
trivial matters? She spoke to Damman briefly, then hurriedly
circled to the back of the wagon. The driver followed. Matt stood,
fuming.

"Mathias! Wilhelm! Get Greta! Send for Elizabeth! Quickly!
Don't hesitate!" His mother's outrageous screams stunned Matt
who looked to Wilhelm for a clue. Was Anna in the bed of the
wagon? Was she dead?

294

He charged to the wagon. As he rounded the back corner of the wagon, he saw that Mother's hand held another hand. The dead hand of little Anna? But the hand was large, brown and hairy. It gripped Mother's small hand in return.

A man laid face up, head to the rear of the wagon bed, his right hand outstretched into Mother's. He cast his eyes upward from his prone position. His thick, dark eyebrows and straight nose were unmistakable, the pointed mustache and sharp beard carefully groomed.

"Father! Is it you? God, how we've needed you." Matt kissed his father on the forehead and took his other hand.

Euphoria swept over Matt in waves. He choked in tearful pleasure as he heard the unmistakable voice for the first time in over two years. "Son, help me turn over, then I'll stand and greet you properly. Pull me part way out." Though his voice held low, it was strong, clear, reassuring. "Take both my hands, and pull."

"Father, are you sick? Don't exert yourself." Matt pulled as instructed and called out to Wilhelm. He saw Greta exit the house, rushing to the yard gate. His father swung his legs around slowly, then righted himself. He sat on the wagon gate. Wilhelm and Greta arrived as he put his weight on his feet and stood.

Wilhelm roared in delight as Greta screamed. Both rushed to hug their prince's neck and collided in the process. Matt and his mother laughed joyously, nervously as they were forced to take second turns.

"Where, where is Anna? I must see my daughter. Mathias has changed so much. And Anna! She must appear as a young lady now. Where is she, darling?" His voice seemed to gain strength from the excitement.

"Can you walk inside, my love?" Her tone resisted a tremor, which only Matt caught. "Anna is away at the moment."

"I'll walk to my own door if it kills me. No power on earth could stop me. God will give me strength." He breathed deeply, blinking tears.

Matt and Mother wrapped Father's arms over their shoulders. *And may God give you strength for the news you must hear, and for the mission that besets us now.*

# Chapter 29

The mixture of joy at the return of his father and the grating misery of explaining the happenings of the day left Matt drained He heard himself repeating, "It's my fault, Father. Please forgive me."

The pain on his father's face deepened as he answered once again, "The kidnappers are to blame, Mathias. No one else." Turning his face toward Wilhelm, he said, "Are you confident of your plan?"

"As confident as circumstances allow, Herr Carl. But please provide your thoughts. You have led many battles successfully."

"I'll swill laudanum and lead out when Ruggers arrives. Mathias, you stay. Your mother needs your protection and comfort."

Wilhelm's alarm showed in his firm voice. "No, Carl, you cannot ride. I won't allow it. You risk infection. We could lose you after all this time that God has kept you alive."

"He's right, Father. You won't go. You'll stay and comfort Mother. I'm a man, and I'll ride to save my little sister." Matt's voice trembled, determined that the mission would go as he said, but dreading the confrontation with his father.

"Thunder!" Father's rage was terrifying. "You two gang up on me. I'm still the head of this family. You asked my thoughts. Now you try to ignore everything I say."

Wilhelm stared at Matt. "Matt, I hadn't planned that you should go." He turned to face the bed. "Both of you are needed to comfort your Maria. You can see she is near collapse."

Matt's mother stood holding the long absent hand. To Matt, she looked suddenly strong, renewed, confident.

He said, "Herr Wilhelm, I'll go with you. I won't make a fool of myself. You won't regret my presence. And Father will remain in bed." An idea struck Matt. "Get Doctor Schmitt here at once. Doctor Hagerdorn, too. Let their opinions decide if you're able to ride. Greta, would you fetch them? Ask them to bring laudanum."

Father's eyes narrowed. "Don't try to trick me, young man. You know well Schmitt will say I cannot ride. He is such a mouse. I'll ignore his advice."

The argument continued for fifteen minutes, Matt trying to defuse his father by protesting the slight insult to Schmitt who had not a cowardly bone in his scrawny body, and his father knew it. Father explained that Schmitt was a coward when it came to the care of his patients and rendered a weak apology for his earlier words. Still, he railed against Matt's going. "Better that I should go and die than for my son, my heir, to do likewise. You are the future."

Matt spotted Greta and the doctors through the front window and rushed to meet them outdoors. "Herr Schmitt, Herr Hagerdorn, he's in grave condition. Please unwind his bindings and examine his wounds. And please agree with me that he can't travel horseback. If you give him laudanum, give it with generous quantities of schnapps so that he'll pass out before the departure tomorrow."

Matt's plea turned prophetic when Schmitt and Hagerdorn examined father's abdominal wound and gasped in despair. "Good Lord, Carl. How have you stayed alive? The wound is badly infected. No! No! You will not ride tomorrow. Maybe never again in your life." Schmitt's furrowed brow told Matt there was no sham in the statement. Now, Matt had to worry over his father's health. He would gladly relinquish his place in the mission if his father could ride – now or ever.

Father rose to his elbows. "Watch me, Schmitt. You have always been so reserved in your medical opinions. You underestimate my strength. Spread my wounds with salve. I'll worry about serious treatment when this mission concludes." He threatened to rise from the bed. Mother screamed. Schmitt tried to push him back.

"All right, Carl! Someone said you had come to an

understanding of God. Yet I see you are as childish as before. If you can walk across the room unaided, and back, I'll agree you can ride." Schmitt stepped away. Matt saw his plan failing. His father would do it.

Father planted his feet on the floor and pulled his hand from Mother's reluctant grasp. Matt could see pain behind those brown eyes, which usually disguised all unspoken feeling. He pushed with both hands and rose. He took two steps, three, buckled and would have fallen flat on his ruptured stomach had not Wilhelm caught him under the arms. He groaned deeply. His face turned pale, tilted upward, revealing clinched teeth. Wilhelm, with the doctors' help, returned him to the bed.

"Willi, can you handle it?" Father gasped, obviously conceding.

"Of course, my prince." Tears rimmed the old soldier's eyes.

"Mathias, do as Willi tells you. I'll kill you if you come back shot." He tried to laugh, but groaned. "Bring back my Anna." His eyes pleaded. "Bring back my Anna."

Matt rolled, stretched, yawned and worried. If sleep ever came it was in that one flash when he saw Anna crumpled in Father's arms. Father looked ancient, weak. Matt couldn't tell if Anna was alive or dead. The sight made him leap gasping. He poured out of the bed before daylight and saddled his horse. He checked the load in Wilhelm's old pistol and looped the powder horn and bullet supply to the pommel. He returned to the house for a food sack and canteen. The only sense of relief he felt was when he exited with the leather pouch – gold coin and blocks – with no stir from his parents' bedroom.

The few minutes before Wilhelm, Arnold and Ernst arrived were the longest of Matt's life. He couldn't wait to ride. But Wilhelm said they must wait for Ruggers. To pass time, they galloped out of the village toward San Antonio, hoping to intercept Ruggers coming in. They did, two hours later.

Ruggers was bent so in the saddle, Matt thought he had been shot, or was in severe pain, like his father. The lined face rose from its stoop. A broad grin creased his black cheeks. "Hail, Juhman friends. You ready to fix them outlaws?"

Wilhelm extended his hand as he spoke. "Greeting, Blacky. You know this is not a normal chase. We have to rescue the girl, even if we don't render justice to the perpetrators." Each man pushed his mount forward, taking the thick, dark hand and speaking softly.

"Blacky, this young man is the son of Prince Carl, and the girl's brother. He will act as you say. He's brave and determined." Matt blushed at Wilhelm's introduction.

Blacky extended a steel and rawhide bear paw. "I meet him few times in Altmann. Little fella. Still mighty young back then. Is you ready tuh hang a man if it come tuh that, son?" The stout guide's voice, so deep and clear it seemed to settle on the surrounding junipers and repeat itself.

Matt cleared his throat. "If it comes to that, yes, sir, I am."

"Show me them foot prints you made. That wuz good thinkun', son."

It gave Matt a chance to free his hand from the powerful grip. He dug the four plaster imprints from his saddle bag and handed them to Blacky. "Hmmmmm. Mmmmmmmm. Mmmmmmmm. One's short a nail and this one's got too many nails. Piece missin' right heah. Won't use these unless we git tuh trackin'. If they's on the San 'Ton-ye, I knows wheah they is. They's frum the old Waldrip gang. What you name, son?"

"Matt Altmann, sir."

"I knowed it was Altmann. I knows yuh daddy real good. How he doin' these days?"

"Not well, sir. He sure wanted to come with us."

"Quit suhin' me, son, and I'll call you Matt. That ain't no Juhman name, though. You papa like them tuh call you Matt?"

Blacky's bland humor disarmed and relaxed Matt. He felt the same was true for Wilhelm and the others. And that voice! He could have sung for a choir if he was born in a different time and place. "Texans gave me the name. I like the sound. Father will get used to it."

"Le's ride, boys."

Four hours through live oak and cedar, ravines, wet and dry, brought them near the drainage of the east branch of the San Antonio. Blacky had watched the ground, getting down periodically, but saying nothing. He raised his hand and dismounted from his tall, lean bay. "Sho' nuff they rode this way. I ought to be the one goes up and calls, but outlaws know who I am, and they figgah out it's a trick. And you goddamm Juhmans ride out heah wearin' soljah clothes, they figgah *you* up tuh sump'm, too. Mistah Will, you got any uthah clothes?"

"I'm sorry. I didn't think of that. Maybe I could tear my clothes and roll them in dirt to disguise the military look. Throw my hat in a bush. I should do the calling."

Still mounted, Matt said, "I'll go up. If they know me, they'll know I have good reason for calling. I want my sister back." Blacky and the others looked up, startled.

"No, Mathias, you must not. Your father will hang me if anything happens to you. I would hang myself." Wilhelm's voice and face showed love and concern.

Silence fell on all. A minute passed. Blacky said, "Makes sense. 'Pends on if Matt got the nuhve tuh do it."

Wilhelm started to speak but Blacky raised his hand as if he had heard a noise in the brush. Another minute passed. "Boy wants tuh do it, Mistah Will, bettah let 'eem. Our best bet."

Wilhelm's uncertainty showed easily in his face. "All right, Matt, but if there's any chance of gunplay, you turn your horse, stay mounted, and run like hell."

Matt moved his horse forward. Blacky took hold of the reins just where they joined the bit and stopped the horse. "If they call back, keep 'em talkin' long as you cin. Thuhty minutes if you cin. I gotta git in position. You unnah-stan', son?"


Matt stuffed the long horse pistol into the deep saddle pouch on his right and buckled the strap. He rode slowly for seven hundred yards until he came to a break in the trees where a circular meadow spread to the edge of the creek. The trickle of water from recent rains dulled the sound of mockingbirds fussing in the hackberries overhead. He eased his horse into the open, a few scarce feet outside the cover, in case he needed it in a hurry.

He drew a deep breath, then another. He surveyed the landscape but saw only a jackrabbit on the opposite edge of the clearing.

"Oscar!" He waited.

"Oscar!" Instinct told him to call rapidly, then retreat to the trees. But he waited again.

"Oscar!"

The next five minutes seemed an eternity but he held his ground.

"Oscar!" His heart sounded louder to him than his call. "Oscar!... Oscar!"

Matt knew Blacky was waiting, perhaps not far behind him, for a sign that contact had been made. The tracker couldn't move into position until he knew where the response came from. Matt was unsure of Blacky's intention, but the question about *hanging* loomed in his mind. Could he, or they, pull this off; actually capture one or more of the kidnappers? Did Blacky mean to haul them in to the law, or was *he* the law? Half an hour passed. Matt lost count of his calls but decided it was time to move upstream and try again. The sound of hooves on stone in shallow water stopped him.

He looked down and realized he had pulled the reins so hard his horse's head was twisted to the side. The animal snorted, or had been snorting for a while. He also knew his hands were shaking. Otherwise, he sat frozen in his tracks.

No rider appeared in the stream, but Matt believed the sound came from above the meadow-cleared view to the bank. He watched the trees on his right, where the rider would appear, if he appeared. He caught the movement of a dun horse in the elms and catclaw where he stared. Like a ghost, it disappeared as rapidly as it came. A clammy sweat oozed from his forehead. But he couldn't raise his hands to wipe it.

"Who calls!?" came a gravel voice from the brush.

Matt tried to clear his throat, but coughed. At first no sound emitted. Then he cried, weakly, "The man who wants to see

301

Oscar."

"What's Oscar to you?"

"You got Anna von Altmann. I want her." He hadn't chosen the words but was satisfied with them once they came out.

The horse in the trees moved again, as if to avoid standing in one spot too long. "Who are you?"

"I'm the man you sent for." Matt sensed an anger building on top of his fear.

"Anybody with you?" *Anybody*! That word told Matt he was dealing with a native, not that it mattered.

"Come and find out. Or does a cowardly kidnapper fear a fifteen-year-old boy?" Matt thought of the words David spoke to Goliath seconds before he slew the giant.

"I hold the cards here, boy. You tell me the truth, or you know what happens. You got a gun?" The word *gun* took on a childish pitch.

"You don't hold anything, boy! Your boss tells you everything you do." Matt regretted the outburst, but words came from his mouth without warning. "I got as many guns as I got friends in the brush. Show me the girl."

"I never said I had the...a girl. You bring a little loose change with you?" The ghostly horse moved again. Matt wished for a revolver and steadiness of aim to empty it into the brush.

"You don't have the girl but your drunken pa has her back in the brush. Go get her, and I'll meet you in the clearing with what I brought."

"I could drop you right now, hotshot. And I will. You ride out in the clear and dump what you got. The girl gits sent home tomorrow."

"I won't drop anything until I see she's alive." Matt's voice roared in a piercing tenor, like his father's, and he knew it. It pleased him. "You'll get the present when I get my si...the girl." *Damn.*

"What'd you start to say? You that other Altmann kid?"

"I came for the girl. I don't reveal my identity to a nobody like you. Go tell your sorry pa I'm gonna hurt you if you don't bring the girl."

"One more smart remark and I'll put a bullet between your eyes, Altmann."

"Prove to me you haven't already done that to my sister. Damn right, I'm an Altmann. I can see every move you make. Now, go get the girl or I'm gonna ride on you." Matt knew he had erred. To reveal his identity was to risk a double kidnapping. But his Altmann patience had run out. He turned and looked around to see if interlopers had approached in the brush. Among the shifting shadows he saw the whites of Blacky's eyes. He jumped.

In a low tone, Blacky said, "Don't push it any more. But hold him another three, four minutes." Crouched against the horse's mane, he wheeled the animal easily, silently, and disappeared.

Matt called back to the brush across the clearing, "Leave a note in her handwriting telling me she's all right. I'll leave the present when I see the note."

"Cain't do that. You leave the money first."

Matt screamed, violating Blacky's instruction. "I know you can't do that because you got no authority. Go tell the drunk what I said. He can do it."

"How do I know you'll leave the money?" The voice in the brush no longer growled but sounded youthful.

"I want the girl more than I want the money. You got nothing to lose by leaving the note. That is if she's alive. And don't try to fool me with that ignorant crap you wrote in town. I know her hand." He wheeled his horse and headed toward his comrades.

Finding no one in the spot where he left them, he studied the ground, shaking his head at the idea that he could track horses like Blacky. But the tracks of at least three horses clearly led off to the north, maybe to circle the kidnappers. He followed in an arc until he approached a tumbling stream which he presumed was the creek, upstream. Horses had crossed. He crossed. Blonde hair around his neck curled upward as a sense of danger tried to override determination. He unbuckled the saddle bag and drew the big horse pistol to his side. He slowed his mount to a snail crawl though he wanted to apply spurs.

Thoughts of what they may have done to Anna floated through Matt's head as he moved silently, slowly, through the pecans and live oaks, occasionally forcing his horse through thick ground cover. A mile's distance from the ravine, he heard voices, stopped and tied his horse. As best his moderate stalking skills could muster from play back home, he moved toward the voices which ceased immediately. He froze. A minute later the voices returned, muffled. He moved again. The voices stopped. He halted again. The voices, or voice, came again, distinct for a split second, then garbled. He waited until certain of the exact direction the sound came from. His own footsteps and heartbeat seemed to cancel out the voices. No use trying to hear them while he walked. He took a bearing and moved straight ahead, crouched, pistol in hand.

Movement through the brush ahead caused him to drop to his belly, terrified that he had been seen. Now, the voices came clearly. "You write the note. Say she's nervous and cain't write good. Say she's fine and nobody's hurt her. Say leave the money like we said or she'll get killed."

The voice from the ghost horse replied, "That Altmann kid said my writin' looked like crap. He'd know it. You write the note, Ed. You know good words better'n me."

Matt peeled his western range hat from his head and rose on his hands. Movement in the foliage revealed itself as three saddled horses. Then three men, partially blocked by the brush came into view. Two had spoken. One had not.

One man, apparently seated until now, rose. He stood a head taller than the other two. Matt could tell it was he who now spoke, a new voice. "I'll write that snot nose kid a note. I'll tell him his sister is dead and he better drop the gold or he'll be dead, too. And he will. I'll be watchin' from behind him with my Sharp's. Soon's he drops the bundle, I'll drop him. You two don't know how to handle anything."

Where's Wilhelm? Where's Blacky and the others? What to do? Stay here until they find him and try to take out one before they kill him? What did he mean, "Your sister is dead?" Now or later? Questions and terrors raced through Matt's mind. Where was Anna if she was alive?

Something he overheard Father say years ago came back. *In a battle situation, you have to give up on your own life, or you will lose it*. He crawled backwards, keeping a wary eye on his adversaries. His horse was farther away than he remembered leaving it. He rode slowly in a continuing left arc around the outlaw camp, hoping to approach from a different direction to spot Anna. His heart bore downward in his chest, fearing that she was dead. She should have been close to the abductors.

Near the opposite side of the encampment he dismounted and crept in close again. A small, one-person, army tent stood staked to the ground. Could Anna be inside? He could lunge forward and jerk the flap back, pull her outside, fire his one shot and try to run. Foolish, Willi would say. So would Father. In an agonizing decision, Matt deserted what could be his sister, returned to his horse, and rode for the spot where he had left his comrades over two hours before.

Where the hell were they?

When Matt exited the brush into the earlier departure point, four pistols jerked into position. He heard the hammers click in preparation to blow him to bits. Never had four faces looked so sweet: Wilhelm, Arnold and Ernst. He could have hugged Blacky whose broad face already broke into a stain-toothed grin.

Wilhelm must have felt the same. He fell from his horse in tandem with Matt and hugged the youth breathless. "Mathias, Blacky told me what you did in that clearing. You should not have put yourself in such danger. Your father..."

"Father does not need to know. Besides, we're not out of this yet. Let me tell you what I heard from the kidnappers." Matt told the story of his stalk to the outlaw camp as Wilhelm blew and shook his head. "I didn't see Anna, so I circled the camp for a look from the other side. There was a tiny tent. I sensed that she was in it but you would think me foolish to rush it."

"Oh, Mathias, Mathias." Wilhelm wilted to the ground. Though Matt appreciated the concern, he resented Wilhelm placing safety above the main priority.

"She's in the tent aw-right. You got good hoss sense, Matt." Blacky's voice stunned Matt, and likely the others. "Make a hell of a tracker one these days."

Matt and others burst in near unison, "Is she alive? Is she

hurt?"

"Alive, yes. Not feelin' too good. We'll git yah little sistah. Don't you worry none 'bout that."

Chill bumps seized Matt. He shook and fought tears. They came anyway. He choked back sobs. "They're going to leave a note. It will say she's dead and they will kill me unless I drop the gold sack. And the big man said he would kill me anyway soon as I drop it."

Every man chattered his view, seeking the next move, unsure but offering solutions anyway. Blacky raised his hand. Everyone fell silent.

Matt rode into the clearing near the creek, where the note was to be dropped. He pushed his horse past the brush and trees into the open. He could scarcely catch his breath. The pounding of his heart drowned the birds and the light breeze in the grass. He rode to the center of the clearing, then circled outward in a close loop. A stone, stacked on another revealed a scrap of paper underneath. He looked around, knowing that a killer lurked in the brush, ready with a large bore rifle to blow away his beating heart. "Anna, Anna, Anna," he repeated in his mind.

He stepped down from his horse and took the note in shaking hands. Deliberately, he read every word, taking his time.

*The girl is dead. You pulled stunt on me and it your fault. Drop your sack because I got a bead on you right now. Git on your horse and ride back where you come.*

Matt could hardly stand for the cold fear that shook his bones like a skeleton in the wind. He staggered around his horse to the right side which held the sack of gold. He reached for it.

The shot burst like a cannon in his ear, his head, his chest. His horse charged ahead as he fell, face down and tore his shirt open looking for a gushing wound.

He saw no hole. He felt no pain. *Am I already dead?* The sound of a thundering horse from the brush caused him to curl in that direction. A tall rider on a tall lank horse bore down on him.

*Blacky*!

"Git on you hoss! We gotta ketch thuh other two." With those words, Blacky charged past Matt. Matt caught his horse and followed, crashing brush as he left the flat and entered the thicket. Shots sounded a quarter mile ahead as Matt caught up to Blacky.

"Will's got 'em on the run. We gonna miss the fun. Le's ride." He spurred his mount and shot ahead, paralleling the creek's rivulet.

Minutes later, Matt spotted the form of a man on the ground ahead, sprawled face up, mouth and eyes open. He thought Blacky would stop. He didn't, but punished his horse for more speed on the uphill grade. Matt glanced at the body, knew the man was dead, and knew it was not the young man who confronted him on the ghost horse earlier. Sweat seared his eyes as he pulled his hat low, trying to keep up.

A mile farther, they rode upon Ernst, who had backtracked to find Blacky or Matt, or both. As they pulled together, Ernst said, "Wilhelm has him cornered in a shallow canyon up ahead. He can crawl out without our seeing him if he tries."

Blacky surveyed the landscape briefly. "He ain't gonna crawl out. Ya'll go back to Will." He turned his horse obliquely to the trail and disappeared into a brushy wash.

Matt and Ernst rode into view of Wilhelm while Arnold crouched behind a natural rock breastwork. Wilhelm waved frantically and motioned downward. They stepped from their horses and tied them.

Wilhelm ran to them. "He's about three hundred meters up there." He pointed behind himself. "He shoots every time we show a feather. We're safe behind these rocks, but we're also trapped. Where's Blacky?"

"He turned off the trail," said Matt.

The three men and one boy took positions among the rocks. Periodically they raised a hat on a stick or jutted it sideways from the rock fortress as though a member were planning to run to another cover. They drew fire from the canyon twice. Wilhelm said the distance was too great for accurate aim from a handgun. But an earlier shot had obviously been that of a rifle. "If he knows we're

307

still here, he has to be careful in plotting an escape. Be patient. Blacky will surface sooner or later."

Matt pondered his father's proverbial impatience. *No wonder. How could anyone be otherwise in times like this?* He sat and leaned against the limestone boulder. He examined the horse pistol, aiming it at cactus, mesquite stumps, moving ground squirrels, wondering if he could fire accurately. He was good with the long barreled rifle under easy conditions. He tried to put his mind in neutral but Anna's face, dirty, bloody, tired and frightened, appeared each time his eyelids closed.

Boom! Pow! A pistol shot followed a rifle blast from within the rock canyon. The men jumped and dared to peek over the rocks. Blacky bellowed from where the kidnapper should have been. "He's movin'! Spread out! Don't let 'eem through!"

Wilhelm motioned for Ernst and Arnold to move right. When Wilhelm darted to the left, Matt followed though not directed. Wilhelm would do anything to keep Matt out of the fight. But Matt felt another of father's traits – determination.

Wilhelm ran along the rock line for fifty feet and dropped into a crouch, looking through a gap in the stones where a prickly pear broke any clear view by the outlaw. Matt ran past his father's faithful companion, hearing a faint cry of alarm, and continued another forty feet. Suddenly, the rock barrier dropped away and Matt entered a strip of low brush. The only cover was three feet, or closer, to the ground. And nothing about it would stop a bullet.

A voice screamed, "He's runnin' to the right! Your left! He's got a gun!"

Toc!

Toc!

The voice and pistol shots were both Blacky's, Matt was convinced. Maybe one shot registered and it's over. Matt eased upward on his hands. An unknown form stood directly in front of him, ten feet away. The man's left shoulder was coated red. His chest heaved. In his right hand a six-shooter dangled but raised quickly as though startled by the sudden discovery in the brush.

Instinctively, Matt jerked the horse pistol ahead of him and fired. The man reeled to his right, screaming. Matt saw his handgun drop in the soil and almost stand upright as the barrel inserted itself in the soft ground. Now Matt saw the terror and pain-stricken face clearly. He was young, a year or two older than Matt, a light colored, thin beard and blue eyes. The young man continued hard breaths and sorrowful moans. He staggered away from Matt, arms flopping helplessly, dripping, pouring blood.

Beyond the wounded man, Blacky's rolling form emerged from the rocks and brush, rushing toward the pair. Wilhelm appeared from Matt's right. Blacky advanced quickly upon his quarry and drew a rope around the man's middle, pulling helpless arms to his sides.

"Ohhhhhh! Don't kill me. I beg you. Don't kill me. Aaaaaagggghhh," the abductor cried. Blacky encircled the bloody arms with several coils of rope and secured them with half hitches.

"That girl aw- right?" Blacky's voice growled as he nearly strangled his captive from the grip at the man's collar.

"Yessir, she's all right. I promise. Just let me go. Please let me go." His voice whined for mercy, crying pathetically between sentences.

"She where she was a hour ago?" Blacky showed no reaction to the pleas.

"Y-Yessir." He licked his lips. His face turned white where dirt and smeared blood were absent. Could I have a drink? I'll...I'll take you there."

"You ain't goin' no wheah. Sombitch like you ain't got no barginin' left." Blacky's words brought a coldness to Matt's spine.

"Le's move to thuh crick, men. Trees down theah." He brutally pushed the young outlaw toward the low ground. The man fell and couldn't rise because of his useless arms and the ropes. Blacky jerked him onto his feet by yanking the rope from behind.

Matt hated the man as bad as Blacky, but something about firing a seventy caliber bullet into his arm had taken the determination away. In any case, Matt couldn't bear the thought of further violence today. The gang who had kidnapped his sister was through. He wanted to ride to Anna. He looked to Wilhelm for an answer as Blacky shoved and kicked the man through cactus, moving ever closer to the large live oaks.

Wilhelm, who served as sheriff in Altmann County, said, "This would not happen in the old country until the court had its say. America is different. Texas is different even more. I'm sorry, Matt, I won't stop this man."

During the clumsy march to the trees, the captive pleaded that the kidnapping had not been his idea. His father, the tall man, had ordered it. He hated his father and tried to kill him once. He had been beaten and mistreated all his life because he tried to do good things. He had never even killed a deer. And he was good to the girl, brought her food and water when his pa wasn't looking.

Matt remembered the threatening tone from the trees when this young man was trying to sound much older. He wondered.

When they stopped under a live oak with a substantial branch ten feet high, the prisoner begged Blacky to shoot him. The scout didn't speak. He loosened the rope around the man's torso and fashioned a hanging noose with three, instead of the traditional thirteen coils. The young man made no attempt to escape, weakened from the loss of blood, and from fear. He sat on the mat of leaves under the tree waiting his fate with rhythmic whimpers.

Blacky threw the loose end of the rope over the branch. Matt wished his shot had killed the boy outright to spare this from happening. The loop plunged over the bent head after Blacky tossed the shapeless hat aside. The silent black man tightened the noose until the boy gasped for air. "Ya'll pick 'eem up and make 'eem stand."

Wilhelm and Ernst reached for his arms. He screamed in pain. They drew back bloody hands and looked to Blacky who roared, "Stand up straight, boy, or they gonna grab you arms agin."

The boy stood, now in open wails. Blacky moved behind him holding the loose end of the rope. He stepped onto a fallen tree and reached upward along the rope, as high as his arms would allow. Matt felt his own head spinning, threatening to take away consciousness.

Blacky leaped from the log and pulled powerfully on the rope until his hands held it steady just above ground level. The boy's body vaulted five feet off the ground. A hideous rasp exited his mouth. His feet flailed wildly like a clown who held his hands in his pockets, because there was no movement from the bullet-crushed arms. A minute later, the flailing feet turned to a pulsating push, both in harmony. They quivered pathetically, then stopped.

Blacky had tied the rope to the tree trunk by the time the last evidence of struggle ceased. No one spoke, but everyone watched Blacky for the next move. He said, as though the young man were still alive, "Iz whut you git fuh stealin' a guhl."

He turned to Matt and smiled. "Go git you hoss and pick up you little sistah. We meet yah back at the clearin'." The man's tranquilizing voice had returned as if nothing had happened. Matt would never be the same. He had been ushered into a man's world, a violent world which he despised. He would sort out the lessons later, but right now, he would make the happiest ride of his life.

# Chapter 30

Maria returned from the window and blinked from the setting sun, her eyes already red from crying. Carl knew she didn't want Matt to go on this dangerous mission but she submitted to his will because she loved Anna so. The terror of knowing she could lose them both showed in her face, not only her eyes but her mouth. Her lips protruded, swollen.

She struggled for a clear voice. "No one in sight, darling. Not yet." The tears came again.

Carl sat on the overstuffed, bow-legged chair, his old favorite. His feet extended on a matching floral cloth ottoman. "Are you sure? Did you look to the south? They'll return from the south rather than the west." He knew instantly that his tone sounded harsh, demanding.

She turned back to the window. "Nothing. I look in all directions when I look. I'm as concerned as you."

Carl extended both hands. "My darling, I know I aggravate you. If only I could walk, or better still, ride." When she leaned toward him he gathered her shoulders and kissed her forehead. Her generous bosom revealed itself from the low-cut house dress. He felt an old stir. He had already felt it in the thirty or so hours which had passed just from being near Maria. It added to his frustration. *But it gives me another reason for living. My Lord and my God, is it possible in your great mercy to give me a glimpse of my family as it was before I left?*

He wondered of the God he had come to trust. His life had started on a road through a living hell the minute he surrendered in honest faith. Since then conditions got worse. But, no, he had nothing at all now if he didn't have God. He would not give up his belief.

Hardly a minute passed before he asked Maria to look to the window again. Daylight would soon fade. She rose to comply when a gentle pounding came at the door followed by a voice.

"Carl, it's Schmitt. I brought a friend you will want to see."

"Open the door, Maria. The blockhead brings company at a time like this."

Schmitt kissed Maria gently on the cheek and asked if there was any word. Hardly waiting for her reply, he stepped aside and ushered in his tall, stout guest. "Carl, you remember Doctor Ferdinand von Herff. He just rode in from San Antonio. I told him of your wounds and he wants to see for himself."

The renowned physician strode to the side of Carl's chair and extended his hand. "Herr Carl, to see you sitting upright lifts my spirits. I know your despair at this moment. Don't lose hope."

Carl always thought the doctor sounded like, even resembled, his companion, John Meusebach. He said, "Equally heartening to see you, old comrade. How fairs our partner, Meusebach?"

"John is fine. Again toying with politics. The man knows no end of mischief he can enter." Carl joined Herff's hearty laughter with a single chuckle before the daggers in his belly stopped him.

Greta entered with a silver serving tray, pitcher and cups for tea. They chatted informally as Maria dashed to the window to glance into the fading sunlight, each time returning, shaking her head as Carl watched her movements while listening to the conversation. Greta and Maria lit oil lamps on the walls and long candles near the men.

Herff said, "Carl, I've seen a number of wounds like yours, where skin is torn away and healing can only take place by the replacement of the loss with scar tissue. I have known a bit of success in helping some patients. Would you allow me to examine?"

Carl didn't want Herff to examine him. He wanted to stay close to the window, determined to be standing upright if and when Matt walked through the door. But Schmitt and Herff were already reaching for his arms to help him to his feet. "Oh, all right, Ferd, but no treatment tonight. I have pressing business, you know."

"Just a look to help me with a prognosis and a course of action."

As they walked him gently toward his bed, Carl said, "Schmitt and Hagerdorn are performing magnificently. They've already reduced the infection I caught on the road."

Schmitt said, "Compared to Ferd, we are both frauds, and you know it, Carl. Listen to the man."

Lying, Carl loosened his belt and pushed his trousers downward to reveal the hideous, lumpy wound. It resembled an abstract painting in blue, red and yellow, covering his lower abdomen from navel to pubic hair, as wide as his entire belly. Herff took a clean linen cloth and covered his hand. He pressed with one finger in various spots, with the palm of his hand in others. Tears welled in Carl's eyes.

"Hmm, there are three places where the skin was turned under and not stitched correctly. I can unroll that skin and create a better covering. Also, I've experimented with grafting, which means I take healthy skin from another part of your body and inlay it. Sometimes it works. Sometimes it does not. My experience tells me that the general health of the patient is a great determining factor in the success of skin grafting."

Carl drew a breath to regain composure as the doctor withdrew his hands. "Schmitt tells me that I'll eventually heal if he can keep infection down. Why should I subject myself to further torture?"

"For your comfort. You'll never be able to lift weight of any substance, such as a grandchild. Scar tissue has no strength. Infections will threaten you all your life." Herff glanced around as though to see who else stood close. Only Schmitt.

"I see that your reproductive apparatus was unharmed. But you will never repose comfortably in sexual intercourse because your abdomen cannot bear the weight that position requires."

"Stop grinning, Schmitt, or I'll rise up and permanently remove that smirk from your face." While Carl couldn't prevent an embarrassed smile of his own, the news alarmed him. He had already been courting ideas of alternate positions. He wouldn't give up his Maria if the experimentation killed him. "Can you

314

operate right away? I mean after Mathias…and Anna…get ho…"

Not a lamp or candle was extinguished as Carl and Maria lay down, wide eyed in their large bed. Greta slept by the door sitting upright, under promise to alert the parents at the slightest stir outdoors. It came at midnight.

She shrieked, "He's back! Maria, Carl, quickly."

She swung the door open and screamed again as the ugly face of Blacky Ruggers thrust itself within a foot of hers.

"Boy and guhl in fine shape, Miz Altmann." He turned and extended a big hand, ushering the two Altmann children into the house.

"I am not Frau Altmann, but they are my children." Greta grabbed Matt in one arm and Anna in the other. Maria had to pry Greta from Anna to take her daughter into her own arms.

Carl watched from the bedroom door where the pain had stopped him. He couldn't go forward or backward, and the nearest chair was ten feet away. In frustration, he cried, "Bring her to me, Maria. Mathias, come."

Maria released the children and they rushed to their father. Matt said, "Get under his arm and give him support." Anna entered the warm sanctuary below Carl's left arm as it closed around her and crushed her to his side. Matt supported him on the right, taking the cane into his own hand. "We'll get you to a chair, Father."

"No, Matt." It was the first time Carl had let the nickname slip. "Stand with me for a bit. I feel no pain when you two are at my sides." He sucked in the fragrance of Anna's rumpled hair.

CB   CB   CB

Several times Carl regretted letting Doctor Herff operate on his wounds. He had run a high fever afterwards for ten days. The swelling was as bad, if not worse, than when Major Gilbert in Northern Georgia had patched him together. He would have to endure the worst of the pain all over again. And the two-inch by four-inch skin voids from near his buttocks grew irritated with every movement of his legs. But Herff visited each month, and insisted the surgery was healing properly, and the time would come…

Despite his pain, Carl rode by carriage up to the construction site of his castle. The great, round keep lacked only a cone-shaped roof. But the roof was no small chore. Workers had to hoist perfectly cut stones sixty feet into the air while workmen on wooden scaffolding manipulated them into place. The stones' weight had to bear against the outer wall, braced against one another to prevent a total collapse. Once all blocks were set, they would secure each other, but the tedious piecing together kept everyone on edge.

Matt accompanied Carl when studies didn't interfere. Carl hugged his son around the shoulders often and spoke affectionately to him. But the sadness on Matt's face lingered after his ordeal above the San Antonio.

Carl knew his son had been robbed of his childhood. He had risen to the occasion, gone against his fears, acted as a man, and witnessed the untamed West as no child should have to do. Carl reflected on his own youth. He hadn't gone to war quite so young, but he knew the effects.

Though he couldn't laugh for a long period afterwards, he believed the experience was beneficial. He took responsibility for his own actions after that, thought like an adult, respected people and property, and sought to right the wrongs he saw in society. Though born to leadership, he believed he would have been as pathetic as his late brother, Julius, had he not known conflict.

Carl took Anna's gleeful squeals, her way of jumping, even indoors, and swirling, as evidence of recovery. How his heart had gone out to her that night – that grim-faced child who had returned from hell. And when Maria called Carl aside and told him not to buy Anna the requested shoes, he smiled. Yes, Maria recognized that limits must be set, lest Anna become a spoiled tyrant. The problems of success!

Carl laughed as he and his friend walked the cobblestones of Altmann Avenue. "Just look at the buyers in town, Schmitt. Most are Texans. The war has been over a few weeks, and already they're back."

With hands clasped behind his back, Schmitt glanced up. "Little is said of the war. No gloating. No pointed fingers. I'm glad."

"Me, too," said Carl. "I could enjoy the jubilation of peace more if there were not one lingering burden pressed on my mind. Isaack Covington – his family murdered by that cut-throat Comanche chief, Fleetaumountec. Willi tells me Fleetaumountec still roams free, though farther west. The more I heal, the more my mind dwells on it."

Schmitt said, "But Carl, that was long ago. Call on your God to relieve you of the seizures of anger you once felt, the night chills of hatred you've told me of."

"True, I don't think as once I did. But as the leader of our colony, I have vowed justice against that monster. I cannot let my friend's death go unpunished."


The following four years passed peacefully for Carl, the happiest of his life, he often said. He watched Matt establish himself, slowly at first, as the stockman for the hilly land above the creeks and canyons where settlers farmed. By the time he had reached eighteen, Carl saw the lad turn the seeming wasteland into a modestly profitable venture. Matt employed his brother-in-law, Elisabeth's husband, Sammy Smathers, as his right hand assistant.

Sammy knew more of open land ranching than Matt at first, but Matt was a quick learner and carefully tended the bookkeeping required for correct financial decisions. Sammy cared nothing for that department, preferring the horseback chores all day, every day, if possible. Carl came to respect his son-in-law as a dedicated worker, accepting his lack of acumen in scholarly endeavors. Moreover, he took great pride in the two grandsons and two granddaughters Sammy and Elisabeth gave him.

When the little ones, ages three and one, were gathered into the house, Maria often remarked that Carl's energy soared as he lifted them from their feet, the toddling girl all the way to his face.

Carl invariably declared with a twinkle, "It's but one gift that Herff's operation gave back to me."

Ever the proud father, Carl praised Matt to Maria, remembering to throw in a word on Anna's beauty or success in school, lest his wife remind him. But a son so strong and handsome! No feeling had ever given such pleasure. Still, Carl felt a sadness that Matt drifted away from German ways. He wore the hat and clothes of the Texans. Though blonde of hair and eyes, his skin tanned golden under the Texas sun. He spoke in the English language more often now than in German. When Carl occasionally called him Mathias, he corrected his father.

Across the dining table, Carl said, "Son, do you care nothing for the German heritage of your parents? You sound and look more like the Texans than us these days."

"Aw, Pa, I care about German ways. But I made up my mind, when you took us to Southern Bavaria back in fifty-five, that I could never live there or be one of them. Texas is our home, and the sooner we accept that, the better off we'll be."

He no longer treated Matt as a child, so he made a joke of the title. "Pa!? Indeed. You would use such a scurrilous name for your father?" Carl knew well the term was Texan. While he felt a tinge of regret for the loss of German tradition he also knew Texas fathers and sons held the title dear.

"Sorry, Pa. I mean, Father. Are you gonna spank me?"

In scolding mock, Carl said, "I've never laid a hand on you, and you know it."

"Yes, you did. That time I misbehaved in church. You took me outside and thrashed me pretty good." Matt laid his knife and fork aside.

"Well, that once. Now that you're grown, do you agree you deserved it?"

As they moved hastily with teacups to the comfortable cushioned chairs near the front window, Matt said, "You could have applied a few less strokes with your belt."

"You'll be a parent some day. See, then, if you can always control your impulses." Carl laughed and grabbed his stomach.

"Not that there is any relationship, but I've been seeing a girl.

318

Nothing serious. But she makes me think that all work and no play is not the way I want to spend my life."

"A girl?" Carl sat up straight in his chair. "When will we meet her? What's her name? German, I hope."

"She's French and part Slavic. One of twelve kids. Just got off the boat."

Carl spewed lukewarm tea five feet in front of his chair, spraying his boots. "Slavic!? Twelve children? I *will* take a belt to you again."

"Father! Settle down before you tear your wound. I was teasing. Besides, I said she's just for fun. Nothing serious. You and Mother are ever ready to play matchmakers. Old country habits you need to dismiss."

"You are sure she's not Slavic? French well, the Alsatians are not bad. But twelve children?"

"I was joshin' about the twelve children, too. She's one of the new families. Yes, from Alsace. While she claims German, I do suspect that she's half French. I'm relieved that you'll be able to tolerate her." Matt wiped his father's boots with a towel.

"But proper matching is so important. Consider the length to which I went to find your mother."

Matt's face lit up. "As I recall, they sent the wrong match, and you married her anyway."

"Hmmph. I did well, nonetheless. Bring the fraulein, and her parents. We'll examine her."

"I'll bring the girl, but not for an inquisition by you and Mother."


Beatrice Louise Kohlenberg was taller than the Altmann women, blonde and blue eyed. At first, Carl thought she bore a resemblance to Matt, himself. But her chiseled face and full mouth, flawless skin told him she was all woman, young, capable of making a weakling of his son. Edward Kohlenberg's face held a reserve, an apprehension. He, too, stood tall, an inch or two above Carl's ample height. His wife, a strong, handsome woman with an open smile, seemed completely at ease with the introductions. Her hair revealed where Beatrice had inherited the light waves, but her husband's high cheek bones showed, in masculine form, where most of the girl's features had descended.

Frau Theresa Kohlenberg spoke first. The accent was decidedly French though she spoke flawless German. "We've much enjoyed the company of your son, Mathias. And we've wondered when we would meet the prince and his household. Our children are quite fond of one another, you know."

"Ah, yes." *Quite fond?* "And Herr Kohlenberg, I trust my son's comportment has been to your suiting."

Kohlenberg spoke in deep baritone as he extended a crusty hand. "Indeed, Prince Carl, though I care little for the long strolls they take in the twilight. In the old country, we would have met you first, and only by mutual agreement would our children form a courtship. And all meetings would remain under parental supervision."

Carl smiled, "A new world, Herr Kohlenberg. The same was true in my past, except in cases of more mature people." Carl thought of his own courtship with Maria. *Well, it was supervised,* he supposed, *by Greta.*

Matt stood, slightly red from the words exchanged. "If I may speak, Bea and I are mature in our respect for one another. The greatness of America is in the fact that young people are given the opportunity to succeed at any age, not just when they grow old, not that any of you are old." More red flashed on his cheeks.

Maria rushed to seat her guests, placing Matt across the open space from Beatrice. "Must you all speak so seriously? We've hardly met. Be seated, Matt, you over here, while I fetch tea. Herr Kohlenberg, perhaps you would prefer wine?"

Frau Kohlenberg answered for her husband. "We both would. But none for Beatrice." Matt joined Beatrice in laughter and boldly moved his chair next to his young friend. He took her hand. Kohlenberg frowned.

Carl tried to get Matt's attention and motion for him to drop the hand holding. Matt either didn't see or ignored his father.

Maria invited Frau Kohlenberg to join her sewing group on Thursdays. Carl inquired of Edward Kohlenberg's occupation –

carpenter and brickmaker. Separate conversations grew as the wine and tea were poured. Carl dropped his usual pomp, feeling a need to impress this commoner who didn't hesitate to speak bluntly.

Beatrice entered the conversation when asked a question. She spoke clearly in a musical tone which pleased Carl's ears. He noticed an admiring smile erasing Kohlenberg's grimace as she spoke. She was not one of twelve, but the only surviving child of the couple who had suffered hardship in the old country, losing three children to the plague after Beatrice was born. Kohlenberg's grandfather had been a baron, but his own father and uncles were fond of gambling. He sold the last of the estate to buy passage for America. Never afraid of work, a careful manager of his affairs, he took readily to the hardships of the frontier, determined to succeed for the sake of his wife and their great pride, Beatrice.

Carl chided Matt lightly after the Kohlenbergs left, to determine how serious he was. "You know it is expected of you to marry in your class. Your mother and I can tolerate this girl, but you promised that the courtship is only in fun."

Matt gazed through the window, watching the family disappear toward the village. "Was there a question in your words, Father?"

"Of course, there was a question. You don't intend to become more serious, do you?"

"Time will tell. She comes from noble blood. Everyone starts over in America. Look at Herr Meusebach. He could have stayed abroad and reveled in faded glory. Now, he's wrestling steers on his farm, and loving every moment of it."

Carl stymied an outburst of laughter. "Meusebach, though I love him, is a bit daft, you know."

Matt turned toward Carl. "He's doing exactly what I want to do. Stocking gets in one's blood like arrogance in a prince."

Carl frowned. "You are a prince by inheritance. Do you perceive yourself as arrogant?"

"You were a prince once, Father. You gave it up to become your own man. I'm doing exactly what you did. If I can succeed in some small measure as you have I'll die a satisfied man."

Carl felt that the buttons on his coat would burst with pride.

Matt had never complimented his father in such a way. He had neutralized all objections to the girl and his chosen vocation — ranching.

Matt continued to see Beatrice, though there seemed to Carl, long periods when he never spoke of her. He traveled to San Antonio, New Braunfels, and Fredericksburg, and spoke of having a good time and the beautiful women. Carl didn't inquire in depth, but always felt a slight depression when Beatrice wasn't mentioned or didn't stop in. At least, Matt was not getting serious yet. Carl and Maria preferred that he wait. He was a few months away from his twentieth birthday.

And Carl was even closer to his seventieth birthday. Maria cautioned him to plan no trips around that time. She and friends would host a grand birthday fest in his honor. At first he argued, not wanting to draw attention to his age. But the excitement he saw in Maria and the children melted his resistance. He consulted with Fuessel on the castle project. Could Fuessel and his crew prepare the first level, clean up the grounds enough, that the party could be held there? Maybe, Fuessel, agreed, but there was a matter Carl would want to settle.

"What matter, Herr Fuessel? Have I fallen behind on your pay?" Carl knew that wasn't it.

"Of course not, Herr Carl. It's your choice of words to be carved on the pink granite columns at the grand entrance. Depending on your verbosity, the engraver can cut the words in two weeks, which is about all the time you have."

Carl's heart leaped. "Gad, my friend, I had planned to take half a lifetime for the inscription. Now, I have two weeks? Nevertheless, I'll try." He had forgotten this item. Years had passed and not a word had come to mind for the stones.

Huge boulders were moved from the yard, the entrance, and the road. The wood floor of the great hall was swept and polished. Dirt and sand, a foot deep in places, was scooped and hauled by wagon out of the construction area. Engineer Fuessel pushed his men long hours to finish the high, pointed, circular keep roof and clear the debris. He installed wall lamps in two rows, one six feet above the floor, another row twenty feet up, each lamp five feet apart, inside the great hall – the ballroom.

The unfinished wall, jagged with massive limestone blocks, would glow like the sun, giving a feeling of strength and security. The guests could tour the keep, walk the winding stairs up the tower, or down into the sub-basement. But no one was to see the secret passages known only to Fuessel, Carl, and a few workmen, most of whom saw only portions of the entire lengths of the passages.

Fuessel told Carl, "You and I are the only two people who know all three of the secret passages. We grow weary with years. You must decide who else is to know."

Carl knew Fuessel referred to Matt. He joked, "There's no hurry, Herr Fuessel. It is one of the few secrets I can claim for my very own. As soon as you've roofed the keep, I'll drop you from its peak and preserve the secret only to myself."

Fuessel grinned. "I'll shout the secrets during my fall. The drop is eighty feet. Carl, it is no laughing matter. Bring your son tomorrow. No, on second thought, stay home and work on the wording. Send Matt to me."

Carl clapped a hand over Fuessel's. "I'm afraid it's too late. Your slack security has allowed the young rapscallion to prowl the castle at night. He knows more of the passages than we."

# Chapter 31

Fleetaumountec took little pleasure in driving off Meusebach's fifty horses. But the ocean people chief had betrayed him. He had not kept White Goose as his wife. True, Fleetaumountec intended that the captive girl go to Gold Hat, but that was before he had come to trust the whites, and he hadn't been present to assure the right man got the squaw. He would have kept White Goose as another of his own brides but for the fact that she was Caddo. All Caddo were cowards. Any son she might give him would likely inherit the trait. Besides, she was skinny.

The chief had long admired Gold Hat for the valor of his tribe in the coastal lands. And when they met on the San Antonio road, and Gold Hat had presented him with seven fluffed skirts for his wives, Fleetaumountec developed a genuine affection for the strange warrior. He considered El Sol Colorado a friend, too. But if he didn't respect the gift of White Goose, he should have returned her to the Indians. The horses served as retribution.

The chief observed, after the treaty with the ocean people, that his band stayed the same numbers for over twenty years. As young warriors grew to manhood, half left to join warring bands in the Northwest. The other half stabilized the band. Other bands had suffered high attrition due to the white man's diseases and bullets.

He told Queno, his only son, "I have been a wise leader to respect the treaty of the whites. Our people prosper while other Comanches eat grasshoppers."

Queno, claiming his white name, replied, "Silly Looking wants to find whites who do not belong to ocean people. I Need scalps for my lodge. Wives do not think me brave."

"All whites between the San Saba and the Guadalupe are ocean people. Go far north or west if you must raid.

Fleetaumountec collected scalps before the treaty. You acted as a loco dog when you had the chance."

Queno spread a wet buffalo hide on the grass to stake it down. "Silly Looking medicine is only strong with Fleetaumountec. You will go with me?"

The chief drew smoke from his mesquite pipe. "Hurt in the hip when I ride for two suns. My lodge is satisfied. My wives want me near. Chiefs at Fort Mason give us beef because my word is true. I see El Sol Colorado on land close to us. He looks through a spy glass on sticks. I will take him colts from the herd we stole. No more war with ocean people or other whites. My people live safe."


Twenty Indian warriors thundered down on the camp before Meusebach could take refuge behind rocks. Loose horses churned dust from among the mounted red men. Meusebach didn't recognize their headdresses as Indians he knew. For once in his life, he felt true terror. He pulled his revolver from its holster, ready to command his team of surveyors to fire.

The Indian leader wore a black felt hat but held no weapon in his hands. While others held bows, no arrows were notched. The faded red shirt of the chief stirred Meusebach's memory. He hesitated to fire until it was too late. The fast moving horsemen surrounded him and his crew of seven. The surveyors looked to their leader, deadly fear in their eyes.

"Don't shoot! I know this chief from years ago." The big man holstered his pistol and raised his hand. "Fleetaumountec." He added in poor Spanish. "You come in peace?"

Fleetaumountec raised his right hand as his horse pulled to a dusty halt. "El Sol Colorado," he said in Spanish, adding in English, "friend."

Meusebach wasn't sure. The last time he'd seen the red-shirted chief, the rascal had driven off fifty of his sixty horses. Had it been nearly twenty years? He had long since forgiven the theft, realizing that to pursue the raiders would have breached the treaty if likely shooting erupted.

The chief slid easily from his yellow horse, but Meusebach perceived that he stumbled to the right as he landed. His long braids were streaked with gray. The broad face bore more numerous and deeper wrinkles than Meusebach remembered. But the stoniness hadn't changed. He could stare right through you while you wondered if he saw you at all. His son, Silly Looking, was now the age Fleetaumountec had been at the last encounter. His face resembled his father. His stoop, shaggy hair and unsteady glance did not.

"Fleetaumountec, friend," Meusebach said, extending his hand uneasily.

The chief took Meusebach's hand and moved his own hand up along Meusebach's forearm, gripping hard, and speaking in gravelly Spanish, "Treaty is true. Bring horses back."

Meusebach's apprehension eased, and while holding his eyes on the stone face, said to his crew, "It's all right, men. Put your weapons away." He smiled at the ridiculous thought that Fleetaumountec could or would return his horses after so many years. "My horses are old or dead."

"Colts of colts." Fleetaumountec motioned to his braves. They shuffled their ponies from around the loose horses but closely guarded the nervous animals from seeking a leader for a bolt in any available direction.

"Men, build a rope fence for the colts," Meusebach ordered. The surveyors brought up posts as several of the Indians dismounted to help string rope.

Fleetaumountec seemed as amused as Meusebach while the two stood side by side, watching.

"You are truly a friend, and a great chief." But a burden bore on Meusebach's heart. He knew the Indians could mount and ride at any second. He had to ask a crucial question, using Spanish, before that happened.

"Fleetaumountec, do you make war on white men who are not ocean people?"

"Before treaty. No more. All white men between San Saba River and Guadalupe are ocean people." The chief didn't change expressions and returned his attention to the construction.

"When you came to my lodge, when you took my horses, you wore new white man boots." Meusebach felt his pulse increase. "Where did you get them?" His question suggested that the chief was lying.

Fleetaumountec, arms folded, looked back to Meusebach. The ominous stare seemed stronger. Meusebach felt that his own legs would give way before the chief answered. Maybe he was trying to recall nineteen or twenty years ago. Maybe his fury was building. "Friend, Ike, on Cibolo Creek, give boots. Present. Friend Ike go to land of gold on Western ocean." The chief touched a finger to his tall hat. "Present. Chief at Fort Mason."

Now Meusebach's heart raced for another reason. Hope. Could it be? Had Carl been terribly wrong in accusing the chief of killing Isaack Covington and family and taking his boots? Was Meusebach understanding the mumbled Spanish? Speaking as he believed the chief would speak, he said, "You no kill white man? Ike?"

Meusebach caught the first and only grimace on Fleetaumountec's face. A curl inward of his hairless eyebrows. The chief dropped his hands from their folded position. Meusebach tried to watch them while appearing to maintain eye contact. "No kill Friend Ike. Friend Ike go with Captain Jack to land of gold. Friend Ike tell me."

Joy flooded Meusebach's mind. If this were true, he would have a first-hand report soon, because Captain Jack Hays of the Texas Rangers had sent a letter saying he would visit Meusebach by fall. He couldn't wait to tell Carl whom he would see in October. Maybe he should ride to New Altmann and tell him now, as soon as the survey was finished.


But the survey dragged when Muesebach learned they had used the wrong starting point and were forced to pull stakes and move the livestock pens. Then, another visitor appeared – Jack Hays, himself. Following a jubilant reunion, Meusebach grasped the diminutive white warrior's forearms and leaned close. "Captain, tell me what you know of Isaack Covington and his family?"

"Well, as you know, they joined my party overland to California. Ike and I entered a few joint business ventures..."

Meusebach's eyes bulged. "As I know? I know nothing! I have thought the man murdered by Indians for nineteen years. How is he now?"

"My Lord, John! You didn't know? We left on short notice, and Ike wanted to go. So, we sent word by old Alejandro Pasqual to tell you and Prince Carl, and ask one of you to tell his business interests in San Antonio. You didn't get the word?"

Pleasure, sorrow and a million questions blended in Meusebach's mind. "We found Alejandro shot to death on the San Antonio road back in 1849, the year you and Covington left. Oh, Captain, tell me he's well now. Carl will go out of his mind with joy."

Hays smiled through his graying black beard. "Not only well, but should be here in a week or two. They planned to leave California right behind me. Ike's got a fine family, you know. Two grown boys. June's as pretty as ever."

Meusebach slammed Jack Hays' body into his own with the force of a bull. Hays gasped, groaned and groped for an opportunity to pull away.

"Wonderful," Meusebach said, crunching Hay's shoulders as he jerked backwards, eyes dancing. "Carl married a young woman about the time you left. They have a fine son and a lovely daughter. But I must tell you, invite you, and the Covingtons. Maria plans a grand birthday party for Carl in October, just a few weeks away. What a surprise it would make if you and they came."


But Meusebach's planned surprise became a barrier to any visit to Carl now. He thought it just as well and poured himself into the construction of pens and a barn for shelter, now that he had twenty-nine horses to protect on the open range. Fleetaumountec rode into his camp, leading hunting parties, on more than one occasion. Meusebach fed the aging chief and his warriors on each visit, and showed him his barn, assuring him that the horses had shelter. The German leader remembered well the rage of the Indian when he suspected that White Goose had not been respected. He could lose his horses again. Fleetaumountec followed close behind Meusebach as they steadied posts, stretched ropes, and thumped the rough-sawn boards of the barn wall.

To Meusebach's surprise, the chief entered the barn behind Meusebach, and commented, "Strong."

"You enter white man lodge without fear. Where you learn?" Meusebach spoke easily to the chief, now, hardly weighing his words, noticing that words didn't offend the man.

"Village of Pedernales. Much presents. Fort Mason. Soldiers give beef inside lodges. Fleetaumountec friend." He ran his hand along the slotted siding.

Meusebach knew the village meant Fredericksburg as he took on a special excitement, near delirium. "Your friend, Gold Hat, built a great stone house on a hill. Soon he gives a celebration for the house. Would you fear to go inside it?"

"Fleetaumountec fear nothing." His ebony stone eyes showed ever so slight tightening of lines. "Presents?"

# Chapter 32

To Carl's amusement, Maria refused to discuss the guest list with him. Each time he mentioned a person he would like, she smiled and tugged at the tips of his mustache. *This Octoberfest combined with my birth date will become a day to remember, if Maria is inviting everyone I think she is.*

Meantime, he struggled with the wording for the cornerstones. He couldn't say everything that came to mind. It must fit the immigrants, the colony, the transition. It must rise to the occasion. He turned callers away while he worked. The writing must be completed tomorrow, or Fuessel would hire more carvers. But their artistry would vary. No, one man must do it all.

On Monday morning, he handed his script to Fuessel, still not satisfied with it. No one to review it for better grammar. No one to strengthen the impact. But, on the positive side, no one could take credit for the wording except the creator of the castle himself, Kronprince Carl Franz von Altmann.

Now, the old impatience set in. Ten days must pass before the grand birthday party followed by a week of Octoberfest.

"Hmmph! They'll all get so drunk they'll forget me, the castle and all I've done for them," he told Maria.

Maria tip-toed and wrapped her arms around his neck. "See if you think one soul has forgotten you when your party begins." She kissed his lips lightly. His arms encircled her waist, still slender, though not so much as twenty years earlier. "No time for romance, my love. Details, details." She lifted his hands from her buttocks and escaped his capture.

"My anxiety is out of bounds. Only your love can set me at ease."

"Go visit your friend, John Meusebach. And tell him to send

330

his Agnes here. I need her help."

"Meusebach. A poor substitute for love." He thought how Meusebach had found the love of his life in seventeen-year-old Agnes Coreth a few years after Carl and Maria. The men had talked long and often of how love smiled on them in latter years. "Yes, I'll send Agnes to you. Perhaps she can gain a reprieve from the paws of that bear she's married to. Poor girl, he's kept her pregnant since the day they wed."

Maria worked with Greta sorting stacks of colored paper and flowery crockery. "As I recall, you got me pregnant the day we married. I wouldn't talk."

As Carl retrieved his Texas style hat, an early birthday gift from Matt, he heard Greta's pitched complaint. "Since the day I disembarked the ship, I've tolerated the crude tongue of that man. I suppose it is my legacy."

Carl lingered at the door to hear Maria's reply. "And you are honored to work for such a man. You live in the house of greatness, Greta."

Carl didn't find Meusebach at home but asked Agnes to join Maria. He fumed that Meusebach was likely caught up in a new project and would ignore the upcoming party.

Surprisingly, Carl slept well the night before his birthday. When he had last viewed the engraver's work, the inscription moved forward nicely. Fuessel had frowned when Carl suggested forcing the man to work extra hours to complete the task, saying a tired engraver is a poor engraver. When Carl suggested that Fuessel simply tell the man to refrain from mistakes, Fuessel had said, "Go home, Carl. You need sleep."

Comfortable and alert that morning, he told Maria, "No, I have decided that the best approach will be to allow all guests to arrive, then I'll make my grand entrance, complete with uniform, new sword and pistol. They'll cheer and applaud for an hour."

Maria stopped with the breakfast dishes in her hand. "Now, Carl, this has been thoroughly discussed. You are to arrive first, take a seat in your throne chair, and receive guests one at a time. Address them cordially, welcome them, one and all. I know you've tried to apologize to most of the Altmanners for your arrogance in the past. But even those you've missed, you'll make welcome."

"But, Maria, darling, there are a few to which I didn't apologize because I still don't like them." While it was true, Carl mainly wanted to see the frustration on his wife's face. He did.

"No more stale jokes." Her eyebrows curled downward. "You'll greet every guest respectfully."

"Yes, dear."

"And you will arrive first."

"Yes, dear." He couldn't stifle a chuckle.

As the sun drooped to within an hour of the western horizon, the Altmann carriage pulled to the castle yard. Carl, Maria, Matt, Anna and Greta exited. Elisabeth and Sammy's carriage stopped alongside the family. Their four children scampered toward the arched entrance. The family walked proudly across the recently cleaned, level ground. Rake marks still showed on the gravel and limestone dust. When they approached the great stone arched entrance, Carl froze.

"Wait! You must be the first to read the inscription." He pointed to the great pink granite block on the left, then swung his finger to the right column.

"Carl, did you write so much it required both columns?" Maria held his arm.

"No, on the left the inscription is in German. On the right, English."

### Castle of Dreams

Dedicated to all Germans who braved the great waters
Who died for their dreams, who held the vision true
Of an earthly heaven, and never wavered.
To those who knew hardship
Waiting to see the Promised Land
Those who gave up kin
In the Mexican, American and Indian wars.
To the kin who perished before their dream drew nigh
So that others could know the dream.

Let no German memory ever fade
From past terrors or present comforts.
Both are our heritage and our right.

God has made it possible
For no man is intelligent without him.

October 1869

Maria's eyes welled. The others joined her. She drew a handkerchief to her face. "Oh, Carl, I've always known you were brilliant, but you've captured the meaning of your castle with absolute genius."

Carl's vision blurred as his frame trembled in Maria's grasp. "I am not brilliant or genius. And never again call it my castle."

Inside the great hall chairs and tables stood in abundance. The old piano, brought from Altmann, stood near the head table. Its new finish gleamed in the light of Fuessel's thousand lamps. Elisabeth and Anna trotted around the tables and sat on a leather covered bench before the keyboard. Softly, they launched into a classic from Bach. Barely recovered from his earlier gush, Carl's eyed reddened anew. "Forgive me, darling. I had not even asked of their music since I returned. Where has the piano been stored?"

"In Elisabeth's house. We plotted to save their debut for this event."

Greta busied herself with the food layout, considering no one her equal. The grandchildren ran free in the great hall. They screamed repeatedly enthralled by the resounding echo of their voices and the thump of their shoes on the thick oak floor. Carl said, smiling, "The hall needs tapestry…in abundance."

A loud, metallic clang, like a bell, burst from the entrance. The grandchildren were into something else. Or were they? Architect Adrian, Engineer Fuessel and John Meusebach entered. Agnes followed. They struggled with a six-foot-long metal object held horizontally, obviously weighing over a hundred pounds.

"Carl, where do you want this damned shield?" Meusebach's

bellow reverberated above the childrens' screams.

"What shield? Are we expecting an attack?" Carl moved toward the mystery.

"What shield, indeed! Your family coat of arms, modified, of course, to symbolize the Americanization of the Altmann family."

Carl stood stunned, overcome with happiness and appreciation. Meusebach had sent it to the old country for refurbishing, commissioned it at his own expense. But, now the braggart could boast to the world that he created the masterpiece. No, that was wrong thinking. Today Carl would appreciate the gift.

The three men stood the shield upright. Its background of gleaming white caused the stark simplicity of the symbols to leap toward the viewer. A calligraphic 'A' centered near the top and separated from the two main features – a cursive cross, and a spread eagle – by a simple line which formed three triangles to house the three parts. Carl chuckled in pride, remembering gaudy coats of arms painted on shields which contained so many pictures he could only conclude that the bearer hoped to confound his enemy. Below the images, obviously Meusebach had commissioned the words which rolled upward twice to form hills like the local terrain, "der Herrschernfamilie von Altmann," The Ruling Family from Altmann.

Carl protested feebly. "John, you should not have. I no longer think of myself as a ruler."

Doctor Schmitt thumped Carl's back from behind. "Of course you do, Old Pomp und Prunk. You're as sassy as ever."

Energized, Carl grabbed his lifelong friend in a half nelson neck hold and bent him down. "One has to rule you, scatter brain, or die from humiliation."

Barrels of beer and wine rolled into the ballroom on carts, supervised by Berta Roth, widow of Carl's friend. Carl felt a tug of melancholy but resisted yielding to the emotion. He had to stand strong this night. He had already seen his control wrenched left and right. He hugged Berta warmly. "Your finest?"

Still attractive past forty, Berta smiled. "For you, my prince."

Carl took his throne chair near the entrance as guests poured in with tons of steaming foods. The Gruens, the Renningers, his former sister-in-law Katheryn and her husband, Christian Linnartz, their grown, married children with them. Hagerdorn and family entered with strudels and cakes.

The Reverend Edward Clemens entered, greeting Carl graciously, praising his dedication to the Lord and the church since his return.

As other guests reached for Carl's hand, Maria said, "Darling, allow the men to move your throne to the front of the hall. We're creating impossible congestion here at the door."

Carl stepped down. Men and boys instantly grabbed the pedestaled chair and waddled with it to the front near the piano. For ten minutes, the New Braunfels entourage paraded through the arched doorway: Nicolaus Zink, engineer; Ferdinand Roemer, doctor and geologist; Hermann Seele, teacher; and Ferdinand Lindheimer, botanist and newpaperman whom Carl had blamed for the atrocities committed against Germans before and during the war. Upon seeing the man, Carl's smile turned to a frown. Lindheimer was one of those Carl hadn't apologized to. The man had published uncountable articles condoning slavery while opposing secession from the Union, a conflict most Texans hated, and thus took their anger out on Germans.

Maria saw Carl's features furrow, or heard an audible growl. "Carl, you must apologize to Herr Lindheimer. He did exactly what you did during the war. He stood up for his convictions."

"That rat bait? Never. He caused our people grief. Much grief." Lindheimer loomed near, bushy white hair shining.

"Then never again call yourself Christian."

Lindheimer extended his hand. Carl stared. Trembled. *Oh, what the hell. There's really only one man, an Indian, I cannot forgive. And I'll forgive him...after I kill him.* Carl extended his hand, slapped the rotund journalist on the back, and welcomed him warmly. Lindheimer's aging eyes smiled with a trace of surprise.

Wilhelm, Ernst, and Arnold, dressed in military attire, passed inside under arch. Their wives led. Carl rose from his seat and embraced each man, kissing the cheeks of the wives. Berta presented a tray of red wine, "From Herr Young's garden," to Carl and the standing soldiers. Carl's jaws cringed as he savored the first mouthful.

Countless villagers poured through the door, most bearing food. The table legs appeared ready to snap. Carl relished the pleasure on each face, gratified that the grand lighted hall was more than adequate for the occasion. Though he wouldn't claim ownership of the castle, he couldn't avoid pride.

The Hanovers, led by Felix Gossett, the unpretentious leader and fellow soldier, entered blowing trumpets, tapping drums, and singing. Their noisy demonstration quieted abruptly to greet Carl.

When the Kohlenberg family walked through the arch, Matt leaped to his feet and ran to them. He took Beatrice's hand in his and led her to the light foods, the hors-d'oeuvres.

Two men in Texas dress appeared at the doorway. The smaller man slapped his large hat against his trousers, whether by force of habit or to shake dust, Carl couldn't tell. He saw no dust fly. From eighty feet Carl couldn't make out their features.

*But I've seen both men. Years ago. They were younger.* It hit him. Samuel Maverick and Ranger Jack Hays. He leaped and ran to them. Roaring hoorahs went up from the three as they slapped backs and raved over one another's age and ugliness.

Maverick said he left the cattle business and grew fat and lazy in San Antonio. Hays, the man with the hat, explained that he followed the gold rush to California in '49. The place had become home.

The trail of arriving guests finally diminished to a trickle allowing Carl to resume his seat, sip his exhilarating wine, calling to Berta for more periodically, laughing with each joke made by the guests, great and small. Barbecue expert, J.L. Kincaid said he should have catered the event. In fact, he had killed a calf the day before and smoked it in New Altmann as a gift to the prince. Iron forger, Triesch, claimed credit for the grill Kincaid used, "an improvement over your inferior San Antonio fires." Kincaid agreed.

Carl shouted a greeting to the deaf stone quarryman, Fritz Braun, and his associate, Speck Vogel. Braun appeared reasonably clean, his hair cut and brushed. Vogel, his former tavern accomplice, sparkled in a new suit. Vogel's bride, at his arm, the former Bertha Wagner, smiled glowingly.

Carl eased back into his chair, thinking how gratifying the evening proved. *Age seventy years! It means nothing...provided I can get a party like this every few days.* He smiled in satisfaction. His guests returned the radiance as though it was meant for each one individually.

Maria approached the throne chair. "Darling, there are a few more guests waiting outside. Please control yourself and act with dignity."

"Why would I act otherwise? Show them in." He prepared for the next round of hugs and compliments, though he had run out of original lines for new arrivals.

Maria whispered to Doctor Hagerdorn. He made for the entrance, disappearing under the archway.

Moments passed. Carl cleared his throat, making his impatience obvious. A full minute passed. The crowd grew quiet, pensive. Shuffling in his chair, Carl waited another minute. "Maria, go see what holds back my next honored guest."

"This guest is not accustomed to entering stone walls filled with the white race. Hagerdorn will persuade him."

"Another minute, and I'll persuade him myself. All are welcome on this grand occasion."

People standing near the entrance moved away quickly, creating a wide corridor. Hagerdorn emerged, followed by five unconventionally dressed men. Behind them came a dozen women whose straight black hair fell in braids along their shoulders. Their long dresses covered their feet. Carl then knew it was a special entertainment group, contracted for the occasion.

The garb, complete with knives in buckskin sheaths and long spears in hand, depicted the dress and manner of Comanche warriors. Would their act involve speech or just antics of the American Indian?

Hagerdorn walked, smiling, toward Carl. His following entourage stopped, seemingly when they saw the throne chair. The broad-faced leader propped his spear on the floor and stared expressionless at Carl.

Anger, bitterness, passion built over many years rose in Carl like a bolt of lightening. They were no traveling comedy act. The graying chief, glaring with his hand on his sheathed skinning knife, was none other than Fleetaumountec. The slouched figure by his side was Queno, named Silly Looking by Hagerdorn.

*How dare Hagerdorn invite these butchers into my castle. How dare Maria know of this and not tell me. How dare these killers stand in front of me and expect no consequences after what they've done.* Carl's hand gripped the .44 caliber pistol at his side. *When he pulled it, may no innocent person be standing behind these cutthroats.* The aging German warrior's fighting blood boiled anew. Christian or not, he had waited for this opportunity for twenty years.

Fleetaumountec raised his right hand and cried loudly, "Gold Hat! Friend," likely exhausting his English vocabulary.

Carl's rage knew no boundaries of decency. At his birthday party or on the open range, justice had to be served. "No friend. You killed my best friend, Ike Covington, his frau and his child. You will pay." He pulled the pistol. Fleetaumountec's eyes widened briefly, then returned to their stoic stare.

Wilhelm, ever alert, leaped and landed both hands on Carl's forearm before he could cock the weapon and fire. "No, Carl, you're wrong. The chief comes in peace. Carl, Carl, listen to reason." Carl struggled to free his hand. "Help me," Wilhelm cried to anyone close. "I can't hold him."

Ernst seized Carl from behind, pinioning his arms. Arnold grabbed the gun itself at risk of taking a shot to his legs or groin. He twisted it from Carl's determined grip.

"Why?" Carl panted. "Why do you stop me? He's our mortal enemy. Close the door. At least take them prisoner, so we can hang them." His face glowed red.

"No, Carl. You don't understand. It's not as you think."

"That is Fleetaumountec," he screamed. "Older but just as murderous. Oh, I understand. You know his crime."

Wilhelm nodded to Hagerdorn, who looked as though he had been switched by an angry schoolmaster. Hagerdorn rushed back to his red guests, passed them and charged through the entrance.

All eyes followed him.

In that split second of distraction, Carl wrested the gun from Arnold's hand, leaped backwards away from the others.

Maria screamed, "No, Carl, for God's sake."

"Clear the wall!" Carl bellowed as he raised the Colt into position. "Everyone to the side."

The corridor of people widened instantly leaving the Indians in the middle. Already, Queno squatted behind a woman. Fleetaumountec tore at the faded red shirt covering his chest as if to bare his heart to the bullet. His face never flinched. Carl cocked the pistol. A lifetime of military training told him not to hesitate.

A white couple appeared in the archway directly behind the warrior chief accompanied by two boys, one around twenty, the other slightly younger. All wore the frontier dress of Texas, clean and proud. Carl shouted in his awesome tenor, "Clear the way."

The white family moved forward without regard to the spine chilling voice of the armed prince. "Mr. Carl, good to see you, old friend. Put down that pistol. You could hurt somebody." The man motioned downward with his hand as he pulled his wide brimmed straw hat from his head.

"Out of the way, you fool. Out of the…" A chill shuddered Carl's frame like he had been caught in the wheels of a giant grist mill. What he saw wrenched his anger left to right with such force, his mind surged. He swayed, light-headed, ready to faint. The man continued to march forward blocking the view of Carl's mortal enemy.

The dark hair, slightly graying at the temples, the kind eyes. The smile of white teeth. *Ike Covington*…back from the dead. The woman was June, slightly stouter than her former self…like Maria. And the boys: One was John, the infant at the time of the attack. The other must be the child who died in June's womb.

Carl folded forward with a deadly groan. It came clear now. He had been so wrong. He had carried hatred for years. It had all but destroyed him. Now, it had certainly made a fool of him. And in front of all his friends in the world.

"Carl, get up. Don't be like this. We come a long ways to see you." Carl felt Covington's hand on his arm. His sobs ran so deep he was embarrassed to raise his face. "Carl...Carl, please get up. You're makin' me blush."

Covington's plea was so simple, so honest, Carl found the courage to look up. "Oh, thank God, Isaack." He choked back another anguishing sob. "Thank God." Then an unsure smile came over his face. "But you are still using contracted words and dropping your 'g's. How will I ever learn English?"

Covington dropped to his knees with Carl and they stood for a long time in that position in a bone crushing bear hug. The audience murmured among themselves until most came to understand what had happened. They broke into thunderous cheers and applause as Wilhelm swept the revolver from the floor. Fleetaumountec, Queno and the others smiled broadly and joined in slamming their hands together.

Carl and his reincarnated friend rose and beckoned Fleetaumountec to come forward. He looked left and right, handed his lance to a woman and marched smartly ahead, back ramrod straight, head held proud. A face of stone stood in front of Carl for an eternal moment. Then, arms fell around shoulders. Carl smelled the sage and cedar of the wild man's clothes, noticing that no body odor presented itself. The chief had cleaned himself carefully for this reunion with a presumed friend. And the friend had turned on him.

In strained voice Carl said, though he knew Fleetaumountec didn't understand, "Forgive me, my friend. Forgive my stupidity." He patted the steel muscle of the red man's back.

Fleetaumountec said, "Friend! Stupidee!" and returned the kind patting.

It was four o'clock in the afternoon when Carl forced himself from bed. Maria entered the bedroom and asked him if he cared for dinner. He said no he would have breakfast now. "It's a bit late, my love. You slept through breakfast and noon. The sun sinks in the west."

"Oh, my life, I wanted to visit Jack Hays, Sam Maverick and the Covingtons. And I hope Fleetaumountec has not left the village. I'll need Hagerdorn's translation."

"Mr. Hays and Mr. Maverick are still in bed, like you, lazy man. Mr. Covington said he would not dare leave without visiting you. Herr Fleetaumountec sat with Greta for an hour, with Hagerdorn's assistance. He wouldn't let your helmet from his lap. I never saw a child so proud of a toy. You were most magnanimous to give it to him and your new sword to his son, Silly Looking."

Carl's eyes rounded. "I did that? I...I mean, of course, I did...that. I...am a generous man." Under his breath, he added, "Stupidee."

A village boy brought word that Hays and Maverick would linger another day in the village. They sent apologies for their laziness. Carl rose and ate. He hadn't drunk that much, but the party continued until daylight. At seventy, he needed his sleep. "Let's sit on the gallery and enjoy the cool air, love," he told Maria. "Where is Greta?"

"She's still writing letters to relatives in the old country, and adoring the cougar claw necklace the chief gave her."

"I'm glad for Greta. Some day she may write a volume." Carl's right arm encircled his wife's shoulders as they strolled to the porch.

They sat in the swing, Carl insisting that the time had come to move into the castle, Maria protesting that only the great hall was finished – partly. They looked up the hill. Moonlight caught the structure's silhouette in perfect detail.

"Do I see a man on the parapet at the top?" he asked.

"I think not, love," Maria replied. "You're still relishing the last evening. Darling, you know I couldn't be more proud of you, even if you almost ruined the evening with murderous intent. Your forgiveness of Herr Lindheimer was magnanimous, but your reversal of anger toward Fleetaumountec earns you a place in history."

Carl loved the flattery. "Darling, did I ever tell you I once lied to you?" *Once? Lightening could strike me.*

"How could you? I never scold you when you tell the truth?" Maria showed white teeth in the moonlight.

"When I lingered in the Altmann castle for a long period while you and the children waited in the carriage. The fact was, and I could never tell you, I forgave Julius for his wrongs against me. For *that* I deserve a place in history."

"Wait," Maria said. "There *is* someone. Look, dear. It's a man and woman. He wears a Texas hat. They're leaning on the wall. Now, he's taken off the hat... I know who it is! It's Matt and Beatrice. Do you see?"

"Now, I do. Yes, it's Matt and Beatrice."

The silhouetted couple sat like stone for a moment. Then the shadows blended into one and held in a passionate embrace.

Carl reached for Maria's hand and squeezed it hard. "Last evening was not my greatest victory." His left hand pointed toward the lovers. "This is."

He leaned forward, squinting. "There's another person on the wall. No, two more. I wonder who."

Maria said flatly, "I'm sure it's Anna and young John Covington. I gave permission to Anna. She wanted so to hear of John's California adventures."

"Hummph!"

# About the Authors

## Denzel Holmes

Denzel Holmes was born on the Pecos River, at Sheffield, Texas, in 1940, the youngest of five, and grew up in the least settled area of the state. As a teenager he hunted jackrabbits, explored uncharted caverns and played guitar.

In college, he studied engineering for two years, quit, came home and married his high school sweetheart, Margie, who remains at his side. For five years he sweated in the Permian Basin oil fields, delivered gypsum board for a lumber yard at Kerrville, ran a service station, and sold life insurance. He graduated with a business administration degree from Sul Ross State University in Alpine. He, Margie, and daughter Berine moved to Dallas where he joined the U.S. General Accounting Office. Housing and Urban Development in Fort Worth moved him and family to Denver in 1970.

The family, including Colorado-born Janet, returned to Temple, Texas, in 1979 with the Department of Agriculture. His career enabled him to travel widely and study America's history first hand, including a stretch with the Sioux tribes of the Northwest.

With encouragement from his writer uncle, Paul Patterson, and retired from government service, he wrote his first novel, *Ride*

343

*Hard to Hondo*, an epic of a Texas family.

During research for *Ride Hard* he met Tom Schleising at Uvalde. Tom took an instant interest in the project and loaned Denzel a number of history books. When Denzel "actually returned them" Tom decided the guy was all right, and the two formed a close E-Mail correspondence. Tom read the draft of *Ride Hard*, and wrote, "Would you be interested in co-writing a novel on Germans who immigrated to Texas in the 1800s?"

Denzel and Margie live in Belton, Texas. Their daughters, husbands and four grandsons live nearby. He is a substitute teacher in the local high school, hunts deer, and is active in his church. He is a member of Writers' League of Texas, in Austin.


## *Tom Schliesing*


Thomas Gene (Tom) Schliesing was born in San Antonio, Texas on April 21, 1941. He earned his bachelor's degree from Southwest Texas State University in 1964 and his master's from Texas Tech University in 1974. He worked with the USDA Soil Conservation Service from 1964 to 1967 as a range conservationist.

Tom taught agriculture at Southwest Texas Junior College from 1967 to 1998 at which time he became, and continues to be, the career center coordinator and an academic advisor.

Tom has been married to Ouida Fillingim Schliesing since 1966. They have three children: Tina, James, and Roxann, along with seven grandchildren.

Tom's hobbies include hunting, genealogy, and collecting historical artifacts. He has served as a volunteer in the Uvalde EMS and Sheriff's Reserve. Tom is a member of the German Texan Heritage Society.

To order additional copies of *Texas Victory*

Name_____

Address _____

_____

$21.95 x _____ copies =          _____

Sales Tax                                    _____
(Texas residents add 8.50 percent sales tax)

Please add $3.50 postage and handling per book    _____

Total amount due:                            _____

Please send check or money order for books to:

***WordWright.biz, Inc.***
***P.O. Box 1785***
***Georgetown, TX 78627***

Printed in the United States
21374LVS00002B/157-195

9 781932 196092